A RECIPE FOR
MURDER

BOOKS BY VERITY BRIGHT

A RECIPE FOR MURDER

VERITY BRIGHT

bookouture

Published by Bookouture in 2025

An imprint of Storyfire Ltd.
Carmelite House
50 Victoria Embankment
London EC4Y 0DZ

www.bookouture.com

The authorised representative in the EEA is Hachette Ireland
8 Castlecourt Centre
Dublin 15 D15 XTP3
Ireland
(email: info@hbgi.ie)

ISBN: 978-1-80314-529-7
eBook ISBN: 978-1-80314-530-3

Before you embark on a journey of revenge,
dig two graves.

— CONFUCIUS

PROLOGUE

It was still a good hour before the sun's rays would creep down the narrow lane. Until then, darkness owned the street. The heavily-cloaked figure shivered, kicked a dislodged cobblestone out of the way, and hurried along a side alley. Emerging onto a wider, more evenly cobbled street, the figure hesitated as if unsure which way to go. But a moment later it was on the move again; down the deserted road, past a line of darkened buildings, then stealing along another alleyway.

The alleyway ended at a dirt track at the rear of the buildings. Turning left, the figure slunk along the low wall to a gate which led into a small yard. Light leaked from the closed door at the back of the building. Someone was already hard at work before dawn. Slipping further along the wall, the figure slumped down. And waited. Waiting was the easy part. After nine years, what was ten minutes? Nothing. And yet everything!

Right on cue, ten minutes later the muffled clatter of a van could be heard. Two weak headlights penetrated the dark as the vehicle drove up to the gate. The driver, cigarette drooping from his lips, got out and walked round to the back of the van. Pulling open the doors, he reached inside with both hands, half-turned his body and straightened up, a sack on his back. He staggered through the gate and dumped the sack next to the building's back door. Returning to the van, he repeated the operation until there were four more sacks propped the other side of the door. Flicking the cigarette butt away, he climbed back in the van and, with a graunch of gears, drove off.

The sound of the engine slowly died away. Darkness and silence returned. The figure emerged and crept through the gate into the yard and up to the single sack to the left of the door. Carefully opening it, the figure produced a cylindrical tin and poured the contents into the sack. Something heavy hit the inside of the door. The figure froze. A muffled curse came from within. Then silence. The figure waited. Then, seemingly satisfied, stirred the sack's contents with a stout stick, resealed the sack, and faded into the darkness.

1

'Clifford, wherever would I be without you?' Lady Eleanor Swift's piercing green eyes stared into her butler's ever-impassive gaze. 'Oh, I know,' she said in mock frustration. 'Not up to my neck in endless lists of preparations, tasks and innumerable decisions I've evidently still to make!' Her fiery-red curls shook as she waved at the array of notebooks, fabric swatches and catalogues pinning her onto the velvet chaise longue in the main drawing room of Henley Hall.

Clifford bowed. 'My apologies then for my disgraceful dereliction of duty, my lady, since the appointment book requires your attention too. The one even Master Gladstone appears to have taken some interest in, if only to rest his over-indulged bulk upon.'

He gently rolled her lazy bulldog further onto his back beside her. Tugging an exquisite ivory silk-covered diary from under the dog's portly form, he passed it to her. Tomkins, her tomcat, shot out a paw from under the heap on her left and snared the silky ribbon marking what was evidently an important page.

She winced. 'Maybe now isn't the best time to tell you, Clifford, but Tomkins here ran off with the lace samples for the ring bearer's pillow.'

His lips twitched. 'On the contrary, my lady, it is most heartening news. Since whichever sample remains least mauled by the ginger menace might be deemed the only one suitable. And thus, one decision spared.'

She rolled her eyes good-naturedly. 'Very droll. Now, look. Mightn't we go at these wedding preparations a little less like a military operation? After all, we're planning my big day, not mobilising the entire King's army! Even though I know from your past with my beloved late uncle, you could probably do just that.'

To the outside world, Clifford was just her butler. In private, he was so much more besides. He had been her uncle's long-serving batman in the army and his unwaveringly loyal friend and confidant. And so he had increasingly become hers in the few short years since she'd inherited Henley Hall at her uncle's passing. He was also the one person whose head she frequently wanted to boil. His measured and meticulous approach being everything she inherently wasn't.

She sat up straighter. 'What I actually meant, Clifford, was could you be just a little less... well, thorough...' She tailed off, fearing she might sound churlish.

'Duly noted.' He added a long entry on a new page of his slim leather pocketbook. Sliding it into his jacket, he stepped away to open the French windows, letting in April's balmy early evening air. The welcome scents of hyacinths, sweet William and jasmine drifted in from the beautifully attended flower borders flanking the striped rear lawn. He turned back to her. 'Henceforth, my lady, the forthcoming wedding of the year shall go down in the annals of history precisely as you see fit.'

'Good,' she said in her best haughty lady of the manor voice. But after a minute of silence, her curiosity got the better of her. 'Dash it, Clifford. What did you write in your notebook?'

He paused in fastidiously aligning the pleats of the cream and gold fleur-de-lis silk curtains. 'Merely a note to post abject apologies to all those who will have attended the wedding ceremony after the inevitable indecorous mayhem which will now accompany my mistress down the aisle.'

She laughed, always secretly delighted by his mischievous wit. Although, in truth, it had seemed subdued in recent days. She peered at him sideways.

'Feeling the full ticket, are you, Clifford?'

He tutted as he turned to the drinks table. 'My lady, I am a butler.'

'Which means you wouldn't say if both your legs had fallen off.'

In silent reply, he presented her with a sherry on a silver tray. Taking the glass, she pointed at the tissue-paper wrapped bundle beside it.

'What's that?'

'Something I found delivered to the front doorstep, my lady.'

She put down her drink and gently slid her now eagerly interested pets to one side. 'Move over, chaps. I don't think it's edible, you know.'

She started to peel back the wrapping, then hesitated. Why, she had no idea. Her hands just seemed suddenly unwilling to expose what was inside. She shook herself.

Come on, Ellie. There'll be a lot more things to unwrap soon.

As she pulled away the rest of the tissue paper and saw what was inside, she felt a wash of relief. Again, why, she couldn't say.

'How sweet, Clifford! It's a little posy of white peonies set amongst some darling yellow flowers I don't recognise. And those clusters of pretty emerald leaves are almost like flat leaf parsley. All tied with a satin green ribbon.'

Clifford pointed at the foliage. 'I believe that is maidenhair, my lady, if memory serves. Actually, a type of fern. A gift from a well-wisher regarding your forthcoming nuptials, one assumes?'

She nodded as she searched through the folds of the wrapping paper. 'It's very thoughtful, but there's no card to say who it's from.'

'Hmm, I wonder why? More pilfering on one of your parts, no doubt.' He gently cupped Tomkins and Gladstone's chins.

She nodded. 'Although the sender might just have forgotten to include it.' A sense of unease crept over her. She shook it off in annoyance. Just pre-wedding jitters, surely? There was still so much to do. 'Now, Clifford, you need to pretend you can't hear me breaking your precious rules of etiquette because I owe you an apology.' She halted his respectful protest. 'I want you to know I do truly appreciate your infuriating attention to detail, galling lists, and meticulous efforts to make sure my wedding day is perfect. Thanks to you, there have only been a few tiny hiccups in the preparations so far. Honestly, I'm just feeling overwhelmed by it all,' she ended quietly.

Clifford bowed from the shoulders. 'Apology unnecessary, but accepted, my lady.'

She beamed. 'Thank you, because in my head, it all sounds so simple. In nine days' time, I potter down the altar of our delightful little St Winifred's Church in the village. Standing next to our wonderful Reverend Gaskell, my fiancé, Hugh, is waiting, looking positively edible in whatever divinely fitted wedding togs he'll have chosen. And then... what? I can't have blundered already?'

Her butler's lips twitched again. 'Ahem, it is not customary for ladies, titled or otherwise, to refer to their betrothed as "edible", as if they intended to devour them over their vows. Unless, of course, they are a spider and Chief Inspector Seldon your prey as well as fiancé?'

She smiled impishly. 'Good point, I should have said Hugh will look positively mouth-watering. So, after the service, we'll come back here and enjoy a wonderful garden party for all the villagers. And then...' She noticed him fiddling with his cufflinks. 'What now?'

'"All" the villagers, my lady?'

'Well... of course, Clifford.' She faltered, hushing her conscience. 'Little Buckford welcomed me with open arms from the moment I inherited Henley Hall. Even with the potentially awkward matter or two which might have arisen afterwards,' she ended airily.

He raised an eyebrow. 'Indeed. Though "awkward" is perhaps not how they viewed their lady of the manor repeatedly stumbling across deceased persons? Particularly when she then pointed the finger of suspicion at several of them on more than one occasion?'

'Tsk, you make it sound like I made a habit of it.' At his increasingly arched brow, she held her hands up. 'Yes, alright. Point taken. But that was before. And as this... this little posy proves, I'm long forgiven.'

But am I, Ellie?

She shook herself again. 'Plus, I'm about to get married. Which will be the start of a whole new life.' Her breath caught. 'Oh, gracious, Clifford! That sounds daunting and wonderful in equal measure. But it's all the more reason to include the entire village in the reception in Henley Hall's grounds, you see?'

He pulled his pocketbook out again. 'And after the garden party, the evening plans remain unchanged, my lady? A champagne reception for the other strata of your guests?'

She pretended not to have noticed that he'd avoided her question. 'The "toffs", you mean?' She smiled at his horrified cough. 'Clifford, we both know that's how Hugh still secretly thinks of them. Poor fellow, I wish he'd stop being daunted that he's "only" a policeman, as he sees himself. The fact he's one of Scotland Yard's most revered senior detectives doesn't seem to ease him feeling out of place amongst the titled classes.'

'Rest assured, my lady, the eminent chief inspector will grow into his new position, alongside his new wife growing adroitly into hers.'

She felt a wave of panic.

Let's hope so, Ellie. I've never grown adroitly into anything!

2

'Are you alright, my lady?'

Eleanor shook herself out of her panicky thoughts. 'Yes, thank you. Now, back to the evening reception.' She tickled Gladstone's tummy for a moment to calm herself. 'I do hope Hugh will invite a raft of people who are important to him. Be they friends, colleagues or distant relations. It's shocking, but even after repeated efforts to carve out time to know more about each other, something always seems to have got in the way. And now here we are, hurtling towards the aisle, with less than two weeks to go, and still with so much to learn about each other.'

'And after a lengthy engagement, my lady.'

'And a very protracted and fractious courtship before that!' she added, knowing he was too respectful to say all that was in his mind. 'I lost count of how many times Hugh threatened to arrest me in the early days.'

'Six, I believe, my lady. But fewer than was warranted as the gentleman is still unaware of several of your more... unseemly escapades.'

'Well, before you lose any more starch from your impeccable collar, pretending they didn't feel a little like the adventures you miss with Uncle Byron, back to the wedding plans again. I intend to take full advantage of Hugh being away on an investigation, stuck on the wrong side of the country for a few days. Thus, I shall bash out as many of your dratted, I mean vital, tasks as possible before he returns and joins us here. Especially as he'll be bringing darling Kofi with him from boarding school.'

She didn't miss the animation in her butler's eyes. While caught up in a nasty business in London, they had befriended a young Gold Coast boy who was thousands of miles from home with no one he could trust to turn to. Given his lack of family back home as well, the British authorities had finally ceded to Kofi's polite but unswerving insistence he be allowed to remain in England to complete his education. And Clifford, whose own childhood had been similarly troubled, stepped forward to be his guardian without hesitation, the two of them forming an immediate kinship.

'I shan't permit you to do anything except spend every minute with your young charge, Clifford, so please don't bother arguing. It's such a treat for both of you that he's coming home.'

He half bowed. 'Too gracious, my lady. Assuming, that is, Master Kofi can be extracted from the eager clutches of your band of aproned elves, of course?'

She hugged her shoulders with delight at his words. Since she'd arrived at Henley Hall, the ladies who made up the female contingent of her staff had embraced every change thrown at them with unbridled enthusiasm. Be that her own unexpected arrival, the addition of a new maid she'd rescued from Scotland, or a cheeky tomcat who regularly drew her easily-led bulldog into mischief. And lately, young Kofi joining them all as part of the eclectic household that was Henley Hall.

Hugh moving in as your husband once we're back from our honeymoon is going to be the real test of their resilience for change though, Ellie!

Ever able to read her thoughts, Clifford shook his head. 'Only in regard to keeping their minds on their tasks, my lady.'

She laughed. 'I'm sure one day they'll lose the giddy school-girl feeling Hugh brings on in them.'

He shook his head. 'Would I could share your confidence on that score. However, shall we continue?' He picked up the appointment book. 'A trip to Chipstone tomorrow for luncheon. Then, in line with your gracious determination to keep as much wedding expenditure as possible in the local area, a trip to Miss Lucetta Moore, the florist.' He checked his notes. 'For discussions over the flowers for the church and those to grace the ballroom here for your reception afterwards.'

She cocked her head. 'Now I know you're not feeling quite yourself.'

His brow flinched questioningly.

'Because, Clifford, my luncheon appointment is with my best friend Constance and unrelated to the wedding. And you distinctly pointed out that it is a dedicated appointment book for my wedding preparations alone!'

He tutted and tapped the cover. 'This is a three-year diary, my lady. To accommodate not only engagements regarding your wedding and honeymoon, but also to assist in plotting the course of the first two years of your newly married life thereafter. Which you professed to be planning some weeks ago?'

She avoided his gaze. 'Clifford! That's too much to even think about on top of the wedding. Please help me not panic, by sticking just to the appointments for the big day for now, will you?'

He nodded contritely.

'Good,' she said in relief. 'On to the catering arrangements then. As you know, Annie Tibbets will be in charge of food for the reception. Our own wonderful cook, Mrs Trotman, will, of course, make the wedding cake itself. And, doubtless, cast her fiercely expert eye over Annie's suggestions. I'm confident, however, that everything that side will go without a hitch, despite a few, well, as I said, minor hiccups so far. I mean, Polly was bound to drop some of the wedding crockery at some point. Luckily, early enough so we can get it replaced. And even though Annie was my second choice—'

'Indeed, she was, my lady. But only because Miss Hester Hopcroft, your first choice, who also lives in Little Buckford, and employs several ladies from the village, declined.'

'Yes. Honestly, I was disappointed Hester felt the wedding was too large a contract for her. But impressed she said so. And I'm still looking forward to enjoying whatever delights Annie conjures up.'

He gave her a sideways look. 'Ordinarily, the magnitude of getting married tends to diminish a bride's appetite, I have heard?'

She feigned horror. 'Then watch and learn, Clifford. Hugh is under no illusions about my robust appetite. And if he were, I'd be doubly sure to put him straight on the day.'

'On that note, my lady.' Clifford clicked open his pocket watch. 'Time has moved on considerably. You have but forty minutes left to dress for the Spring Supper and be in Little Buckford.'

'Oh my word, yes! I'd almost forgotten it's tonight. My head's fuller with all the wedding planning than I'd thought,' she said lightly, trying to hide the guilty feeling that washed over her.

His eyes twinkled. 'Unlike your plate needs be at each stage of the supper, my lady.'

She opened her mouth to offer a pithy reply, but then realised she actually had little idea what the Spring Supper was about.

'Come on. Bail me out in advance with an explanation so I don't mess up what I'm supposed to do. I haven't been in the village for any previous ones, as you know perfectly well.'

'The Spring Supper, my lady, is a centuries-honoured tradition in Little Buckford. It is the villagers' way of welcoming in spring and all the abundance it is hoped she will bestow upon the parish. A favourable growing season has been critical to the livelihood of the residents since the early twelve hundreds.'

'And still is.'

'To some, yes.' Uncharacteristically, Clifford hesitated before continuing. 'In short, the villagers throw open their doors for the evening and offer some form of refreshment in their homes for anyone who steps across the threshold. The key point is for everyone in Little Buckford to visit as many other villagers' houses as possible and partake of a little of the offerings in each. Whilst exchanging words of goodwill for the forthcoming season.'

'Ah! I see. So, all the villagers go from house to house, eating a little supper in each?'

He nodded. 'In essence, yes, my lady. The community-spirited evening has been a privilege to attend in previous years whenever his lordship and myself were not overseas at the time.'

'Or more recently, away with me.'

He held up his pocket watch again. 'Less than thirty minutes to change now, my lady. Unless you wish to miss the event for the fifth year running?'

'Definitely not!' She wriggled her slender form out from under her pets' cuddle. 'I just wish Henley Hall wasn't so far out of the village so we could partake as well and open the house to everyone.'

Clifford raised an eyebrow. 'With Silas unusually absent until just before your wedding day?'

Silas was Henley Hall's mysterious gamekeeper-cum-security guard. He had been inherited, like the rest of her staff, from her late uncle who had amassed many enemies in the criminal underworld and elsewhere. However, he was so elusive, she still hadn't set eyes on him.

She shrugged. 'The villagers aren't going to run off with the silverware! They come here every year on Christmas Eve to eat and make merry as you know perfectly well. And nothing's gone missing yet.'

Thinking the posy might look pretty in her bedroom, she scooped it up. 'I must admit, the whole village getting together will be just the tonic I need to clear my over-busy thoughts.'

'Would that could be guaranteed!' her sharp hearing caught Clifford mutter as his suit tails glided out of the room.

She tutted to herself at his remark as she mounted the stairs. But in her bedroom, she stared at the posy now on her dressing table and shook her head slowly in frustration. What was wrong with her?

Why can't you shake this feeling of foreboding, Ellie?

3

As they arrived in Little Buckford, Eleanor gaped through the passenger window of her Rolls Royce.

'What on earth, Clifford?'

She was unable to take her eyes off the unexpected crowds criss-crossing the diminutive high street of just seven small shops, one public house and a reading room. Nestled deep in the Chiltern Hills, it was usually a sleepy village, through which the rural inhabitants ambled as if haste had never been invented. But tonight, patched Sunday best outfits surged in every direction, rousing exchanges ringing out over the peal of St Winifred's church bells.

She shook her head in disbelief as Clifford eased the stately car to a stop again to let more chattering villagers pass.

'I thought the annual May Fair had everyone animated, Clifford, but it seems this welcoming in of spring is an even more important tradition. I mean, normally life in the village moves at the pace of an elderly slug!'

'Indeed, my lady.'

He doffed his impeccable bowler hat to each of the passing

female villagers. She didn't miss the fluttery effect his distinguished features brought on in most of them, as always.

Suddenly, she tapped the dashboard.

'Ha! Your wily ruse, as I now realise it was, failed. Tsk! You need to seriously up your game, Clifford.'

He eyed her sideways. 'In what regard specifically, may I enquire?'

'In your relentless efforts to cram me into the mould of a respectable titled lady, you made this evening's Spring Supper sound a far more sedate affair on purpose. In the foolhardy expectation I might therefore approach the whole thing in a decorous manner. But instead, I shall hurl myself into the festivities with unbridled gusto as the rest of the village is doing.'

'The unusual aspect being?' he said drily.

She smiled sweetly, pointing at him. 'One wet blanket from Henley Hall joining the merry throng will be one too many, don't you think?' Secretly, she delighted in the idea of witnessing her ever-dignified butler cavorting heedlessly just once. 'You could let a little starch out of your collar tonight, Clifford. When in Rome and all that?'

'Where we are most definitely *not*.' His lips pursed. 'Something the disgracefully unruly element of your female staff need reminding of, evidently.'

He pointed at the four women who were perched along the side of the local milkman's cart. They were clutching each other and laughing raucously, their legs swinging as it rumbled over the cobbles.

'That will teach you to insist the ladies couldn't ride down with us in the Rolls,' she teased, knowing they would actually have been uncomfortable doing so. 'Now, please park here so I can join the fun.'

Clifford cut the engine and came around to open her door. She leaped out, whispering, 'Please afford the ladies some leniency tonight. It's such a treat for them to be out.'

'Whoa there,' the milkman called to his horse, bringing the cart to a stop alongside them. 'Best of the evenin' to you, m'lady. Mr Clifford.'

'And to you, Mr Wilkes.' Eleanor noted he was dressed in a serviceable brown jacket and jauntily tied red-and-white spotted neckerchief, instead of his customary blue-and-white milkman's overall. 'Come to enjoy the Spring Supper too, I see. And by starting on the way here,' she added, smiling at the line of flushed cheeks behind him headed by her motherly, grey-curled housekeeper, Mrs Butters. At the other end of the cart sat Mrs Trotman, her saucy-humoured cook, and the scourge of Clifford's unenviable task of maintaining order below stairs. Lizzie and Polly, her two young maids, sat between them, both with uncontrollable grins on their faces.

'A most motley collection of additional wares among your offerings tonight, Mr Wilkes?' Clifford said playfully.

'You're right there.' Leaping down, the milkman's hazel eyes glinted under his mop of red-brown curls. 'It's the rummiest thing. Do you think I could find a taker for 'em on my way here? Couldn't even get tuppence a head!'

'You cheeky rascal,' Mrs Trotman huffed. 'You just haven't got the bottle for the likes of us, Milky.'

Even Clifford joined in the amused groan at her pun.

'Be off with you, women, afore you curdle.' Wilkes chuckled, setting a crate down for them to step onto and offering Mrs Butters his arm.

Over the general bustle around them, Eleanor noticed Polly gazing wide-eyed at a lean youth with roughly cut, but neatly combed, blond hair. He was turning his cap in his hands as he hovered a couple of yards away. Taking in the mature set of his shoulders, and the band of fabric added to the bottom of his trousers, she realised he was actually closer to adulthood than adolescence.

'Is that... no?' she murmured to Clifford. 'Surely he's not the scrawny young chap who used to be sweet on Polly a year ago?'

'Almost two now, my lady. During which he has behaved nothing but honourably towards her. His name is Jack Browne, if you recall?'

Her ladies flustered into a line and curtseyed to Eleanor as the milk cart rumbled away over Wilkes' cheery promise to collect them there at ten o'clock. It was only then she noticed, swinging from a ribbon on each of their wrists, a four-inch, yellowish bell of intricately woven wheat stalks.

'Ahem, ladies.' Clifford fixed them with a firm look. 'Which of you would care to explain why you arrived in such a manner?'

''Twas all on account of sparin' your nerves. And the household purse, Mr Clifford,' Mrs Trotman said innocently. 'We knew you'd be frettin' buckets at the cost of having to pay Charlie-the-Carriage his taxi fare for bringing us all the way down here and back. So, we hitched a free ride. Anything for you, Mr Clifford. You know us.'

'All too well,' he said wryly. 'Jack, my boy.' He beckoned to the young man.

Jack shot over and bobbed his head respectfully to Eleanor. 'Evenin', m'lady. Summat I can do for you, Mr Clifford?'

Her butler nodded. 'Indeed. It's a ghastly task, Jack, but might I burden you with accompanying her ladyship's staff this evening? And keeping them in order?' he added in a stage whisper.

Eleanor spotted Polly's cheeks burn with delight and the others nudging each other. Jack's blue eyes shone eagerly. ''Twill be a pleasure, Mr Clifford.'

'Speaks the voice of inexperience. So good luck. There'll be a medal waiting if you survive.' Clifford gave an exaggerated shudder, sending everyone into fits of laughter.

Eleanor watched her ladies shuffle Polly to Jack's side of

their line before linking arms and herding away up the high street.

She turned to Clifford. 'Thank you. But honestly, I'm amazed you broke your cherished rules like that.'

'I "adjusted", not broke the rules, if you will forgive the correction. The truth is, Polly is fast approaching the age when she may make her own decisions.' He busied himself looking both ways along the street, muttering, 'And would I am never the man to bury my head in the sand.'

Feeling as though she had been quietly chastised, Eleanor shook herself.

Let it go, Ellie! He's got a lot on his plate with all his normal duties and trying to make sure my and Hugh's wedding goes off without a hitch. He's bound to be a little... on edge. Like all of us!

She clapped her hands, then stared down at the woven bell she had missed him slipping over her wrist. 'Oh! There's a plaited cluster of wheat ears hanging in the centre, just like a proper clapper.'

'For the ringing in of spring, my lady. Made from the final bales of last year's harvest.' He looped his own over his gloved index finger.

She pointed up and down the street. 'Now, my guru on local life, where does one start in visiting the houses taking part in this marvellous tradition?'

'Ahem, as the lady of the manor...'

She groaned. 'Just lead the way, please.'

To her surprise, instead of setting off to the few larger houses around the village green, he led her to two tiny terraced flint cottages. Sandwiched between the cobblers and the bakery, they were the only dwellings on this side of the high street before the vicarage. The low blue door of the first was thrown wide open. She stepped over the threshold into a small sitting room filled with a chattering crowd. It was furnished with a simple wood dresser and pretty cloth-covered table, plus a bench seat, set with patchwork cushions either side of the unlit fireplace.

'Ding dong, hark the cuckoo's song,' Clifford called over her shoulder.

'All the smiles of spring, do more well-wishers bring!' came a jovial female voice in reply.

The people in the room jiggled their wheaten bells high above their heads in unison. Eleanor hurried to join in, feeling horribly like the new girl at school. A comely, sixty-ish woman in a flower-print cotton dress flustered over from the group around the table. She smiled at Clifford, patting her grey-white waves, then nodded shyly to Eleanor. Holding out a tall glass of rosy-pink liquid, she said, 'Welcome, m'lady.'

'Thank you, Mrs Jenkins,' Eleanor replied, having caught Clifford murmur the name seemingly without moving his lips.

The room turned suddenly quiet, all eyes staring expectantly at her. She looked hopefully at Clifford, but was met with his ever-inscrutable gaze. 'Umm... Blessed April sun, Little Buckford shine upon?' she said hesitantly.

A sharp collective intake of breath met her reply.

'Cor lummy! Rain as needed, once fields is seeded,' a throaty male voice countered. The room breathed a sigh of relief, the ruddy-faced man receiving a raft of hearty claps on the back and murmurings of a close call avoided.

'Yes, that too, of course,' Eleanor said brightly to hide her embarrassment.

Mrs Jenkins pointed at the table. ''Taint what you're used to, I'm sure, but if as you could bear to try, m'lady? For luck, see?'

Eleanor smiled back. 'I thought you'd never ask.'

To her relief, the chatter started to flow again. However, the conversation lurched from one local topic to another like a drunken ship in a storm, leaving her with little she could latch on to. All the more so, as she detected a hint of tension in the air.

Oh dear, Ellie, maybe whatever omens they trust in aren't proving favourable for spring? She sighed to herself. *Let's hope you don't jinx it even more!*

Chipping in with a positive word here and there when she could, she savoured the pastry turnover she'd been given, which oozed delicious pink fruit over her fingers. A smiley old chap she vaguely recognised waved the plate at her.

''Twill make Mrs J's week, m'lady, to tell all 'n sundry your ladyship was munchin' on her rhubarb bumpers. Go on! 'Ave another.'

'If you think so,' she whispered back, taking a second of the quaintly named pastries, purely for the sake of her hostess, she told herself. Her drink of generously spiced ginger ale felt an unhappy chaser to wash it down with, but tasted too good not to finish. Aware of a few new arrivals behind her, she gave her wheat bell an exuberant pretend ring.

'Ah, Mr Mayhew. Good evening,' Clifford said. The gaunt man had long been a widower and was something of a prickly character. But only because of his fierce pride in trying to feed his numerous children without recourse to charity, Eleanor knew. Something she had helped with a few years earlier by buying land for allotments and coaxing him into accepting a small stipend to manage them. Which gave him at least one reliable source of income.

'Is your eldest son, Mew, with you, Mr Mayhew?' she said genially, remembering the villagers' penchant for shortening names and words, the lad's full name being Matthew Mayhew. 'I haven't seen him for... ah! There he is.'

She tried not to gawp as he stepped out from behind his father. His facial features had matured, the stubble on his top lip showing he was now grown up like his friend Jack. But the malnutrition that had dogged those growing years had taken their toll, she thought sadly. He was no taller than when she'd met him before. Feeling guilty again for her own markedly different privileges, she floundered for words.

Clifford came to her rescue. 'Been beating the bounds with the reverend today, gentlemen?'

'That we'ave as is tradition.' The sinews in Mr Mayhew's rawboned neck flexed. 'With the lads proper, mind.'

She noted Clifford's brow flinch fleetingly, which only added to her bafflement.

'Sorry. Beating the what?'

Mr Mayhew frowned. 'The bounds, m'lady.'

'The parish boundaries,' Clifford explained. 'A tradition that has stood since the thirteenth century, when maps were rare and costly or non-existent. Hence a group of villagers, including all the young boys, walk in procession along the parish boundaries, marking the way stones by beating them with wands made of willow.'

She smiled at Mew. 'Goodness. That must have taken all day.'

'We was done just afore St Winifred's bell rung it was jam 'n fold time, m'lady. Teatime, that is,' he added at her blank look.

'Four and a half hours. Most efficient, Mew,' Clifford said. 'Especially with you all needing to cross the bridge to mark the other side.'

Mew's Adam's apple bobbed. 'Umm, we was told not to, Mr Clifford.'

'By Reverend Gaskell?' To Eleanor's ears, Clifford's voice contained a hint of vex.

'Can't remember rightly by who, Mr Clifford.' Mew ducked his head and murmured, 'If as you'll excuse me, m'lady.'

As he darted away, she realised Clifford was discreetly indicating the door.

Evidently time to move on, Ellie.

'Such delectable treats, Mrs Jenkins,' she said as her hostess passed.

'Too kind, m'lady.' Mrs Jenkins beamed. 'Thank you for comin'. 'Twas an honour. And you too, Mr Clifford.'

Eleanor stepped back out into the street and spun to face her butler, arms folded.

'Clifford! How could you have forgotten to tell me I need a ready springtime greeting up my sleeve?'

'Did I, my lady?' he said impassively, but his eyes twinkled. 'Apologies. Greetings in the plural are required, however, as it is considered bad luck to repeat one already offered in a previous house.'

'You terror!' She hid a smile, pleased to see him back to his usual mischievous self. 'At least I shall take solace in knowing you'll be squirming all evening at having to break your golden rule of eating in front of your mistress.'

'Perhaps.' He waved her on. 'But for now, the next house awaits with who knows what surprises inside...'

4

Eleanor dredged her brain for a suitable seasonal greeting as she stepped over the next threshold. The room was crowded with people struggling to fit around a narrow settle seat, a treadle sewing machine table and a tall, open-fronted wood cabinet.

'On spring's bountiful flourish, may everyone... nourish?' she sang out hopefully.

'Including the weevils, so prevalent this time of year?' Clifford whispered teasingly. As a woman hurried over – who could have been the twin of her neighbour, save for her plumper curves tightly tied in an apple-green crossover dress – he called out, 'And may your eggs stand on end, Mrs Browne.'

'That doesn't even rhyme,' Eleanor murmured, as the room waved their wheat bells.

'And may your swallows keep muddin' up a good 'un,' Mrs Browne replied cheerfully.

'African migrant birds who build their nests below the houses' eaves here. A potent symbol of good fortune for the season,' Clifford translated for Eleanor.

'Never heard it needin' explainin' afore,' the woman said, blinking at her. She fumbled in her pocket and pulled out a pair of spectacles. 'Oh lummy! Beg pardon, m'lady. Didn't realise it was you with Mr Clifford. Welcome over to me table, won't you both? Mind, 'tis only dripping wheels with a cup of frumenty, if as that's not too lowly?'

Eleanor smiled reassuringly, having no idea what either was. 'Not at all. In fact, they are my two favourite things. However did you know?'

Pleased she'd made less of a spectacle of herself this time, she joined in the general chatter in the room. Despite looking the simplest of fare, the 'dripping wheels' were crispy fried spirals of batter filled with tender slivers of beef and gravy. And her cup of 'frumenty' proved to be a frothed milk drink, seasoned with cinnamon and sugar. But the milk and meat seemed to be unhappy bedfellows, as her stomach grumbled.

When she'd first entered the house, she'd vaguely been aware of a slight tension in the air, similar to the first house they'd visited. Now she felt the room charged with it. Looking around, she spotted two unfamiliar men she was sure hadn't been there when she'd arrived. But she hadn't heard any exchanged greetings or noticed any wheat bell ringing. Both of them had lank dark hair that disappeared into their collarless shirts, with no jackets covering their trouser braces. They were tucking into the dripping wheels, glancing over their shoulders at the others in the room as they did so.

She shrugged to herself.

None of your business, Ellie.

But as she mingled, a small voice told her maybe as lady of the manor, it was?

However, the room was so crowded she soon lost sight of the two men. With relief, she spotted someone whose face was not only familiar, but one she could actually put a name to.

'Evening, Miss Tibbets,' she said on reaching the petite, auburn-haired woman who would be doing her wedding catering.

'Oh goodness!' the woman replied breathlessly. 'Fancy you coming across me here like this, my lady. Whatever must you think?'

Eleanor was confused. The woman's normally pallid complexion looked a little paler than usual, perhaps. But she was well turned out in a dark-blue pinafore dress over a white blouse with a thin lace edging to the collar and cuffs. Eleanor held her concerned grey-eyed gaze with a reassuring smile.

'I think you're joining in with this delightful village tradition, just as I am. Nothing else.'

'Not at the expense of planning for your wonderful wedding day, though, I promise,' the woman said earnestly.

Eleanor shook her head. 'Miss Tibbets. May I call you Annie?'

The rigid set of the woman's slim shoulders loosened a little. 'Yes please, m'lady. I've done alright striking out my own, but 'tis nice not to be forever reminded of it.'

Not wanting to pry, Eleanor hastened on. 'Then, Annie, please understand I have every confidence in you.' She mentally crossed her fingers at her fib. She lowered her voice. 'Between you and me, Mr Clifford has all but banned me from interfering in the catering arrangements!'

She laughed, which Eleanor was pleased to see made several years fall away from her face. 'Forgive me saying, m'lady, but it still catches me out that you're not quite what we all imagined.'

'My lady?'

She jumped. 'Clifford! How can you still sneak up behind me without...?' She raised her hand before he could reply. 'I know. You're a butler.' She turned to Annie. 'Time to move on, I believe. We'll meet again as arranged to discuss the catering arrangements?'

The woman's reply was lost as a man's voice across the table called out, 'What'd I tell you? Here's trouble!'

Before she could ask what the man was referring to, the lank-haired men she'd noted before tried to push their way towards the door. Only to be blocked by a line of frowning faces. Both seemed early-thirtyish now she studied them. They were lithely hewn, from manual labour, she assumed. It struck her that neither had any of the stocky, strong-shouldered farming traits that predominated in Little Buckford. Nor the ruddy outdoor complexions. The taller of the two jerked his shoulders, releasing a curtain of straggly long hair from his shirt.

''Scuse us, why don't ya?' he said with a curled lip and a nasal twang to his words Eleanor couldn't place. 'We wanna get past.'

'To barge your way into another house? You've eaten enough free food for tonight, I'd warrant,' Mr Drinkwater, the dairy owner, growled.

'And the bridge is that way!' the man scowling beside him added, pointing down the high street outside.

She blanched, realising it was the usually mild-mannered owner of the general stores, Arthur Brenchley.

'And what if we don't fancy goin' home yet?' the second one growled, as they rolled up their sleeves, revealing menacing forearms covered in a raft of cuts.

'Oh gracious!' she gasped as a scuffle broke out.

'Disgraceful,' Clifford muttered, spinning her by the shoulders with his fingertips and steering her out of the front door as the other women retreated to the safety of the kitchen.

In the street, she turned to him. 'Thank you, my ever-chivalrous knight. But in manhandling me out of there, you seem to have forgotten your promise to be less overprotective of me?' she said firmly.

Checking through the window that the skirmish was not getting too out of hand, he gestured for them to head up the steep, narrow cobbled lane leading to more cottages.

'I admittedly escorted you out in an uncustomary fashion,

my lady. Which could not have been further from "manhandling", however. Nevertheless, my apologies for such.'

'Don't misunderstand, Clifford. I appreciate your solicitude but...' She tailed off, both of them pausing in the shadow of the porch over the butcher's shop to watch as the two men were ejected from Mrs Browne's house. A small group of villagers stood outside until the interlopers disappeared from sight around the corner in the opposite direction to Eleanor.

'It's a shame they obviously weren't invited,' she said uneasily. 'They just seemed hungry.'

Clifford cleared his throat. 'They did not need an invitation.'

She looked up sharply. 'But that means they must live in Little Buckford?'

'Not to the thinking of the old guard of the village, my lady.'

Now she understood his remark to Mr Mayhew's son, Mew. About the parishioners' procession needing to have gone over the bridge as part of beating the bounds. And his flinching when told they had stopped short of doing so for possibly the first time since the thirteenth century. The old, dilapidated mill complex across the river had been purchased by a firm some hundred and seventy miles north that was involved in the pottery trade. Once the renovations were complete, some five months previously, the owner had shipped the workforce down from the north as well. Their accommodation, shopping, and even schooling for the children was all provided within the complex.

She had been aware of the planning application the year before. And the subsequent public meetings in the nearest town of Chipstone, where the council had passed the application and granted the firm's licence to operate. But it had all occurred when her life had been over-busy with a series of trips abroad. To say nothing of getting engaged. Nor the handful of murders she'd unwittingly become embroiled in solving. Compounding her decision to keep her distance had been her earlier brush with politics when standing for election as the area's first female Member of Parliament. It had made her determined not to get caught up in any more Machiavellian machinations. The upshot was, she had never actually been to the complex over the bridge herself.

The real reason for her unease, however, was that she knew in her heart that her beloved late uncle would have visited the new villagers and made sure they knew him. And, as lady of the manor, she too had responsibilities. Responsibilities which, she now admitted to herself, she'd sidestepped.

But tonight isn't the night to try and sort that all out, Ellie.

'Come on, Clifford,' she said over-zealously. 'We've many more houses to visit yet.'

To bury her guilt, she threw herself into the festivities with extra fervour in the blur of homes they visited over the next few hours. In truth, her stomach was growing more unhappy with each new dish she ate. But she was determined to do something right tonight. And this supper mattered enormously to the village residents, all of whom seemed honoured their lady of the manor had taken the time to welcome in spring in their home.

Trying to outdo Clifford with her good luck greetings kept her mind off the events in Mrs Browne's house. Later, she spotted the lank-haired men in the shadows heading back down into the centre of the village. She looked the other way, telling herself again, tonight was not the time to get herself involved in more unpleasantness.

Finally, they'd visited every house in Little Buckford, including the larger dwellings around the green and the more outlying higgledy-piggledy clusters of thatched cottages dotted along the winding cobbled lanes.

'Just the vicarage left, my lady,' Clifford said as they came full circle to the swing gate into St Winifred's Church at the top of the high street.

'Thank goodness, I shall sleep like a log after all this social-ising and eating.' She yawned.

As they passed through the grounds and under an arch in the yew hedge, she could see the front door of the vicarage, a yellow-stone building topped with decorative chimneys. It was wide open, as usual. Reverend Gaskell, Little Buckford's vicar, kept an open house year-round, save for the bitterest of winter days. Before she could step inside, his familiar thatch of tousled grey hair and thick spectacles above a clerical collar appeared on the threshold.

'Lady Swift! Mr Clifford! Hurrah!'

'Let spring begin, bringing nature's heartiest bounty there-in,' she called quickly.

'May the devil's coach horse thunder through your days. And may all your winds be chelidonian,' Clifford added.

'Dash it! I can't possibly compete with that,' she muttered, following the beaming reverend along the sunny ochre-painted passageway.

'It's not supposed to be a game of trumps,' Clifford whis-pered back.

'As if you weren't going at it like it was!' she hissed.

'We can take the opportunity to discuss your wedding service wishes over the refreshments,' Reverend Gaskell said, misinterpreting a particularly loud gurgle from Eleanor's unset-tled stomach as hunger. 'My wonderful housekeeper, Mrs Pegg, has made a mountain of crisp bacon dumplings and lovage scones.'

'Chelly what winds?' They both spun around as two women stepped out of the vicarage into the late evening air. 'Ever the silver tongue, Mr Clifford.'

'"Chelidonian", Miss Hopcroft,' Clifford said. 'Greek for warm spring winds. Or favourable, in short.'

The two women nodded to Eleanor. 'Good night, m'lady,' they chorused.

'And to you, Hester,' she called to the retreating footsteps. One of them being Hester Hopcroft, the woman she'd originally asked to do her wedding catering. 'And to...' She turned to her butler. 'Quick, Clifford. Do you know her friend's name?'

Before he could answer, Reverend Gaskell bobbed around her to stand between them. 'That was the new schoolmistress from across the bridge. A recent friend of Miss Hopcroft's.' He tapped his forehead. 'But, oh dear, how disgraceful of me. I've forgotten the young woman's name already.'

Eleanor's sharp hearing caught Clifford murmur, 'And the fact your parish lies *both* sides of the river, Vicar!'

She pretended not to have heard. But her traitorous heart whispered, *And as lady of the manor, so does yours, Ellie.*

5

The following morning, Eleanor felt completely wrung out as she came to. Not surprising, after being up most of the night with an unhappy stomach. Too embarrassed to confess she'd obviously overeaten, and with no regard to the mixture of foods she'd consumed, she had tried saying nothing and holed up in her bedroom. But with his ever-unfathomable wizardry, Clifford had knocked at intervals throughout the night, leaving yet another digestive remedy on the bureau outside. At just gone two in the morning, she'd lurched out of her door, despite her sallow and sweaty condition, so she could thank him. And ask for something a little stronger.

Thankfully, her system now felt more settled as she lay staring up at the patches of sun dancing on the plaster roses of her bedroom ceiling. Still unable to face the thought of eating anything, however, she swung her feet out from under her covers, rubbing her sore stomach.

'I can't blame you for abandoning me, chaps.' She bent gingerly to stroke Gladstone and Tomkins, where they lay cuddled together on a soft wool blanket on the floor. Clearly stolen from the end of her bed as a better option than sharing her eiderdown after her third urgent lurch up and into the bathroom. 'Well, on the positive side, at least there's nothing left inside me to expel in an unladylike manner now!'

Despite the warmth of the April morning, she wrapped her thick ankle-length robe over her pyjamas. She hoped it would help combat her sporadic shivers as she headed downstairs in her slippers. Tomkins bounded ahead while Gladstone lumbered down sleepily, dragging the blanket with him.

'Good morning, my lady,' Clifford's disembodied voice said as she reached the bottom of the stairs. 'It appears you may have forgotten to bring something with you?'

'Yes. Most of my insides,' she groaned. 'At least that's what it feels like.'

She heard him tut. 'I rather meant any hint of decorous attire.'

'I thought it worth suffering your razor-witted admonishments in order to hurry down and tell Mrs Trotman not to waste her efforts preparing me breakfast. I can't face it.' She turned in a circle, feeling testy. 'Oh, stop hiding, Clifford. You can clearly see me from wherever you're lurking, anyway.'

His impeccably suited form materialised from behind the plinthed marble bust of Gladstone that her eccentric late uncle had commissioned. Eyes averted, he said, 'I could not, in fact, my lady. I imagined, due to previous experience, that you might still be in your nightwear. But that was not the entire reason for my remaining out of sight.'

'Well, as long as it wasn't to quell your nausea at seeing my sickly visage.'

'Alas, I have been found out, gentlemen,' he said mischievously to her bulldog and tomcat, restoring some of her good humour. Coaxing the blanket from Gladstone, he folded it meticulously over his jacket sleeve. 'Though, if I may point out, my lady, I have not suffered any such symptoms from the Spring Supper evening.'

'And how is that supposed to make me feel better?'

Without waiting for his no doubt ready quip in reply, she shuffled off towards the kitchen. Batting away his insistence he could relay the message for her, she trudged the full length of the passageway, which felt a mile too long this morning. But she would not be swayed. Like him, all her ladies worked tirelessly for her. And she wanted to apologise personally if they had already started preparing her breakfast.

As she neared the kitchen door, Clifford glided around in front of her. 'My lady, please. I fear you may not be sufficiently recovered to venture beyond.'

She took a tentative sniff and shook her head. 'Stop fussing. I can't detect any whiffs of bacon...' She faltered as her stomach cramped in protest at the thought of the salty, crisp, fat-edged slices she would usually devour with paprika and caramelised onion relish. She straightened up. 'It's no good. You won't deter me, Clifford.'

With a resigned shake of his head, he stood to one side.

'Oh my stars! And lookin' worse 'n last week's kippers run through the mangle,' she heard her housekeeper gasp as Gladstone shouldered his way through the door.

'For heaven's sake, don't mention fish, Butters!' her cook replied.

Evidently, all your staff know the extent of your inelegant bathroom activities in the night, Ellie. Marvellous!

Taking comfort at least she now needn't pretend, she watched as her four ladies went through their usual routine of forming a line and curtseying. But uncharacteristically, with all the energy of limp dishrags. Their grey faces blinked back at her, none of them standing smartly, or even upright. She realised their hissed comments had been about themselves, not her!

'Oh goodness, ladies, you too?' she exclaimed in concern.

''Fraid so, m'lady,' Mrs Butters wheezed. 'Only Joseph is fine, as he never went to Spring Supper.'

Joseph was her elderly gardener who was more comfortable in the company of plants than people.

Mrs Butters swallowed quickly. 'Begging your pardon for us all looking so shocking, though, m'lady.'

Eleanor waved the apology away. 'Gracious, you shouldn't be out of bed, let alone trying to plough on with your duties. On which note, I came to say no breakfast, please.'

Her bulldog let out an indignant woof and marched over to the quilted bed by the range to sulk at the lack of sausages on offer.

'Quite, Master Gladstone,' Clifford said with barely disguised amusement as he held out a chair for Eleanor. 'One more fit only for the slop and scraps bucket, I fear.'

All five women ran a hand over their tummy with a queasy wince.

'Hilarious, Clifford! Now, any more wily ruses you can find for shoehorning references to food and eating into the conversation is strictly forbidden. Understood?' Eleanor sunk into the seat.

'Spoilsport,' he muttered as he laid the blanket over the arm of her chair. He stepped to the range. 'Despite her ladyship being present, perhaps you had all best sit at the table on this singular occasion, ladies? Before you crumple underneath it.'

Looking relieved, they put down the bowls and cloths they had listlessly picked up and came over to slide into their seats.

'I don't suppose any of you fancy the back door being open, do you?' Eleanor said. 'Even with these occasional chills, I'm feeling rather over-warm at the same time.'

Her four ladies nodded gratefully. Polly rose unsteadily to be the one to do so.

'No. Allow me,' Clifford said in a playfully martyrish tone. 'As the only still serviceable member of staff.'

Eleanor gave him a good-natured huff. 'Stop enjoying our plight, you toad. None of us realised the perils of our overindulgence in the Spring Supper refreshments. And if you could also stop looking so dashedly bright and chipper, it would help. Especially as you can't have got more than a few snatched winks of sleep yourself.'

He bowed his head contritely but then picked Tomkins up from where the cat was batting the cheese dish on the dresser and waltzed him over to the range.

She smiled affectionately. 'Actually, Clifford, a doubly big thank you for all your nursing ministrations last night. I didn't realise at the time you were gallantly attending to all five of us with your magic potions.' She winked at her ladies. 'I shall purchase you the full frilly nurse's outfit. And a cauldron!'

Despite their pallid faces, they managed a giggle.

Clifford's lips quirked as he kept the tray he was now holding out of her reach. 'Touché, my lady. Perhaps I had best dispose of these, however?'

Looking at her staff, she tapped the table for him to dish out whatever he had conjured up. He set down the tray of five tall handled glasses, the light spirals of steam offering no hint of what the dangerously green-looking liquid was.

She shuddered. 'As much a penance as a cure?'

'Sadly, nothing more subversive than a restorative for your depleted electrolytes. A blend of puréed spinach in oat water with basil, ginger, honey and a pinch of sea salt.'

'Well, they'd better be lifesavers, Clifford. Or you may have a couple of dead bodies on your hands before long!'

6

'Ay, ay, girls! All cream and no flies, as always,' a voice called over the sound of boots stomping along the side path.

''Tis Milky Wilkes, m'lady,' Mrs Butters said. Unnecessarily, as the milkman appeared on the back step.

'Not today, thank you.' Clifford strode over and waved the milkman away.

'Be off with me double quick, is it, Mr Clifford?' Wilkes grumbled, no sign of his normal, relentlessly cheerful manner. 'Without even me usual cuppa? And after I ferried her ladyship's gaggle down to the village and back up last night. Well, there's thanks for you!'

'Gaggle? You rascal,' Mrs Trotman said weakly.

'Mr Wilkes definitely deserves at least a cup of tea. At the very minimum,' Eleanor called to Clifford.

'Ah, 'tis her ladyship.' Wilkes chuckled. 'Slummin' it in the kitchen too, mind, m'lady. Whatever would folks say?'

'Nothing, Mr Wilkes,' Clifford said firmly, still blocking the doorway. 'Just as you will not breathe one word about it.'

'If as it'll get me a cuppa and the sale of a quart of milk or two, surely I won't.' He sighed. 'I'm still stuck with more 'n half a cartload this mornin'.'

Mrs Butters looked up from the table, a frown on her face. 'How come, Milky? We're almost at the end of your round.'

'That you are. On account, however, of over half the village havin' been up all night after the Spring Supper, stuck on the lav—'

'Mr Wilkes!' Clifford said. 'Your tea will be served on your cart this morning. If you would kindly wait—'

'Hang on!' Eleanor interrupted. 'I want to hear what he has to say.' She jumped up. And then hastily sat down as her legs seemed to be made of jelly.

Clifford blanched. 'A covering, at least, my lady. Please.'

'What?'

'Pyjamas, your ladyship,' Polly whispered, making Eleanor look down at herself.

'Ah, yes. I forgot.' Sweeping Gladstone's pilfered blanket from the arm of her chair, she draped it round her like a cloak, pushed herself up again, and shuffled to the back door.

Clifford reluctantly stepped to the side.

'It's the latest fashion, Mr Wilkes. From Paris,' she said at the milkman's bemused look.

Wilkes whipped off his cap and gave her a sage nod. 'Makes sense, m'lady. I've heard tell more often than not the French are the sort to be found mostly in bed. Mind, whether it's theirs or not, is another story.'

She hid her smile, knowing Clifford would be horrified. 'Please tell me more about everyone feeling unwell. Minus the, er... physical details.'

Wilkes ran his hand through his mop of red-brown curls and leaned against the door frame. 'Well, it's just what I said, m'lady. Most folk are up and about. Barely. And lookin' like death warmed up. And a few 've got it so bad, they're still in bed.' He pulled a face. ''Tis a case of food poisoning alright.

And one as has run rife because everyone was in and out of each other's houses last night. Someone served up summat decidedly dodgy last evening and no mistake.'

'Goodness, how unfortunate!' She threw Clifford a pointed look. 'And some people might have been quick to judge that it was self-induced by overindulgence!' She noticed the milkman was still looking glum. 'You don't seem at all your usual self, Mr Wilkes. Perhaps someone close to you is poorly?'

Wilkes' jaw tightened. 'No! None of my lot are.' He threw out a sorry hand. 'Oh, 'pologies for that havin' come out soundin' sharp, m'lady. Only 'tis tearin' at my innards fierce enough, as if I'd got the sickness myself to hear folks' accusations.'

'Accusing you? Surely not? Of what?'

He thrust his hands angrily into his overall pockets, nodding grimly. 'Over half my customers have cancelled their orders sayin' my milk was the cause! The cheek of it! More likely that Sidney Giggs is to blame. Forever hawkin' his stinkin' fish round the village. 'Twas bound to happen sometime.'

Eleanor tried to hide her stomach griping at the image the milkman's words had thrown up. Particularly as Giggs was the fishmonger to Henley Hall. She gave Wilkes her best reassuring smile. 'Well, no such thoughts that your fine dairy products are to blame here. I shall be delighted if you would deliver your normal order.'

Taking her cue, Clifford nodded. 'Please bear with me, Mr Wilkes. I shall bring the jugs out to you presently. Along with remuneration, tea and a slice of something sweet.'

Wilkes broke into a smile for the first time. 'Mighty kind, m'lady! Your faith in my knowing what's what with keepin' milk is highly appreciated. That'll teach folk when I tell 'em the most important person of Little Buckford is wavin' my flag!' He left to wait on his milk cart with more of a spring in his step.

Clifford turned to the ladies. 'I believe her ladyship will

have no need of your diligent efforts this morning. Nor I, thank you.'

As the door closed behind the four of them, leaving Eleanor alone with Clifford, she groaned. 'I hope you've more of your wonderful tonic remedy. I think we'll all be needing it. And speaking of remedies...' She left that hanging.

'Quite. In light of Mr Wilkes' news, my apologies for misreading the rampant gluttony I witnessed last night as the cause of your digestive upset, my lady.'

She couldn't help laughing. 'You monster! Having a robust appetite does not make one a glutton.'

His lips quirked. 'Nor a lady.'

She laughed again, then clutched her stomach. 'I say, in all seriousness, Clifford. It struck me as rather odd, and out of character, that Wilkes was so vehement in pointing the finger at Giggs, the fishmonger, didn't you? Wilkes always seems such a genial chap.'

'Indeed. However, the two gentlemen ply their trades at the same back doors. And use the same, ahem, bawdy sales patter.'

'Ah! Rivals, you're suggesting? They each fancy themselves as Little Buckford's only back-door lothario, do they?' She frowned. 'I can't help wondering where the food poisoning did come from though? In fact, even with everyone trying to visit as many houses as possible for the Spring Supper, I can't see them all having gone to every house.'

'Though we did,' Clifford pointed out.

'Yes, but only because you harped on about as lady of the manor, I couldn't be seen to be snubbing anyone.' She tapped her chin thoughtfully. 'Not meaning to point any fingers, but I wonder who the most popular people in the village are? Because it seems likely the offending food was served by one of them.'

'Not necessarily, if you will forgive my offering a contrary view.'

She waved for him to elaborate.

'My lady, the Spring Supper is a most revered tradition in Little Buckford. But as in every village, and town, the world over, the chance to poke one's nose inside a grander home than one's own invariably proves too tantalising to resist.'

'Oh my, then thank goodness Henley Hall is too far to have taken part in the festivities so no one can point the finger at us.' She shrugged. 'Hmm, the vicarage and the larger houses around the village green would have seen most visitors in that case and therefore...' She tailed off with a knowing look.

'Most likely the fare in one of those establishments was to blame, my lady.'

'But hang on, that means we're wrong. As you just pointed out, we went to every house, including those, so how come you didn't succumb?'

At his enigmatic look, she folded her arms. 'I know how, Clifford! You didn't eat a morsel all evening, did you?'

'I really couldn't say, my lady.'

'You don't need to. Because I know and fully respect your fastidiousness about the little you ever seem to eat. And your precious rules of not eating in front of me. But the entire point of the Spring Supper was to partake of refreshments all together to bring good luck for the season.' She waggled her finger at him teasingly. 'You do realise you've likely blighted the whole spring now? And probably brought the pestilence of food poisoning down on the village as judgement!'

He rolled his eyes good-humouredly. 'Excuse me changing the subject, my lady, but do you wish anything before you retire for the rest of the day to recuperate?'

'Retire? I couldn't possibly. I've got two people to see in Chipstone, as noted in that appointment book you so thoughtfully provided. And I've something important to discuss with each of them.' She felt a pang of nerves. 'Especially with the first one. So I shall be washed, dressed and looking the picture of health. Well enough anyway, by the time you've done the necessaries and then brought the Rolls around.'

His brow flinched. 'If you are sure you are sufficiently recovered, my lady?'

'Tsk, Clifford! It's going to take a lot more than a little soured cheese curd or over-ripe herring to thwart my determination to carry on regardless.'

Actually, not that much more, her stomach griped. She hurried away to the door through to the main house to avoid him seeing how green her mention of food had made her feel. As she went, she mused that it really had been bad luck so many had been struck down. And so violently.

It makes you think, Ellie...

She shook her head gingerly. 'No, it doesn't,' she muttered. 'There's no time for unfounded speculation. More importantly, fingers crossed, you make it there and back without disgracing yourself!'

7

The imposing Georgian façade and liveried doorman of the Eagle Hotel reminded Eleanor it was by far the grandest building in the small market town of Chipstone. The only establishment respectable enough for the more well-to-do to dine in. And certainly, for anyone with a title. It enjoyed an admirable reputation that had stood since its sixteenth-century origins as a coaching inn on the route to London. The cobbled courtyard was ringed by black-timbered stables and precariously leaning outbuildings. Originally used to house the horses, the largest now housed the hotel's second, more down-to-earth, bar, affectionately nicknamed 'the Nest' by the locals.

As Clifford parked the Rolls, stepped around, and opened her passenger door, she bounded out more brightly than she felt.

'Now, as I've made clear the entire way here, I shan't need you on standby for an urgent dash back to Henley Hall's er... facilities. So, please enjoy a tipple in the Nest, rather than waiting in the car for me.'

'Too gracious, my lady,' Clifford said in that tone, which she knew meant he had no intention of doing anything of the kind.

She sighed. 'I don't suppose they serve stubborn donkeys anyway.'

At the end of the carpeted vestibule, the dining room was just as she remembered with its burgundy-flock wallpaper and exuberant array of horse brasses. It must have been several years since she'd been there.

Was it really as long ago as that, Ellie? Time really has flown.

She glanced around the room, looking forward to seeing her friend again, but not to what she needed to ask her.

Her uneasy thoughts were interrupted by the welcome feel of an arm sliding into hers and a familiar kiss on her cheek.

'Constance!' She beamed, too pleased to see her best friend not to pull her into a hug without a thought for decorum.

'I've missed you too, love,' Constance said. 'But remember, I'm half a foot shorter than you. Which means I'm balancing on tiptoe, with probably more than the hem of my petticoat on display.'

'Tsk! Hardly an appropriate way for a countess to behave,' Eleanor teased.

'Don't remind me!'

Eleanor pulled back and searched her friend's cornflower-blue eyes. 'Sore subject?'

Constance wrinkled her nose. 'A little, perhaps.'

'Your quietest table, please,' Eleanor said to the hovering waiter. She looped her arm in Constance's, waving to the tell-tale bump of the baby on the way. 'Come, my wonderful friend. Sit. Let it all out. Likewise, your beautiful hair.' She pointed at the blonde wisps visible under her friend's unexpectedly sensible navy hat. The one that matched her uncharacteristically conservative dress and jacket. 'No wonder you're a little melancholic. You've pinned your spirited waves up too tightly.'

Constance chewed her lip as she took her seat. 'Promise you won't tell me off?'

Eleanor laughed. 'Sniffy admonishments are Clifford's department, not mine, remember?'

'Still squabbling with your wonderful butler, I see.' Constance sighed. 'I hope he at least stays on after you're married, so you've one bit of certainty.'

'What?' Eleanor blanched at the unthinkable idea of being without him. 'Constance, you don't seem quite yourself?'

They were interrupted by the waiter returning to take their order.

Eleanor glanced at the menu, but the descriptions of the dishes made her still unsettled stomach churn.

'Anything light and simple that the Eagle's illustrious chef recommends, please,' she said weakly.

Having ordered the same, Constance unpinned her hat. Far from the waist-length cascade of blonde waves Eleanor had always admired, a restrained cluster dropped demurely to only halfway down her friend's neck.

Hiding her horror, she reached over and mussed it out a little. 'I think it's very chic. You look like Clara Bow on the silver screen.'

Constance shook her head. 'No, I look like a matronly married lady who's going to have a child. And I've stopped gazing into the mirror, because I don't recognise me at all.'

Eleanor felt a wash of dismay for her friend. And a pang of worry that it might soon be her feeling like that. 'Pity, because the girl I'm looking at is just as beautiful on the inside as she still looks on the outside.'

Constance smiled. 'Thank you, love. We are always girls underneath, aren't we? I think that's the problem.'

'Darling, your hair will grow again,' Eleanor said gently. 'I'm sure Peregrine adores it in any style, though. How is he, by the way?'

'Since we were married? Busy. Distracted. And... different.'

Constance's face lit up a little. 'But still gorgeous and loving, when he can find a few minutes to spend with me.'

Eleanor had quickly grown fond of Peregrine, now Lord Davencourt. He was a good man, even-tempered and kind. Handsome too. But most importantly, to Eleanor's mind, he adored his wife. But he had inherited an earldom and a vast estate, all of which he needed to juggle around his demanding mother – the dowager countess and Constance's mother-in-law.

Eleanor sipped her water and studied her friend closely. 'Want to tell me about it?'

Constance nodded gratefully. 'Only I don't want to sound negative. Especially as you're busy preparing to walk down the aisle yourself. It's just that, well, married life isn't...' She fiddled with her napkin. 'The thing is, I had no idea there are so many things Peregrine and I think differently about. Very differently. We talked about how we envisaged things being after we were married, obviously. But all our words have mostly turned out as fine theories that don't translate into real life.'

Eleanor patted her hand. 'I imagine it just takes a bit more time to get used to.' She hated how lame that sounded. 'But you know I'm the worst one to give advice. My first marriage only lasted six weeks. So you're already doing way better than me.'

It had been a whirlwind romance and a fairy-tale wedding in South Africa with a man who turned out not to be the respectable army captain he'd said he was. But Eleanor was at peace with the whole episode now. By a twist of fate, she had learned the real truth. That he'd loved her and no one else up to the point he died.

Constance, obviously reading her thoughts, squeezed her arm. 'I'm so sorry. I didn't mean to make you think about... that. You must feel this is terrible, what with you having been head bridesmaid for my wedding.'

Eleanor laid her hand over her friend's. 'Nonsense.'

Their food arrived.

'Lovely.' She tried unsuccessfully to quell the nausea at the exquisitely presented dish of flounder fillets on a bed of asparagus, dressed with a delicate parsley butter sauce. Valiantly clutching her knife and fork, she picked at the bits she hoped her groaning stomach would find least offensive.

'How about telling me what you are up to at the moment?' Eleanor said, hoping to lighten the conversation.

Constance beamed back at her. 'I'm rather excited, actually. I've set up a charity and action committee. Only, it's not the usual sort of thing a countess is supposed to get involved in.' She rolled her eyes. 'So you can imagine the relentless remarks from Peregrine's mother. But I'm determined. It started when I saw this workman chap, you see. He was struggling along the road on crutches having lost both his legs from the knees down.'

'Gracious, poor soul!'

'Exactly. The worst of it is, it happened on account of the stairs in his horribly neglected lodgings giving way.' Constance looked sheepish. 'It made me realise that even before I married Peregrine, and became a countess, what a privileged life I've lived. So I'm working on getting the most impoverished buildings in the area improved.'

'I say, that's amazing. You know you can absolutely count on my support in any capacity,' Eleanor said ardently.

Constance shook her head. 'Thank you, love. But no. You must be up to your neck in your own good causes. You've always been so busy fighting for others. That's why I admire you so much.'

Eleanor felt her cheeks flush guiltily, but Constance seemed not to notice as she leaned forward. 'Umm... I have got one horribly awkward thing I need to say, though.'

Eleanor winced. 'Me too. Fancy a walk?'

They both pushed away their barely touched plates and headed for the door.

As they reached the vestibule, Eleanor spotted Clifford at the reception desk, sorting out the luncheon bill on her account.

'We're just going for a stroll in the park, Clifford,' she said. 'I'll see you at the bandstand in about fifteen minutes.'

Chipstone's public gardens lay not far from the Eagle. A large oval grassed area, intersected with paths and beds of blooming spring flowers, it had been donated to the town by a philanthropic resident over a century before.

Eleanor and Constance paused behind a couple of dozen elderly parkgoers in deckchairs listening to the musicians play in the octagonal bandstand. Elgar swirled out across the gardens, as stately and reassuring as Buckingham Palace.

She turned to her friend. 'Who first?'

'Me, please.' Constance reached up and hugged Eleanor by the shoulders. 'Love, it's about your wedding day. The thing is... just in case you wanted to ask me to be, you know, head bridesmaid...' She tailed off, then spoke in a rush. 'I didn't want to presume, especially as you hadn't asked me yet, but in case you did, Peregrine has to go abroad for some business to do with the estate I don't understand. And he's told me he desperately needs me to go with him. I'd be back in time for the wedding, of course. I wouldn't miss that for the world. But I'd be away for all the rehearsals and fittings.' She looked up at Eleanor. 'I'm... I'm so sorry. But naturally, I'll tell him no if you want me to?'

Eleanor could barely contain her relief. It was exactly the topic she'd been dreading broaching, which is why she'd foolishly put off asking her friend. Although she knew from her own four years running... well, watching Clifford run Henley Hall, that Peregrine's estate and its tenant farms would be unlikely to have business in another country. Peregrine was almost certainly trying to make peace with his beloved wife and whisk her away somewhere unspeakably romantic so they could work through their problems.

She grasped Constance's hands. 'Honestly, darling, I was

dreading asking if you... if you would mind awfully *not* being head bridesmaid?'

'Of course not!' Constance cried, looking as if a great weight had been lifted from her, too. 'You silly thing. You could never offend me. I just want your wedding to be perfect for you.' She slapped Eleanor's arm. 'Which means it will probably be a fabulously unorthodox affair that will outrage high society.'

Eleanor laughed. 'Unfortunately, not with my infuriatingly pernickety butler helping me plan. His firm hand has kept any snags to a minimum so far. Although we have had a few things go wrong. You know, deliveries not arriving, a few things dropped by...' She shrugged. 'Well, it happens. And a couple of other minor setbacks.'

Constance slapped her arm again. 'Of course things are going to go awry when planning such a monumental event. Even with your infallible butler to hand.'

Elgar came to a measured close. As they clapped along with the other parkgoers, Eleanor heard a familiar voice.

'Two of my patients just admitted, yes.'

She couldn't mistake that taut, slightly tremulous tone. Nor the brusque delivery. She spun around to see Doctor Browning, Little Buckford's long-standing physician, his burgundy bow tie lying askew against his collar as always.

Browning tapped his white-coated companion with his cane. 'But be prepared for more, do you hear?'

The man, obviously a counterpart from the hospital, nodded. 'Yes, Doctor. And what is your diagnosis of the patients admitted so far?'

'Suspected food poisoning.'

Eleanor's brows shot up. *Oh goodness!*

8

'Doctor Browning?' Eleanor called, almost colliding with the white-coated man as he strode off, clearly keen to get back to the hospital.

'Who's calling?' Browning grumbled, tottering forwards and hooking his wire-rimmed spectacles over his ears to peer at her. 'Oh, it's you, Lady Swift.'

She nodded. 'And my good friend, Lady Constance, Countess Davencourt.'

Browning held up a tremulous hand. 'Enchanted, I'm sure. But forgive me, I've no time for chatting. Not that I am a man inclined to such frivolous pursuits anyway,' he added tartly.

Eleanor smiled placatingly. 'I know, Doctor. On both counts. But I simply must ask. Did I hear you correctly? That two people have been admitted to Chipstone Hospital with food poisoning?'

The elderly physician's lips met in a thin line. 'Nothing wrong with your hearing, evidently,' he said testily. 'Like the rest of you. You've the constitution of a rhinoceros, as I've said before.'

'I didn't know they got food poisoning too,' she said sweetly. 'Like I did last night. It kept me up constantly, actually.'

'Hmm, so that's it? Lady Swift, all my other patients seek my professional advice in my surgery. Not by accosting me in a public park!'

She fought the frown that threatened. 'I didn't hail you to ask for an impromptu consultation, Doctor. Only to ask if the people admitted are from Little Buckford? And if so, who they are?'

Browning frowned. 'If you must know, they are from the village, yes. Two serious cases of the near epidemic caused by someone's shoddy food hygiene at the Spring Supper. Miss Annie Tibbets and Miss Joyce Dunne. But in their condition, neither will appreciate a fruit basket, even from the lady of the manor.'

She rose above his terseness, knowing it stemmed from her having trodden on his venerable medical toes on more than one occasion. 'Goodness, I know Annie, of course.' She stifled her immediate concern that the woman was doing her wedding catering. 'But Miss Dunne, I've never met her.'

'Nor I, previously. Evidently, she is the new schoolmistress across the bridge.'

'Ah!' Eleanor's thoughts ran back to Clifford's teasing over how much she herself had eaten at the Spring Supper. Her frown reappeared. 'It seems odd those two ladies should have eaten so much more than anyone else to the point of being stricken so badly, doesn't it?' She remembered the lank-haired men tucking into the dripping wheel pastries as if they hadn't eaten properly for a week.

Browning eyed her irritably. 'Not to me, since I am their attending doctor! But what do I know? I've only been an expert physician for nigh on fifty years! Now, if you will excuse me.'

He doffed his homburg and stomped away with the aid of his cane.

Constance grimaced. 'Golly! He's prickly. But I know that look of yours, Eleanor. Something important has happened. So I shall leave you. Especially after you never said you'd been poorly last night, you naughty thing! Not that I gave you a chance, sorry. Thank you for listening, love. Get better and I'll telephone you tomorrow and make another date for lunch.' Blowing a kiss, she stepped away across the grass.

Eleanor waved distractedly, caught up in her concern for the two women admitted to hospital. Her own symptoms had been hideous enough, and yet she'd obviously been one of the lucky ones.

She closed her eyes heavenward and sent words of gratitude.

'There but for the grace of God, indeed, my lady,' her butler's measured tone cut into her thoughts.

Her eyes flew open in surprise. 'Clifford! I didn't see you lurking. Eavesdropping on my conversation with Doctor Browning, were you? Or are you running the gauntlet of reading my thoughts again?'

He tutted. 'Neither, my lady. Principally because I neither lurk nor eavesdrop. And, besides, your thoughts are too indecorous a place to venture into. Again,' he ended with a shudder.

She laughed. 'In which case, how did you know what I was thinking?'

'Simple deduction from the doctor's irate grumblings to himself as he passed me.'

She grimaced. 'I do seem to ruffle his feathers easily. But I should have asked him for something to settle my stomach. No matter, you can take me home, and I'll rely on one of your magical concoctions again.' She held up a finger as he went to reply. 'That is, once I'm finished at my next appointment. As well as needing to discuss floral bouquets and whatnots with Miss Moore, I think I've worked out who I owe the belated thanks to. You know, for that sweet little posy which was left on the doorstep?' For some reason she couldn't fathom, she desperately wanted to know who'd sent it to her. 'So enough fussing, I'm fine,' she lied unconvincingly, the morsels of lunch she'd eaten already dancing the fandango in her stomach.

The florist was in one of Chipstone's less affluent neighbourhoods, the hotchpotch of houses and shopfronts all in need of some serious love and attention. But that only made the florist's window display of beautiful blooms and verdant greenery shine out all the more, like a beacon of hope among its neighbours.

As the bell tinkled and Eleanor stepped over the threshold, the perfumed air she would normally relish seemed cloying in her queasy state. Nevertheless, she called out cheerily, 'Hello! Lucetta?'

'Lady Swift, is that you?' Lucetta Moore's head bobbed out from behind the moss-green curtain that led through to her workroom. With her long fair curls loosely tamed by a sweet circle of delicate wildflowers, she looked as if she'd just popped out of a fairy tale. Eleanor smiled, wishing she could emulate such natural beauty on her wedding day. Far from it looking affected, the florist had the knack of wearing her floral artistry as naturally as hair itself.

Lucetta stepped out with a welcoming smile and ran her hands over the front of her calico apron. 'M'lady, I'll understand completely if as you've come to say you've changed your mind?'

Eleanor gasped in mock horror. 'Not at all! There is no way my fiancé can escape from marrying me now.'

Lucetta laughed. 'I meant over me doing your flowers, not you getting married! Really, I've such a lowly little shop compared to the famous florists in London and even Oxford that most ladies in your position would use for such an important event.'

'But far more expert knowledge and skills than all of them put together,' Eleanor said genuinely. 'Including, somehow, understanding exactly what I'm looking for when, in all honesty, I have no idea myself.'

Lucetta smiled again. 'Then where would you like to start, m'lady? The arrangements for the church, for your ballroom, or your bouquet?'

'Please lead me through them in that order. Although,' she winced, 'I should have said before, my bouquet might not be needed. Umm, from you, that is.'

'No problem at all,' Miss Moore said easily. ''Tis your day to do with as you wish. And you must make the most of it. Goodness, I can't imagine even the lady of the manor ever getting a whole day that's entirely hers to unfold as she pleases. Not with all the responsibilities she has.'

Eleanor felt her cheeks flush. 'Ah, yes. But there is maybe something else wonderful instead you could create for me? But only if you honestly think I could pull it off with even a tenth of your effortless grace?' She hesitated, feeling unsure of herself. At Lucetta's encouraging look, she pointed at the woman's floral hair garland.

'Oh, m'lady, you'd be an absolute picture!' Lucetta cried. 'With your beautiful red curls and, forgive me saying, your green eyes being even more striking than real emeralds.' She moved around the shelves, selecting a few blooms, soft springs of various greens and a selection of tiny buds ranging from cream to white. Holding them up to Eleanor's cheek in turn, she frowned. 'Having met so many times afore in Little Buckford, I'd have said the creamier cherry blossom would match your skin tone. But it seems the ivory of baby's breath does so today, m'lady.'

Eleanor winced. 'Ah, that might be because I had a slight bout of something last night. It sort of washed me out, as it were.'

'The food sickness, m'lady? You got it too, then?'

Eleanor nodded. 'And I just heard poor Annie and the

new schoolmistress from across the bridge have been admitted to the hospital. But gracious, I should have checked that you're feeling alright? We didn't bump into each other, but with you living in the village too, I imagine you were at the supper?'

'That I was. But, to my shame, I only nibbled a little all evening. Always do. I get so nervous, needing to make conversation with so many people.' She gestured around the blooms filling her small shop. 'I've spent too many years with mostly flowers to talk to, you see, since my husband, well, left and then passed on, as you know.' She bit her lip. 'Only, if as I can beg you not to tell anyone about me not eating much? 'Tis believed to bring bad luck on the season.'

Eleanor leaned in and whispered, 'You have my word. And, confidentially, I know someone who ate even less than you, so you'll be blameless if any unfortunate seasonal outcomes occur.'

'Oh, thank the heavens.' Lucetta let out a long breath. 'How about I send you a few samples for your hair design?'

Eleanor clicked her fingers, pleased to have been reminded of the other reason she'd kept this appointment instead of crawling home as her battered body was pleading for her to do. 'That's what I meant to say. Thank you for the—'

'Ma, there's trouble! But it's not my doing afore you start,' a gruff male voice called.

Eleanor turned to see Alvan, Lucetta's twenty-something son, standing in the doorway raking his blond hair out of his blue eyes.

'Not now, Alvan,' Lucetta hissed. 'Beg pardon, m'lady.'

'That's alright.' Eleanor waved at him. 'Hello, Alvan, we haven't bumped into each other for ages.'

Alvan had the good grace to look abashed. 'Sorry not to have realised 'twas you, m'lady. Not surprising you haven't clapped eyes on me, mind. Seeing as you're a proper lady like, and I'm nowt more than a hardworking labourer as folk think is forever courting trouble. But it weren't my fault this time, I swear!' he protested to both of them.

Eleanor spotted Clifford materialise at the sudden commotion. She shook her head discreetly. She'd come across Alvan's unfortunate inherited temper once before. It fizzled out as quickly as it flared. When all was said and done, he was a good-hearted young man who'd grown up in difficult circumstances.

Lucetta rubbed her hands over her face. 'Alvan, I said *not now*. Can't you see I'm busy with Lady Swift?'

'But, Ma, who else am I supposed to go to?' he grumbled dejectedly, suddenly looking more like a lost little boy than a belligerent young adult.

Eleanor's heart went out to him. She smiled at Lucetta. 'In truth, I was looking for a way to make my hasty excuses without mentioning why... exactly.' She gave her a knowing look.

Lucetta nodded back in sympathetic understanding. 'Please do hasten home, m'lady. Soon as you're feeling better, pop along any time and we'll perfect your floral wedding wishes.'

As Clifford eased the Rolls away from the shop, he half-turned to Eleanor. 'Was it Miss Moore who sent you the posy, my lady?'

She frowned. 'Dash it! I didn't get to ask.'

'But you discussed the floral arrangements?'

'Er, a little. Poor Alvan needed her more than I did.'

Her butler's brow flinched. 'It is your wedding day at stake, my lady.'

'True. But with you as my personal wizard, it will all come together somehow.'

Despite it drawing ever closer, Ellie, and with so much still to arrange.

She grimaced at the gurgle from her stomach. 'Oh crumbs. I say, Clifford, can't you drive any faster?'

. . .

Back at Henley Hall, the news that her ladies were feeling considerably better allowed her to indulge in two blissful hours of worry-free snoozing on her favourite chaise longue. She woke a little stiff, but far more herself. And with two doting furry faces gazing into hers.

'Hello, chaps.' She reached out from under the soft woollen blanket she didn't remember falling asleep with, to cup the chins of her bulldog and tomcat, who were both balancing on her front.

'Gladstone, old chum, you're rather weighty for my stomach though,' she groaned.

She caught the sound of her butler's quiet cough from the other side of the closed door.

'Come in, Clifford. I'm perfectly respectable,' she called out.

He entered cautiously. 'Mmm. Debatable, my lady. Given your conversation with the milkman this morning was conducted in your nightwear.'

'Lucky fellow!' she said impishly.

His lips twitched. 'Perhaps. However, I shall ask your present visitors to wait while you change into something more suitable.'

'Visitors?' She groaned, glancing at the mantel clock. 'Who can it be at this hour of the evening?'

'The police.'

Her eyes lit up. 'Tell me Hugh's come back early!'

'Alas, no. It is, in fact, Sergeant Brice and Constable Lowe from the Chipstone Constabulary.' He peered at her sideways. 'Did something... untoward occur today while you were with Lady Constance that you perhaps failed to mention?'

She shook her head, a sense of foreboding welling up again in her stomach to replace the dull ache of food poisoning. 'No. Nothing. So what on earth can they want?'

9

Fluffing out her tousled curls, Eleanor hurried to the drawing room in the left-hand tower flanking the grand entrance of Henley Hall.

'Sergeant Brice and Constable Lowe, good evening,' she said overenthusiastically. Despite their ages differing as greatly as their physiques, the two policemen were both turning their helmets in their hands, looking equally uncomfortable at being in the, admittedly rather imposing, room, she assumed. The sweeping Wedgwood-blue settees, custom-designed to fit the curve of the tower along with the light-oak panelling of the walls, did give the space an undeniably illustrious air. Even her bulldog and tomcat didn't seem to relax either man as they scrabbled up their trousers.

'Ah! Usual greetin's welcome in a moment, Masters Gladstone and Tomkins, but not right now, eh?' Brice said, straightening up from tickling both their heads.

Eleanor smiled. 'Apologies for the terrible two, Sergeant. Please take a seat and a spot of tea while you tell me to what I owe the pleasure of you both coming all the way out from Chipstone?'

Brice ran his hand over the strained buttons of his uniform jacket, his thick moustache quivering as his lips moved. 'Mighty kind, m'lady. But we're on duty.'

She sensed a whiff of something ominous in his manner. 'Naturally, ever diligent as you both are. I'd still rather you got comfortable on the settee while you tell me what this is about, though?'

With a poorly disguised nod of relief to the fresh-faced Lowe, Brice hitched up his trousers and plonked his portly form down, Gladstone and Tomkins immediately nestling either side of him. He cleared his throat. 'Beggin' your pardon for comin' unannounced, m'lady. And for... well, perhaps as I'd better get to that in a minute. Only it's on account of us, that's Lowe and me, lookin' into the upset, you see?'

She didn't.

Clifford held out a cup of weak ginger tea to her, then turned to the policemen. 'The, ahem, digestive upset plaguing Little Buckford after the Spring Supper has brought you here, perchance, gentlemen?'

'Right on the nose, as always, Mr Clifford,' Brice said in a grateful tone. Despite his earlier protestations, he accepted a cup of tea, his face lighting up as Clifford added a slice of fruit-cake to the saucer with a pair of silver tongs. 'No. The furry ones is alright,' he whispered as Clifford made to remove her pets.

Eleanor was baffled. 'Forgive a silly question. Or two, actually. But why on earth does an unfortunate bout of food poisoning need investigating by the Chipstone Constabulary? It obviously wasn't deliberate. And why isn't our own village policeman, Constable Fry, conducting enquiries even if, heavens forbid, it was?'

Brice held up a podgy finger. 'Ah! Ever the sharpest sandwich in the picnic, m'lady. Or however the sayin' goes. In the case of the second question, Constable Fry is one of those as has been struck down severe enough so as he can't leave the la— er, house.'

She winced, knowing too well how awful that felt, even more glad that seemed behind her now. 'Poor fellow. But do enjoy your refreshments, gentlemen. They're quite safe. Henley Hall wasn't part of the Spring Supper. And feel free to ask anything you wish. Constable Lowe included. I won't bite.'

'Though that might depend on the nature of the visit,' Clifford murmured.

She pretended she hadn't heard and smiled at the young officer, remembering his Buckinghamshire accent was even broader than Brice's. His elongation of 'a' to 'ah' and 'o' to 'ohw' she always found delightful. 'Well, Constable, what's this about?'

Lowe glanced at his sergeant and received a magnanimous nod, partly Eleanor thought with a quiet smile because his superior's mouth was too busy savouring her cook's delectable fruitcake to speak.

'Thing is, m'lady, it was Constable Fry as rang Sergeant Brice, and asked for our help. When he heard 'bout poor Miss Tibbets and the other lady, Miss...' Lowe stared at the ceiling. 'Miss Dunne, that's it.'

'Being admitted to hospital, yes, I heard that too. So unlucky for both of them. I do hope they're recovering quickly with expert medical care?'

Brice swallowed hastily. 'When did you hear of it, m'lady? If as it's not rude to ask, of course?'

'Not at all. It was this afternoon, about two o'clock. Doctor Browning told me when I bumped into him in Chipstone Park.'

Brice's expression turned more earnest. 'Ah! Then I'm afraid I've an unhappy update. That Miss Dunne is stable, alright, but poor Miss Tibbets has tumbled even further downhill.'

She shook her head. 'Gracious, that's terrible! I must visit both ladies first thing tomorrow morning.'

'Ah, no can do, m'lady,' Constable Lowe said apologetically. 'No visitors allowed. Hospital doctor agrees with your Doctor Browning, you see.'

'He'd be a braver person than me if he didn't,' she murmured to Clifford as he topped up her tea. She took a sip, still trying to fathom why she was having this conversation with the two policemen, who were now looking decidedly shifty as they stared at their boots.

'Sergeant Brice, please get to the heart of the matter,' she said firmly.

Brice hesitated, then seemed to decide. 'The problem, m'lady, 'tis like this. Constable Fry telephoned me, and in a voice as weak as a babe in swaddling too, mind.' He shook his head. 'And him normally bein' built stronger 'n two carthorses sewn together.'

Eleanor restrained her natural impatience. Despite his bumbling manner, Brice was a good and dedicated policeman. Just one out of his depth on much beyond the petty misdemeanours the locals of sleepy Chipstone generally got up to.

'Yes, Sergeant?'

Brice grimaced. 'Thing is, m'lady, Constable Fry's worried as how the bad feelin' in the village might escalate. If anyone else ends up in hospital with the sickness, like Annie Tibbets. And havin' stopped off at the first front door only, I'm of the mind he's more 'n right!'

Eleanor frowned. 'The first front door you knocked on in Little Buckford?'

Brice nodded again, looking embarrassed. 'That's why when the door slammed on us, I said to Lowe it'd be better without us pokin' our noses in. Well, you can see how us goin' from door to door delvin' into where this 'ere food poisonin' might have come from would be like petrol to a lit rag, m'lady?'

He tugged on his jacket collar. 'Specially as Chipstone police aren't so popular in Little Buckford.'

'Plus, m'lady,' Lowe said, 'unless as someone's broken food hygiene regulations in a shop or a business, then, well, it's not police jurisdiction.'

Brice clucked his tongue at him. 'Alright, Lowe, you've no need of stealin' me thunder. Nor spoutin' the law at her ladyship. Lummy, with her record of diggin' 'bout in police business, her ladyship likely knows the law better 'n me and you.'

'Only through having repeatedly flouted it so comprehensively,' Clifford murmured.

She realised the two policemen were staring expectantly at her.

'Say as you will, m'lady?' Brice said.

'Will what?'

'Whether you'll ask around the village and find out where the food poisoning came from?'

Clifford arched a brow, a sure sign he was unhappy with the request.

Eleanor was also unhappy. She shook her head slowly. 'Sorry, Sergeant, I can't.'

The policemen stared at each other.

'But, m'lady, you've got that way of gettin' folks to open up that we haven't,' Brice said. 'And you've always been a champion for Little Buckford. Leastways, in the not-so-distant past.'

His words bristled her. Unfairly, her conscience whispered, because he'd unwittingly hit a sore nerve that had become increasingly raw in the last few days. She used to know almost everyone in the village. At least to say hello to. But what with her being away so much and it having grown in the last few months or so, she felt out of touch. Particularly with everyone and everything over the bridge. And quietly, she felt guilty about it. Too late, however, her reply flew out, more harshly than intended.

'Evidently, I need to repeat myself, Sergeant. My answer is no, I'm afraid. Because much as I appreciate your confidence in me, it may have escaped your notice that I am knee-deep in preparations for my fast-approaching wedding day!'

Brice shifted uncomfortably. 'To the chief inspector, I know, m'lady. And all the area's cheerin' for you both. Only, I'm honestly worried that the two halves of your village might come to blows over this food poisonin', you know?'

She shook her head again, more forcefully this time. 'I'm sorry, but I've made my decision.'

Brice rose hurriedly, his jowls wobbling as he nodded. 'Course, m'lady. Sorry to have taken up your time askin'. We'll be runnin' along now.'

Having seen the policemen out, Clifford stepped back into the drawing room, his expression as inscrutable as ever. 'More tea, my lady?'

She suddenly felt very tired. 'Stuff the tea, Clifford. Please get your admonishments over with.'

He tidied the discarded cups onto a silver tray. 'As your butler, my lady, it is far from my place to hold, let alone render, an opinion on your words. Or decisions. However, I do believe the strain of severe food poisoning on top of all the preparations for your wedding has taken its toll. You need fewer responsibilities, not more.' He held her gaze. 'Will there be anything else?'

She rubbed her face in her hands. 'No, Clifford. Thank you.'

As his coat-tails glided out the door, she dropped onto the settee, wishing it would swallow her up. But she couldn't get a creeping feeling of guilt... and foreboding... out of her mind.

10

The following morning, feeling fully restored, Eleanor gave herself a good talking-to over breakfast. She hated maudlin self-indulgence. It was an anathema to her innately direct and honest approach to everything and everyone. Including herself. So, she admitted to her mountain of toast and jam that, although she hadn't changed her mind, she could apologise to Sergeant Brice. After all, she had rather brusquely turned down his suggestion she investigate the unfortunate outbreak of food poisoning.

While eating her delicious griddle scones topped with light scrambled eggs, an idea struck. She could ring Brice that afternoon. Which left her free to pop down into Little Buckford this morning. The great outdoors had always been her haven, her escape; it would restore her spirits and at the same time, her perspective.

'And while I'm at it, I can make my first attempt at reacquainting myself with the villagers,' she whispered to her pets under the table. Sneaking them the sausages and kippers her stomach still didn't fancy, she straightened up. She just needed to play it right.

'I shan't need the Rolls, thank you, Clifford,' she said airily, as he stepped back into the morning room.

'As I suspected, my lady. Your other "vehicle" is waiting for you at the base of the entrance steps. Regrettably.' He sniffed before gliding away again.

Dash it, Ellie! How does he manage to be so disapproving and so thoughtful at the same time?

Pleased, however, he didn't seem to have guessed why she preferred not to take the Rolls, she finished her breakfast in record time and hastened up to her bedroom.

She was soon attired in her favourite cycling wear, made by her expert seamstress and housekeeper, Mrs Butters. A stylish divided cycling skirt in sage green with matching jacket. The skirt's generous pleats front and back and overlay panel which buttoned down the centre gave her the freedom of movement offered by trousers while still maintaining decorum. To her mind, anyway. To Clifford, the very notion of her being seen on a bicycle gave him nightmares. And that despite his genuine awe that she had once cycled across the world, alone.

She shook herself. That world seemed a lifetime ago now.

Twenty minutes later, the imposing gates at the end of Henley Hall's half-mile long treelined drive came into view. As she pedalled under the tall arch, Gladstone let out a series of excited woofs from the olive-green trailer attached to the side of the bicycle. It had been a wonderful surprise from Joseph, her gardener. Next to his inseparable friend, Tomkins' eyes were equally bright with excitement. Both of them sat with their paws up on the thickly padded, curved-front cowl, which served as an extra safety feature for her precious pet cargo, along with their made-to-measure harnesses.

As she turned onto the small country lane leading down into the village, the wind was more blustery than she'd anticipated, but still mostly behind her. That meant later she would have to battle a headwind on the way up the steep, winding hill back to Henley Hall. Hoping her stamina would hold after the draining effect of her stomach upset, she decided it was worth the risk. At least at that moment, she was freewheeling down. And, as a last resort, she could always walk back up, pushing her whole charabanc with plenty of rests.

Although in her heart she wanted to catch up with the locals, the village common and duck pond arrived all too soon. She quickly leaned down and placed a hand over Gladstone's eyes so he wouldn't see the ducks waddling across in front of them. Then she pedalled on around to the start of the high street.

To her confusion, Little Buckford's shopkeepers were gathered outside the butcher's shop, along with several other villagers. Even with the universal penchant for gossip, she'd never seen such an ardent-looking discussion under way. Her bicycle bell dinged of its own accord as her wheels juddered over the cobbles towards them. Every head turned. She spotted Dylan Penry, the heifer-framed butcher, flap his meaty hand at the others. As if fearing she had something contagious, the shopkeepers hurried back to their respective premises, the other villagers dispersing.

Eleanor fought a frown. She wasn't in the mood for tricky conversations. However, Penry re-emerged to chivalrously hold her handlebars as she dismounted. Needlessly, in fact, as the attached sidecar made the perfect stabiliser.

She smiled at Penry, realising now that he had hurried back out in case she'd thought the gossiping group had disbanded because of her arrival.

'Good morning, m'lady. Out pedalling your fine wheels, I see. And with the terrible two aboard,' he said in his delightful Welsh lilt as he ruffled her pets' ears. Although it sounded a little flatter than usual.

'I have, Mr Penry. However, I should really swap the lazy

pair for a couple of horses who could pull me back up that wicked rise to Henley Hall.'

Penry cocked his head. 'Like me to watch them while you go about whatever you've, er, planned, m'lady?' he said in an unconvincingly nonchalant tone.

She hid her smile at his nosiness and unhitched her bicycle basket. 'No, thank you. Because I shall need you behind your wonderfully well-provisioned butcher's counter to conjure up the items on Mrs Trotman's list. I pilfered it while Clifford wasn't watching.'

'Ah, that's the best news since I opened up this morning,' Penry said earnestly as he escorted her inside. 'But playing cat and mouse with your butler though, m'lady, well, well.'

She laughed. 'Trust me, sometimes it's just easier.'

'Is that so?' He pushed away a pile of neatly stacked wrapping papers on the wooden counter. 'Now, what can I get for you?'

His deflated manner made her realise how far he was from his usual self. Not wanting to pry, she rummaged in her jacket pockets for the list. Then tried her skirt. 'Ah! Here it is. A little battered and crinkled but still legible, hopefully.'

Casting his eye down the paper, Penry brightened. He turned to his butcher's block, deftly slicing and chopping. 'A goodly list, thank the heavens! At least some of my meat won't go to waste now.' At her questioning look, he sighed. 'M'lady, you're the only customer I've had all morning. And likely as not, will probably still be the only one by the end of the day. No one's buying today.'

'After the bout of food poisoning that coincided with the Spring Supper?' she said, trying to be diplomatic.

Penry's expression clouded. 'There was no coincidence, if you'll excuse me saying, m'lady. Over half the village was struck down, only a few hours or less after eating in all and sundries' houses that evening. And some is blaming my meat!'

'I can't imagine why,' she said genuinely, waving a hand at the immaculate glass-fronted cabinets filled with precise cuts on shiny trays, all divided by fresh green herbs. 'You run the most pristine butcher's shop I've ever been into.'

'Mighty kind, m'lady. And being a shrewd 'un, as you've proved many times before, you'll agree with me who's really to blame, I'm sure?'

She felt put on the spot. 'Oh, goodness. I wouldn't dream of speculating who it was. And it hardly matters anyway. It was just an unfortunate, er, mistake.'

'Like that, is it?' Penry looked at her askance, which was so out of character for him, she blanched as he turned back to the beef joint he was stringing for her.

'I'm afraid I don't understand?' She loaded the parcels he had wrapped so far into her basket.

Penry blushed. 'Didn't mean to speak out of turn, m'lady,' he said gruffly. 'Only it's obvious it came from over the bridge.'

'But, Mr Penry, I didn't think any of the new villagers over the bridge had taken part?'

'Maybe, m'lady. But as we say in the valleys, "Things turn sour when you play with fire!" Mark my words on that.'

She grabbed the last of the parcels, feeling the urge to escape his uncustomary lack of goodwill. But before she left, she had to ask. 'Have you heard any more about the ladies who were taken to hospital?'

'Not a word, m'lady. Poor Annie Tibbets. She was only in here the afternoon of the Spring Supper, giving me a heads-up on what might be needed for your wedding catering. Once you'd approved it all, course.'

'There were two of them taken to hospital,' she said pointedly. 'A Miss... Miss Dunne, I believe, was the other lady?'

'If you say so, m'lady.'

She dug out her brightest smile. 'Well, I'm pleased you yourself seem to have avoided any ill effects?'

He nodded. 'Not surprisin'. I'm built like two sides of beef strung together. Plus, I'm one for eating only as I do every day.' He waved a firm hand around the shop.

'Mr Penry, you've no need to convince me. I really do believe your fine produce isn't responsible for this outbreak. Thank you for the extra ham bone for Gladstone. Good day now.'

She escaped out into the blustery wind, feeling a few spits of rain in the air. She sighed.

The weather, Ellie, like the mood in the village, seems to be turning increasingly sour!

11

Eleanor wheeled her bicycle awkwardly across the cobbled street and parked it opposite, outside the baker's. Having assured Gladstone and Tomkins she'd only be a minute, she pushed the shop door open.

'Good morning, Mr Shackley?' she called cheerily.

'Is it?' came the unexpected reply through from the back room where the ovens were.

She was horrified by the lack of welcome. Then it dawned. He was teasing her.

'Yes, it is still morning, Mr Shackley. Has Clifford been telling you again that I usually finish breakfast just in time for lunch?'

'Mr Clifford?' Shackley's flour-covered face poked around the doorway. 'Lawks, 'tis you, m'lady! Forgive me hollering at you like that.'

He hurried out, looking rather unsteady to her mind.

'That's alright. Only if you weren't teasing me, what *did* you mean?'

He let out a long breath. ''Tis no use pretending. I've had no more than three people cross my threshold this morning. And all of 'em came not to buy even a crust, but to give me an earful.' He picked up a thick blue order book. 'Then three more had the face to come in and tell me straight they was cancelling their orders for the foreseeable future. Most other folk took the coward's way of shoving their accusations through my shop's letter box.' He flapped at the papers. 'No bread. No flour. No buns. No cakes. No nothing. Until further notice!' He sighed. 'I assume you've come to do the same, m'lady?'

Eleanor shook her head vigorously, spotting that his usual radish cheeks were close to being as pale as his sacks of flour. 'Mr Shackley, I haven't come to cancel anything. On the contrary, I'm here to purchase everything on Mrs Trotman's list.'

'Really, m'lady?' he said, looking relieved.

'Yes, really. It's here somewhere...' She rummaged in her basket, then scrabbled in her pockets. Coming up empty, she realised with dismay she'd never taken it back from Penry. Not relishing the idea of returning, she sent her cook a silent apology. 'I seem to have mislaid it. Never mind, I remember it was plenty of the usual, please, with generous amounts of all your stickiest treats as well.'

Now who's the coward, Ellie?

'Right you be, m'lady.' Shackley busied himself filling a half-sized paper sack with loaves. 'Forgive me, I'm not myself at the moment. I should have trusted you'd be cheering us this side of the bridge. That food poisoning couldn't have come from anywhere but t'other side, could it?'

She groaned silently. 'But none of us even crossed to that side, Mr Shackley. Far less ate over there. So that can't be where any of the tainted food came from, can it?'

'There are ways, m'lady,' he said darkly.

She hurriedly switched the conversation to her wedding preparations.

''Tis too good of you to be inviting the village proper up to

Henley Hall after the service.' Shackley tapped his nose know-ingly. 'With you being your usual shrewd self and keeping the list to only that, there'll be no repeat of the Spring Supper awfulness, thank goodness.'

She felt herself bristling. Her wedding day was hers to plan, with Hugh's input too, obviously. Not that her fiancé wanted anything except exactly what made her heart skip with delight. And yet here was the village baker, poking his nose in on who she should invite! She frowned. That didn't sound like the Morace Shackley she'd liked from day one of inheriting Henley Hall. He was usually the epitome of affable and peace-loving.

'Feeling alright, Mr Shackley?' she said.

'Not great to tell the truth, m'lady. But much better than afore. That food poisoning got me good and proper. My Eliza-beth too, she's still tired out after it. I told her to stay upstairs and rest.'

Eleanor was fond of his wife. Like him, she was a gentle soul, always the first to visit anyone who was unwell in the village. 'Goodness, please give her my very best, won't you? And say to ask if she needs anything at all. Clifford's a wizard at knocking up miraculous remedies. Some of them don't even make one shudder.'

'I'll pass on your kind wishes, m'lady.' Shackley held out the paper sack and a large box to her. His jaw tightened. ''Twas bad enough, trouble coming over and making half the village sick. But giving it to my wonderful Elizabeth, too. That's too much!'

She took the sack and box. 'Well, thankfully not as badly as the ladies admitted to hospital.'

'Thanks be, indeed. That poor Annie Tibbets.'

'Oh, didn't you hear? *Two* ladies were taken in.'

Shackley shrugged. 'I did, m'lady. What of it?'

'Nothing,' she mumbled. She had decided last night not to get involved, she reminded herself, so she bid him a hasty farewell.

She turned and almost collided with the owner of the general store who was standing on the step into Shackley's bakery. 'Oops, sorry, Mr Brenchley! How are you this fine morning?'

'Perturbed, m'lady. If as you really want to know.'

Suddenly fearing she didn't actually want to know, she glanced at her watch as St Winifred's bells rang out the hour. 'Goodness, is that the time? Do excuse me. I really must be... anywhere else,' she ended in a mutter, throwing the sack and box into the trailer beside her and mounting the saddle. She waved as she set off, her head down.

Perhaps we'll get a more positive reception at the Dog and Badger, Ellie?

Little Buckford's only legally licensed public house embodied its publican; solidly built, down to earth and no frills. But plenty of heart if one looked hard enough. And, unfortunately for her, staunchly traditional. She wasn't allowed in the main bar, only the room at the rear reserved for women. And only then if accompanied by a man. That it was affectionately known as 'the Parlour', however, softened her irritation. But today she put her views on women's rights out of her mind. Rounding the corner, she spotted Stokes placing several bench seats and mismatched tables on the small square of grass in front of his pub.

'Setting up for the lunchtime rush, Mr Stokes?' she called out.

His tired face broke into a frown as he tugged on the hem of his smart but faded grey cardigan.

'I'm afraid there's no meals going, m'lady, if as you was hoping so?' he said in his familiar hoarse voice, gravelled by decades of standing amid clouds of cigarette smoke.

'I was, actually.' She'd hoped something light might help

fuel her back up the hill. Stokes' game pies were legendary. 'Trouble with your stove, is it?'

'Not a bit. Haven't bothered to turn it on. Folk aren't eating so much as even a steak and ale pie. Not after that awful doings at the Spring Supper.'

She should have been more prepared, she knew. 'Yes, of course. And, umm, please forgive me if it's the wrong thing to say, Mr Stokes, but I was very sorry to hear about Annie Tib— I mean Annie.' She blushed, cursing her runaway tongue.

He shook his head. 'No, you were right calling her by her maiden name, m'lady.' His brow furrowed. 'She chose not to be known as Annie Stokes no more, after we, you know, separated.' He waved his hand dismissively. 'Anyway, I tried ringing the hospital this morning, but they wouldn't say anything. At least Doc Browning had the mind to come tell me yester afternoon she hasn't rallied yet.' He looked away. 'There's a fine how d'you do when a man can't ask after his own wife. She still is, you know. Leastways on paper,' he muttered, looking down at the bench.

Eleanor winced. 'I'm so sorry. I didn't mean to cause any upset...' She tailed off, wishing she'd never come down to the village at all. 'Can I buy you a drink?' she said, floundering for anything else to say.

He looked up, almost smiling. 'In me own pub?' He shrugged. 'Why not, m'lady. What'll you have?'

'Something cold, without alcohol or bubbles, please.'

Stokes tutted. 'You should have stopped off at the river and just lain down in it, m'lady. Would a' done as good a job.' He disappeared inside briefly as she sat down at the table, returning with a still lemonade for her, and what looked like a large brandy for himself. Taking a seat, he drummed his fingers on the table. 'Terrible doings, that supper business.'

'Well, most of us are recovering quickly,' she said, trying to inject some positivity. 'And we did all welcome in spring. So you should be fine for a bumper crop of hops to replenish your beer barrels.'

''Tain't the point, though,' Stokes gruffed, waving at the near empty high street. 'Look how bad it's affected the village. Just as that wretched lot over the bridge planned by messing with our centuries-old traditions, too. The blooming nerve of it!'

She sighed to herself. Short of leaving her drink and flouncing off, she really had no choice but to answer.

'I admit some shopkeepers mentioned their businesses have been adversely affected, like yours, Mr Stokes,' she said carefully. 'But who exactly from over the other side do you think is responsible?'

'Them two as started the scuffle in Mrs Browne's house,' he growled.

She sipped her drink, finding it far more refreshing than the conversation. 'But I was there at the time and didn't see anything untoward.'

He thumped the bench top. 'Ah! But you was poorly after, if I understood, right, m'lady? See? Stands to reason. Them two louts tampered with the food what Mrs Browne had made special for the Spring Supper. And then did same in t'other houses in the village.'

She tried, and failed, to keep the frown off her face.

'But why, Mr Stokes? What reason would they have to do such a thing?'

He rolled his eyes as if she was a small child. ''Tis obvious. They was put up to it, and paid no doubt, so as Penry and Shackley's customers'll be forced to buy their food from the new shop over the bridge!'

A familiar cough made Eleanor spin around in relief.

'Yet the shop over the bridge does not sell fresh meat, Mr Stokes,' Clifford said smoothly. 'Only tinned. And the only goods akin to bread in any way are all packaged.'

Stokes shrugged. 'Morning, Mr Clifford. Right you be. But they'll start selling it now, I'll wager.'

She fought hard to keep a frown off her face. 'Please, Mr Stokes. Let's keep this unfortunate incident in perspective. It was an accident, nothing more.' But even as she spoke, she felt a flicker of doubt herself. Forcing it down, she continued. 'At the very worst, it was simply carelessness in the way someone had stored the food they made for the Spring Supper.'

A collective gasp rang out. Eleanor turned to see a group of villagers had gathered behind her, shaking their heads in unison.

'Time to go, my lady,' Clifford muttered.

She opened her mouth again, but caught his cautioning look.

He's right, Ellie. Otherwise, things might turn ugly in Little Buckford!

12

Without another word, she hurried her bicycle across to the Rolls and, with Clifford's help, positioned it onto the mounting points he'd had added to the back of the car. As they drove away with Gladstone and Tomkins on her lap, the last thing she saw in the rear-view mirror was the group of villagers standing in the road. They were looking after her, still shaking their heads in silent admonishment.

'Thank you for coming along when you did, Clifford.' She buried her face in her tomcat and bulldog's soft foreheads where they lay snuggled against her front. 'Dash it, I'm trying, but I don't seem to be getting anything right at the moment.'

He shook his head. 'Purchasing inordinate amounts from each of the shopkeepers was at least well-intentioned, if misguided, my lady,' he said gently.

'Even though you're quietly horrified at my running errands at all.' She smiled. 'Are we friends again, then?'

'A titled lady and her butler?' He sniffed, his eyes twinkling though. 'Tsk! That would never do.'

As he swung the car's stately bonnet around the rear of

Henley Hall to unload her bicycle in the far garage, she looked across to the kitchen step.

'Oh, that's so sweet!'

Polly, her youngest maid, was clutching a bunch of forget-me-nots, clearly a gift from her admirer, Jack Browne, who was hovering with his cap in his hands a few feet from her.

'Ah! Young Jack has evidently taken the opportunity to see Polly while delivering some packages for your wedding garden party. And to say with flowers what I doubt he has still yet to find the courage to say in words.' Clifford reversed the car. 'Rest assured, Mrs Butters will be within chaperoning view, my lady. However, our arrival would certainly mar the snatched moment for the young pair. My apologies for thus returning you to the front of the house.'

'Don't be daft, you softie,' she said.

As he opened her passenger door, two large trucks with smart burgundy-lettering along the sides slowed on seeing them.

'Sorry, governor. Looks like we missed the tradesmen's entrance,' one driver called out.

Clifford held her pets back from bounding over and waved for the drivers to wait there. 'The marquee has arrived, my lady. Given it will take some days to erect with the flooring as well, if you will excuse me to instruct the assembling team on its precise location?'

'Of course. But goodness, the marquee! That arriving, more than anything else, feels like the wedding is really going to happen in a week's time.' She felt a little breathless.

'Too late to wriggle out of it now,' Clifford said teasingly.

The thought of burying herself in wedding preparations sounded a wonderful diversion from her uncomfortable conversations in the village. And, in truth, imagining the marquee erected on the rear lawn was too magical not to fill her with excitement. It felt like a turning point.

The only important thing is that Hugh wants to marry you more than anything in the world, Ellie!

She turned to her pets. 'Come on, chaps. We've got heaps of wonderful things to do.'

She bounded up the entrance steps, followed by Gladstone and Tomkins.

'Oh my stars, 'tis such a treat to see you looking better, m'lady,' her housekeeper's voice enthused from behind the tall stack of beautiful pink-and-cream striped boxes she was carrying.

'You too, Mrs Butters.' Eleanor took the top half and scanned her housekeeper's motherly face. 'Assuming you really are, and not just ploughing on with your duties as always?'

'Ach, scout's honour, m'lady,' Lizzie said with her delightful Scottish burr as she joined them. She was carrying three large velvet-covered cases, each adorned with an embossed silver ribbon across the top corner. 'We're all as right as ninepences bobbin' in champagne now!'

'Thanks to Mr Clifford and his witch's concoctions.' Mrs Trotman chuckled from the other side of the hallway. She rested the enormous cake stand she was carrying on the banister rail. 'Wouldn't be surprised to see him flyin' over Henley Hall on the scullery broom next full moon, m'lady!'

They all laughed, Eleanor loudest of all, as she'd suggested that very thing to her butler recently.

'Wait for me,' Polly called, skipping around the corner from below stairs, draped in emerald and gold silk chair sashes. She skidded to a wide-eyed halt on seeing Eleanor. 'Beg pardon, your ladyship, I didn't realise as you'd arrived back.'

'Good,' Eleanor said, which seemed to baffle her youngest maid.

'Now, ladies. How about you join me for a catch-up in the main dining room? Clifford has insisted that is the only area large enough for the wedding's base of operations.' She beckoned them all to huddle in close. 'Because I've got a change to the plans I want to ask for your help with.' She lowered her voice. 'But confidentially. Just between us girls. So I'll save it until last.'

Over the next few hours with her ladies, she ticked off the raft of tasks and decisions meticulously listed in Clifford's planning notebook. Including choosing the final sets of table decorations for both the ballroom and the marquee, plus deciding on the linen and silver napkin rings for the evening reception. And, to her bemusement that such a thing was optional, the piping style of the icing for her wedding cake.

Mrs Trotman smiled at her. 'And don't you worry, m'lady. If as Annie Tibbets needs more of a hand with doing your catering after being taken with the food poisoning, I'll find time without trouble.'

'And Polly 'n me is all primed for pitchin' in with any extra as would be needed kitchen-wise this end,' Lizzie said.

'With Mrs Butters keepin' us on track,' Polly added solemnly.

'Thank you, all. Poor Annie. I imagine she'll certainly be rather tired for a few days, at least. I shall visit her the moment I'm allowed to,' Eleanor said.

As they moved onto admiring the embroidered ribbons and lace Mrs Butters had lovingly crafted to match the bodice of her wedding dress, Eleanor spotted all her ladies welling up.

'Don't start me off,' she whispered.

Polly dabbed at her eyes with the hem of her apron. 'M'lady, 'tis a wonder you want to include the likes of us in plannin' your most special day.'

'Indeed. Since there is no mischief to be decided upon,' Clifford said playfully, as he passed in the corridor accompanied by eight men in overalls, all carrying potted cream and apricot rose trees.

Eleanor waited until their footsteps had receded towards the ballroom. 'Ah, on that note. Mrs Butters, is it too late to press your wonderful sewing skills into conjuring up four extra-special outfits...'

Thankfully, that evening, Clifford hadn't made a fuss over Eleanor's request for a simple supper tray to enjoy in Henley Hall's cosiest room, 'the Snug'. She felt it was the least she could do to spare her ladies even more work alongside all the wedding preparations still going on around her.

As the mantel clock struck nine, he handed her a small sherry on a silver tray. 'Bravo for your progress today, my lady. I cannot say the same my side, unfortunately. As you know, we were due a delivery from Whitlows of London of the bespoke embossed wedding guest books for the marquee and ballroom. Guests will be eager to scribe their heartfelt wishes for your future happiness in both, I am sure.'

She nodded. 'And?'

'And they are insisting they delivered the items. Apparently their delivery van broke down so they sent them by another company who disgracefully left them without informing anyone late last evening. However, I have not been able to locate the items, suggesting they are either lying or—'

'Or someone took them?' She thought for a moment, a cold feeling creeping up her spine once more. 'I'm sure not, Clifford. It's bad service, certainly, but don't worry about it. We can get them to send some more in time.'

He nodded. 'Absolutely, my lady.' Then arched a brow. 'Is there anything else on your side I need to be informed of?'

'No.' She held up his planning notebook with both hands to make the point of how weighty it was. 'I ticked everything off neatly as I went, so you can see exactly what's what.'

'Ahem, "neatly" for a spider dipped in ink, perhaps?' He peered at the open page through his pince-nez and tapped the entry she'd spotted he had recently underlined. 'If I might be so bold as to suggest telephoning Lord Langham soon to ask him to give you away, my lady? As his lordship was your late uncle's oldest friend, it is only proper. And he will be expecting too, naturally.'

'I haven't forgotten,' she said, sipping her sherry.

The sound of the doorbell ringing more fervently than usual made them share a look. She winced. 'I rather hoped to spend the rest of the evening trumping you at chess and toasting progress with a glass of our favourite port.'

Clifford's lips quirked. 'As inappropriate an offer as it is tempting, my lady. Whomever it is, I shall say you are not at home.'

He returned quickly. 'Regrettably, it appears you need be at home, my lady. I have been informed whatever the matter is, it cannot wait.'

'Oh gracious, what now?'

In the doorway of the reception room, she faltered. 'Doctor Browning? Good evening. And Sergeant Brice too, how unexpected. I tried to telephone you to apologise this afternoon, but you were out.'

The portly policeman ran a hand over his hair. 'Lummy, m'lady. Can't ever be 'pologies for anything needed from your good self.'

'Yes, there is—'

'Maybe. But not now!' Browning cut in sharply. 'I failed her.' His already stooped shoulders slumped. 'Annie Tibbets is dead.'

'Oh no!' Eleanor's hand flew to her mouth. She closed her eyes and silently sent heartfelt wishes heavenwards. Recovering herself, she sank down onto the settee. 'Firstly, Doctor, how is Miss Dunne, the other lady admitted with food poisoning?'

'She is stable at the moment.'

'Thank goodness for one mercy. And I'm in no doubt you did absolutely all you could for Annie, Doctor. And the hospital staff, too. But could you bear to tell me what happened? Please do sit. Both of you.'

Browning creaked stiffly down onto the opposite settee, Brice following suit nervously. The doctor let out a long breath.

'For the first time in my medical career, I need to hold my hands up and say I made a gross misjudgement. The food poisoning the villagers have suffered, including yourself, Lady Swift, was likely not accidental. But malicious.'

Eleanor's jaw fell. 'But who would do a monstrous thing like that? And why? It's unthinkable!'

'Yet it has occurred,' Browning said gravely. 'Of course, I can't be entirely certain until the exact cause is discovered. But a number of my patients who experienced severe symptoms of food poisoning also suffered other symptoms, not commensurate with food poisoning. Particularly irregular and lowered heart rates.' He tapped his walking cane on the floor. 'In short, the widespread illness was likely no accident.'

Eleanor's hand strayed to her chest.

Clifford's face was etched with concern. 'Is her ladyship in any delayed danger, Doctor?'

'Or my ladies, more to the point?' she said.

Browning shook his head. 'No. Of that, we can be confident. You, Lady Swift, as I have oft noted, have the most robust of constitutions. And if your staff were in any peril, from the start they would have suffered with more than just significantly upset stomachs. They would also have experienced irregular heartbeat and the like, such as I have now noted in too many of my patients. Perhaps you felt a few flutters yourself, Lady Swift?'

She nodded. 'I thought it was wedding nerves getting the better of me.'

'No. It was the effect of whatever substance the culprit used to cause illness to the villagers.'

Eleanor felt sickened by the idea anyone would do such a

terrible thing. 'Then why did poor Annie pass away? Because she ate more of this poison, Doctor?'

'No. Annie had a heart condition. Bradycardia has dogged the latter part of her adult life.'

'A low pulse, or heart rate,' Clifford translated.

'Ah!' Eleanor said. 'I thought she was often out of breath.'

Browning nodded. 'Her heartbeat was very low. Less than sixty per minute. Even with the hospital administering her usual atropine medication, it was too much for her already weakened heart.'

'Sergeant Brice, can it really have been a deliberate act to inflict illness on the villagers?' Eleanor entreated the policeman, wishing somehow he could make all of this go away.

His thick moustache twitched as his expression turned sombre. ''Fraid so, m'lady. The good doctor 'ere has taken me through a lengthy explanation of the medical side of it all. Only some snippets of which I grasped, I'll hold me hands up to that. But still, I don't see as there can be any doubt.'

She shook her head, still in disbelief. 'But what could possibly have been the reason for such an attack? Someone with a grudge against the whole village?'

He swallowed hard. 'I don't rightly know. But I'm more convinced 'n ever now that the poor woman's gone, the old villagers and that new lot over the bridge will clash. Especially if the news gets out that the poisoning was malicious.'

She grimaced. 'I agree. The village was already rife with rumours about that earlier today.'

Brice nodded. 'I think as folks will put two and two together.'

'And make five. Or twenty, or anything else they want!' Browning said earnestly. 'They'll be baying for blood now Annie's dead! We have to find out how and where the food poisoning happened.'

Clifford stepped over. 'Without inflaming the situation any further.'

'Spot on, Mr Clifford. Then us police can swoop in and act,' Brice said. 'But none of that'll happen unless...' He tailed off.

Eleanor didn't wait for any of the others in the room to articulate the only solution. She was the lady of the manor. And she felt responsible for what had happened. Even her wedding planning would have to take second place.

'I'll admit I'm shamefully out of touch with the village, particularly with those over the bridge, gentlemen. But I shall do my very best to find the source of whatever poisoned the villagers and killed poor Annie,' she said passionately. 'And the culprit. Or culprits.'

Clifford caught her eye.

He's right, Ellie! How are you going to make this work so close to your wedding?

She bit back a groan. The truth was, if there were any more dramatic developments in the next few days, it was becoming increasingly hard to believe there would be a wedding at all!

13

Eleanor paced the room, all eyes following her intently.

'We can't afford to waste any time,' she muttered. Drawing level with Doctor Browning, she felt a second wave of worry wash over her. 'And not only because the villagers might turn on each other once the cause of Annie's death gets out.'

'Shrewd as ever, my lady,' Clifford muttered, clearly having followed her thoughts.

Brice stared between them, his puzzled frown deepening. 'What is it I'm missin'?'

Before she could answer, Browning jumped in tautly. 'Lady Swift has realised that a range of heart conditions similar to that of Annie Tibbets could be affected with equally fatal results. Conditions most prevalent in the elderly. Of which I am one!'

She gave him a placating smile. 'Doctor, we're working on the same side here.'

'For a change,' he muttered. 'In short, Sergeant, there could be more deaths if we do not find the source soon!'

She rolled her shoulders back, determined to do whatever she could to sort out the hideous situation. 'I know it's getting late. But let's begin by agreeing on our starting point?'

Clifford glided over with a tray bearing steaming coffees for the three of them.

'Obviously, that must be to find the source of the contamination first, so no further poisonings occur,' Doctor Browning said firmly. 'Then hunt down those responsible!'

Sergeant Brice nodded, but his blank expression gave away how at a loss he felt. 'But with the sickness bein' so widespread across the village, it would take an age to investigate the food in all the houses as took part in the Spring Supper. 'Twas almost every home this side of the bridge, I understood.'

His words made Eleanor click her fingers. He'd shone a light into the dark abyss she'd been staring into. 'It would, indeed, Sergeant. You're brilliant!'

'I am?' he said incredulously. 'Er, thanks for noticin', m'lady. But do carry on explainin' why.'

She turned to the doctor. 'Can you identify a particular part of the village where the majority of the poisoning victims came from?'

Browning thought for a minute, his forefinger tapping across his lap as if mentally walking around Little Buckford. 'No. Quite the opposite. The worst cases were from all areas, including the more outlying clusters of cottages on the furthest lanes.'

'Perfect!' she exclaimed, much to the collective surprise of the room. 'I'll explain. The point of the Spring Supper is to visit as many of the homes taking part as possible. Agreed?'

Everyone nodded.

'But given how engrossed in conversations everyone was in each house Clifford and I stepped into, I'd say there's no way most of them got around even half the village that evening.'

'So, you're saying that the contaminated food must have come from only half of the village?' Doctor Browning said.

She shook her head. 'No. I'm saying it likely came from almost every house.'

Clifford stepped forward. 'Gentlemen, her ladyship is right. Little Buckford is too widely spread for anyone of a, shall we say, country-esque pace of life to have made it more than half the way around. But those who became ill are spread all across the village. No one could have visited so many houses and tampered with the food in each. Certainly not those two men from over the bridge. They would have been noticed and ejected again. Permanently. No. The substance that led to the poisoning must have been added to the food *at source*.'

Eleanor nodded vigorously. 'Exactly. Which our resident expert should be able to set us in the right direction of.'

Clifford stepped to the fireplace and pulled on the bell sash three times.

A moment later, Mrs Trotman flustered in, drying her hands on her cook's apron.

'M'lady, is there summat you... Oh lawks, evenin', sirs. Beg pardon, I didn't realise as you was still here,' she said to Doctor Browning and Sergeant Brice. 'Is it more coffee as is wanted, Mr Clifford?'

Eleanor shook her head. 'No, Mrs Trotman, it is your unrivalled expert knowledge. On all things culinary.'

''Twould be my pleasure, I'm sure, m'lady,' her cook said, failing to hide how delighted she was to be asked.

Eleanor gave the briefest outline of what the four of them had just finished discussing, ending in the gentlest words she could find to break the news of Annie Tibbets' death.

Mrs Trotman gasped. 'Oh lummy! Poor Annie. And her never anything but kindness itself.' She thought for a moment. 'So you think someone messed with the Spring Supper food offerings on purpose? 'Tis an awful notion, alright. I'll help anyway I can, m'lady. Just say the word.'

The others all deferred to Eleanor with a wave of their hands.

'We think whatever made the villagers ill, us included, Mrs

Trotman, was in too many foods eaten at the Spring Supper for it to have been added afterwards. So it must have been added *before* they were made. And we're hoping you might come up with a theory as to how?'

Mrs Trotman clapped her hands. 'Oh, and I thought you had a challenge for me. But that's easy, m'lady. There's only a few ingredients as go in almost every kind of nibbles, treats and finger food. Or appetisers, as is the posh term.'

Notepad poised, Brice shuffled forward on his chair. 'And them few things is what, Mrs Trotman?'

'Water, flour or milk, Sergeant,' she said confidently. 'Stands to reason they'd be the base of most everything dished up at the Spring Supper too. Them three ingredients is the least expensive of all in everyone's kitchen. Though milk is perhaps least likely of the three of bein' your guilty ingredient. On account of it being the thing to spoil afore everythin' else, see? So it's used less.'

Were it not for the horror it would cause Clifford, Eleanor would have hugged her cook. 'Mrs Trotman, I knew you'd be the one who could fathom what none of us could. Thank you.'

As she returned to the kitchen, Eleanor said, 'What do you think, gentlemen?'

Browning rocked forward in his seat. Then back again. 'I can find no flaws in your argument, Lady Swift.'

Clifford held up a finger. 'If I might add something regarding water supply, which might hasten things further still? Not being an affluent village, the vast majority of Little Buckford is reliant on two public handpumps. These draw water from the only natural chalk spring in this area of the Chiltern Hills that remains all year. To contaminate a slow-moving body of water such as the spring's groundwater source would require a huge amount of contaminant.'

Eleanor nodded. 'Plus, everyone would have been ill. Not just those who attended the Spring Supper.'

Sergeant Brice leaped up, letting out a long, low whistle. 'So 'tis the flour we need be questionin'?'

'Unfortunately, without me.' Doctor Browning rose unsteadily, leaning on his walking cane. 'I must make another round of those still stricken.' As he reached the door, he turned back. 'And I hope you find that source before I have to attend to any more deaths, Lady Swift. Mine included!'

14

In Little Buckford's high street, Clifford eased the Rolls to a stop behind the Chipstone police's sole official vehicle; a small converted delivery van. Painted black, it had the word 'POLICE' added in block white lettering along each side. Three formidable locks ran across the back door. Sergeant Brice climbed out of the cab, while Constable Lowe clambered out of the rear.

Looking up at the windows above Shackley's bakery, Eleanor bit her lip. The curtains were all drawn. Not even the faint glow of a lamp filtered out.

Brice frowned. 'I hope as this baker bloke hasn't decided to up and away, m'lady. That'd mean Lowe and me havin' to force entry.'

She blanched. 'Sergeant, I'm sure that won't be necessary. I suspect he and his wife have simply retired for some much-needed rest.'

Clifford's brow flinched. 'Indeed. It is only two hours until midnight and Mr Shackley usually begins his daily bread baking at half past four each morning.'

Brice waved his truncheon. 'Not to worry, this'll wake him.'

Before she could stop him, he rapped it forcibly on the door. 'Open up! Police!' he hollered, head thrown back. 'You upstairs! Let us in!'

She and Clifford glanced at each other in concern.

'Sergeant, we don't need to wake the whole street,' she hissed.

The sound of a sash window being opened hurriedly made her look back up.

'Who's that causing a ruckus down there? Decent folk are trying to sleep!'

'Chipstone Police! Get down 'ere quick!' Brice bellowed.

The sash dropped like a stone, the glass rattling in its frame.

In a trice, Morace Shackley wrenched open the door of his bakery and shot out with his arm around his wife's shoulders, both swathed in a blanket over their nightwear.

'What's on fire, Officer?' he said breathlessly.

''Tain't no fire. 'Tis about all that trouble at the Spring Supper. There's good reason to believe your flour is what poisoned everyone,' Brice said firmly.

'What!' Shackley cried. 'My flour! How dare you!'

His wife turned to Eleanor. 'M'lady, thank goodness you're here. Morace said as you were good enough to come in this morning and buy all Henley Hall's usual order and more when no other folks had. Please tell this policeman he's wrong?' she pleaded.

Eleanor winced. 'Elizabeth, I would do if I was sure myself, but...' She tailed off.

The Shackleys gasped and stared at each other.

'Stand aside,' Brice commanded. Beckoning to the wide-eyed Lowe, he charged inside.

Shackley shot in behind them, shouting, 'Whatever you're thinking, it's madness. And this is Little Buckford, not Chipstone. Our own Constable Bob Fry would never behave like this!'

Eleanor silently agreed with him, wishing Fry hadn't been one of those struck down with food poisoning. She stepped in hastily after the others, hoping to defuse the situation.

'Mr Shackley, Elizabeth, listen... Oh goodness!' She faltered at the sight of the baker and the sergeant wrestling with each other for the sack of flour behind the counter.

''Tis not a scrap wrong with it, I tell you,' Shackley yelled. 'That's the one I keep for selling to folks for their home baking.'

'Ah! The same folks as got sick at the village Spring Supper? On account of cookin' with this, like as not!' Brice used his extra bulk to wrench the sack free from Shackley's grip. 'Lowe, lock this in the van. Then come back sharpish 'n help me get the rest.'

'The rest! But all t'other flour Morace uses only for the bread or cakes we make,' Elizabeth cried weakly.

Darting around her, Lowe ducked out with the sack and Brice marched through to the back room.

'I warn you, sir, resistin' is a bad idea,' Brice grunted as he tried to swing one of the remaining sacks onto his shoulders with Shackley in the way.

'Now you're threatening to arrest me, is that it?' the baker shot back. 'Oi!' he shouted as Lowe darted in with the agility of his younger years, scored another sack, and made good his escape to the van.

Brice paused in following him with his own hard-won sack. 'No arrest planned for you, sir. Leastways, not yet. We are only here to arrest your flour. I mean, confiscate your flour.'

'But there's nothing wrong with it, I tell you!' Shackley protested.

'So I heard you say, sir. Milled it yourself, direct from the field, you'll be tellin' me next?'

Shackley gritted his teeth. 'Of course I won't. It gets delivered each morning from the mill over westways. Same as it has since I started my bakery here over seventeen years ago. Why,

the driver even knows to deliver it to the covered store in the
yard, so as not to cause me to open the back door and waste the
heat of the ovens.'

'I'm still takin' it all, sir. For testin',' Brice said, marching on
towards the street.

Eleanor was momentarily lost for words. Or what to do that
could hope to soothe the understandably incensed baker. Clifford appeared beside her, his eyes chivalrously averted from
Elizabeth in her nightclothes. Before either of them could offer
any calming words, the Shackleys ran past them together after
the policemen.

'Oh dear,' Eleanor said with a sigh. Dashing out into the
street, she realised faces were now poking out from all the open
windows on both sides and a small crowd had gathered.
Coming to the Shackleys' aid, Penry and Brenchley were trying
to barricade the back door of the police van.

'What the heck's going on?' Brenchley called to Shackley.

'Folks as should know better is trying to ruin me, that's
what!'

As the Shackleys glanced pointedly at her, Eleanor
wondered with a sinking feeling if she might have been
included in that statement.

'I'd stand aside if I was you, gentlemen,' Brice said grimly,
setting down the flour sack so he could swing his handcuffs in
the other two shopkeepers' faces pointedly. With a scowl they
stepped over beside Shackley, who was comforting his wife
while still shouting they were being victimised.

'No need for such talk,' Brice called back. 'But your bakery
needs to stay closed until we've had all this flour tested. And
only after I give you the all-clear can you open again.'

'And who's going to compensate me for all that business
lost? Who, I ask you?'

'That's not police policy, sir,' Brice said dismissively. 'However, if it is found that this 'ere flour went bad due to your negli-

gence and that's what made them poor folk ill and Annie Tibbets to shuffle off her mortal coil like, well, then, it is police policy to slap you in jail! Now, out of my way!'

Shackley's cheeks turned scarlet with rage. He squared up to Brice and growled, 'Some policeman you are! Siding with those trying to ruin me. Them lot from over the bridge are responsible. Anyone with their wits about them could see that! Two of their wretches came to the Spring Supper and caused all this.'

'Hear! Hear!' the crowd cried.

As Lowe reappeared, saying he had the last of the sacks, Penry stepped forward menacingly, his large physique dwarfing even Brice's portly form. 'And am I to expect you forcing your way into my butcher's shop in the small hours too, Officer? Confiscating my meat and closing my only means of making a living?'

Brice shook his head, busying himself with checking the three door locks, now all the sacks were secure inside. 'Not for the moment, sir. Assumin', that is, there's nowt wrong with your meat?' He hauled himself up into the driver's seat and leaned out of the window. 'But you've all made a sorry spectacle of yourselves. And in front of her ladyship. And when 'tis her you should be thankin' for all this! She put us on to your baker's bad flour there.'

With a wail of tortured gears, the van rumbled away over the cobbles.

Elizabeth's lip trembled. 'So you support the Chipstone Police then, m'lady? I can't believe it!'

She broke off into sobs. Her husband pulled her to his side, the scowl on his face making his next words unnecessary.

'M'lady, we none of us ever thought we'd see the day. You, of all people, taking t'other side?' He shook his head. 'Beg pardon for saying, but your uncle, Lord Henley, would turn in his grave!'

The bakery door slammed shut. The sound of bolts being drawn in anger made Eleanor hang her head in dismay. She looked up to find the crowd dispersing down the street, muttering.

She groaned, feeling wretched for the Shackleys. 'Oh, Clifford, what a hideous mess! This is exactly why I didn't want to get involved when Sergeant Brice first asked me. And we haven't even started searching for the culprit yet!'

He opened the passenger door of the Rolls, permitting himself the luxury of a quiet sigh. 'Well, whether or not you wanted to be, my lady, it seems you are involved now. Up to your likely still burning ears!'

She nodded miserably. She'd worried only a short while ago that if any more dramatic events occurred, there might not be a wedding. Well, there was definitely going to be a funeral. Poor Annie's! And as Doctor Browning said, unless they acted fast, hers might not be the only one!

15

Eleanor woke with a groan. Two days ago, she had promised herself today would be a full morning-till-evening session of wedding planning. With no interruptions. She had even written it in Clifford's ivory-silk diary in letters large enough to fill the page. But after the debacle at the bakery last night, she felt terrible. The Shackleys' insistence that she had betrayed them, and, by inference, all of Little Buckford this side of the bridge, had stung badly. In admitting to herself that she had fallen short of her responsibilities to the village, and by trying to do the right thing, she had inadvertently cast herself as the villain of the piece!

The April weather seemed to empathise with her unsettled state as it lurched between short sharp showers and patchy periods of weak sunshine before she'd even finished breakfast. The wind the night before had woken her several times as she tossed fitfully in bed and now, outside in the garden, she could hear the canvas sides of the marquee flapping fretfully against the supports.

She looked up as Clifford returned with more coffee and a frown.

'What's wrong?'

He pursed his lips. 'Before the workmen left last night, they had erected most of the superstructure for the marquee and attached one of the panels. It seems, however, they had not secured it properly.'

She nodded. 'I know. I can hear it flapping around from here.'

'Precisely. Unfortunately, you can hear it so clearly because it seems to have caught on an exposed strut in the night and ripped into several pieces.'

'Oh, no! Do they have spare sides?'

He shook his head. 'Regretfully, no. I spoke to the manager on the telephone just now and he informed me it is their largest marquee and thus they only have one. No panels from their other marquees would fit. However, he has promised he will try to use his contacts with other similar companies to find us a replacement as soon as possible.'

'There you go!' she said extra brightly. 'I'm sure they'll find one in time, Clifford.'

Her butler's frown failed to lift, however. 'I'm sure they will, my lady.'

'So why the long face still?'

He hesitated. 'I examined the damaged panel and would have thought it more... robust.'

She didn't fail to notice the brief look of concern that passed over his features. She shrugged more nonchalantly than she felt.

'Well, it seems it wasn't. As Constance said, things are bound to go awry with such a monumental event. Even with your infallible hand at the helm. So let's not cry over spilled milk!'

After finishing breakfast, she hurried to the dining room, her mind still brooding on her conviction that she'd let the village down. Surrounded by boxes, samples and as yet unticked lists, she reminded herself dwelling on it would help no one. But the immediate question of how to reverse the situation still occupied her thoughts.

You'll find a way to make amends, Ellie... somehow.

However, by eleven, things took a turn for the worse. Doctor Browning had called. He told her they'd had more hospital cases overnight. And even though no one was currently hovering at death's door, the disturbing news preyed on her mind as she tried to make inroads on the mountain of wedding tasks spread out on the table and floor. A mean-spirited voice kept needling her. Telling her a woman had died and more had been hospitalised. And yet here she was, messing around with trivialities.

'It's not messing around,' she muttered to herself angrily. 'Hugh would be here helping too, if he could only get some time off. It's spending just a little time to make sure one of the most important days of my life goes without a hitch!'

But the mean-spirited voice disagreed.

Needing a break, she rose and joined her tomcat and bull-dog, where they were delighting in a game of tug on the deep-buttoned ottoman seat.

'It would be nice to have as little to worry about as you terrible two do,' she said wistfully, just as Clifford glided in with a silver tray of elevenses.

'Alas, it is worse than I feared,' she caught him murmur to the tiered selection of delectable-smelling pastries as he headed back towards the door.

'Where are you going with those?' she protested.

'To Mrs Trotman, my lady. With an apology on my part. I can see I should have ordered jam roly-poly for my mistress instead. With lashings of custard, Clifford, naturally!' he added teasingly, in a remarkable impression of her cook.

She laughed, her pensive mood broken. 'I am not behaving like a child, Clifford. Well, maybe a little.'

She beckoned him back with the pastries. Accepting a selection of Stilton, sausage meat and caramelised-onion savouries, she sighed, overcome by nostalgia.

'These are perfect, thank you. I remember you conjuring up versions of these as a distraction for me after Uncle Byron took me in as his ward. But I'm not the troublesome nine-year-old who plagued your days back then any more, despite your insistence I need jam roly-poly!'

He tutted. 'Age is immaterial, I have learned. Effective methods are still effective.'

She sighed. 'Clifford, I'm sorry for having been a worry blanket of late. We both wish this awfulness in the village had never happened. But I put my hand up, and my head above the parapet, to try and help. And I've got to live with the consequences. It's something you can't undo on my behalf. Even though I know it's quietly eating you up not to be able to wave your usual wizard's wand and make it all go away.'

'Indeed. And, most importantly, it is marring your wedding day preparations.' He gestured around the room.

She nudged his arm. 'Which I was just getting to, only please pretend you can't hear me for a moment?'

Hands over his ears, he nodded.

She crossed her fingers, hoping her voice would hold. 'The fact you want to move heaven and earth to make my wedding beyond perfect and nothing less than fit for a true princess means the absolute world. Especially as Hugh can't be here for most of the planning and preparation. And especially as you've stepped in unbidden, in Uncle Byron's stead. Because he can't be here either. Which is pulling at both our hearts equally. So perhaps...' The lump in her throat halted her from continuing.

Clifford too, evidently, as he turned and busied himself rescuing the tug-of-war ribbon from her pets. After a minute, he said gently, 'So perhaps today, progress might be made... together? And rather more chaotically than one might usually countenance, my lady?'

She nodded eagerly, wishing he would cope with her pulling him into a heartfelt hug just once.

Amid their usual good-natured squabbling, they rapidly ticked off more and more on the preparations list. She made a series of telephone calls and chose from among the myriad samples and catalogues. She even settled on the final design for the monogrammed boxes in which a slice of wedding cake would accompany every guest home.

And the mean-spirited voice kept quiet.

With Gladstone and Tomkins bounding exuberantly under her and Clifford's feet, the tour of the marquee, torn panel aside, had her brimming with ideas for the layout of tables and decorations. All of which Clifford noted in meticulous sketches with approving nods.

Chatting with the overalled workmen was also fun. Especially as her ladies appeared with mountains of well-deserved tea and freshly baked biscuits. Plus a raft of reasons from the ever-saucy Mrs Trotman why the four of them needed to stay until it was time to clear the cups. At Eleanor's quiet plea that her ladies would never have the company of such burly good-looking chaps again, Clifford hadn't intervened. Instead, with a sympathetic grimace to the workmen, he had left to check progress in the ballroom while she went off to unearth her treasured, silver-haired gardener, Joseph.

She found him engrossed with more workmen in fitting a new pump to the fountains of the ornamental lake to create a spectacular backdrop display for the evening wedding festivities. Once they were alone, she asked him if he would make her wedding bouquet.

'Lummy, m'lady,' he said, his eyes welling up. 'I'd 'ave thought you'd get a fancy London florist to do that. It'll make these ancient hands and heart proud fit to burst to do so.'

Delighted, she slid quietly back into the house, needing to complete one more task without Clifford hearing. Up in her bedroom, her telephone call to Langham Manor and Lord Langham himself was connected.

'Ah! Harold, hello. It's Eleanor. I've something I've been burning to ask you...'

After her telephone call, she set off for the ballroom where she met Clifford.

'You know, I've ticked so much off the list this afternoon it's quite wonderful.'

'Including?' He hovered his fountain pen over one underlined entry.

She nodded. 'Yes, Clifford, I have just got off the telephone with Lord Langham. You can stop worrying.'

'Indeed. Since your luncheon meeting with Lady Constance in Chipstone must also have proved successful. I noted you have ticked that bridesmaids and dress fitting arrangements are all under way?'

'Of course,' she said airily, hiding a nagging worry that no matter how many items she ticked off her lists, her and Hugh's plans for their big day already had a hole torn in them the size of the one in the marquee's side. And just like the marquee, she wasn't at all convinced it would be mended in time!

16

By early evening, she'd done all the wedding planning she could for the day and recovered with a hot bath. Then came down the stairs to relax in what Clifford decorously referred to as her 'house pyjamas'.

'A shockingly unsolicited telephone call for you, my lady,' he hissed with a wince as she reached the bottom step.

'Surely, I've applied myself to enough today? Get rid of them, please!' she hissed back.

He nodded and spoke into the mouthpiece she realised in horror he hadn't been covering. 'Regrettably, her ladyship has no more capacity for interruptions this evening, Chief Inspector Seldon. If you would be so kind as to call at a more suitable time?'

'Hugh!' she cried, grabbing the telephone.

Her fiancé's rich chuckle rumbled out, delighting her ears as always. 'Hello, Eleanor. Been tormenting your beleaguered butler even more than usual, I gather?'

'Oh, he loves it. It salves his conscience over teasing me remorselessly.' She laughed as, eyes twinkling, Clifford glided away. 'Please tell me you aren't telephoning to say you can't come back the day after tomorrow as planned?'

'I'm not. Nothing will stop me being there.'

'Good! Because Clifford is desperate to see darling Kofi.'

'Is that the only reason?' Seldon's voice sounded hesitant.

'No, silly, I'm teasing! Even talking to you long distance is torture. I wish you were here already. And as I don't want to have to carry you up the aisle on our wedding day because you've wasted away, tell me you've eaten something since I last saw you?'

'Eaten? Er, yes. Now, tell me you're enjoying yourself?'

'Fibber!' She shook her head ruefully. Giving it up as a hopeless job, she filled him in on progress on the wedding preparations, save for the secret of her dress. 'But, Hugh, I so want you here in case I'm ploughing on with things you'll be horrified by.'

'Darling, if it's what you want, I want it more than I can say. All I really want in the end, though, is you as my wife.' His voice was so tender she could almost feel his arms reaching through the telephone to embrace her. 'I haven't got long, so tell me, how have you been, my love? As irrepressibly impossible as always?'

'Tsk! Now I know you're imagining the wrong girl joining you at the altar! As it happens, I've been fine, thank you. Oh, aside from a bit of food poisoning. But never mind that,' she said hurriedly, not wanting to explain over the telephone.

Seldon's tone was filled with concern. 'Eleanor... There's something you're not telling me, isn't there?'

She sighed. 'There's just a teeny matter of someone having tampered with the food offerings at Little Buckford's Spring Supper. More than half the villagers were ill. It seems it might have been the flour. Luckily, Henley Hall wasn't affected as Mrs Trotman had over-ordered the week before, so was still using the old, unaffected flour. Anyway, Sergeant Brice has asked me to help get to the bottom of it. And we made some progress last night. So there's nothing to worry about,' she said brightly, hoping he would drop the matter before she blurted out that Annie Tibbets had died. He'd only concern himself unnecessarily.

'Brice? Poor fellow!' Seldon's tone was a mix of surprise and quiet amusement. 'Oh, blast it! My second in command is calling for me. I'll have to ring off with the beguiling image of you running rings around the well-intentioned but lumbering Brice. I'm coming!' he called tersely to someone at the other end. 'Eleanor? I'll try to call you back.' The sound of a whispered kiss being blown was followed by the line going dead.

She sank down onto the seat beside the telephone table, hugging her shoulders at having at least heard his voice. Clifford reappeared and replaced the handset on its cradle.

'Better now, my lady?' he said softly.

'Yes, thank you. Although I wish he was here, instead of running himself ragged, being the best detective in the country.'

'A sentiment I believe the gentleman has noted on more than one occasion regarding his betrothed, albeit in regard to amateur sleuthing?'

She nodded. 'True. But the three of us have made quite the team on several cases.'

'Most assuredly. However, since no further progress can be made on the regrettable matter of the Spring Supper tonight, perhaps your thoughts can rest now? Over unladylike quantities of dinner, no doubt.'

'Pff! Heaps more than that!'

They had only got a few yards along the passageway when the jangle of the telephone bell stopped her.

'Hurrah! Hugh said he would try and call back.' She raced to answer it, sliding the last few feet in her excitement. 'Hello, darling!' she breathed.

'Oh lummy! Beg pardon, I must have the wrong number,' a

familiar voice said so loudly she held the earpiece away an inch. Her cheeks coloured.

'Ah, Sergeant Brice, good evening.'

In the reflection of the gold-framed mirror above the telephone table, she caught Clifford pinching the bridge of his nose.

'Pretending it was a wrong number did not appeal then, my lady?' he whispered.

She flapped a hand for him to be quiet. 'Sergeant Brice, you've come through to the right number. It's Lady Swift here.'

''Tis really you, m'lady? Well, there's a rummy thing. Fancy Mr Clifford leavin' you to answer your own telephone?' Brice's voice bellowed out.

She gave a mock tut. 'I know, shocking, isn't it?' She hid a smile at her butler's long-suffering expression. 'But butlers can be wickedly tricky. Now, I'm sorry, but Chief Inspector Seldon isn't here, if you're hoping he is?'

'No, m'lady. I've an update. On the flour as we confiscated.'

'Already?' She urged Clifford closer. 'And?'

'Well, blow me if you weren't right, m'lady. Poisoned! Leastways, the sack as Mr Shackley insisted he only kept for sellin' to the villagers for home bakin'. There was dried, er... one moment.' The sound of papers rustling followed. 'Ah! There you are, you rascal of a page. Dried monkshood seeds, m'lady. That's what was in it. And they are mighty poisonous!'

'Excellent work, Sergeant. But, however did you find out so quickly?'

'Ah! I asked meself what would you do, m'lady? Ask a man who knows his way around the ways and means of poisons, so you would. So I took the lot to an old apothecary herbalist bloke, way out t'other side of Oxford who I remembered was on our list of reputable oddballs.'

'I'm not sure the science of herbalism quite qualifies the poor chap for that accolade, but well done for initiative,

Sergeant. Gracious though, the problem now we officially know the flour was deliberately poisoned is—'

'I know what you're goin' to say, m'lady. 'Pologies for interruptin', of course, but Annie Tibbets' passing is now manslaughter!'

She swallowed hard at the awful thought, an unpleasant sensation telling her it might end up more horrible still.

Brice cleared his throat. 'Which you'd be within your rights to say is entirely a police matter. And that you're walkin' away from the whole nasty mess, m'lady. 'Twould be more 'n fair if you was to wash your hands of the matter. Only, you saw the hostile reaction down in the village when me 'n Lowe confiscated the flour...' He trailed off.

She hesitated.

You spent all night and all morning wishing you'd never got involved, Ellie. Here's your chance to bow out gracefully.

Behind her she felt her beloved uncle's eyes looking down at her from the portrait hanging at the head of the stairs.

She stood straighter and shook her head.

'Sergeant Brice, I wouldn't dream of going back on my word to help. I'll be in touch very soon.'

Brice's relief was still ringing around the marble entrance hall after she replaced the handset.

'Bravo, my lady,' Clifford said, coming to her side.

She looked up at him. 'I hope I've done the right thing.'

'Indubitably. Since in who else but their lady of the manor can Little Buckford put their faith at this critical time?'

She grimaced. 'Let's hope they see it that way. I'd better tell you everything Brice said.'

He shook his head. 'Not necessary. I imagine the badgers at the far end of the estate heard his strident voice. Dried monkshood seeds? Malicious, indeed!'

'Ever the walking encyclopaedia, Clifford. What do you know about the plant?'

'That its name derives from the shape of its flowers, being hooded like the cowl traditionally worn by monks. It is native to much of England. And Europe. It has also been a cultivated garden plant since before sixteen hundred, if memory serves. However, if ingested, it is toxic to humans. Very toxic!'

'So, it's wonderful stuff if you have a malicious streak?'

'Unfortunately, yes. Hence, throughout the annals of time, it has been steeped in mythology, linked with witchcraft and favoured by poisoners. The Roman naturalist, Pliny the Elder, claimed its origin was the spittle of Cerberus, the hellhound brought from the underworld by Hercules. He also referred to it as, ahem, "woman's murder".'

She shuddered, her previous unsettling feeling returning.

'In that case, Clifford, I suggest we treat it as murder and hunt down those responsible!'

17

The cottage Clifford pointed out as Annie Tibbets' home washed Eleanor in a wave of sadness. It seemed a perfect reflection of the woman herself; petite, with a soft pale exterior, and topped off by a neat dark-golden thatch which shone almost auburn in the shaft of early evening sun. Even the traditional patches of exposed flint reminded her of Annie's grey eyes.

They shared a look. 'Visiting the scene of the crime, in this case the victim's house, is definitely the first action in a murder case, Clifford.'

He nodded. 'And in the inimitable words of my mistress, there is no time like the present.'

And maybe, just maybe, Ellie, we can sort this awful matter out before Hugh gets back the day after tomorrow.

She peered along the path, past the one adjoining cottage to where it led off around the corner to more grey-roofed homes. Why did she know that, though? Of course! It wasn't the first time she'd been there, she realised.

'Clifford, even with us having come from the other direction, how did I miss that this was Annie's home when we called in as part of our Spring Supper visits?'

'I imagine because when we arrived, as with the owners of many of the houses, Miss Tibbets was out enjoying the Spring Supper in another home.'

She stared at him. 'And left her own open for everyone to come and go?'

'Naturally. Little Buckford is a tight-knit community. Locking one's door has always been far from common practice, as you know.'

She smiled, comforted by such trust. 'And everyone knows everyone, of course.'

'Aye, afore, but not any more!' a sharp female voice called.

'But neighbours are still nosy enough to make the best guard dogs,' Clifford whispered.

Eleanor vaguely recognised the formidably built middle-aged woman in a mustard-coloured apron blustering towards them.

'Dash it! How are you going to use your dubious lock-picking skills now?' she hissed.

He tutted. 'That was never the intention. Unlike having a plan ready for once we're inside, hmm?'

'We'll think of something,' she muttered.

He swept his bowler hat off as the woman reached them. 'Good evening, Miss Ingelby,' he said silkily.

To Eleanor's mind, Miss Ingelby feigned surprise. Badly. 'Well, of course, if I'd known as it was you, Mr Clifford, I'd never have hared down the path to pin your ears back for havin' no business here.' She fanned her generous chin with the blue gingham tea towel she was clutching. 'And m'lady, too. Good evening.'

'May I offer my condolences over Annie's passing? It seems you were neighbourly towards each other?' Eleanor said.

Miss Ingelby flapped the tea towel at her. 'Oh, Annie 'n me was more 'n that, even though I'm fairly new to the village and Annie had lived here all her life. Well, "new" in Little Buckford terms, m'lady. Anyways, folks said as we were more like sisters than neighbours.' She faltered. 'Mind, it doesn't always do to listen to folk. Though there was plenty bein' said in the high street this mornin' over that ruckus at Shackley's bakery last night. Policemen, a horde of 'em, draggin' out all the flour, bread, buns, the lot, apparently!'

'It's a wonder the village drums weren't heard up at Henley Hall,' Clifford murmured to Eleanor.

She nodded, appreciating he was trying to lessen her dismay at the rumours having ballooned so wildly, and so quickly.

Miss Ingelby looked at Eleanor coyly. 'Silly me, someone might have mentioned as you was there, too, m'lady? Course, I'm not one for tittle-tattle. Never know who might get trampled by the wrong hooves, see?'

Eleanor groaned silently. Whatever they said to this woman would undoubtedly be all over the village before breakfast tomorrow.

'Indubitably, Miss Ingelby,' Clifford said smoothly. 'Which is precisely why we were hoping you would come to her lady-ship's rescue? It's a most delicate matter, you see.'

The woman's curiosity was sparked as fiercely as if he'd held a burning torch to it. She leaned in conspiratorially, so much so that she tripped over her own slippered foot.

'Apologies, Mr Clifford. How clumsy of me.' She disentangled herself from him with flushed cheeks.

He tutted. 'No harm done, dear lady. However,' he lowered his voice, 'perhaps we'd best talk inside?'

From her apron pocket, she slid out a black iron key. 'I only locked up in respect of Annie's passin', you understand? I was always in 'n out. She'd sometimes come over all dizzy. Breathless too. 'Twas on account of her heart problem. Summat with a complicated name.'

'Bradycardia, perhaps?'

She nodded. 'Sounds familiar, Mr Clifford. I used to help her out with a few bits around the house or into bed when she had one of her turns.'

'What an exemplary neighbour you are,' Eleanor said genuinely, following her inside.

There was no hallway, just two stone steps down into the sitting room. Two more on the opposite side led up into what had to be the kitchen. Eleanor remembered thinking on her Spring Supper visit how cosy the house felt. The walls were a sunny-yellow ochre, even with some spare shillings for a repaint needed. The two armchairs facing the fireplace had been re-upholstered in colourful patchwork fabric, while a matching cushion nestled into the curved back of the wooden chair, whose arms dipped in the centre from decades of supporting weary limbs.

It was pulled up to a narrow table covered with neat piles of notepads, the jam jar in the middle home to a handful of pencils and pens. Within easy reach of this improvised desk, four shelves set in the arched alcove were filled with what she assumed were cookbooks, given Annie's business was catering. Which also explained the notes and sketches pegged onto the looped strings pinned into the thick ceiling beam above. Annie had evidently been a visual girl, and one painstaking in creating the menus she provided for her customers.

Clifford gave an imperceptible flick of his eyes towards the kitchen.

Eleanor stepped past the neighbour, artfully directing the woman's gaze in that direction. 'Miss Ingelby, I'm so grateful to you for letting us in. You see, Annie was doing the catering for my wedding.'

'So as she told me, m'lady. Set her all of an excited fluster, it did. She'd bought some extra bakeware. Come and see.'

She led Eleanor into the tiled kitchen. Clearly it had been

home to a hard-working cook. It was spotless, organised, and well-stocked. The gleaming copper pans hung from the beams in rows, the plethora of baking utensils and wooden spoons crowded together in jars, and the oven tins stacked in decreasing size. Miss Ingelby's brow furrowed.

'What did you say as you'd come for?'

'Actually, we hadn't quite got to that.'

Clifford came to her rescue. 'Miss Tibbets had been due to meet with her ladyship today. To discuss the wedding menu, the magical day being so close now. However, given the tragedy...'

Miss Ingelby looked sympathetic. 'Lummy, m'lady. I'd not put two and two together. Your most special day ever gallopin' up at you, and no one to cater it?'

'Absolutely. But still, it feels wrong to be thinking of anything but poor Annie,' Eleanor said honestly.

'I'm sure as she won't be thinkin' so, lookin' down on us. Not that she's had time yet to pass over proper, mind.' Miss Ingelby's hand flew to her chest. 'Have you come to ask her spirit for the wedding menu, m'lady?'

'Good gracious, no.' Eleanor seized on Clifford's cue. 'I was just hoping it might be alright to take any notes she'd made? Naturally, I'll send payment to whoever she has bequeathed her house and effects to. I imagine you know who that is?'

Miss Ingelby looked away, running her tea towel along the tiled edge of the sink. 'No, m'lady. I can't say I do.' She glanced up. 'It's a pity, though. What with no one to do your catering now for your most precious day.'

Clifford jumped in. 'Her ladyship is determined to spread as much of the wedding expenditure locally as possible. But it seems Annie was the only local caterer willing to take such a task on.'

Miss Ingelby nodded knowingly. 'Doesn't surprise me, Mr

Clifford. That Hester Hopcroft is t'only other one around. And she's got a knack of lookin' the part, but is a canny mare behind it, by all accounts.'

Eleanor fought a frown.

So much for not being a gossip!

Miss Ingelby was looking thoughtful. 'Well, if it's Annie's notes for your menu you wanted, m'lady, they'll be no good to anyone else, will they? No other folks is goin' to have such a big, expensive do around here.'

Eleanor caught Clifford discreetly patting his coat front. 'But where would Annie's planning notes be, I wonder, Miss Ingelby?'

The woman thought for a moment. 'Most likely they'll be on her desk over there, I suppose.'

Knowing they weren't thanks to her butler's infallible sleight of hand, Eleanor followed slowly, trying to think of a way to get some minutes without this woman watching. She had no idea what they were looking for, as Annie had simply been a tragic victim, her heart giving out. But maybe something would strike a chord and help them figure out how to track down the poisoner. Or poisoners!

Over at the desk, Miss Ingelby was staring across the notebooks she had spread out. 'That's rummy, there's nothin' here with your name on, m'lady.'

Clifford shrugged. 'Being so diligent, maybe the lady was working on them in her... ahem, sleeping quarters? Or in the pantry for extra inspiration? Perhaps you might accompany me to the latter, Miss Ingelby, for propriety. While her ladyship checks upstairs.'

Not giving the woman time to think, he steered her back up into the kitchen.

Ah, Ellie! That's why Clifford hid Annie's menu notes. To give me an excuse to check Annie's bedroom.

Opening the low door at the end of the room, she hurried

up the dog-leg wooden stairs, almost tripping over the corner stool on the one wider step halfway up. At the top, she ducked under the roof beam and stepped through the only door. She stood there undecided. Clifford's ruse had given her breathing space.

But what exactly do I do with it, Ellie?

18

In the steeply pitched eaves, Annie's bedroom was cosy but cramped, the thick dark-wood beams running across the ceiling reducing head height even further. Eleanor glanced around, taking in the plain pink-cotton curtains and the jug and bowl on the washstand. Nearby sat a spindle-backed kitchen chair with curved arms, a red wool blanket draped over it, ready to warm the woman who would never sit there again. The bed was jammed against one wall, the sheet, pillows and quilt a tangle.

Of course, Ellie. Poor Annie was hauled out of bed and rushed to hospital.

Something beside the candle on the tiny night table caught her eye. She walked over to it. A cardboard medicine box, lid open. It was divided into seven sections, the days of the week written in neatly inked lettering above each of the glass vials. Eleanor peered closer; Monday to Saturday's vials were empty and set back in their allotted section upside down. But Sunday's was missing. Flipping the lid over, she read the name stamped in red ink on the front: 'Atropine.'

'My lady, please hurry!' Clifford hissed from the top of the stairs. 'I have run out of ploys to buy you more time.'

'Then slip in here quickly. Something is niggling me.'

Her butler slid around the door frame, looking decidedly uncomfortable.

'What do you make of this?' She pointed at the box.

He arched a brow. 'Hmm, that ordinarily Miss Tibbets was meticulous in taking her heart medicine. Very sensible since bradycardia can cause bouts of disorientation, or dizziness, as her neighbour noted. Doctor Browning mentioned it was atropine the lady was prescribed.'

'Then where is Sunday's vial? The one she would have taken—'

'The night of the Spring Supper?' A fleeting look of concern crossed his face. 'Hopefully caught in the distressing confusion of bedcovers?'

He dropped to his haunches to scour under the bed as she pulled the covers apart, then ran her hand over the bottom sheet.

'Nothing!' Her ears pricked. 'Footsteps!'

He quickly passed her a pristine handkerchief and a notepad with her name on.

'There you are, Mr Clifford,' Miss Ingelby said as she entered the room.

Eleanor dabbed at her eyes. 'He knew how upsetting I would find this.' She smoothed out the covers as if she'd remade the bed as a mark of respect. 'I hadn't realised poor Annie was taken so ill here.'

Miss Ingelby glanced away. 'Luckily, I came to check on her early that morning. 'Twas me as sent for Doctor Browning. All of a flap I was too, seein' as I couldn't wake her. Not that it stopped her from passin' on, poor soul.'

'You likely did all you could the night before?' Eleanor said coaxingly.

'Course! When I got back from visitin' some others' houses at the Spring Supper, I found Annie was home afore me. I popped round, and she wasn't feelin' at all right then. That's why I helped her into bed.'

'And helped her take her medicine, too?'

'Well, I waited till she'd taken it, same as usual. She was so careful with it. She turned the spent vials upside down. To make sure she never took two in one night by mistake. When she was feelin' dizzy with it, she liked me to wait as an extra check if I could.'

'So kind of you. Perhaps she was even more disorientated than usual though, since she seems to have thrown that one vial away.' Eleanor pointed to the empty day.

'No, she put it in the box, wrong way up, as always. See?' Miss Ingelby flustered over to the night table, then frowned. 'Leastways, I could have sworn I saw her do it.'

'Perhaps the lady threw it away later that evening?' Clifford said.

'No, I'd stake everythin' she didn't. Annie was as bad as I've ever seen her that night. So tired and breathless, she'd never have managed the stairs back down. Even with that stool I suggested she put halfway.' She shook her head slowly. 'Plus, Mr Clifford, that followin' mornin', I found her exact as I'd left her the night afore. With the counterpane still tucked up to her chin.'

Eleanor felt a prickle down her spine.

So what happened to the empty vial, Ellie?

'We must leave you to your evening, dear lady.' Clifford gestured for Miss Ingelby to lead the way downstairs. 'Her ladyship has found the pad with Miss Tibbets' notes and menus for her wedding that you and I were searching for. So, thank you for your help.'

As Clifford and Miss Ingelby descended the stairs, Eleanor took the opportunity to lag behind and quickly search under the red wool blanket on the chair. She shook her head. Nothing. No empty vial.

After leaving Annie's house, Clifford drove straight to Doctor Browning's at the head of Cowgate Lane without a murmur, despite the late hour. The concern in his eyes told her he felt as unnerved as she did.

'I've never wanted to be more wrong in my life,' she muttered, stepping out of the car.

'Fingers crossed, my lady.'

As he gestured down the path to the rectangular, red-brick addition to the austere, grey-stone house, she shook her head. 'No point hammering on his surgery door. At this hour, he'll probably be ensconced in his sitting room, smoking his pipe in his pyjamas and slippers.'

'All the more reason to ring the surgery bell, therefore. Lest all decorum be lost tonight,' Clifford said in a clipped tone.

'Says the man who lured Miss Ingelby into Annie's pantry for another chance she might fall against you,' she teased to lighten the mood. 'Did she, by the way?'

He ran a horrified finger around his starched collar. 'Might we forgo any further such troubling images, my lady?'

'For now, yes. But I will get the full confession from you later.'

She strode down the path, thinking the hand-painted sign KEEP OFF THE GRASS! perfectly summed up Doctor Browning's lack of bedside manner. At the surgery door, she yanked on the bell rod harder than intended, almost pulling it free of its mounting. After half a minute, a light snapped on in what she knew was the doctor's small consulting room, beyond the waiting area.

'I'm coming!' his taut voice filtered out to them. 'A late hour for an emergency, though. So it had better be a serious one!' The door opened, revealing Doctor Browning doing up the last buttons of his coat, the blue and white stripe of his trousers leaving no doubt they were his pyjama bottoms.

'Lady Swift, why am I not surprised?' he said testily, rapping his cane on the tiled floor.

'I'm very sorry to call so late, Doctor. But I think you'll agree this qualifies as an emergency. A serious one.'

His watery eyes glared back at her behind his spectacles. 'I fail to see how. You are your usual picture of rude health. Whatever it is can clearly wait until surgery hours.'

'If you insist. Though it's not about me. It's about Annie Tibbets,' she said, feeling that icy prickle in her stomach. 'And why she died.'

'Annie?' he repeated in a wavering tone, rocking back on his heels as he flapped a hand for her to step inside. Closing the door, he faced her, looking suddenly even older. 'Lady Swift. Please explain?'

'Sergeant Brice telephoned me an hour ago. Dried monkshood seeds were found in the flour he confiscated from Shackley's bakery.'

'I know. He telephoned me too.' His brow creased further. 'I felt it odd, as I have only heard of poisoning, accidental mind, through such seeds around Autum when they are found on the plant. But it confirms the food poisoning was malicious.'

'It might be worse than that,' she said grimly.

'Worse? Good heavens!' He swung his cane at the two hard wooden waiting chairs. 'Sit! If only for my sake.' He sank stiffly down onto the seat next to hers and held her gaze. 'Well?'

'I have a question. About monkshood seeds. Specifically, how they adversely affect the body if ingested?'

His brow furrowed. 'Principally, by lowering the heart rate.'

She stiffened. 'A coincidence then that Annie Tibbets suffered from lowered heart rate already? And was taking atropine as treatment for it?'

His jaw tightened as he glared at her butler. 'Mr Clifford, have you really dragged me from my fireside to rub salt in the guilt I feel for not realising this in time to prevent Annie's death?'

'Categorically not, Doctor. Please hear her ladyship out,' Clifford said.

Browning eyed Eleanor hesitantly. 'Very well. What then?'

'Clifford and I have just come from Annie's house. Where we discovered that in the box of her atropine vials, one was missing. The one from the night of the Spring Supper.'

He shook his head. 'But Annie was fastidious about taking it.'

Eleanor nodded. 'Exactly. And I am not suggesting she didn't take it.' At the doctor's increasing frown, she continued. 'Suppose that the vial Annie took is missing because it was removed afterwards by the same person who put monkshood seeds in Shackley's flour?'

The doctor's brow furrowed further. 'But why on earth would they?'

'Because they had also tampered with Annie's medication. Maybe by removing some of the atropine and adding dried monkshood seeds?'

The doctor's glasses fell from his nose. 'But, with what Annie ingested from the Spring Supper as well, that would have been a double dose. It would have...'

'Killed her,' Eleanor finished for him gravely.

Clifford cleared his throat. 'With her death looking unquestionably no more than an unfortunate reaction due to her existing medical condition.'

Doctor Browning nodded hesitatingly. 'Yes, it would never have been questioned but for your snooping, Lady Swift. Thank goodness you are incorrigible in that regard.'

'You sound like Clifford, Doctor!' She swallowed the bristled feeling of having been chided and congratulated in the same breath. 'If we're correct, I can only assume the heartless wretch who did it snuck back into Annie's cottage either that evening after Miss Ingelby had left, and Annie was asleep, or sometime early the following morning. They checked she had taken the atropine, and then removed the empty vial to eradicate the risk of her death being thought suspicious.'

'I agree. Traces of the poison would almost certainly have remained, even if the vial was wiped clean,' Doctor Browning said thoughtfully.

She bit her lip. 'Can you arrange a post-mortem on poor Annie's body, Doctor?'

'I can. And I will. I'll telephone Sergeant Brice immediately with the instruction to do so as quickly as possible. Though I fear it will only show traces of monkshood poison in her bloodstream, which we know already.' He rose unsteadily, even with the aid of his cane. 'You realise what this means, though?' She failed to hide the shiver that overcame her at what she knew he was about to say. 'Some madman poisoned the entire village just to cover up Annie Tibbets' murder!'

19

The wheels of Eleanor's bicycle spun at half their usual speed the next morning as she pedalled down Henley Hall's long drive.

It's time to venture over the bridge, Ellie, and meet the newcomers.

Or 'interlopers', as the villagers clearly regarded them. But the fact remained that she had reconfirmed her intention to help the police. And she couldn't dismiss the fingers being pointed as being unfounded rumours without checking for herself.

Just supposing they were right, Ellie, and the poisoner, or poisoners, did come from the other side? Which meant, so did the murderer! Something deep inside her told her she was right. There was no need to wait to find the missing vial. Annie had been murdered. She was sure of it!

She took a deep breath. Not deep enough to smooth her growing frown, however. Why would someone want to murder a woman like Annie? How could they possibly profit from it? This was Little Buckford, after all! The inhabitants unified by a centuries-old way of life she had found increasingly comforting since inheriting Henley Hall. But as far as she'd seen, chocolate box scenes of rural life never depicted malicious poisoning or murder. But even before the awful events of the Spring Supper, the village was no longer quite the same. Times were changing. The trouble was, she had fallen in love with the way things used to be. But if she was to have any relevance to her beloved Little Buckford in the future, she needed to learn to love it how it was now.

As she bumped over the cobbles in the high street, she over-heard Arthur Brenchley addressing a huddle of people outside his general stores.

'Dried seeds, the word is. Poisonous. Found in Shackley's flour, so they say!'

'Put there by those two from over bridge!' someone shouted.

'More likely planted by those bent Chipstone coppers!' someone else shouted back.

She pedalled away as fast as she could. This was not the time to try to extend an olive branch. Though, how the news had leaked out, and how the truth was being twisted so quickly, was a mystery.

And a disaster!

She surged up the rise of the high street, wincing at the closed bakery, shutters down. And above, the Shackleys' curtains still tightly drawn, despite the late hour.

It was only at the bridge she slowed as the former disused stone and brick paper mill loomed into view. It had closed overnight, almost forty years ago. It had been one among hundreds of similar casualties across England when the devel-opment of more sophisticated machinery allowed greater production in fewer mills. Or so Clifford had told her. And he was rarely wrong.

From the main monolithic mill building itself came a sound like a muffled giant hurling boulders in a temper. Dominating the hotchpotch of connected stone buildings, a tall dark chimney released sporadic plumes of ash-grey smoke into the sky to join the few clouds scudding by.

Was Annie Tibbets' murderer really inside that complex?

'Only one way to find out,' she said to the river rippling past as she cycled on over the bridge.

At a division in the road, she took the right-hand fork, which joined a fast-flowing tributary of the river. The old mill had been left empty to the elements for decades, and the ravages of time and nature still stood out like sullen scars. Large cracks ran up the walls, the windows which had glass in were caked in moss among the swathes of thick ivy, and those that didn't resembled hollow eye sockets.

It looked a soulless place to work. And live, she thought, remembering someone had told her the other woman admitted to hospital, Miss Joyce Dunne, was the schoolmistress for the works. Children meant families. And since none of the newcomers had moved into old Little Buckford, they must all be housed somewhere within the labyrinth of weathered stone and brick buildings. And so must the new shop! Stokes had been adamant that the poisoning was a direct ploy to drive the old villagers to spend their money there.

That's it, Ellie. That's got to be the best place to start.

She cycled under the vast ancient entrance arch, hoping the whole thing wasn't about to crash down on her head as its wind-battered look suggested it might.

''Ere, watch out!' a coarse voice grunted, making her jump. She jerked to a stop as her bicycle collided with an already dented barrow. It was filled with some sort of thick, whitish slop, which she came close to joining face first. A wiry man of about forty in rolled-up shirtsleeves and turned-up trousers unhooked his thumbs from his patched braces. 'Get yerself some eyes, woman! Someplace I'll not be in trouble for yer lack of 'em.' He heaved on the handles of the heavy barrow and lumbered away with it.

'Nice to meet you too,' she muttered dismounting.

She considered trying one of the three sets of pitted iron steps that led up from the flagstone yard. Shielding her eyes, she looked up. Ah! The second, third, fourth and fifth floors had a series of gantries that butted heads at corners and then criss-crossed over the main section of the yard itself. And swarming over them was an army of men, and the occasional woman, in stout boots, overalls and aprons, weaving back and forth on every level, laden with barrows, carts and buckets.

'Of course. Everyone's hard at work,' she muttered. No one would be keen to be caught slacking while answering her questions.

Then she spotted him. There was no mistaking that sneering look and curtain of straggly long hair brushing against the collarless shirt. Nor the curled lip grasping a drooping cigarette. He was definitely the taller of the two men who had been warned off by the villagers on the night of the Spring Supper.

She hesitated calling out, opting to follow and see what he was up to instead. This proved harder than she'd expected as he shot up one of the pitted iron staircases with gazelle-like strides and raced along the long gantry leading off. Determined not to leave without some answers, she hurried after him.

The gantry led into a vast brick entrance hall, which itself led to the inside of the giant chimney. The heat was intense even in the hall; the source being two massive pits filled with burning coal and broken flints and, unsettlingly, bones. Her quarry had hastened past, however, along the narrow walkway. Below it, the river's tributary was now gushing down a channel towards the enormous, ponderous mill wheel.

A short flight of worn stone steps led down, another up. She had missed which way her quarry had gone.

'Dash it!' she grumbled under her breath.

Just as she was about to opt for down, a cigarette end flew

out of the upper doorway, landing at her feet with a hiss. She mounted the stairs and hurried along the narrow passageway, managing not to look concerned as the man stepped out from behind the door, blocking her way back out.

'We don't do tours, lady,' he said in a sly tone, which was impressive, she thought, given he was as good as shouting over the noise.

She feigned disappointment and raised her voice too. 'What a shame. I imagine you're all far too busy. Which is why I won't keep you long.'

'Keep me?' He laughed, then ran his tongue down the inside of his cheek. Holding up his forearms to display a network of angry fresh cuts and old scars, he added, 'What could a lady like you want with the likes of me? Your class and mine can't 'ave no business.'

'Now that really is a shame,' she said, genuinely this time. That seemed to stump him for a moment. 'But you know, it feels rather churlish to be shouting at you when I haven't even introduced myself. I'm Lady Swift.'

He shrugged dismissively, but then laughed again. 'Then you definitely ain't 'ere hopin' for work.'

She sent a silent prayer of gratitude heavenwards for her many blessings as she pointed at the cuts on his arms. 'It looks jolly hard. And painful too.'

'Flint. It's mean, alright. Can do some nasty damage when it's sharpened.'

She fought a frown.

Was that a veiled threat, Ellie?

She swallowed hard. Over the satanic din of the mill, no one would hear her call for help...

20

Just as Eleanor was seriously considering beating a hasty retreat, the other stranger from the Spring Supper appeared from the other end of the passageway.

'Oi, Natty! What's keepin' you?' He stopped on spotting Eleanor. 'Aye, aye!' he added with such lascivious gusto, she shuddered.

However, she reminded herself she was there to catch a murderer and wasn't going to leave until she'd got what she came for. 'Natty and I were just talking, actually.'

He stared at her in surprise and then looked daggers at his friend. 'What in hell is this? First-name terms with her now, is it?'

His friend scowled. 'Don't be soft. I didn't tell her me name, you just did, you ar—' He had the good grace to contain whatever expletive had been about to follow, she noted in surprise. Slapping his shirt front, he said, 'I'm Nathan Kemp, but folks call me Natty. He's Lucas Villin.'

'Delighted to meet you gentlemen,' she lied, wishing she was anywhere else but alone with these two. 'I wanted to ask you both about the Spring Supper you came to over the bridge?'

'Don't know what you mean,' Lucas scoffed.

'Strange, because I saw you there myself,' she said firmly.

He blanched. 'Alright, but hush!' he hissed.

Natty nodded and herded her down the passageway. 'We can talk in the pan room.' He seemed to catch her hesitation. 'Lady, we ain't gonna do nothin' to yer.'

The pan room turned out to be a large rectangular space lit by the weak light seeping through the grime and thick white dust covering the large windows. Eight huge circular wooden vats with a long rotating arm at their centre were half filled with milky-looking liquid and square blocks of stone over which hundreds of flint and bone pieces tumbled in the turbulent waves.

It was even noisier than where they had been, which unnerved her, given no one else was in the room. Then Lucas stepped over to a bank of switches and pulled down two of the eight levers. The noise diminished gradually as the nearest mixing arms came to a stop.

'We didn't do nothin' at yer supper,' Natty said to her, his dark-eyed gaze a mixture of anger and defensiveness. 'And we weren't there to cadge free food like yer lot accused us of, neither.'

'S'right. We just went 'cos...' Lucas shrugged. 'We fancied it.'

She pulled a face. 'I want to believe you, gentlemen, but I'll be honest, I'm struggling to.'

Natty's shoulders slumped. 'Alright. Happens we might have gone for the food. Only chance to get anythin' hot 'n proper. But we went to see what's what over yer side as well. We ain't ever been south of Chester before. Would 'ave been nice to have got even a hello, rather than aggro. We've no bones to grind with yer lot, but they were fit to beat us with theirs.'

She gave him a smile. 'Now, I'm feeling less disbelieving. And I'm sorry you didn't see the villagers at their best. Tell me, what do you know about the food poisoning so many suffered with after the supper?'

Lucas shrugged. 'That one of yer lot caused it. Only reason we wasn't sick was 'cos we eat rot all the time.'

'Rot?'

'He means rubbish food,' Natty said. ''S'all we can get in the shop 'ere with the tokens we're paid in. And he's right. It must have been one of yer lot as mucked with the grub, 'cos it weren't us.'

'Hmm, now why do you suppose anyone might have done such a spiteful thing?' she mused out loud.

The two of them shared a look.

'Must be someone in yer lot has a grudge agin the rest,' Lucas said blandly.

Natty nodded.

Eleanor was about to ask if they'd known Annie Tibbets, but her words dried on her lips as a beetroot-faced bull of a man stormed in.

'What in bloody hell is the problem, you two cumberlins?'

She didn't miss the look of fear that passed between the two men. The beads of sweat running down the new arrival's face splattered on the floor as he waved his meaty fist at Lucas and Natty. His already squinting eyes narrowed even further as he saw her.

'Tell me I'm seein' hallucinations?' he said darkly.

Natty swallowed hard. 'I'll explain, Mr Oxdale.'

'No, you bangin' well won't! She's no business bein' 'ere. And yer skivin', the pair of yer. That's a day's tokens docked. Each of yer.'

'But grinders 'ave only been off couple of minutes,' Lucas protested.

In reply, a bubble of spit joined Oxdale's other fluids on the floor, which turned her stomach, but made her furious all the more.

'Mr Oxdale, is it?' she said tartly. 'I would like to explain. I'm Lady Swift.'

'I don't care if you're the Queen of blummin' Egypt. I'm the manager of this factory. So, out with yer, woman. Or you'll get a taste of me boot on the back of yer fancy skirt.' He seized her arm.

She grabbed the little finger of the hand holding her and swiftly twisted. Oxdale yelped and hastily let go.

'I'm quite capable of making my own way, thank you,' she said firmly.

With a stiff nod to the other two, she started towards the door.

'Start up them grinders, or I'll do it with yer heads!' Oxdale barked at them, following her out, shaking his smarting finger.

Eleanor stalked out along the passageway and down the steps to the narrow walkway. Oxdale blustered up behind her, bellowing.

'We won't take no interference from over the bridge, woman!'

Spotting that three men manhandling heavy barrels onto a barrow cart were well within calling distance, she held her ground.

'No one's interfering. Like it or not, you and I live in the same village, Mr Oxdale,' she shouted back over the noise of the mill.

'Well, I don't like it!' he growled. ''Specially when nosy types like yer come round 'ere distractin' the lads from production.'

She calmed down a little. 'For that I apologise. And it was entirely my fault the two grinding machines, or whatever they are, were turned off. I'll pay for each of the day's tokens the men have been docked.'

'No chance. 'Cos how else is they gonna remember I'm in

charge?' He cocked his chin at her. 'Say, what was yer botherin'
Natty and Lucas with anyhow?'

'I just asked what I intend to ask everyone. *Both* sides of the
bridge,' she said pointedly. 'About how the food at the Spring
Supper could have caused so many people to be ill. Perhaps you
know something?'

He nodded conspiratorially, leaning in uncomfortably close
to her. 'Too right, I do.'

Her heart leaped. 'What?'

'I know that it's nothin' to do with anyone 'ere!' he splut-
tered in her face. 'There's been no trouble this side. If yer lot
want to poison each other, go ahead. More the merrier. Serve
yer all right for makin' us less welcome 'n flea-bitten dogs.'

Eleanor bit her tongue. He had a point. And a strong one,
she admitted to herself. She for one certainly hadn't done her
duty, even as a neighbour, let alone as lady of the manor.

*And you couldn't have picked a worse time to try to correct
that, Ellie!*

'Mr Oxdale, for my part, I wholeheartedly apologise,' she
said earnestly.

'Like I care, woman,' he grunted. 'Get gone!'

'I'll leave. But, first of all, I want to ask about Annie
Tibbets.'

'Want all yer like, woman. I don't know nothin' 'bout
her... whoever she is.' His scowl deepened. 'I'll tell yer one thing
I know for sure, though. The part of the village yer from over
there is redundant.' He nodded in the direction she'd originally
come from on her bicycle. 'And it'll soon be gone, swallowed up.
It's just a useless waste of space and time, left over from history.
Like ladies of the manor!'

21

In the yard she collected her bicycle and cycled off. But only until she saw Oxdale stride away in the opposite direction. Then she quickly returned. Spotting a gaunt man with a slight stoop, she headed for him. In his arms he held what looked like... a cow's head?

'I say, excuse me?'

'Hollerin' at me, was yer?' he grunted, his gnarled face twisted in a frown.

She put on her best disarming smile. 'Goodness no. I was just trying to get your attention. I'm Lady Swift. Nice to meet you.'

'What?' he boomed, turning his grey-haired head sharply enough to release a cloud of creamy white dust. The same creamy white dust that covered everything on this side of the bridge. He stood so close to her, she could see the thick clump of bristling hairs sprouting from his ear. 'Speak up, snicket. It's deavely in me 'ead,' he bellowed.

Having no idea what that meant, except that he was possibly hard of hearing, she was about to try elsewhere when she realised he was waggling his ears at her.

'That's quite the party trick,' she said, raising her voice to match his.

He grunted again, but his eyes brightened. 'Lifetime of grindlestones and knapping do that.'

She assumed 'grindlestones' and 'knapping' were something to do with the working of the mill. Before she could speak again, he thrust the thing he was carrying at her. Only then did she recognise it was an enormous chalk-white boulder. The two jagged knurls on top she had mistaken for cow's ears, the exposed section of inner grey flint as its nose. She let out a breath of relief.

'Very nice,' she shouted. 'Now, can you direct me to the mill shop?'

'Frem folk, you are then. If you've need of askin.' He swung a dust-covered leg towards the other end of the yard. 'It's down there,' he bellowed, before vanishing through the door again.

A moment later, she was standing at the narrow-barred iron gate that evidently served as the entrance to the shop. A rough, hand-painted sign nailed above declared: TOKENS ONLY! NO TICK! THE MANAGEMENT.

None the wiser, she leaned her bicycle against the wall and pushed the gate open.

'Hello?' she called out, almost twisting her ankle on the worn step.

Silence. She looked around. The shop was reasonably stocked, but there were none of the display cases and shelves filled with baskets of fresh produce she was used to in Little Buckford's high street. Here, the entire inventory for sale was displayed in old wooden crates, stood on end and stacked six high in an octagonal shape in the middle of the stone floor. All of it packaged in tins, cardboard drums and stiffened paper packets. Two words on more than half of all the labels leapt out at her: MODERN CONVENIENCE

She felt a frisson of dismay. Was this the future? Lunch and dinner reduced to wielding a tin opener or tearing open a packet and dropping the contents unceremoniously onto a plate? She shuddered, grateful for Mrs Trotman's staunch determination that food should be fresh and tasty above all.

And it wasn't just the food. In Arthur Brenchley's general store, even the more everyday essentials – candles, soap, cloths and the like – were available in several varieties, and to purchase singly if need be. Here, every item was of the most basic kind and bound in twos by string. Instead of a counter and till, an unvarnished table stood just far enough from the wall for someone to stand behind, two stiff ledgers lying on top. But what really intrigued her was the large wooden box bolted securely to the wall behind with a slit in the front. Her curiosity got the better of her. She stepped over quietly and tried to lift the lid. It didn't budge.

'Even a hammer won't open it, miss,' a soft female voice said. Eleanor spun around, her cheeks flushed with guilt at having been caught in the act. A pale girl of about twelve with captivating blue eyes was staring back at her. With her strawberry-blonde hair and sprinkling of freckles, she was as pretty as a picture. Except for her haircut that seemed to have been done using a pudding bowl as a guide.

The girl tugged shyly on her patch-pocket pinafore dress, but her gaze was sharp and questioning.

Eleanor smiled sheepishly. 'Please forgive my shocking nosiness. I couldn't help wondering what it's for?'

The girl stared back at her in obvious surprise. 'It's for the tokens, course.' At Eleanor's puzzled look, she waved a hand around the shop. 'That's how everyone pays for what they need.'

'Ah, of course,' Eleanor said, remembering what Natty had told her. 'I'm Lady Swift. From over the bridge.'

'My name's Rosine Crory.' A stomp of heavy boots made the girl's eyes widen. 'And that's me dad comin'! He's—'

'What's them wheels doin' leanin' agin our wall outside, my girl?' A stony-faced man in black trousers and mismatched brown waistcoat over his grey shirt barked as he stepped into the shop.

Eleanor was about to explain when her breath caught. The poor fellow was missing the bottom half of his right arm, the sleeve of his shirt flapping uselessly. 'The bicycle is mine,' she said genially. 'I'm Lady—'

'This shop is only for the millworkers. Men or women,' he growled in an uncompromising tone. 'But you obviously ain't one. So what's your business?'

'Actually, I came to say hello and welcome you to Little Buckford. And apologise profusely for not having done so sooner. It was very remiss of me,' she only half lied. Her ulterior motive for having mustered the resolve to come today would clearly need delicate wording.

'No one's goin' to trick Jared Crory with bunkum!' he scoffed, thumbing his chest. 'You came here up to no good. Well, listen hard. You're not gonna mess with my goods over here, like your lot have got up to over the other side!'

He stepped over to his daughter and put his arm around her shoulder protectively.

'Wait a minute,' Eleanor blurted out. 'What do you mean by that?'

'Just what I said. All that talk of food poisonin' at the celebration supper was rot! One of you lot did it deliberate. Clear as anythin' it is.'

She hesitated, momentarily lost for a reply. She hadn't expected everyone this side of the bridge to be aware of the food poisoning rumours. Slapping her forehead, she groaned.

Of course they would be if one or more of them is responsible, Ellie!

She dragged up a smile for Rosine's benefit. 'How did you enjoy the Spring Supper?'

The girl went to answer, but then hesitated. Her eyes flicked to her father. At his frown, she closed her mouth, busying herself with her pinafore instead.

'Neither of us went,' Jared said firmly. 'You lot made it clear none of us was welcome.'

Eleanor couldn't deny that.

'Oh, but a few of your colleagues did come.'

'Maybe. But happens as we was too busy anyhow. From mornin' of Spring Supper, Rosine and me had to set out the stock in here. We was busy all day and then we was home all evenin'. Together.'

Eleanor fought a frown.

That sounded rather... rehearsed, Ellie?

Rosine shuffled into her father's side. 'Me dad's right. That's just as we did, miss.'

'How nice,' Eleanor said, unconvinced. 'Did either of you know Miss Annie Tibbets, by any chance?'

'Never 'eard of 'er!' Jared growled. 'Now, it's time you left, or bought somethin'.'

'I'd love to. But I haven't any tokens. As you pointed out, I'm not one of the workers,' she added a little snippily.

Jared glared at her. 'Sure that bicycle's yours? 'Cos, strikes me you've come chargin' in 'ere on yer high horse! We can count and know what brass is, woman.'

'I wasn't suggesting otherwise.' She reached into the nearest crate and grabbed a tin and a drum of something. 'How much do I owe you?'

'Shilling 'n fourpence,' he snorted, taking the money and surreptitiously placing it in his pocket, she noticed as he stomped out.

Rosine shrugged apologetically. 'Miss, don't think bad of me dad. After his accident, the manager took him off his job of pan room foreman and stuck him in the shop, which gives us less to live on.'

Eleanor tried to hide her concern. 'Did he have the accident in the factory here, then?'

'No. One we was all in before. Back home.' She looked wistful. 'Me dad doesn't trust anyone down here. That's why he was mean to you.'

Eleanor smiled at the girl. 'Well, I hope we can be friends, Rosine?'

'Me too, miss,' the young girl said shyly. She glanced cautiously in the direction her father had gone. 'I don't think all folk is bad on yer side of the bridge like Dad does,' she whispered. 'I—'

'Rosine! Come here now!' Jared's voice called from the back of the shop.

The young girl's cheeks coloured as she hurriedly turned away.

'I'd better go. Good day, miss.'

Eleanor sighed. With this level of distrust on both sides of the bridge, how was she, or the police, ever going to catch Little Buckford's mass poisoner and Annie's murderer?

22

Outside, Eleanor dropped her unwanted purchases into her bicycle basket and took stock. Her visit so far couldn't exactly be chalked up as a success. She forced herself to focus on the positives. It had always been her method for not giving up when things got tough. After a moment, she sighed.

Being grateful no one has let down your tyres, Ellie, can't really be the only positive, can it?

She decided her wisest strategy was to retreat and try again later. And maybe lick her wounds just a little, she admitted to herself.

'Nonsense, Ellie!' she muttered. 'What's got into you? Now, who else can you speak to?' After a moment, her furrowed brow cleared and she set off, pushing her bicycle rather than riding it to avoid any further collisions with slop-filled barrows.

A few minutes later she was standing between two cramped terraces of what looked like brick storehouses. The low-pitched roofs were barely a foot above the doors, which were in dire need of painting. Long lines of washing filled the narrow space between each row, suggesting she had stumbled into the mill-workers' housing. She shuddered at the sight of two damp-blackened sheds marked 'Men' and 'Women', probably the only sanitary facilities available. She also noted two ceramic troughs with hand pumps. However basic, at least they had to be a blessing at the end of a long, hard, dirty day's toil. Especially as it hinted that none of the houses had running water. But, then again, neither did many of the houses in Little Buckford itself.

She reversed her bicycle and headed down the next alleyway. Dodging around a multitude of metal drums, piles of ropes and stacks of buckets, she came across something much more uplifting than the previous rundown housing; the unexpected sound of children at play.

'Ah, that must be the schoolroom,' she murmured. In truth, it had more the hallmarks of a converted, but still dilapidated, barn with wide arched windows and a large paved area in front enclosed by iron railings. Amongst the children, a harassed-looking woman in head to toe navy with pinned-back brown hair was staring up at the sky as if wishing she could fly away.

Supervising playtime can't be an easy task, Eleanor thought, given the forty or so children ranging in age from three or four up to around twelve, she guessed. Games seemed to be of the make-do kind; rhymes were being chanted, girls skipped arm in arm, and boys raced after each other. There was one marked out hopscotch grid, a few skipping ropes, and the odd hoop and ball. The sandpit was a low crate filled with earth, spoons being used as improvised spades.

As she approached, the children nearest the railings thrust their hands through and waved.

'Come to help me team win, have yer, ducky?' a cheeky-faced lad of about seven in badly fitting, hand-me-down clothing said with a grin.

She laughed and bent down and quacked, which drew a round of giggles and more children racing up to the railings.

She pointed at the stick and worn ball he was holding. 'Do you know I'd love to try and help you win whatever game that is. But I'm really only good at cycling and elephant polo,' she said honestly.

'Elephants! Tell us, yer've really seen one, miss?' a hollow-cheeked girl of about ten gasped.

Delighting in their wonder over something her time scouting safari routes in South Africa had made seem common-place, Eleanor beamed at them. 'Ah, well, yes, I have. Elephants are amazing animals. And wonderfully nosy about what you've got in your pockets, which tickles like you wouldn't believe!'

The children held their arms out as impromptu trunks and tickled each other exuberantly, dissolving into fits of giggles.

A shadow fell over her. She looked up to see the schoolmistress standing there.

'Good morning. Forgive me interrupting the children's play, but I...' Eleanor paused, vaguely recognising the face smiling back at her. From the Spring Supper, she realised. Although the woman's features seemed a lot paler and more exhausted. 'Gracious, you must be Miss Dunne?'

'Yes, that's me. I'm the schoolmistress here for my sins.' She spoke in a more clipped, 'educated' tone than the others Eleanor had met so far that morning. But it was still softened by a tinge of the universal nasal accent she had noted in the rest of the mill complex. 'And you're Lady Swift, I think I heard the reverend say?' she added.

'I am. Delighted to meet you.' Now Eleanor thought about it, even though she'd come looking for the schoolmistress, she was surprised the woman was back at work and not still in hospital.

'And you. But do call me Joyce,' Miss Dunne said, putting down the bell she had been holding to offer her hand through the railings. 'I've never lived anywhere with a lady of the manor before.'

Eleanor shook it warmly, noting how cold and limp the woman's hand felt. 'Oh, we're nothing special, Joyce. Certainly in my case. I was just blessed with the kindest uncle who left me his house and title. But no real instructions on how a titled lady is supposed to behave,' she added with a wince.

'I did wonder about the bicycle.' Joyce laughed, but it was clearly an effort as she tailed off quickly and leaned against the railings.

Eleanor scanned her face in concern. 'How are you after your unfortunate illness from the Spring Supper?'

Joyce swooshed the children back to their games. 'Honestly, not very good at all. It worsened so rapidly after I returned home, someone called the doctor and he insisted I was carted straight to hospital.' She fiddled with the cuff of her plain navy cardigan. 'It's lucky really that I felt so uncomfortable I didn't stay at the supper very long and eat more. Otherwise, I would probably have been far worse.'

'Goodness, I suppose that was one blessing.' Eleanor grimaced to herself, but she had to ask. 'I hope it wasn't the reception you got in the houses you did visit that made you feel uncomfortable?'

Joyce shrugged apologetically. 'I'd be lying if I said it wasn't. No one actually said anything unfriendly, but I got the feeling that was because I was with Hester. That's Miss Hopcroft. No one spoke to me directly, you see. Except the reverend, but even he'd forgotten my name by the time we left.'

'Oh, gracious! I'm so sorry. Perhaps you wish you'd never come to Little Buckford?'

The woman started, as if fearing she'd caused offence. 'Oh no!' she said vehemently. 'What I mean is that... that it's obviously a very traditional sort of village and we've all rather landed on you uninvited.'

Eleanor admired her attitude. 'Are you positive you should be back at work already, though? Or even out of the hospital?'

'Between you and me, Lady Swift, no to both. But I insisted the hospital discharge me this morning with some extra medication.' Joyce sighed as she gazed around the hurly-burly of the playground. 'I'm the only one employed to teach the children. So if I'm not here, they get left at home. Even those that are too young, which worries me enormously. But what can their parents do? Any days they don't work, they don't get paid. So none of the family eat, the children included.'

'Gracious, what a responsibility that must feel,' Eleanor said genuinely. Quietly thinking it all grossly unfair.

'It's the least I can do for the poor things. They're having to make do with too few stimulating resources, as you can see. They do get bored quickly. And that leads to trouble.'

As she spoke, a cry echoed around the schoolyard.

23

Eleanor and Joyce glanced in the direction of the cry. A scuffle had broken out. Blood trickled down one boy's knees and another's shins. The stockier of the two was tormenting his far punier counterpart, who was clearly trying to hold back his tears.

'Edwin Oxdale, come to me now! You too, Percy Pane,' Joyce called in a stern voice. She turned to Eleanor. 'There's always one bully, unfortunately. And ours is Edwin.'

Eleanor couldn't help noticing how solidly built the boy was as he reluctantly stomped over like a sullen bull calf. 'Son of the manager, is he, by any chance?'

Joyce nodded.

Oxdale's words came back to Eleanor. '... just a useless waste of space and time, left over from history. Like ladies of the manor!' She shook them out of her head.

Left over from history or not, Ellie, you've a job to do.

Joyce looked glumly at the bell. 'Not for the first time, I shall have to cut playtime short for the rest of the children just because of Edwin. Which means a hellish afternoon ahead. They'll all be fractious from not having run off enough pent-up energy. But I need to see to those nasty-looking grazes and can't be in two places at once.'

Eleanor leaned forward. 'Can I help? I used to be a nurse during the war, you know?'

Joyce's cheeks flushed. 'No, no, I didn't. But no, thank you. Basic first aid was included in my schoolmistress' training,' she added a little stiffly. 'It pays to be able to scold and patch up cuts and bruises at the same time.'

'Of course. I didn't mean to suggest I might know better. Only to help, as your job looks exhausting, even if you were feeling in top form,' Eleanor said gently.

'I'm sorry.' Joyce gave her a wan smile. 'Would you really help? Just for ten minutes?' At Eleanor's ready nod, she let out a sigh of relief. 'If you could just watch this lot until I'm finished with the two boys, I'd be immensely grateful.'

Eleanor hurried around to the gate in the railings, which Joyce was now unlocking. 'Children! Best behaviour for Lady Swift!' she called behind her as she steered her two patients into the schoolroom.

Left with almost forty curious and eager faces, Eleanor beamed as they raced over to crowd around her calling, ''Ello, lady!'

'Hello, boys and girls,' she called back. 'Now then, what games can we play together?'

She darted forward and gently extracted two toddlers who were getting lost in the exuberant crush. The grip of their little hands in hers made her smile. And her heart skip.

'Cor, miss, yer really gonna play with us?' the cheeky lad she'd first spoken to said.

'I most certainly am. But,' she lowered her voice conspiratorially, 'how do you all fancy a few new games?'

Eager heads nodded.

'Excellent. Now, we will need some chalk. Perhaps there's

some insi— Ah!' She gave the three boys, who had sheepishly pulled handfuls of coloured chalk from their pockets, a knowing look. 'Thank you, boys. I'm sure I can trust you to return what's left over to Miss Dunne's desk when we're finished?'

'Yes, miss,' they mumbled, looking relieved.

From the back of the group, a familiar pale-faced girl with striking eyes stepped forward.

'Ah, Rosine! You're just the person I need.' Eleanor beckoned to the shopkeeper's daughter, which made the girl's face light up.

With an eager audience, and her best efforts to juggle some long-dormant creativity and inexperienced supervision of children en masse, Eleanor set to with the chalk.

'That's it,' she said to the group of seven to ten-year-olds on the left side of the playground a few minutes later. 'Keep going. Younger ones, you need to draw more squares to fill the grid. Older ones, fill in the numbers up to a hundred, please. Rosine, be ready to add the snakes and the ladders when they're done.'

To her delight, the gaggle on the other side was laughing so hard the enormous circle she had tasked them with chalking was looking decidedly wobbly. 'Perfect,' she said, glossing over its imperfections. 'Now, please add six different shapes inside it with plenty of space between each one. Now, little ones, we're going to play... puddles and pillows.'

The unbridled glee of her entourage of hand-holding toddlers was adorable, especially as they clearly had no idea what she was talking about. Not surprising, as she was making it up as she went along.

In truth, she was sorry when Joyce stepped back out from the schoolroom. Even though it must have been closer to twenty minutes, not the ten she'd suggested. The schoolmistress hurried over.

'I do apologise, Lady Swift. Dredging an apology out of

Edwin took forever. You must be tearing your beautiful fiery-red curls out by now... oh my!' Her hands went to her chest as she turned in a slow circle, taking in the scene. Some children were counting enthusiastically as others stepped up the ladders and slid down the snakes, depending on the number of squares called out to them by a child with a blindfold. Others were arranged in teams bouncing the ball on whichever of the different shapes in the circle the allotted caller shouted out. And the littlest ones were all chuckling their hearts out as they wobbled from chalked pillow to pillow, mostly landing in the chalked puddles on purpose.

'And all without a hint of an argument anywhere. Lady Swift, what a... an incredible gift you have with children,' Joyce said, with something in her tone Eleanor couldn't place.

'Goodness, purely a case of me being the novelty for them, I'm sure.' Eleanor winced. 'I probably should have checked first though, that chalk marks are allowed on the playground?'

Joyce laughed. 'If it makes them interested in learning and cooperating, you could have used paint and daubed it over the windows!' She set down the bell she had been about to ring. 'I think the maths lesson I had planned for the next session will work perfectly with your wonderful additions.'

'And you, a tiny breath of rest?' Eleanor said, hoping to discreetly steer the conversation back to where she needed it to go.

Joyce leaned against the railings again. 'I admit I'm finding today even harder than I anticipated.'

'I don't suppose you know or have heard anything that might help work out how that terrible food poisoning happened?' Eleanor said lightly.

Joyce rubbed her hands over her cheeks. 'I wish I did. All I've heard is a host of rumours about the villagers the other side of the bridge being responsible. It's awful to think someone might have done it deliberately. But, golly, I can't complain. I was sorry to hear about that other poor lady. Annie Tibbets, I think her name was?'

Eleanor nodded sadly.

'She was going to do the catering for your wedding too,' Joyce said in a sympathetic tone.

Eleanor was surprised she knew. Evidently, it showed on her face.

'Hester mentioned it,' Joyce said. 'When she was telling me you had asked her to be your caterer first. She's been very kind in treating me like a new friend. She's even come across the bridge a few times to see me.'

So, Ellie, people from different sides of the bridge can get on.

'I would like to ask Hester to consider doing the catering again,' Eleanor said. 'But it feels wrong to be trying to replace Annie. And I don't want Hester to feel pressured.'

Joyce shook her head emphatically. 'It's your wedding day, Lady Swift. And every girl knows there is nothing more precious than that. Especially' – she faltered, taking a moment – 'those of us who'll never have one, in all likeliness. And,' she hurried on, 'you've kindly helped me this morning, so I'd love to return the favour. Give me time to tell Hester later today that I'll help with it. Then, I'm sure she'll say yes. It just felt too scary a job for her to take on before, I think.'

Eleanor sighed with relief. 'Gracious, that's so thoughtful of you. Especially as I imagine, after a day being a schoolmistress, you're probably ready for a set of earmuffs and your eiderdown.'

Joyce nodded. 'Yes, but not so much that I would turn down any opportunity to build a bridge of friendship between the two halves of the village.' She picked up the bell. 'I'd love to chat with you for hours, but I really ought to get back to teaching this lot as much as I can.'

They shook hands again. Eleanor left amid a rousing cry of disappointment from the children.

She wheeled her bicycle away, feeling rather shamed.

Even an exhausted schoolmistress has found the gumption to do what you haven't as lady of the manor, Ellie.

'Thank you, Joyce,' she murmured aloud. 'You've taught me a more important lesson today than you'll ever teach the children.'

24

Eleanor arrived at Henley Hall's imposing entrance as Clifford stepped onto the driveway, pocket watch in hand. She jammed her brakes on, a shower of gravel raining down just short of his meticulously polished shoes. He sniffed, snapping the watch closed.

'Finally, my lady.'

He took her handlebars as she smiled sweetly.

'If I'd known you were timing my excursion to the village and back, Clifford, I'd have pedalled more slowly.'

He rolled his eyes. 'Touché. However, you would then have missed the surprise.'

She dismounted, frowning. 'Surprise? Mmm. If it's a good one, why are you looking so pursed-lipped?'

'I wonder,' he said drily, gesturing down her cycling outfit. She winced, noticing for the first time it was streaked in coloured chalk. 'Perhaps, my lady, you might at least hasten to the guest cloakroom before joining everyone on the rear terrace?'

More mystified than ever, she raced inside to tidy herself

up. Hearing voices raised in excitement, however, she changed direction and hurried to the kitchen.

'What fun am I missing, ladies?'

'Oh, my stars!' Mrs Butters bustled over. 'We've been fretting buckets as you'd be too late, my lady.'

Mrs Trotman, Polly and Lizzie set down their bowls and cloths and joined her housekeeper, nodding.

'Too late for what?' Eleanor knelt to enjoy her bulldog and tomcat's exuberant welcome. 'Yes, you both look very dapper, chaps. But why you're decked out in colourful neckerchiefs is a mystery.'

Mrs Butters made a show of pinching her lips closed.

Clifford strode in. 'To the terrace, ladies. Quickly!'

Caught up in their excitement, Eleanor picked up her skirts and led the charge. As she stepped out of the main drawing room's French doors, her hands flew to her chest. Swinging from the two stone balls at either end of the terrace's balustrade was a lovingly painted banner. Framed with streamers and balloons fluttering in the breeze, it read: WELCOME HOME MASTER KOFI!

Mrs Butters looked even more motherly than usual as she said, ''Tis the first proper time the young lad will have been here in what feels like too long, m'lady.'

'And Mr Clifford said it might be alright to make a wee bit of fuss,' Lizzie added. 'Seein' as he and Mr Seldon are comin' for your wedding, m'lady.'

Eleanor hid a smile. 'The groom usually does attend too.'

'We'll all be together. Like proper family,' Polly breathed.

'Albeit a most eclectic one,' Clifford murmured, but Eleanor could see his eyes were shining at the prospect of spending time with his ward.

Despite everything being too special for words, a slight frown crossed her face.

'But why the hurry, Clifford? Hugh and Kofi aren't due until tomorrow.'

In reply, he held a finger to his ear. 'The sound of the chief inspector's Crossley motor car, I believe.'

'Hugh's coming early?' she cried in delight, picturing his chestnut curls, warm brown eyes, and divine athletic form.

A moment later a car appeared, a smartly dressed, ebony-skinned boy hanging out of the passenger window waving wildly. As soon as it stopped, Kofi tumbled out of the door.

Eleanor barely had time to reply to her fiancé's equally eager waving before Kofi darted up the steps. Reaching down to receive Tomkins and Gladstone's euphoric kisses, he laughed at their neckerchiefs. He looked up, beaming.

'I am so happy to see you all. What a beautiful welcome.' Ever the epitome of exquisite manners, he headed straight to Eleanor first, left hand behind his back, right one extended. 'And it is such an honour to be invited to your wedding.'

She pulled him into a hug. 'Kofi, this is your home. You don't need an invitation for anything. And we've all missed you dreadfully. Most especially Clifford,' she whispered.

His bright brown eyes radiated happiness as he peeled off to receive the ladies' flurry of welcoming clucks. Eleanor felt her heart squeeze with affection as Kofi turned and walked towards Clifford, then broke into a run and threw his hands around his arm.

'Hello, young friend,' Clifford said, discreetly patting the boy's head.

'Who fancies a celebration cup of tea?' Eleanor croaked, while beckoning to Seldon who had been hanging back.

He joined her and looped her arm in his. In the drawing room, he closed the French doors behind them, making sure they were alone, save for Tomkins and Gladstone both scrabbling up the legs of their favourite policeman. He bent down and stroked their ears.

'Hello, you terrible two. Could you give a man a minute with the girl of his dreams?' He straightened up and pulled her into his chest, burying his face in her red curls. 'Eleanor, I couldn't get here fast enough to hold you in my arms.'

She pulled back teasingly. 'Without so much as a "Good day, my lady" first? Be off with you, Chief Inspector!'

He kissed her passionately. 'How's that for a hello?'

She pretended to think it over, trying to regain her breath. 'I really couldn't say, Hugh. You'll have to do it again before I can decide.'

He did. His rich chuckle afterwards set the butterflies off in her stomach as usual.

She reluctantly pulled back an inch. 'Now. Your turn to confess. What are you doing here? You've never been early. Ever.'

He scooped her hands in his. 'I know, I've always been late or had to cancel altogether. Which is just one of many reasons I haven't given up the idea of leaving the police force. But let's not talk about that now. In short, I took a chance and left my second in command, Morrison, to finish up the case we were on. He's a good man.'

'So you telephoned my scallywag butler and plotted this between you, including collecting Kofi early, I suppose?'

Seldon grinned. 'I've no idea what excuse Clifford gave. But when I arrived at Kofi's fancy boarding school, the young fellow's trunk was already packed. And his term's report was signed and his headmaster waiting to tell me what a fine credit he is to the school.'

'I'm not surprised. He's as remarkable as he is adorable.'

'Something I've been itching to tell a certain lady since I arrived.' He scanned her face, looking bemused, then pointed at her clothes. 'Dare I ask why Little Buckford's favourite titled lady is liberally smeared in chalk?'

'Later, yes.' She wished she didn't need to sour lunch with

news of the awful recent events, but at least she had some breathing space first. She tugged him towards the kitchen. 'Now, you're looking as deliciously handsome as you are dreadfully overworked. Which means the ladies will be dying to treat you as much as you do them.'

He shrugged in confusion. 'Me treat them? How?'

She laughed. 'Do you know, I hope you never work it out.'

The kitchen was a hive of activity and mouth-watering aromas as they stepped in. Her ladies tried to keep their composure, but failed as they did every time Seldon came within ten yards of them.

Oblivious as ever, he held a chair out for Eleanor as Kofi joined them at the table.

Clifford glided over. 'Tea and cake for eight with, inevitably, no regard for the rules, it seems, Mrs Trotman.'

'And before luncheon, Mr Clifford, tsk!' Kofi said cheekily, which made them all laugh.

She leaned towards the boy and whispered loudly, 'I've been meaning to send Clifford back to butler school for ages. And I shall make it a priority now since he and Hugh have colluded against me again.'

'Colluding, Clifford? Is that what we do?' Seldon said, joining in the fun.

'To date, Chief Inspector. However, we did discuss upping it to full scale conspiracy in future,' Clifford parried to the table's amusement.

In a blink, they were all furnished with the perfect cup of tea and a generous slice of two different, but equally irresistible-looking cakes.

'Banana bread with peanuts!' Kofi cheered. 'My favourite cake!'

'And your wonderful fruitcake, Mrs Trotman. Which is mine,' Seldon added.

As Eleanor's cook fanned her flushed cheeks with the hem

of her apron, Clifford rose and raised his cup, prompting everyone to follow suit.

'To her ladyship. And all the other unruly members of the menagerie that is Henley Hall.' He gave Seldon a knowing look and whispered, 'There's still time to back out, Chief Inspector.'

Seldon nodded and made as if to jump up from his seat. 'If I drive and you read the map, they might never catch us.'

'You rotters!' Eleanor chuckled, through the laughter ringing around the kitchen.

Later, in the smaller of the dining rooms, Seldon waited chivalrously for her to settle into her chair and then sighed.

'I vote for getting this business out of the way immediately, Eleanor,' he said resignedly.

'Hardly the way to approach any wedding decisions left to be made,' she joked, noting her butler retreating towards the door.

Seldon held up a hand. 'Oh no you don't, Clifford! Whatever has happened, you're in on it too, I'm sure. Eleanor, I know that look of yours. Too well, unfortunately.' His tone softened. 'Because it means you've waded into an unpleasant matter with no thought for yourself again. Am I right?'

'Perhaps a little, Hugh.'

He sighed. 'I knew it. If it's to do with the food poisoning you mentioned on our telephone call, I shall drag Brice the length of Chipstone by his uniform buttons for having got you involved!'

'It's not his fault. He's shown some uncharacteristic initiative, made sound judgements and been very diligent.' She winced at the memory of the furore he had caused when rather heavy-handedly confiscating Shackley's flour. 'If, perhaps, a trifle overzealously at times.'

'Says the mistress of such,' Clifford murmured, pouring her

a glass of wine and whipping the lid from the silver salver on the table. 'Venison and field mushroom Wellington. Accompanied by roasted button potatoes, creamed cauliflower with flaked almonds, butter sautéed runner beans and red wine gravy.' He glanced at her. 'And unladylike proportions of all the above.'

Seldon chuckled. 'Perhaps a one-minute reprieve for the lady to tuck in before telling us the rest of the tale, then?'

After savouring several mouthfuls, she laid down her fork. 'The long and short of it, Hugh, is that someone purposely poisoned the flour used by pretty much the whole village for the Spring Supper. With dried monkshood seeds. And poor Annie Tibbets died from it.'

His expression turned grave as he pulled his official notebook from his jacket pocket. 'That makes it, at minimum, manslaughter!'

'Perhaps, Hugh. Perhaps more. But slow down. You need to hear the rest.'

She filled him in on everything they'd learned. He listened intently, making copious notes in his short efficient strokes. When she'd finished, he sat back.

'Officially, we can't say for certain if it was manslaughter or murder. But I agree with you. That missing medicine vial does make it seem that murder is most likely.' He frowned. 'Unfortunately, until we find it and can verify whether or not it holds traces of those... monkshood seeds, you said? Until then,' he continued at her nod, 'it's possible that the other poisonings were solely to cover up Annie's Tibbets' murder, as you believe, or that she died purely as an accidental result of them.' He glanced up at her. 'But what is your intuition telling you?'

'That Annie Tibbets was murdered!' she said without hesitation.

He held out his hands. 'Then we proceed with that assumption until it's proven otherwise. Your gut feelings have shown their worth too many times before.'

'Thank you,' she said genuinely. 'That means so much! But we still need a two-pronged approach because we need to catch the murderer *and* stop any further poisonings while doing so.'

'By "we" I assume you mean the police, Eleanor,' he said firmly.

'I think you might have forgotten why Sergeant Brice came to me in the first place, Hugh.'

'Because of the unsettling fact you've got more experience solving serious crime than he has?'

'No. Well, maybe a little. But mostly to defuse the tension between the two sides of the village, not inflame it. Because that's what will happen if either side gets wind it's a murder investigation. Even Doctor Browning agreed with Brice, which is why he also came to try and persuade me to investigate. And he's far from my number one fan.' Seldon went to open his mouth, but she held up a finger. 'Hugh, this is Little Buckford. And I am their lady of the manor. So, please explain to me precisely how you are going to tread carefully enough to ensure all-out war doesn't erupt? If it does, you'll be left with just Lowe and Brice. Who have already admitted that they are out of their depth. Even our own Constable Fry might not be out of bed yet, he suffered terribly with food poisoning himself.' As he let out a long breath, she added, 'And you'll have to solve it and patch the village back up in time for us to enjoy our wedding day. It's only the most magical day we'll ever have, after all.'

Seldon groaned. 'Clifford, I shall need a detailed lesson on how to handle this level of devious argument, please?'

Clifford bowed. 'Would that I could, Chief Inspector. But there is no answer to it I have found. Especially when one finds oneself in, ahem, agreement with the rationale behind it this time,' he ended apologetically.

Seldon pursed his lips. 'You too!'

She continued eating, letting him come to his own conclusion.

'Blast it!' he muttered a minute later. 'Alright, Eleanor, I agree this case needs delicate handling. Which makes it all the more ironic Brice came to you.' He glanced at her teasingly. 'Little Buckford's resident rhinoceros of subtlety!'

She let out a mock huff. 'Well, you'll just have to tag along purely as my fiancé on this case. And let the rhinoceros show you just how delicate and discreet she can be!'

25

Clifford lifted the edge of the tablecloth to reveal Eleanor's investigations notebook.

'Right. A suspect list to start.'

She turned to a fresh page.

Seldon raised a finger. 'A thought first. We don't have a clear time for which alibis are needed. And, from all you've told me, I'd say it's a long window, unhelpfully.'

She nodded sombrely. 'Of course. Shackley insisted his flour delivery was left outside his bakery as usual on the morning of the Spring Supper. So it was most likely tampered with then.'

'That being any time from four thirty a.m. onwards, I estimate, Chief Inspector. As Mr Shackley noted, the arrangement is in place to save losing heat from the bakery ovens by opening the door to receive the delivery.'

Eleanor nodded. 'And Annie's medication was most likely doctored during the Spring Supper that evening, Hugh. It would have been easy for someone to nip upstairs unnoticed. But Annie wasn't discovered unconscious by her neighbour until breakfast time the following morning. I assume the missing vial was probably removed later that night, or in the early hours of the following morning. So yes, a long time-span to check where the entire village was!'

Seldon made a note then looked up. 'Before we tackle suspects, Eleanor, there's one more thing to consider, I'd say. The poison used. What do either of you know about these monkshood seeds?'

'I've never heard of them before. And wish I never had,' she said emphatically. 'Clifford, tell Hugh the potted history you gave me about them.'

Again, Seldon listened without interrupting.

'... and was known historically as "woman's murder",' Clifford ended soberly.

Seldon pointed his pen at him. 'Hmm, which we mustn't let skew our thoughts about the perpetrator. It's a myth that poison is largely a woman's weapon. Yes, they have favoured it over other methods of murder for centuries. But statistically, most poisoners have still been male, by far.'

Eleanor was surprised. 'I had no idea. But back to our present bout of poisoning. Doctor Browning mentioned he'd dealt with a few cases of children eating the seeds, but no fatalities, thankfully. But only ever when the seeds are out, which is...' She tapped her forehead.

'Autumn time, according to the doctor, my lady,' Clifford said.

Seldon's brow furrowed. 'But it's April?'

Eleanor shuddered. 'Exactly. Which means that whatever the wretch's intention, they likely planned their scheme well in advance.'

Seldon nodded. 'Last year! And as Clifford mentioned, monkshood is not a rare plant in this area. Or any other. So, anyone in the village could have easily obtained and dried the seeds last year. Then added them to the flour when it was outside Shackley's bakery only a few days ago!'

She nodded dispiritedly. 'And pretty much anyone could have gained access to Annie's house the evening of the Spring Supper.' She shrugged. 'As it seems that almost everyone had the means and opportunity to commit these crimes, let's consider motives instead. For Annie's murder first, on the understanding the poisoning was only to hide it.'

Seldon nodded. 'Alright. So, clear motives for Annie's murder?'

Eleanor grimaced. 'Basically, none at the moment. Nothing specific anyway. I know of no one in the village who wanted to do her any harm.'

Seldon looked thoughtful. 'Well, if not hate, there's always greed as a motive. Did anyone stand to benefit financially from her death?'

She wrinkled her nose. 'I don't imagine she had much money to leave anyone. Although if the house was hers, I suppose it must be worth something? But it's quite small and simple and this is Little Buckford, not Chipstone.'

Clifford nodded. 'So, not worth a great deal, Chief Inspector.'

Seldon ran his hand around the back of his neck. 'Then we'll just have to start from scratch and speak to anyone who knew her or might have information about her and see what we can dig up. Someone wanted her dead, it seems, so there's a motive somewhere. For the moment, let's move on to the poisoning itself on the assumption that if we find the poisoner, we find Annie's murderer.'

She looked down at her notebook. 'In no particular order, let's start with Lucas Villin and Natty Kemp. They're two of the new villagers, employed in the old mill over the bridge, Hugh. They were both at the Spring Supper. And when I grilled them earlier, it was just the three of us—'

'Eleanor! What on earth were you thinking?' Seldon interrupted.

'Hear, hear!' Clifford muttered.

She folded her arms. 'Chaps, we've been through this. And you both as good as promised not to be so overprotective. I can only charge at whatever I'm doing. It's the way I'm made.'

Seldon smiled ruefully. 'Noted. So, Villin and Kemp, you said. Any motive unearthed for the poisoning?'

'Not from my conversation with them, dash it! But the rumour in old Little Buckford is that they were probably paid by someone on the new side to stir up trouble over here.'

'Then we need to follow up with Villin and Kemp in person,' Seldon said.

She grimaced. 'It won't be easy. The factory manager, Mr Oxdale, is not only built like a bull, he has the temper of one too. He made it abundantly clear he won't stand for any of his workers being questioned.'

'I'm sure you'll find a way! Who's next?'

Eleanor shrugged. 'I spoke to the shopkeeper, Jared Crory, and his daughter, Rosine. She's delightful. He isn't.' She caught Clifford's pointed look. 'Yes, I admit I didn't have the best reason for meeting him for the first time. But he needn't have suggested he'd actually throw me out of his shop.'

'Any motive for poisoning Shackley's flour?' Seldon waited, pen poised.

She sighed. 'Again, only hearsay. That he might have done it to lure the villagers this side to buy everything from him, instead of from the shops on the high street.' Her thoughts flew back to Jared's terse replies. 'Gracious though, I only asked him if he'd attended the Spring Supper, but he insisted he, and his daughter, hadn't. Then immediately gave me a full run-down of their movements from early before breakfast, right through to last thing that night.'

'Setting up an alibi?' Seldon said.

'Certainly smacks of such.'

Clifford signalled to Lizzie and Polly who had appeared in the doorway. They stepped in and began clearing the plates. Seldon hesitated as he glanced at them.

Eleanor shook her head. 'It's fine, Hugh.'

Clifford nodded. 'I believe the ladies proved recently on our supposed Christmas "holiday" in Yorkshire that they are sufficiently robust in matters of a regrettable nature.'

Seldon gave the maids a warm smile, which made them blush. 'Actually, you all proved to be a great help as well.' He returned to Eleanor. 'Right. This Jared. Or rather, his daughter. Rosine, wasn't it? Did she back up his alibi?'

Eleanor see-sawed her head. 'Yes... and no. But Rosine's only about twelve, bless her. She agreed with him at the time. But after he'd stomped out, she almost let something slip, then suddenly clammed up. She swore she hadn't been at Spring Supper.'

''Twas a fib!' Polly gasped, almost dropping the stack of plates she was balancing. 'Lummy, beg pardon, your ladyship. It just flew out afore I could stop it.'

They all turned to her.

'That's alright. Please tell us why you think Rosine wasn't telling the truth?' Eleanor said encouragingly.

'On account of me and Lizzie seein' her in the village proper the night of the Spring Supper,' Polly said ardently.

'You're sure? Because I didn't realise you'd met her.'

Lizzie stepped forward. 'Ach, it was her and no mistake, m'lady. We'd seen her and her dad in his cart going through the high street some weeks back. He'd stopped it to fix summat with the wheel and we said hello to her then.'

'Well done, ladies. That will be all.' Clifford sent the delighted maids off with a flick of one white-gloved finger.

Seldon tapped his notebook. 'Hmm, I'd say you need to talk to this Rosine girl again, Eleanor.'

She slapped her forehead. 'And I was with her without her father there.'

'Not like you to miss an opportunity to charge in with more questions,' Seldon said, only half teasingly.

'I was rather caught up, actually.' She smiled at the memory. 'In trying to entertain about forty children aged between three and twelve with nothing more than my imagination. And some chalk.'

'Ah! Now I see.' Seldon pointed at her still colourfully streaked clothing, then shook his head. 'No, I don't. But I can't tell you how much I wish I'd been there to watch.' He flipped back a page. 'The factory manager next. Oxdale, wasn't it? Get anything from talking to him?'

She grimaced. 'Worryingly so, actually. He said something about the old village being redundant. And that it would soon be... "swallowed up", that was it.'

Seldon frowned. 'Sounds like there might be plans to extend the factory over to this side of the bridge, perhaps?'

Clifford nodded. 'It does, Chief Inspector. Which perhaps is the strongest motive for the poisoned flour so far, if I might be so bold?'

'Go on.'

'Regrettably, the villagers on this side were unified against the new arrivals well before the Spring Supper unpleasantness. It would be to the advantage of anyone wishing to expand the factory to fracture that unity, to more easily divide and conquer.'

Seldon jotted a note. 'Good points. Any planning applications for expansion would naturally have to go through Chipstone's town council again. I'll get Brice to check with the town hall.'

'So Oxdale could have paid Villin and Kemp to tamper with

the flour?' Eleanor mused. 'Sadly, I think most people over there might be tempted to do anything for money. The accommodation looked rather desperate. And the workers are given tokens to spend in the only shop, in lieu of salary, or at least a proportion of it, it seems. The shop, like everything else, is owned by the mill. So I imagine it can charge whatever prices it fancies.'

Seldon frowned. 'That's merciless. What does this factory produce, by the way?'

'Stony porridge, as far as I could make out.'

Clifford tutted as he served her a dessert of brandied pears and goat's cheese mousse. 'The factory is, in fact, engaged in the grinding of flint and bone to a fine emulsion.'

Ah! The white slop the man spilled out of his barrow, Ellie.

'This is then added to the clay employed in potteries elsewhere,' Clifford continued. 'The process results in a substance which adds a purity of whiteness and strength to fine porcelain without loss of translucency.'

'Is there anything you don't know, Clifford?' Seldon said wryly.

'A great deal, Chief Inspector. Most notably, who the evil perpetrator of the poisoning is.'

Seldon looked pensive. 'Me too. And we haven't got much that feels solid yet. Who else have you spoken to, Eleanor?'

'Over the bridge? Only the schoolmistress. Joyce Dunne.'

'Miss, Mrs?' he said, writing busily.

'Miss. And she probably will be forever, apparently. At least, that's what she hinted when we were talking about our wedding, Hugh. Poor thing. I suppose it's tricky in her situation.' At his questioning look, she shrugged. 'Without meaning to sound judgemental about the others, she's clearly more educated than anyone else I spoke to over there. And not...'

'Rough and ready, my lady?'

She nodded. 'Exactly, Clifford. But Miss Dunne was a

victim of the poisoning too, Hugh. She was admitted to hospital just after Annie Tibbets was.'

'Oh! I see.' Seldon started to cross through her name, and then paused. 'There's always the outside chance she poisoned herself to deflect suspicion. But unless she has a known motive?' At Eleanor's headshake, he nodded. 'Then it's unlikely. So, who else could be a suspect?'

Eleanor was acutely aware she had only named people from over the bridge so far. 'Off the top of my head, someone with a grudge against the old villagers in general? Or with a grudge against Shackley alone, perhaps, seeing as it was his flour that was poisoned?'

'Or he poisoned it himself?' Seldon said.

'I can't see that, Hugh. He would have nothing to gain, even if he was brazen enough to do it. His entire livelihood has been closed down until further notice as a result. Unless, of course, he had a hidden link with Annie Tibbets, but that seems unlikely. It would have got out by now. The villagers are impossibly nosy!'

She caught Clifford and Seldon sharing a look.

'Hilarious! But I'm only inquisitive when justice needs serving up,' she said defensively.

'Well, keep it up, please. With caution.' Seldon looked earnest. 'Now, who might know anything about a general grudge? Or one against just Shackley?'

'Possibly Constable Fry. Or Reverend Gaskell,' Clifford said.

She nodded again. 'Good idea. I'll speak to both of them.'

Clifford looked uncomfortable. 'Ahem. Perhaps Mr Stokes ought to be on your list as well, my lady?'

Seldon tapped his forehead. 'Stokes... Stokes. Oh, no! Not the landlord of the Dog and Badger public house? I had to question him once before over some matter or other.'

'Of which he was entirely innocent,' Eleanor added. 'However, Clifford's right. If we're to explore all avenues, Stokes is Annie Tibbets' estranged husband. And now I think of it, he was the one who pointed the finger most fervently at Villin and Kemp.'

'Perhaps to throw suspicion off himself?' Seldon sighed. 'If he's anything like before though, even if I could ask anything officially, he'd lie and fob me off.'

'Constable Fry and Reverend Gaskell will be your best bet again then, Chief Inspector. Regarding the, ahem, state of mutual harmony, or otherwise, that existed between Mr Stokes and Miss Tibbets.'

Eleanor made a note of that, too.

Seldon looked thoughtful. 'What about this neighbour of Annie Tibbets? She had a key to the house, you said?'

'She knew Annie's habits, too. And had her trust, especially when Annie was feeling unwell,' Eleanor added.

Clifford held up a finger. 'Plus, she did dodge the question when you suggested she might know who would benefit financially from Miss Tibbet's passing, my lady.'

Seldon waved his pen. 'Ah! Perhaps she is a beneficiary then? Another question for the reverend and Fry. And Eleanor, perhaps you could talk to this neighbour again?' At her ready nod, his pen hovered over his page. 'Her name?'

'Miss Ingelby.' Eleanor glanced at Clifford. 'Or Phyllis to my butler here. When they were cosied up in Annie's pantry together.'

'Chief Inspector,' Clifford protested. 'I did no such thing.'

'I'm sure you didn't,' Seldon said, trying to hide a smile.

'I'm not making that up! He's incorrigible, Hugh,' Eleanor whispered.

Seldon laughed. 'Now, that is something you both have in common!' He looked serious again. 'Any more for our list? No? Then how about we go and thank Mrs Trotman for that wonderful lunch, Eleanor? And then, before we dive into any more of this unpleasantness, you give me a preview of our wedding day?'

'I rather think that's supposed to wait until our honeymoon, Chief Inspector,' she said innocently.

His cheeks turned beetroot. 'I meant the preparations you've done while I was away!'

26

Eleanor was savouring every minute of riding down to the village beside Seldon. Just the two of them. Except, that was, for Gladstone and Tomkins, the furry pair having bolted into his car and made it clear they weren't leaving.

Her shoulders rose with happiness. It wasn't just watching the breeze from Seldon's open window tousling his chestnut curls making him look so irresistibly handsome. He was more garrulous and animated than she'd ever known him to be, his unbridled enthusiasm over the wedding preparations even more special because of it.

'I can't wait to set your suggestions into motion, Hugh. They're all so romantic,' she breathed.

'With everything you've done, it's going to be the perfect day I've been aching for you to have, Eleanor.' He took one hand off the steering wheel to squeeze hers. 'From us taking our vows in St Winifred's Church in the village with Reverend Gaskell. To the marquee with all the thoughtful arrangements you've planned so the villagers can really let their hair down. And then I shall get to waltz you around that fairy-tale ballroom all night long, among even more people who think the world of you. As my wife,' he ended tenderly.

She gasped. 'Well, not quite all night. We're off on our honeymoon on the stroke of midnight, remember?'

'We most certainly will be!'

'But the part at Henley Hall will run like clockwork. Or at least most of it. Because my wonderful but infuriatingly scrupulous butler thinks he's keeping a tight rein on all the arrangements.'

Seldon chuckled. 'What are you planning that Clifford doesn't know about, you scamp?'

'Oh, only some minor details that really will make it my dream day come true. But they needn't be a secret from you, Hugh.'

He shook his head. 'No, please don't tell me. I fell for the most irrepressibly spirited and unorthodox lady ever born.' He craned around to whisper to her bulldog and tomcat. 'Don't you two let on to her, but I'm almost resigned to a life filled with alarming surprises!'

At her mock gasp, he gave her a roguish look. 'Besides, don't think I haven't arranged a surprise for you on the day, too.'

That clinched this moment as one she never wanted to end.

Evidently for Seldon too, as he sighed on turning into Little Buckford's high street. 'Blast it! I wish we didn't have to spoil the treat of sorting the wedding catering out together by wheedling in questions about Annie Tibbets' death.'

'Me too, Hugh. But the sooner we do, the sooner we can get back to Henley Hall and hopefully grab some time just for us.'

He nodded eagerly. 'Which way to this Miss Hopcroft's house, then?'

'Left, then right. She lives in Short Inch lane.'

'Which is actually seven miles long, if I remember correctly?'

She laughed. 'Welcome back to Little Buckford, Hugh!'

Hester Hopcroft's home was a rather plain dwelling compared to Annie Tibbets' sweet little cottage. The hard centre left until last in the chocolate box. With only a functional strip of stone paving separating it from the road, the squat brown house was topped off by grey tiles. And set with one begrudged-looking window above and to the side of the liver-coloured front door. In reality, Eleanor knew from her previous visits that the house extended further back than it looked. Not surprising, given it had originally been one of the barns of the farm at the end of the track.

Seldon came around to open her door. As she stepped out, her nostrils tingled as a delectable meaty aroma, overlain with golden onions and herbs, wafted on the breeze.

Hester flustered out of the house, untying her pristine cream apron. She bobbed her head of wiry-brown hair with a hesitant smile. 'Afternoon, m'lady. Sir. Or is evening just starting now? I've been that caught up in my kitchen, Father Time could have spun the hours that quick without me noticing.'

'Gracious, I hope we haven't kept you waiting?' Eleanor said.

She shook her head. 'Not a bit. Mr Clifford popped by earlier to say as it's a rummy thing, but the clocks in Henley Hall can be rather deceitful at times.'

Eleanor hid her smile at her butler's mischievous wit, then lost the fight as Seldon whispered in her ear, 'Score one to Clifford!'

'This is my fiancé, Mr Seldon,' she said, remembering not to highlight he was a senior police detective.

He smiled genially. 'Delighted to meet you, Miss Hopcroft.'

Eleanor noted the red circles on the woman's cheeks deepen.

''Tis a pleasure to meet you, sir. Please, be welcome inside. All of you.' She pointed at Gladstone and Tomkins, whose noses were pressed plaintively to the passenger window of the car. 'No need to leave those sets of whiskers waiting outside.'

'If you're really sure?' Eleanor was grateful for any chance to make this as informal as possible. 'I warn you, though. Neither have quite mastered the etiquette of polite manners.'

'All the more reason then, m'lady. I miss having paws about the house.'

Seldon opened the door and let the excited pair out. Hester cooed as she bent to pat each of their heads, but missed both as they charged on inside. As Seldon and Eleanor followed them, Hester called, 'Best be sure to duck a bit, sir— Oh, too late!' He rubbed the top of his head ruefully as Hester winced. 'Them ceiling beams is almost as thick as if they'd laid the whole tree trunks across, sir.'

Inside, the furnishings were as practical and no frills as Eleanor remembered from the Spring Supper. And just as spotless. A long mat of woven grasses and reeds ran down the middle of the tiled floor, while two armchairs covered in buff-beige calico faced the pot-bellied stove. A pair of faded pink and blue wall tapestries had been repurposed to make good the worn raffia of the four chairs around the table tucked in the corner. Everywhere, wicker baskets were filled with books, newspaper and kindling, mending, sewing and knitting paraphernalia, and even shoes, slippers and boots. In the alcove, a centrepiece of vibrant bluebells arranged in an enamel jug gave the room a homely lift of cheer and much-needed colour.

Gladstone lumbered after Tomkins as they started in on their exploration with gusto.

'You're obviously busy, so we won't keep you long, Hester,' Eleanor said.

Their hostess looked disappointed. 'Long enough to take tea, hopefully? Or I can easily warm some of my home-made elderberry and mint pressé if you prefer?'

Eleanor smiled. 'Ah! Mrs Trotman makes something similar

on the eve of autumn's equinox. Clifford told me my late uncle used to join in with the elderberry picking in Henley Hall's wild fruit garden if he was home at the time. Only, between us, that's only partly why she tends to lace it with generous amounts of eye-wateringly strong spirit that she's distilled!'

Seldon grimaced. 'For "strong", read lethal.'

Hester laughed. 'Your Mrs Trotman is lucky to have so much fresh produce in Henley Hall's herb gardens and greenhouses.'

Eleanor noted Seldon's brow furrowing. 'I had no idea elderberries have such a long season, Miss Hopcroft. Possibly from April as it is now until September, I imagine it must be, if Lady's Swift's uncle enjoyed gathering them for the autumn equinox celebration?'

Hester looked away. 'Hmm? Oh, well yes, they're not out yet, sir. But 'tis easy enough to dry them and keep them good for months. I've learned to do that, as some greedy folk around here strip the bushes rather than leaving some for the rest of us. Now, what did you decide on to drink?'

'Tea would be lovely,' Eleanor said quickly.

A few moments later, Hester returned with a teapot, jacketed in grey and blue striped wool. 'Beg pardon for not being able to offer cake or biscuits to go with this, m'lady. Only after that awful news 'bout Shackley's flour being poisoned, I've not dared bake so much as a biscuit or suet dumpling since.'

Grateful for the perfect lead into her questions, Eleanor took her tea. 'Not to worry. And my apologies. I should have offered my condolences before. Being in the same business, you and Annie Tibbets were probably friends?'

Hester petted a guilty-looking Gladstone as he appeared from somewhere he clearly shouldn't have been. 'Oh, we rubbed along just fine. Even with us being in sort of competition, you might say. Annie liked to work all on her own, mind, no matter how many she was catering for. Whereas I'd rather

share a few shillings around the other women as are excellent
cooks in the village. Lummy, only those I trust from this side of
the bridge, naturally.'

Eleanor let that go, because she was suddenly distracted.
'Oh goodness! Gladstone has stolen your slippers. I'm dreadfully sorry.' She wrestled the soggy footwear from the bulldog's
reluctant jowls, silently cursing that he'd broken the flow of
their conversation. Hester looked as if she was trying to pretend
it didn't matter. 'I'll replace them, of course,' Eleanor added.
'But it will have to be first thing tomorrow as it's late.'

Hester smiled. 'Oh then, 'tis no bother at all. Perhaps he'd
spotted as they was a little worn out anyways.'

'Like poor Annie was last time I saw her. It was at the
Spring Supper.' Eleanor hoped that hadn't sounded as shoe-
horned into the conversation as it felt.

Hester nodded. 'She wasn't one built strong. Sometimes as
pale as a ghost she was. And short of breath, too.'

'Perhaps she was taking medicine for it?' Seldon said
smoothly.

Hester frowned. 'Couldn't say, sir. I'm not one for poking
my nose in or for tattle. Not like her neighbour, that Miss
Ingelby. She's got a tongue looser than a herd of starving cows at
an open gate!'

Seldon's lips twitching told Eleanor he'd remembered her
recounting a not dissimilar slight having been delivered the
other way around. She put her cup down.

'It's lovely you got on so well. I can picture you and Annie
visiting each other's houses regularly. Two professional catering
ladies swapping tips and menu suggestions. I happened to pop
upstairs when I was round at her house, actually. I'm minded to
get a rocking chair rather like hers. Any ideas where I might?'

'Why 'tain't a rocker... can't be, I mean,' Hester faltered. 'I
never went up there, but with her feeling dizzy sometimes,
seems an odd sort of chair to have? Matter of it was, I only

visited once or twice. And not for donkey's years,' she said defensively.

Unable to work out how to phrase her questions more subtly, Eleanor ploughed on.

After all, Ellie, there's a mass poisoner and a murderer to catch!

'Was Annie popular with everyone in Little Buckford, Hester? Most people have one or two enemies, no matter how pleasant they seem.'

Hester's eyes narrowed. 'Rummy sort of question, m'lady. But I never heard of her having had a ruckus with anyone. And it's hard not to hear gossip even if one always turns an ear away.'

'I only meant with Little Buckford being so small and close-knit. It's easy for different personalities to clash,' she added quickly.

'Close-knit it was. Afore! But now as that lot over the bridge is among us, we can only expect more trouble,' Hester said in a pointed tone. ''Cept for the schoolmistress, mind. That Joyce Dunne is a good sort and good company, too.' She stepped over to where she'd left the tea tray on the table. 'It was very thoughtful, m'lady, I'm sure. But I didn't realise as you'd come here just to talk about Annie?'

Seldon nudged Eleanor's leg with his knee. He was right. She needed to back off.

'No, no. I didn't. I'm just not very good at finding the right words sometimes. And we don't want you to feel pressured, now that Annie has passed away,' Eleanor said truthfully.

'But we do want to ask you if you might reconsider doing the catering for our wedding?' Seldon said.

Hester's face cleared. 'Ah! I did wonder if it was that. 'Specially after Joyce nipped round this afternoon to say you'd mentioned it to her. Do you know, though, m'lady, I'm glad you've asked. When I thought about it, Joyce was right to give me a friendly scolding for being a ninny in saying no the first time. She thought I'd been unnecessarily modest in thinking it was too big a contract for me. And she was kind enough to offer to help if I said yes to you this time.'

'So, might you?' Eleanor said hopefully.

''Twould be my pleasure!'

'That's wonderful news,' Seldon said.

Eleanor nodded in relief. 'Absolutely. We can meet again properly to talk about menus. Perhaps tomorrow?' At Hester's nod, she smiled. 'Good! Please do bring Joyce with you. Mrs Trotman has also offered to pitch in if you need any additional help. And Clifford is insisting at least part of the evening refreshments must be the sort of thing one orders from London in fancy boxes. So they'll just need unpacking and displaying in line with his precise direction. If you can bear that?'

Hester laughed. 'Of course. Mr Clifford laying down the law to you, though, m'lady?' She patted her hair. 'There's something of a silver-tongued rascal about him on the quiet, I thinks.'

'Oh, only so as you'd notice.' Eleanor lunged after her cat. 'Oh goodness, Tomkins! You've unwound Hester's wool, you pest!'

27

Seldon was looking thoughtful as they drove away with Tomkins and Gladstone cuddled in Eleanor's lap.

'Dash it! That wasn't my slickest questioning,' she said.

He nodded. 'Maybe. But to my shame, I hadn't anticipated she might be so sharp-witted either. My attention was partly distracted elsewhere.' He leaned sideways and brushed his lips over her cheek. 'Fiery-red curls, too beautiful for words, and disastrously beguiling. What hope do I have of ever thinking straight with you next to me? Although I liked it better the other way around, when you were my apprentice on a case.'

Ducking to avoid the swipe she aimed at his arm, he cracked his head against the side window.

'Ouch!'

'Oops! We should call in on Constable Fry next. If only in the hope he's got some ice,' she said innocently.

Little Buckford's police station was simply the Fry family's front room. A table served as a desk and pride of place for the official black police telephone. A shelf held paperwork. And his wife did her best to keep their delightfully busy toddler triplets out of the way of business.

Today, she had lost the battle before Eleanor and Seldon had taken a step along the red-brick path to the front door.

'Oh lawks, I'm so sorry,' she called as three identical tiny boys in matching blue dungarees dodged past her, calling out over each other.

'Gracious, please don't be. It's always a treat to see them,' Eleanor called back, hunching down to receive their welcoming arms around her neck. Seldon pinched his suit trousers up to sink down beside her.

'Hello, gentlemen. Still the scourge of Little Buckford's police force, are we? Oh, gosh, I get the full welcome too, do I? Umm, thank you,' he said with a soft-eyed look as they tried to scramble into his lap, giggling all the harder.

Mrs Fry scurried down the path. 'Goodness, whatever must you think? Only they've been so cooped up, what with Bob having been awfully poorly with the food poisoning, they're about ready to go pop!'

'Is he back on his feet yet?' Eleanor said.

'Up. And in me uniform too, I am, m'lady,' Fry's deep-chested voice reached her from the front door. She looked up to see a wan version of the carthorse of a man Fry normally was. Still, he strode down to greet them, offering Seldon something close to a salute. 'Beg pardon, Chief Inspector. Only the little 'uns have got her ladyship pegged as a soft touch,' he said, looking every inch the proud dad.

Eleanor laughed. 'Excellent. I'm hoping to learn some new tricks from them to torment Clifford with when he's being infuriating. Which is often, by the way.'

Seldon scanned the constable's face. 'Fry, are you sure you're fit to be on duty?'

'That I be, Chief Inspector. Might be a bit slower 'n usual for a day longer, but if I'm breathin', I'm policin'!'

'Good man.'

'In that case, can we talk in your office, please?' Eleanor said.

'With pleasure. Only you'll excuse me nipping off for a mo' to help Mrs Fry with the tea things, I hope?'

Seldon held up a halting hand, clearly about to say they'd just had tea. But given one toddler was still swinging from it giggling, he lowered it again resignedly.

'Tea would be lovely, thank you,' Eleanor said brightly.

Fry looked delighted. He pointed at the car. 'I don't suppose you've got Master You-Know-Who in the chief inspector's fine motor vehicle, by any chance?'

'Yes. And his furry ginger partner in crime. But they're both supposed to be ruminating on the errors of their ways after misbehaving at Miss Hopcroft's.' She hid a smile, knowing what was coming next.

'They wouldn't enjoy doing that while playing with the boys in the back garden, I suppose?' Fry pleaded.

Seldon closed his eyes and took a deep breath. Then at her quiet cough, he nodded. 'Allow me to release the monsters, Constable.'

Amid the sounds of excited woofs, miaows and toddlers' squeals, Seldon stepped into the front room with a pained look. He lowered his voice.

'Eleanor, I had hoped to make this swift. In the vain hope of there being enough evening left to whisk you back to Henley Hall and enjoy more wedding talk together.'

She sighed. 'That is genuinely too tempting for words, Hugh. But this is Little Buckford. And it can only operate on two things; a pot of perfectly hot tea and time to chat.'

'With just a dash of poisoning and murder!'

She shook her head. 'You know it's quicker to do it the villagers' way in the end, Hugh.'

He nodded but still fell into his familiar pacing, which was more a switchback of immediate turns given the diminutive room. She sat down and tried to muster some patience herself.

'Ah, tea up! Good 'n hot too.' Fry wobbled in with the tray a few minutes later. 'Nothin' like wettin' the whistle for thinkin' sharpest.'

Seldon glanced at Eleanor as she sipped hers, then took his cup without complaint.

Fry nodded to her. ''Tis handy you havin' called, m'lady. I was plannin' on doin' the same to you. Only, I'll be honest, the fierceness of the hill up to your beautiful house has been hauntin' these still weary legs, as they're reliant on a bicycle.'

'You could have telephoned.'

'Ah! that I could, m'lady. But truth is' – he looked down at his boots – 'I felt I should say in person I'm sorry as you got caught up in the kerfuffle over Shackley's flour bein' confiscated. Not that I'm sayin' owt about Sergeant Brice's methods, course. Though Mrs Fry said as the rumours have been streakin' round the village like hornets with their tails afire.'

Seldon perched on the edge of the desk. 'Which is why we're here, Constable. But confidentially and unofficially. Especially me. Because if the villagers find out Annie Tibbets was in all probability murdered...' He nodded at Fry's wide-eyed look.

'I'm all ears.' The constable pulled out his notebook.

Between them, Eleanor and Seldon brought him up to speed. Including their initial list of suspects and Eleanor's forays to the factory over the bridge and Annie Tibbets' house. 'So finding that missing medicine vial is critical,' Eleanor said. 'But anything that small could be easily hidden.'

'Or destroyed, m'lady.'

She groaned. 'You're right, Constable. And what's making this harder is all the rumours running rife. Anyone we try and talk to already has a hundred wild theories filling their head.' She threw her hands up. 'Even Wilkes had been infected by it. To the point of blaming a fellow tradesman! He was adamant that Giggs is to blame. And he's always remained resolutely neutral in the past. If only for the sake of not adversely affecting his sales.'

'Wilkes? Giggs?' Seldon waited, pen poised.

'Stanley Wilkes,' Fry said. 'Known as "Milky Wilkes" on account of bein' the milkman, Chief Inspector. And Sidney Giggs is the fishmonger. I'd agree 'bout Wilkes not normally bein' one to bad mouth anyone.' He grimaced. 'Save, that is, for Giggs. There's bad blood between 'em and no mistake.'

Seldon frowned. 'Is it relevant to this case, though?'

'I'd say it might be. Given they came to blows over... Annie Tibbets.'

Seldon jerked straighter.

Fry nodded again. 'Annie and Stokes went their separate ways 'bout two years ago. Not that she left the village, mind. Once in a blue moon, she'd go to the pub, but otherwise, I don't think they ever meet up now. Or met up, I should say.'

'Not easy in a place as small as this to avoid someone?' Seldon said.

''Tis if you buries yourself in your business, Chief Inspector. As Stokes has. All the more so, once Wilkes started seein' Annie, if you know what I mean?'

Eleanor frowned. 'Then what's Wilkes' beef with Giggs?'

'Word is, m'lady, that Annie threw him over for Giggs. Leastways Giggs was tryin' to lure her away from Wilkes like a starved snake.' He tapped his desk with his truncheon. 'I had 'em both in 'ere for a very stiff word on account of 'em brawlin' in the alley behind Penry's butcher's shop.'

'Gracious! Proper fisticuffs, was it?'

'Giggs was wearin' a shiner of a black eye for a few days that Wilkes had given him, m'lady.'

Seldon looked up from his notes. 'Fry, you knew Annie better than her ladyship. Was she the sort to... er, you know?'

Fry stared at him blankly. 'To what, sir?'

'Waggle her physical assets at more than one man at a time?' Eleanor said, biting back a smile.

Seldon buried his head in his notebook. 'Yes. That.'

Fry tugged on the collar of his uniform. 'Not wantin' to speak ill of the deceased, but lettin' 'em both woo her on her back step? Well, strikes me as she had that sort of streak. But she might 'ave been just tryin' to make Stokes jealous.'

'Good point. I'll need to talk to Wilkes and Giggs,' she said. 'Next, Constable, can you think of anyone who might have a grudge against the village in general?'

'Or against Shackley particularly, since it was his flour that was poisoned?' Seldon added.

Fry chewed on his lip, deep in thought. Finally, he slapped the desk with his bear paw of a hand. 'Not a one. To either.'

'Alright, that's a theory demoted down the list then,' Eleanor said. 'What about Miss Ingelby, Annie's neighbour? Have you heard any rumours about Annie promising to leave her anything?'

'Ah, that I have... of a roundabout way. Tongues has been waggin' for a while that old Phyllis Ingelby was takin' advantage of Annie somehow. 'Twas never anythin' solid, mind. Just that she seemed unnaturally keen on bein' neighbourly toward her. But you 'as to remember, Phyllis Ingelby is still a newcomer to the village, like yourself, Lady Swift.'

Seldon nodded, made a note, then frowned. 'We've just come from Miss Hopcroft's house. Have you heard or noticed anything about her being in straitened circumstances recently?'

Eleanor looked at him in surprise.

Where's Hugh going with that, Ellie?

Fry rubbed his chin. 'Hester? She's never had much in the way of money, but nothin's changed there that I know of.'

'Alright. We'd better find a way to dig deeper on that then,' Seldon muttered.

'Hugh?' Eleanor said. 'Are you thinking that Hester's

circumstances might have recently changed so drastically that it was worth killing Annie to get back the contract for our wedding catering?'

He shrugged. 'It's a long shot but a possibility we can't ignore. She could have suddenly got into debt. Or was maybe being threatened. Who knows?'

Eleanor shook her head to herself.

Have I just engaged the services of a poisoner, and maybe even murderer, for our wedding reception, Ellie?

Having rescued the triplets from the terrible two, or the other way around, Eleanor wasn't sure, Fry escorted her and Seldon out to the car.

'Ah, Constable!' a fretful female voice hailed.

Eleanor turned to see a young mother hurrying over, clutching the hand of a boy of about four.

'It could have been so much worse, Constable!' the woman said breathlessly as she stopped in front of them.

Seldon took a step back, ever respectful that Fry was Little Buckford's appointed officer, she knew. Eleanor did the same.

'Hello, Mrs Smith. What's the trouble?' Fry said.

She nodded at the young boy. 'He could have lost a finger when he picked it up 'stead of his ball as rolled in the bushes, that's what. It's so sharp where it's broke. I think you need to go and check there's no more. Though why she'd have dumped 'em, I can't fathom.'

Fry frowned. 'Wait up, if as you know who owns whatever 'tis, why not go to them with it?'

Mrs Smith paled and crossed herself as she hissed, 'I can't. She's dead.'

The hairs on Eleanor's neck prickled. Seldon stepped forward but said nothing.

'What did young Freddie pick up?' Fry said keenly.

'This!' Mrs Smith let go of her son's hand to pull a handkerchief out of her pocket. 'I seen Annie Tibbets with 'em when we

bumped into each other at Doctor Browning's not long back.
Freddie found this one in them bushes just across the road from
Annie's garden gate.'

Eleanor gasped as Fry peeled open the handkerchief to
reveal one half of a glass tube. 'Part of Annie's missing medicine
vial!'

Wide-eyed, Fry handed it carefully to Seldon. 'There's a
stroke of luck. Freddie, well done, lad!'

'What?' Mrs Smith grumbled. 'Teachin' him to pick up
dangerous things? There might 'a been drops of medicine left
in it.'

Or far worse, Ellie!

With Gladstone and Tomkins safely tucked up in the Rolls,
Eleanor and Seldon followed Fry as he escorted the woman
back to Annie's house, where the boy pointed out exactly where
he'd found the vial. The three of them searched the bushes carefully, until Eleanor exclaimed and held out the other half of the
vial. Fry assured the woman there were no more in the bushes
for Freddie to find and sent her on her way.

Once alone with Seldon and Eleanor, he held his hand out
for the handkerchief with the two vial halves.

'Shall I send them off for analysis immediately, sir?'

Seldon nodded emphatically. 'Absolutely.' They all stared
at the broken vial. 'Until we get the results, we won't know for
sure if the medicine was poisoned. But I'd say there's only one
likely way this ended up in those bushes. Someone was
disturbed leaving Miss Tibbets' house and got rid of it quickly
because they couldn't afford to be found with it on them.'

Eleanor nodded grimly. 'Which confirms what my intuition
already knew; Annie Tibbets' death was definitely murder! But
why?'

28

Why was her head pounding?

Wrenched from deep sleep, Eleanor lay there, grimacing. She hadn't overindulged the night before, had she? No. She and Seldon had stayed up late. True. Delighting in such rare private time together. But only with a few glasses of wine. Nothing more. Then he had finally conceded to Clifford's insistence it would be acceptable for him to stay overnight now the wedding was so close. So, he had kissed her goodnight and left for one of the guest bedrooms in the west wing, while she'd retired to her bedroom.

Then why was her head pounding? And why was it intensifying?

She groped for the alarm clock, disturbing Tomkins and Gladstone cuddled up beside her.

'Five thirty!' she groaned.

This must be a bad dream, Ellie.

Her bedroom door swung open. Mrs Butters poked her head around.

'Beg pardon, m'lady. But 'tis urgent and you didn't hear me knockin'.'

Eleanor squinted at her, bleary-eyed. 'Oh! So it was you?' She registered that the pounding had indeed stopped.

Mrs Butters stepped hesitantly into the room. She was dressed in her button-fronted dressing gown, the hem of her nightdress peeping below.

'Where's Clifford?' Eleanor said in a grumpier tone than she intended.

'I heard him leave for London half an hour ago with Master Kofi, m'lady. 'Tis Constable Fry on the telephone. He wants to speak to you urgently. I told him as you was aslee—'

'I'm coming!' She threw the covers back and tugged her robe out from under her bulldog and tomcat. Fighting with the sleeves, she stumbled down the stairs.

At the telephone table in the entrance hall, she swept up the handset.

'What's happened, Eleanor?' Seldon appeared from the west wing, tying the sash of his borrowed navy dressing gown over the matching pyjamas. 'Oh! Excuse me, Mrs Butters.' He averted his eyes.

'Oh, for heaven's sake, Hugh! We'll all be living together soon enough.' Eleanor beckoned him over to share the earpiece. 'Constable, is something wrong?'

'I should say so, m'lady,' Fry's voice came down the line. He sounded agitated. 'There's been more poisonings!'

'What!'

Covering the mouthpiece, she sighed. 'It looks like today's wedding preparations will have to wait, Hugh.'

And the wedding only four days away, Ellie.

He nodded grimly. She wrenched her attention back to the matter in hand.

'Constable, Chief Inspector Seldon is right beside me. We'll be with you as soon as we're dressed.' She dropped the handset back onto the cradle.

Seldon groaned. 'You might have mentioned that, with your

butler acting as chaperone, we slept at opposite ends of Henley Hall!'

'Where we need to be again now!'

She pushed him towards the west wing and turned to the stairs. The shrill ring of the telephone stopped her. She swept up the handset again.

'Yes, Constable Fry?'

'No, 'tis Brice, m'lady,' the sergeant's voice boomed around the expansive marble hallway. 'Fry has just telephoned me. I suppose me and Constable Lowe had best hurry over?'

Eleanor threw Seldon a knowing look. With a resigned sigh, he held his hand out for the handset.

'Brice, Chief Inspector Seldon here. What? ... Ah, yes, it's lucky I arrived so early at Henley Hall this morning, as you say. Just a suggestion, Brice. This is your case, but seeing as I'm already in Little Buckford, I could save you the trip and assess things with her ladyship first?'

'Oh, if you would, sir, I'd be more 'n grateful.' The relief in Brice's voice was unmissable. 'Us Chipstone uniforms are like red rags to a bull over there at the moment.'

Not surprising after the flour incident at Shackley's, Ellie!

'Right. I'll telephone you later, Sergeant.'

In record time, now wearing a slightly mismatched jacket and skirt, Eleanor led the charge out of Henley Hall's front door with Seldon on her heels. She shivered as she noticed another small parcel under the grand porch but hurried on towards the garages, pulling her collar up against the unwelcome rain. Despite her sudden unease, whatever it was, it would have to wait.

The road down to the village was a swirling river as more April showers broke above their heads. The windscreen wipers flicking back and forth marked time as Seldon took the sweeping curves down the steep descent in the gloom as fast as was sensible with the Crossley's weak headlights. Day was breaking, but the overcast sky and rain made everything merge into grey.

'Last night you said you hoped we'd get word of something definite today, Eleanor.' He pulled up outside Fry's gate.

She grimaced. 'I certainly didn't mean anything like this!'

Before she could climb out, Fry appeared. He squeezed into the back of the car and tipped his helmet at the front seats.

'Beg pardon for disturbin' you, and good mornin', m'lady. Chief Inspector.'

Seldon was already pulling away as Fry yanked his door closed. 'Which part of old Little Buckford are we heading for?'

Fry shook his head, spraying water into the front. 'None, sir. I've had no report of any more poisonings this side. The caller insisted as they was all over the bridge this time.'

'In the mill complex?' She felt the now familiar icy prickle in her stomach.

'That's it, m'lady. Over half the workers, men and women, is struck down with food poisoning, apparently. Them that isn't, is threatenin' retaliation.'

Seldon glanced at her. 'Then we're unlikely to get a friendly reception!'

A few minutes later, after they'd rumbled across the bridge, Eleanor was thinking Seldon's words had been an understatement as the crowd in the mill's central courtyard surrounded them.

'Lock your doors!' Seldon said forcefully.

'Hugh, no one this side knows you're a policeman,' she hissed, trying to hide how unnerving she found the tightly packed faces crowding at every window.

'That's one good thing,' he muttered.

'Constable,' she said over her shoulder. 'We forgot to tell you we suggested to Sergeant Brice he and Lowe didn't come over.'

Fry nodded stoically. 'Quite understand, m'lady. No

offence to the sergeant, of course. But 'twas a wise decision, given how angry this lot look.'

'They've a right to be,' she said genuinely. 'They're confused and scared. And probably wishing their factory had never moved here. So, even though the missing vial has been found and we all expect the results to come back positive, we mustn't give any indication that we think Annie Tibbets was murdered. It will inflame the situation for sure.' The two men nodded as she wound her window down an inch.

'Good morning, everyone. We've come purely to try and help. Not to butt heads with any of you.'

'Help!' a stocky man sneered through the gap. 'Yer lot over there has done enough already!'

He was elbowed aside by a craggy-faced man with a scar across his cheek. 'Playin' with fire yer is! Messin' with our only means of makin' a livin'!'

A painfully thin woman whose face was pinched with bitterness poked her finger through the window's gap. 'That's right. If folks 'ere can't work, they go hungry!'

'Then please, you've all got even more reason for us to cooperate to catch whoever is responsible,' Eleanor said earnestly, sounding more confident than she felt. 'I'm sure there is some way we can help. I need to speak to Mr Oxdale.'

She jumped back as the factory manager's sweaty bull face reared up at the glass. 'Well, he don't want to talk to yer! Interferin' old skirt like yer has no business over 'ere! Get lost!'

'Let it go, Hugh,' she murmured as Seldon lunged for the door handle at her being insulted.

She held Oxdale's gaze. 'You've got sick people here. And I'm not going to crawl off and pretend I don't care, no matter how much you want me to. I came to help. Because as I mentioned to you yesterday, you and I, and all of these people, live in the same village. And I understand why they're angry.'

Oxdale snorted. 'They're angry 'cos yer lot haven't a decent bone among yer!'

She resisted the urge to point out he was the one bullying his workers. 'I'm only asking you to back everyone off enough for us to talk like reasonable people, that's all.'

'Which sounds more like a polite request than causing trouble, perhaps, Mr Oxdale?' a voice said tentatively. Joyce, the schoolmistress, pushed her way forward. She swallowed as his eyes narrowed at her. 'And it would let those that aren't unwell get back to keeping production going as best they can,' she added.

Eleanor was sure she could hear the cogs of Oxdale's brain whirring as he scowled at Joyce and then her through the window. 'Yer've got one minute, woman,' he growled, rolling his shirtsleeves further up. Raising his meaty arms, he gestured for the crowd to shuffle back a few yards. She reached for her door handle, feeling Seldon's cautioning hand on her arm.

'Eleanor, there's only three of us.'

'True, Hugh. But they're not going to lynch us.'

Hopefully, Ellie!

29

As Eleanor and Seldon stepped out of the car, she turned to Fry.

'Constable, do you mind staying put? I think your uniform might not be seen as quite the peace flag I'm aiming for.'

Fry settled back in his seat. 'Will do, m'lady. Just call though if as you want backup.'

She nodded gratefully and turned to find Seldon close to her side. 'Good luck,' he murmured.

She faced the crowd, the rain running down her face not helping her focus.

'Everyone, I'm sorry not to have met you all before. In far better circumstances,' she called out, cursing the constant racket coming from the factory. 'I'm Lady Swift. And this is my fiancé, Mr Seldon. I wish I could explain what has happened but...' She waited for the angry mutterings to diminish. 'But the important thing is we've seen how serious this food poisoning can be on the other side of the bridge. So if anyone feels unwell, it's imperative the doctor is called. And if symptoms worsen, get the person to hospital in Chipstone immediately. Especially if they have a heart condition.'

The man with the scarred cheek leaned forward. 'And how is we to afford the doctor's fee?'

She held her hands up to quiet the immediate furore of agreement at his words. 'I'll cover any doctor's costs for those who need it.'

She spotted Jared Crory turn around, as if in disgust, and shoulder his way to the back of the crowd.

'No, yer won't, woman! There'll be no charity accepted,' Oxdale bellowed at her. 'Not after it was yer lot as made my workers sick.'

His already red face was matched by the incensed flush to his neck as he turned to the crowd. 'Back to work, everyone. Now! Or you'll be docked for it!'

The stomp of boots and murmurings receded. Doors slammed. They were left alone with the schoolteacher.

'I'm sorry you had that response, Lady Swift,' Joyce said glumly.

Eleanor beckoned for Fry to join them. 'Well, I'm not sure I blame them. This is a hideous thing to have happened.'

'It is. Even some of the children are ill.'

'Oh, goodness!' Eleanor's heart leaped to her mouth. 'Not seriously, please tell me?'

'Not at the moment. Fingers crossed,' Joyce said shakily.

Seldon was looking more troubled by the second. Eleanor nodded discreetly to him.

'Joyce, would it cause you trouble with Mr Oxdale if you spoke to us?'

Her eyes flicked to Fry, but then she shook her head resolutely. 'It shouldn't, m'lady. My job is a sort of no-man's land around here. I'm neither one of the factory workers, nor management, even though the mill still pays my wages. Please, come with me to the schoolroom. We can talk there. But I can only spare a few minutes, I'm afraid.'

The three of them followed Joyce as she led them to the

school, across the playground, and into the dilapidated barn that acted as the sole classroom.

Inside, the teacher's desk faced eight long worn tables and benches, each of which held a battered box of writing slates. Two faded maps were nailed to the back wall. A dejected-looking clock looked lost where it hung. The small pile of folded blankets in the corner suggested to Eleanor that was where the toddlers most likely spent their days.

'I'm sorry there are only the hard benches, but do please take a seat,' Joyce said.

Eleanor perched on the end of one, hastily sliding further along it as it tipped violently. Seldon and Fry both gestured they would stand.

Eleanor gathered her thoughts. 'First of all, are you alright, Joyce?'

'Yes, thank you. Fortunately, because I got food poisoning so badly before, I'm still on the diet the hospital suggested. Whatever was contaminated, I haven't eaten or drunk it. For which I'm extremely grateful.'

'Is there a works' canteen here?' Seldon said.

'Golly no. There are no perks like that, Mr Seldon. I can't think how people have got sick this time.'

'You haven't heard anything that might help us trace what has been contaminated? It really needs to be identified and taken away, you see?' Eleanor said.

'Yes, of course. But all I've heard since everything erupted in the early hours are even more rumours now about it being someone from your side of the bridge, Lady Swift. I'm sorry to be blunt, but there it is.'

Eleanor bit her lip. 'Don't be. I'm only interested in making sure no one else falls foul of whatever is going on. Have there been any different deliveries or visitors to the mill complex, do you know?' She caught Seldon's quiet nod. She was asking the same questions he had in mind.

Joyce thought for a moment. 'Again, I don't think so. But I'm with the children all day, as you know. I've only heard the usual trucks grumbling up with more deliveries. And the others rumbling away, filled with barrels from the end of the production line. But there's always the most fearful racket going on and with the children shouting in the playground when I'm outside, well!' She held her hands up apologetically. 'Honestly, anyone could have come, and gone, and I'd have been none the wiser. I only realised you had come yesterday, Lady Swift, because I spotted the children talking to you.' Her eyes flew to the clock. 'Good heavens! It's almost seven. I have to collect the ones that are well enough for lessons.' She shook her head sadly. 'And a lot that aren't, no doubt. Their parents will be too fretful of not completing their shift in the factory to stay at home with them, ill or not. Will you excuse me?'

'Yes, of course. And thank you for your help,' Eleanor called after the hurrying schoolmistress.

The familiar brown tweed jacket and askew burgundy bow tie of Doctor Browning appeared in the doorway. He hastened in with the use of his cane, his tottering steps on the stone floor ringing round the schoolroom.

'Doctor. Thank goodness.' Eleanor rose to meet him. 'I should have thought to call you before we dashed over here.'

'Yes, you should have,' he said in his ever-tremulous tone. 'But for the fact you would have found I'd already left.'

'Hmm. You did well then, Doctor, to miss the angry reception her ladyship had to endure. To the point of being pinned inside my car,' Seldon said.

'Perhaps.' Browning shook his black doctor's bag at him. 'But this opens doors, gates and even barricades that are otherwise locked and barred.'

'Unlike a police uniform, on occasion.' Seldon shared a wince with Constable Fry.

'I'm just glad you felt able to come, Doctor,' Eleanor said genuinely.

He eyed her irritably. 'Lady Swift, I may fall short in your ability to ruffle feathers. But I assure you, I can exceed even your stubbornness when it comes to honouring the Hippocratic oath I swore on becoming a doctor! Nothing would have kept me away.'

'Good!' she said brightly, partly to hide the bristled feeling every meeting with him seemed to give her. 'Because at this point in time, I'd say the four of us in this room are the only ones who have a hope of containing this situation before it gets much worse. And the only ones who can get to the bottom of what's really going on. But we need to do it together,' she ended pointedly.

At Seldon and Fry's firm nodding, Browning rocked back on his heels. 'Well, of course,' he said tautly. 'I only hope we can.'

She nodded. 'As you came to find us, I can only assume no one is too ill to need hospitalisation?'

'No. At least, not yet. And none have a heart condition that I know of. Although, I have not had time to check thoroughly. Many were hesitant to allow me in.'

She retook her seat, flapping a hand for the doctor to join her. Seldon strode over and shut the door.

'Well, chaps,' she said. 'It strikes me as odd that all the cases of poisoning last time were in old Little Buckford. And this time, they're all on this side. Is it just me, or does that suggest the poisoner is targeting a victim here? For murder,' she ended in a whisper.

'It's too similar not to make it a distinct possibility,' Seldon said gravely. 'A mass poisoning used as a smokescreen again. And then... a death to follow.'

'Like poor Annie's.' Browning's tone was so self-reproachful, Eleanor risked patting his arm, amazed at his brief nod in response.

Fry put his hand up, then tugged it down at Seldon's head-shake. 'We need all the thinking we can get, Fry. So just speak up, man.'

'Very good, sir. Suppose this weren't the work of the original poisoner?'

'Excellent suggestion, Constable. It could be a copycat poisoning, you mean. But why?'

Eleanor frowned. 'It seems more likely it's the same poisoner to me. Maybe their idea is to kill someone either side of the bridge to set the two halves of the village against each other for their own evil purposes?'

Browning shook his head. 'But we'll only know that for sure if—'

The door burst open. They all spun around. Joyce stood there. Eleanor was about to ask what had brought the school-teacher back when she registered the look on the woman's face. She swallowed hard.

'Who?'

30

Outside in a deserted alleyway, Eleanor tightened her coat against the rain as Fry and Browning waited for Seldon to finish speaking.

'OK. This isn't good. Someone dying so quickly after this second set of poisonings suggests our killer may be getting increasingly bold. Or desperate.'

She shook her head to herself. Whatever faults Lucas Villin may have had, he hadn't deserved to die.

'Chaps. We need to interview Kemp. He was always with Villin when I saw him. Maybe he has some sort of idea why the poisoner targeted his friend?'

Seldon grimaced. 'That might be, Eleanor, but we were almost lynched when we first arrived. And that was before anyone knew of Villin's death. The schoolteacher told us Oxdale is keeping the news quiet only long enough for us to get out of here and back over the other side of the bridge.'

Browning nodded. 'You three should leave. I will examine the body and let you know my findings, Chief Inspector.'

Eleanor shook her head. 'I'm not leaving yet. We need to concentrate first on what was poisoned so we can isolate it, before there are any more deaths. But we've a bigger hurdle than with the first poisonings as the only food the workers can obtain here seems to be tinned or packaged.'

Seldon looked thoughtful. 'That certainly makes it harder to work out how anyone could cause an outbreak of poisoning on such a scale.'

'And,' she grimaced, 'it means we need to speak to Jared again, as he runs the shop. And quickly before he hears about Villin's death.'

Browning waved his cane. 'Do what you must. But I need to leave now and examine Mr Villin's body.'

Seldon nodded grimly. 'Normally, I'd accompany you, Doctor, but we three need to get out before we become the target of a mob!'

He nodded and hobbled away as Eleanor, Seldon and Fry set off for the shop.

'You again!' Balancing a crate from the stack he was unpacking awkwardly, Jared Crory glared at Eleanor as she entered. His gaze flicked to Seldon and Fry. 'Comin' in gangs to cause trouble in my place is your game now, I see!'

She shook her head. 'There's only three of us, Mr Crory. That's hardly a gang. I would have come with more, but there was only room for two in my bicycle basket.'

His scowl deepened. 'I'm not interested in more of yer bunkum. Anyways, I seen yer arrivin' in that black car.'

She smiled sweetly. 'You've found me out! So let me intro-duce the rest of my "gang". This is my fiancé, Mr Seldon. And this is Constable Fry.'

Crory frowned. 'Bein' crippled with havin' lost the best part of one arm doesn't make me blind, or stupid.' He cocked his chin at Fry. 'I can see that one's a policeman with no business bein' 'ere!'

'He does when people are being poisoned wholesale and someone is hiding the truth!'

She bit her tongue before she blurted out about Villin. She pretended to study the tinned food on sale. 'What a selection you stock, Mr Crory! Quite extensive. Like the tale you told me.'

Seldon stepped closer to her as Jared dropped his crate on the table.

'What did yer mean by that?' He sounded more concerned than belligerent.

She held his gaze, ignoring his question. 'You lied. About neither you nor Rosine having attended the Spring Supper. How is she, by the way? Not ill with food poisoning, I hope?'

'Leave her out of this,' he growled. 'I won't stand for yer causin' her any trouble.'

Eleanor tutted. 'Then you shouldn't have lied, Mr Crory. Because I know she was at the Spring Supper.'

'No yer don't!'

'Yes, I do. Because two people I trust implicitly saw her there. Which means you were almost certainly there too. I'll ask her myself.' She turned to the unpacked crates on the floor and whispered, 'Hello, Rosine. It's quite safe to come out.'

For a moment, there was silence. Then her strawberry-blonde hair, blue eyes and sprinkling of freckles appeared from behind the crates.

Eleanor smiled at the young girl. 'My friends and I are only trying to stop anyone else from getting sick, Rosine. Do you believe me?'

She nodded hesitantly.

Jared darted over. Seldon stepped in front of him.

'Take it easy there, Mr Crory.'

Jared scowled and pulled Rosine protectively into his side.

'Alright, so yer found me out. But I only did it to shield her.'

'Which is exactly what we're trying to do!' she said in exasperation. 'Trying to shield her and all the other children out there from this mad poisoner!'

Jared's jaw clenched. 'There's been too many rumours runnin' rife from yer lot 'bout the poisonin' bein done deliberate by someone this side. Me daughter is nothin' but good. But there was no tellin' what yer lot would trump up 'bout her havin' a hand in causin' the sickness if they knew she'd been there that evenin'. That's why I lied and said we was here together.'

Rosine pulled her father's arm tighter around her, her bottom lip trembling. 'I promise it's true this time, miss. I didn't mean to give me dad trouble. And he didn't go to the supper, I swear. Was only me. And a friend from lessons. But we only went to the first house over the bridge, then came straight back.'

'Why was that?' Eleanor said.

'Because everyone just stared at us like we was strange. And no one said nothin' to us.'

Eleanor was dismayed any of the old villagers would have let their distrust of the newcomers spill over to the children. 'I'm sorry you didn't get a lovely welcome, Rosine. It was wrong. And a great shame. But well done for finally telling me the truth. It's difficult to admit to having lied.'

'She should never 'ave needed to, but for yer lot makin' trouble.' Jared's expression darkened. 'And now the one as poisoned yer lot first has poisoned decent folk over 'ere.' He thumped the table. 'Just to get me closed down! Yer should be grillin' that baker, not me and my daughter. He's responsible, I tell yer!'

'Mr Shackley, you mean?' Eleanor wrinkled her nose. 'Come, come, Mr Crory. Can you back that accusation up?'

'Too right, I can! 'Cos I got it on good authority that Shackley's been tryin' to get other foodstuffs supplied to him to sell in his bakery. Only his credit ain't good enough with the suppliers.'

'Which you know how?'

'Because the stupid fool 'as been askin' the bloke who supplies me! So it's clear as the mill stream, he poisoned his own flour to fuel the rumours yer side. Then he's put his stinkin' poison in somethin' over 'ere to get me and my shop blamed so it gets shut down. And then he'll get supplied alright, 'cos he'll get all the trade from this side which'll sort his credit right out. He ends up sittin' pretty and I get done for it all and hauled off to prison!' His voice shook as he grasped his daughter's hand in his. 'It's alright, me girl, I won't let that happen. No matter what it takes to stop him!'

Could that be true, Ellie? Surely not?

She hesitated. 'Mr Crory, one last question. And please remember Constable Fry is listening. Did you lie to me before about not knowing Annie Tibbets?'

'All I knows of her is that I heard she was the poor woman who died,' he said quietly. 'Because the poisonin' got out of hand.' He glared at Fry. 'Which is what yer should have stopped!' He shook his head as Eleanor picked up some tins.

'Yer ain't buyin' nothin' this time. We don't want yer brass. Get out!'

Walking away from the shop, Eleanor's thoughts were churning.

Seldon turned his collar further up against the increasing rain. 'What did you make of Crory's words, Eleanor?'

She thought for a moment. 'Honestly, I believed him wholeheartedly when he said he'd lied to protect Rosine. She is all he's got, I think.'

'And his theory about Shackley being responsible?'

She shook her head. 'It makes no real sense. Even if Shackley had wanted to, stealing Crory's customers was doomed to fail. They get paid, at least in part, in tokens. Not in shillings and pennies.'

Fry stroked his jaw. 'Mind, if that Crory can take tokens instead of money, why couldn't Shackley?'

Eleanor groaned. 'You're right.'

Seldon rubbed his chin. 'Actually, I can't believe the mill would honour them, as it did with its own shop. And I doubt there'd be enough profit in it for Shackley. Still, we have to pursue every possibility. Fry, when we get back, please telephone Sergeant Brice immediately and tell him I'd like him to check Shackley's credit at the bank in Chipstone. And see if he can dig up anything about outstanding debts with any suppliers.'

Fry nodded. 'Right, sir. The minute I walk in the door, it'll be done.'

Seldon grunted. 'Now let's get out of here while we still can. I'll just have to return after Doctor Browning has telephoned his report to Fry to see Villin's body for myself. Hopefully when things have calmed down a little.'

Eleanor set off leading the way, using the huge chimney as her reference point. After criss-crossing two more alleyways, she turned a corner and halted, Seldon and Fry almost running into her. Before her was a yard, but not one she recognised. This had to be the delivery yard for the factory's raw materials. The doorways of the long run of storerooms were crowded with stacks of packing crates the size of double beds. Dominating the yard were towering mountains of flint boulders and ghoulish mounds of bones, all of which looked poised to landslide onto those below. A regiment of shovel-wielding men in dusty and stained clothing were filling a series of long barrows. The unrelenting clang of metal blades scraping up stone and bone mixed with their grunts. The work seemed back-breaking.

About to hail one of them for directions, her breath caught. She waved for Seldon and Fry to duck out of sight behind a stack of barrels.

'I've just seen Kemp looking very shifty,' she whispered. 'Maybe I can talk to him quickly now, as he seemed closest to

Villin?' She peeped again and groaned. 'Dash it! No wonder the men are shovelling like billy-o!'

It wasn't the second wave of poisoning having reduced the factory workforce by half that accounted for the workers' inhuman work rate. Oxdale was overseeing them! From her hidden vantage point, she could see his bullish form lurking between the open door of the first storeroom and the stack of packing crates in front of it. Watching and waiting to pounce on anyone letting up their furious pace, she was sure.

But then again, Ellie, he only works for the owner. He'd probably lose his job in a moment if production slipped by even a fraction.

'Fancy informing Fry and me why we're skulking like rats in this rain?' Seldon murmured.

She tuned in to just how much the damp was penetrating her own clothing.

'Sorry, chaps. It's Oxdale. He'll see us if we approach Kemp.'

About to suggest they intercept Kemp at the yard exit, her words froze. Oxdale's meaty fist was waving. But not at her, she realised. He was beckoning to Kemp. And the way he was doing it made her sure something terrible was afoot...

31

'Constable Fry! Please go back to the entrance and keep watch,' Eleanor whispered. 'Signal if there's trouble.'

He nodded. 'I've a fair imitation of a kite's whistle in me, m'lady. How's that for a warning call?'

'Perfect. Just make sure no one sees you.'

Peering between the barrels, she caught a glimpse of Kemp's curtain of straggly hair disappearing inside the storeroom. Seldon tapped her hand.

'Be careful,' he whispered.

She nodded. Crouching like a cat, she slunk to the last of the barrels and risked a quick scan of the yard. All the workers' heads were down. This was her chance.

She darted for the stacks of giant packing crates and slid her slender frame in between the first and second rows. Straining hard, she could hear nothing inside the storeroom, however. She needed to get closer. But if she left the safety of her hiding place, she'd be spotted for sure.

'Ah! Perfect,' she murmured. The bottom three planks of the last empty packing crate between her and the storeroom were hanging off. She should just be able to squeeze inside...

She caught her breath as her skirt hem caught on the exposed nails. Unnecessarily, she realised, given the sound of continued shovelling. Wrenching it free, she wriggled the rest of the way inside. Through the gap between the planks on the other side, she could see Oxdale's stout stomach protruding between his trouser braces. Craning down until her cheek was almost brushing the floor, she could now see Kemp too. She pressed her ear hard up against the gap.

'Sacked on the spot, I said! Spread the word that's what's waitin' for any worker caught talkin' to anyone from the other side of the bridge.' Oxdale's tone was menacing. 'Out on their ear'oles, they'll be. Without time to draw breath. Do yer hear me?'

'Louder 'n grindlestones breakin' flints in pan room, sir. Not that I'd give anyone of 'em what talked to t'other side the time of day. Not after what happened to Lucas! I'll get goin' right away.'

'Stay where yer are, yer crewdlin',' Oxdale growled. 'Meetin' tonight. Usual place. Eight o'clock. I want every man there, got it! And agin, no one's to talk to any of them over the bridge about it. 'Specially that local copper or that interferin' harpy of a woman who thinks bein' lady of the manor means she's above the likes of me. Now, it's yer job to spread the word. Likewise 'bout me itchin' to sack anyone as goes agin what I've said. Now, get goin'!'

Eleanor held her breath as Kemp hurried out of the store-room. But to her horror, Oxdale didn't follow him. Instead, his boots scuffed on the ground as he lumbered over to lean on the crate she was hiding in.

Her nose stung from the smoke of a cheap cigarette. Just as she feared she would sneeze, a sharp cry rang out, followed by angry shouting. Oxdale marched past her, oblivious, bellowing questions about what the hell was going on?

Still holding her breath, she darted back to the broken planks and wriggled out.

Seldon's concerned expression met her as she slid back behind the line of barrels.

'Mission accomplished,' she panted. 'Admittedly, by a whisker.'

'And the judicious use of the elastic band of my notebook!' Seldon hissed, clearly eager to clutch her to him but stepping back as Fry appeared at his elbow.

'So it was you who made that man cry out, Hugh?'

'Yes, one of the shovellers. Poor chap. Got him right on his neck with a piece of flint.'

She wrinkled her nose. 'Not quite the usual knight in shining armour ploy to rescue the damsel in distress. But appreciated, nonetheless. I might have been caught there otherwise.'

'Or discovered by Oxdale, more worryingly.'

She held her finger to her lips. 'Speaking of the devil...'

Having finished berating the poor worker Seldon had hit, Oxdale had turned his wrath on the rest of the workers.

'Get shovellin'! I'll be back to check how much yer've shifted the minute I've checked in on the front yard.'

'Excellent,' Eleanor murmured to the others. 'Now we just need to find a different route there to the one he takes and happen upon him as if we were never here. Because, believe me, he would be furious if he knew what I'd just overheard!' She recounted what she'd learned.

Seldon shook his head. 'Eleanor. We've already risked enough. After Villin's death—'

She raised her hand. 'We'll catch him alone, Hugh.'

Seldon, seemingly having grasped the vast factory's complex layout more quickly than she had, led them back to the main entrance yard. Oxdale was already there.

'What in hell's teeth is yer still doin' 'ere?' Oxdale growled. 'I told that schoolmistress to tell you—'

She feigned surprise. 'Ah! Mr Oxdale. We meet again.'

'I'll give yer one minute to haul yer ar—'

'Mr Oxdale!' Seldon barked. 'Please remember, there is a lady present.'

'Yeah, a ruddy nuisance of a one, too,' he snarled, raising his hands. 'These fists is just itchin' to throw her back over the bridge.'

Seldon and Fry stepped forward together, making quite the intimidating pair.

'I'm a peaceable sort of officer, Mr Oxdale,' Fry said. 'But mishandlin' a lady will see me arrestin' you with pleasure. Forcibly.'

Dwarfed by the two men, Oxdale stepped back. 'Yer've no business still bein' 'ere. Sling yer hooks!'

Eleanor shrugged. 'If by that you mean leave, well, that depends entirely on you.'

'What rot is this now?' he snarled.

'Not rot. But that's most apt wording. Because the rot threatening to damage Little Buckford is something I can't sit back and watch. No matter which side of the bridge it occurs on.' She cocked her head, watching his expression closely. 'Deliberate poisoning is a nasty business, Mr Oxdale. Especially when it results in manslaughter!'

She gave herself a mental slap on the back for remembering not to refer to Villin's death as murder.

His gaze flicked away fleetingly. 'Like my workforce ain't aware of that now! After one of 'em is dead!'

'Mr Oxdale!' Seldon growled.

She sighed. 'I have no desire to trade insults with you. Only to try and stop anyone else from getting ill. Or dying. Now, what can you tell me about the poisoning on this side of the bridge?'

Oxdale looked at her mutely and folded his arms.

Eleanor turned to Fry. 'Oh dear! It looks like all my protestations that Mr Oxdale is innocent of any involvement must have been wrong.'

Fry's brow furrowed, then quickly smoothed as he caught her drift. 'Looks like it, m'lady. I've me handcuffs ready, don't worry.'

Oxdale's eyes widened. 'Hold up! I've 'ad nothin' to do with this poisonin' caper.'

'Good. Then you won't mind answering my question,' Eleanor said forcefully. 'Would you like me to repeat it?'

He stared at her malevolently. 'No, I wouldn't, woman. So I'll tell yer what I know for gospel. That there's a conspiracy on yer side of the bridge. To damage mill's profits by poisonin' workers. And clearly even the police can't be trusted not to side with them that's guilty!' His fleshy jowls wobbled as he jabbed a finger at Fry. 'As manager of this mill, I have no choice but to take whatever measures the owner sees as fit to protect his, and his workers', livelihood. And their lives! Now GET OUT!'

Seldon drove the three of them back over the bridge, looking deep in thought.

She tutted. 'Get it off your chest, Hugh. Aside from wanting to tell me off for being impetuous, what are you thinking?'

He shrugged. 'That this blasted case can't get any further away from us than it already has! So, thoughts? From both of you.'

Heavy though it was over Villin's life being taken, Eleanor's heart skipped. One thing she admired most about her fiancé was his lack of ego. Despite being a senior chief inspector, his respect for lower-ranking officers doing their level, if limited, best never wavered. She nodded to Fry to start them off.

He thought for a moment, obviously proud to be asked. 'Well, it strikes me, m'lady, that Oxdale is unlikely to be responsible for the latest poisonin'. On account of it causin' havoc with his production rate. But' – he held up a finger – 'on the other hand, if he's really so frantic to keep his workers to the grindstone, why didn't he take you up on your offer to pay the doctor's bills?'

'Brilliant, Constable!' Eleanor cried. 'I didn't think of that at the time.'

Seldon glanced at her, looking concerned. 'Probably because you were addressing an angry mob, Eleanor.' He turned to Fry. 'I didn't register that either. Good man.'

Fry beamed. 'Thank you, sir. 'Cos the times my triplets bein' poorly all of a once has torn through a stack of shillin's for the doctor would make your eyes water.'

His words made her realise the advantage of having people from different social classes and life experience on the team. Seldon too, evidently, as he caught her eye and nodded.

'Right,' he said. 'Eleanor, why would Oxdale poison his own workers and then stop them getting medical attention?'

She tapped her chin. 'Normally, Oxdale would be the last person I'd suspect, given his factory is now operating at only half production. But he probably had the easiest access to add the poison to whatever they... drank!' she blurted out. Fry and Seldon stared at her questioningly. 'You saw the shop, both of you,' she continued eagerly. 'All the food is packaged. To poison it would mean tampering with hundreds of packets or tins without it being obvious, as you mentioned Hugh. But the water supply! There's certainly no running water in the houses. And there's no natural spring on that side of the bridge that I saw. Which means all the drinking water the workers use has to come from a source controlled by the mill. Which in reality means it's controlled by Oxdale!'

Seldon nodded thoughtfully. 'And the source is obviously the river, I assume. From there it would be easy to pump it into water storage tanks.'

'That then feeds into those central troughs with pumps I saw outside the workers' houses,' Eleanor added eagerly. 'Oxdale would only have needed to contaminate one.'

'And if there isn't much built-in infiltration, which I doubt there is, the water would be too cloudy for it to be noticed. Or tasted. Outstanding deduction, Eleanor!' Seldon said.

'Thanks, Hugh. What I can't fathom, though, is why Oxdale would want to kill Villin by poisoning him? With an additional dose administered somehow, like poor Annie was given, I imagine. Why didn't he just work him to death instead? I'm pretty sure he couldn't even be prosecuted for it!' she said in disgust.

'I think I know.' Seldon pulled the car to a stop outside Fry's front gate and turned to face them both. 'Actually, Oxdale's temper might be exactly what trips him up. Just as it's caused him to let slip a few things he never meant to. Unless he's an excellent actor.'

Eleanor and Fry shared a look and shook their heads. 'Gut feeling says no to that, Hugh,' she said.

'I agree, Eleanor. So here's my theory. You told me that Oxdale had said something about the old side of Little Buckford being redundant and that it would be swallowed up. Well, if our initial theory about the owner of the factory planning to expand significantly is correct, Oxdale could be looking at a very plum job; more power, more money. But only if—'

'He has much greater control from this point on!' Eleanor blurted out. 'Which the factory owner is most likely to agree to if the mill and its production appear under threat as he's hundreds of miles away in Cheshire. Especially if one of the workers actually died!'

Fry swallowed hard. 'Lummy, then what's Oxdale planning next?'

Her expression hardened. 'There's only one way to find out. We have to be at that mill meeting!'

32

As Fry hurried into his police house to telephone Brice, Seldon drove away, taking the left-hand turning leading off the village green.

Eleanor looked around. 'Hang on. Where are you going?'

'Back to Henley Hall to get you a change of clothes,' he said firmly.

She pursed her lips. 'Hugh. I may be the luckiest girl in the world. And I'm sure I really don't deserve you and Clifford, undoubtedly England's two most caring men. But the tear in my skirt is hardly noticeable!'

'Possibly. But I'm still taking you home to change so that you don't catch a chill.'

'Ah! In that case...'

She leaned across and jerked the steering wheel right. The car swung violently around to face back up the high street, tyres squealing on the wet cobbles.

Seldon stared at her. 'Eleanor! Explain, please?'

'Hugh, Reverend Gaskell keeps his fire roaring year-round. Plus his housekeeper, Mrs Pegg, conjures up delectable nibbles in a blink of an eye. So we can both dry off while discreetly grilling the reverend on what he knows about Annie Tibbets' murder. Under the auspices of having popped in to talk about our wedding service.'

He shook his head with a resigned smile. 'You are impossible.'

'Best stay alert. I haven't even started yet!'

He drove them up the rise to the vicarage in the continuing drizzle and parked. As she alighted, Reverend Gaskell's cheery voice rang out.

'Lady Swift! And Chief Inspector Seldon! Welcome!' Looking up, Eleanor spotted the reverend's tousled grey hair and clerical collar leaning out of a window. As he waved, his spectacles slipped from his nose. She stepped forward and deftly caught them.

'Thank you!' he called down. 'Please make yourselves at home in the drawing room. I shall let Mrs Pegg know we have company.'

His head ducked out of sight.

'Let's hope without his spectacles he doesn't fall headlong down the stairs,' Seldon murmured, making her wince at the thought as she led him along the ochre-painted hallway. At the end of the cheerfully patterned carpet runner she always thought as jovial as the vicar himself, she turned in to her favourite room in the vicarage. The view of the garden from the drawing room's arched windows gave a glorious vista of vibrant bushes through which a winding stone path led around a plethora of spring flower beds. Beyond the box hedge at the far side of the vicarage, St Winifred's Church stood staunchly as it had done for over eight hundred years, its slim spire piercing the grey sky.

She settled into one of the honey-coloured armchairs near the fire with a sigh. 'This is such a serene spot. I hate to sully it with talk of murder.'

Seldon grimaced, putting his finger to his lips.

Reverend Gaskell paused midway through the doorway, the tray of crockery clattering.

'Goodness, dear friends. Did I hear you correctly?'

She winced back at Seldon in apology, then turned to the vicar. 'Regrettably yes, Reverend. Only forgive me for not having introduced the matter more gently.'

'So much for discreet grilling,' Seldon murmured.

Reverend Gaskell shook his head sadly. '"Ye have heard that it was said by them of old time, Thou shalt not kill; and whosoever shall kill shall be in danger of the judgement." Matthew chapter five, verse twenty-one. Please tell me no one has suddenly been taken in the second round of poisoning over the bridge?'

She winced again. 'Unfortunately, yes. A chap only about my age called Lucas Villin, poor fellow.'

Reverend Gaskell shook his head in self-reproach. 'Doctor Browning telephoned me this morning. He said none of the afflicted workers were in imminent, mortal danger, so I had planned to venture across the bridge after I'd delivered my afternoon service. But now I will go to offer shared prayers with Mr Villin's family if he had any, immediately after you leave.' He cast his eyes down. 'I admit the tension between the two sides of the village has been troubling me for some time. And I confess I have shied away from the problem, mostly for fear of igniting more friction. But in truth, I should have been making regular visits long before now.'

Eleanor nodded. 'As I should have.'

He looked at her with a grandfatherly smile. 'Dear lady, you have had your wedding to plan. To say nothing of preparing for married life.'

A comfortably proportioned fiftyish woman in a cherry-patterned apron entered the room carrying a tray. Eleanor's nose twitched at the tantalising aromas.

'Gracious, Mrs Pegg. We didn't mean to put you to any

trouble,' Eleanor said genuinely, despite being secretly delighted at the delectable spread the woman was placing on the table between the settees.

'Tsh! 'Twas no bother, m'lady. Only begging your pardon for presuming. But as it's so close to lunchtime and last time Mr Clifford called, he mentioned hearty portions are favoured up at Henley Hall...' She tailed off, her cheeks colouring.

Reverend Gaskell came to the rescue. 'Mrs Pegg, you still amaze me with your creativity in the kitchen. What delights have you kindly brought for our guests?'

The housekeeper rallied herself. 'Why, 'tis only gardeners' fingers, ladybirds and a litter of pigs in blankets with an after of chapel kneelers and merry-go-rounds. 'Tis the best I could manage without using... you know.'

With a shudder, she bobbed her head to Eleanor and Seldon and closed the door behind her.

Eleanor shrugged at Seldon's quizzical look. Reverend Gaskell spread his hands.

'Bless her! She has managed to feed me without using so much as a spoonful of flour since the, er, problem at Mr Shackley's bakery. And we've been having fun together naming her creations. Please help yourselves.'

Eleanor didn't need a second invitation. She picked up what she assumed was 'gardeners' fingers'; shredded dark cabbage baked with egg and cheese, flecked with herbs. Next, she tried a 'ladybird'; a griddled potato round with beef, topped with a tangy red damson relish. And to finish, several pigs in blankets; a miniature sausage, cosseted in bacon. All were equally delicious. As she dabbed her mouth with her serviette, the vicar spoke.

'Now, dear friends. Please speak without hesitation. How can I help?'

'Thank you,' she said. 'The first thing is, it must be kept confidential that Hugh is investigating. Officially, he is only accompanying me as my fiancé. And also what we're about to discuss must be kept between us only. Oh, and Constable Fry and Doctor Browning, of course.'

Reverend Gaskell nodded. 'Understood. My lips are sealed, dear friends, rest assured.'

'Wonderful. Because we need to ask you about Annie Tibbets, who we are sure was murdered. As we believe Lucas Villin has been.' She explained briefly about the missing vial of atropine they'd later recovered and why they supposed Villin to have suffered the same fate as Annie. 'But naturally,' she continued, 'we can only really ask about Annie as I doubt you knew Villin?'

He shook his head sadly. 'Unfortunately, I have never heard of the gentleman until now.' He sighed. 'Poor Annie. Such a sweet and kind soul, for the most part.'

Seldon's brow flinched. 'Did the lady have a darker side, perhaps?'

'Not originally. She was a warm and generous-hearted person. And certainly a loyal member of St Winifred's flock. But I admit to being surprised at her behaviour in recent weeks.'

'Is that regarding Milky Wilkes and Sidney Giggs, perhaps?'

Eleanor pictured the milkman's hazel eyes glinting under his mop of red-brown curls and the fishmonger's equally eye-catching chiselled features framed by a raven mane.

The vicar sighed. 'Even being a man of the cloth, it is not easy to entirely dismiss rumours. Particularly having seen the lady being equally, umm... friendly, let's say, with both on subsequent days.'

'Understood, Reverend,' Seldon said quickly.

'But that is not what saddened me most, I confess,' Reverend Gaskell continued. 'I had not thought it possible for Annie Tibbets to use such language as I wish I had never heard fly from her lips last week!'

'Can you tell us more about it?' Eleanor said. 'Or does it fall under the sanctity of discussion between a clergyman and his parishioner?'

'No, no, dear lady. Her outburst was not directed at me but at... oh goodness, I don't wish to create suspicion where it is not due, however.' He dropped his cup back onto the saucer.

'Fact based and objective is the only way I ever investigate, Reverend,' Seldon said. 'Especially in the case of murder. The stakes are too high to send an innocent man or woman to trial.'

Looking somewhat comforted, Reverend Gaskell handed around the desserts; baked rice pudding squares patterned with fruit slivers, and cinnamon baked apple rings.

Ah! Chapel kneelers and merry-go-rounds, Ellie.

He cleared his throat. 'I overheard Annie rowing with Mr Stokes, her estranged husband. In the Dog and Badger public house, of which he is the landlord. Oh, but, of course, you'll remember that? We toasted your engagement to Lady Swift in the parlour room there. It was in that very room I overheard their argument. But goodness, I wasn't eavesdropping. Merely caught in the wrong place at the wrong time, having nipped in to change a booking for the village history society.'

'Gracious, we'd never have considered you were listening deliberately,' Eleanor said encouragingly. 'What were they arguing about?'

Reverend Gaskell hesitated. 'Well, that I can't say. Their raised voices, coupled with Annie's unexpectedly colourful language, made me turn and flee, I admit. I'd obviously happened in at the tail end of the disagreement, it seemed. And I'd only just ducked out of the side passageway when Annie stormed out from the parlour entrance and disappeared down the street. But that's not much help to you at all, I'm sure, Lady Swift?'

'On the contrary, Reverend. That's the most reliable piece of information we've gleaned so far!'

Back in Seldon's car, Eleanor let out a long whistle. 'Even though they were separated, maybe Stokes still had feelings for Annie? Maybe he was possessive of her and thought she was flaunting Wilkes and Giggs in his face as it were?'

Seldon nodded slowly. 'Possibly. Which would give him a motive for her murder. Which means we need to question Stokes about his row with Miss Tibbets. And that will make us about as welcome in the pub as more food poisoning!'

33

Eleanor held her hands up placatingly. 'Mr Stokes, I can assure you Mr Seldon isn't here in his official capacity. He's not even on duty. You see, with our wedding coming up so soon, he's actually managing to spend some time with me, instead of at his desk.'

Stokes slowly folded his arms. 'Not meaning to offend, m'lady, but I can smell being fed a line as easy as stale beer. Standing behind this bar all these years, listening to drunken nonsense spouted as gospel, has done that. This is clearly about the poisonings. I've heard there's been more over the bridge. So you'd better come through to the back. Save us all more wasted time pretending otherwise.'

She winced. Seldon had been right about their welcome.

The room Stokes led them to gave her a glimpse into how much hard work it took so the locals could idle away an evening savouring a pint or two. Racks of dirty glasses sat on the side of a double ceramic sink, rows of bar towels pegged above it. A small workbench was littered with a disassembled brass beer pump, tools, and a large earthenware flagon in pieces, laid out as if waiting to be glued.

The three of them shuffled in as best they could. Most of the floor space was covered in half-unpacked crates and buckets filled with what looked like oven shelves and burner plates soaking. Stokes shut the door.

'Sorry about bringing you in here, but I've already lost too much business with no one eating here after that first bout of sickness. I can't risk folks thinking I'm under suspicion. 'Tis a struggle keeping going at all, if I'm honest. This poisoning affair has rocked me hard.' His head fell to his chest. 'And that was afore... afore my poor Annie passed over.'

'I'm sorry again for your loss.' She felt torn. Stokes sounded genuinely upset. But was he hanging his head so he didn't have to meet her gaze?

'Time heals, folks say,' he said glumly.

'They do. I only hope you managed to truly clear the air with Annie before it was too late? Though there wasn't much time in between, of course.'

He jerked upright. 'Between what, m'lady?'

'Between the fierce argument you had with each other and her passing away.'

As Stokes went to protest, she pointed at the far door. 'The argument you had in the parlour through there. Just before the Spring Supper.'

'We might have had a few sharp words, but that was all,' he said dismissively.

She didn't miss his eyes flicking to the workbench, however.

She turned to Seldon. 'Gracious, Hugh. It seems we'd better make sure any sharp words we have after we're married take place well away from Henley Hall's chinaware!'

At Seldon's bemused look, she pointed to the broken flagon.

Stokes groaned and rubbed his hands over his face. 'Alright, maybe Annie and me had more of an argument. And a fierce one, I admit. But you can't blame a bloke for not wanting to dwell on that. Everyone says a thing or two they don't mean when their temper is provoked.'

She grimaced. 'Evidently hard enough for you to break something?'

He shook his head. 'That were Annie, m'lady. Not me.'

'Forgive me being blunt, Mr Stokes, but what on earth had you done to make her so angry?'

'Me? Oh, I only told her like it was. She came here angling for summat as wasn't any business of hers any more. I mean, I'm the only one of us two grafting away in this pub nowadays,' he said tautly.

Eleanor didn't reply, letting the silence grow uncomfortable until Stokes threw his hands out.

'Bah! A man's got nowhere to go after a while but to put his foot down and say, "No!" Annie came asking for money, see? And she tried laying down the law that it was still her right whenever she was needing some. She left me just a week short of two years ago. Two years! Which is time enough to have lost the right to bleed me dry!'

Walking away from the pub, Seldon glanced at her, his lips as puckered as his brow.

She raised her eyebrows. 'Has Clifford been teaching you that stuffed goose look he reserves for me when he thinks I could have been more subtle interrogating someone? Or do you need a large dose of prunes?'

'Eleanor!' His cheeks coloured. 'Please, can we manage at least one hour in the day without the conversation sliding into awkward topics? Besides, I wasn't pulling any kind of face.'

'What is it then?'

He tucked a stray curl behind her ear. 'I can't bear the thought of us ever having properly cross words after we're married. Promise we'll find another way to sort any disagreements?'

She reached up and kissed the tip of his nose. 'I promise, Hugh.'

He looped his arm through hers and let her lead him down Little Buckford's high street to the village duck pond.

'Well done in there with Stokes, by the way, Eleanor. I hadn't even twigged the broken flagon might have been a casualty of their argument.'

'Thank you,' she said, watching the mottled brown female ducks being hotly pursued by the iridescent green males. She held her hands up apologetically to the quacking gaggle quickly forming in front of her. 'Sorry, my feathered friends, I've no nibbles for you today.'

Seldon stared at her. 'You actually come and feed these things?'

'Sometimes, yes, you hopeless city boy. But only if Gladstone and Tomkins aren't with me because then it's bedlam.'

'It's not far off that without them.'

He pointed at the fighting that had broken out between the males. She watched the two closest jab each other in the chest with their beaks.

'Wilkes and Giggs,' she murmured. At Seldon's questioning look, she explained. 'Those ducks fighting got me thinking. If Stokes is as upset by Annie's death as he seems, he'd almost certainly have been jealous about Annie moving on to a relationship with another man. Especially if it was two different men at once.'

He nodded. 'You said as much in the car. To be fair to the lady, though, it's still only conjecture, Eleanor.'

'Agreed. Which is why we're going to find out from the horses' mouths themselves!'

'Wilkes and Giggs? But where are they?'

She shrugged. 'Giggs doesn't live in the village and usually only delivers his fish in the evening, so I've no idea where he might be at the moment. Wilkes lives here and should be out on his rounds, but again, where I've no idea. Oh! But there's a woman who might.' She waved eagerly across the pond. Mrs Fry waved back, accompanied by her triplets jumping up and down. Eleanor thought they looked cuter than ever in their matching wool sailor tops and knickerbockers as they hurried over to greet her.

'For me? Thank you, boys.'

She took the handfuls of pink bunny-tailed grasses they held out while Mrs Fry peered up at the sky, considering the question.

'Depends if it's afore or after midday as yet?'

Seldon checked his pocket watch. 'Five minutes after, Mrs Fry.'

'Ah! Then 'tis easy, Chief Inspector. Milky Wilkes is certain to be heading down Cowgate Lane after seeing Doctor Browning.'

'Gracious, is he ill?' Eleanor said.

Mrs Fry laughed. 'Old Milky? Never! But he would be if he's ever late delivering the doctor's milk for his afternoon tea when surgery closes. If you hurry, you'll just catch him somewhere thereabouts.'

'Thank you. Enjoy your walk,' Ellie called as she and Seldon hurried back to the car.

A few minutes later, they passed the doctor's house. There was no sign of a milk cart and horse, but around the next bend they spotted it stopped further up the lane.

To her surprise, Seldon pulled up a fair distance from it. It was her turn to look at him enquiringly.

He pointed to either side of the road. 'There are no houses anywhere I can see on this stretch, which means he may have stopped for a...' He fiddled with his jacket cuff.

She caught on. 'Oh! You mean he's probably nipped behind a tree for a—'

'Yes!' Seldon said quickly.

Before she could reply, the sound of shouting drifted over.

She wound her window down as Wilkes stepped into view, waving his fist.

'Goodness! It looks like he's arguing with someone,' she muttered.

'Bad timing then, blast it!'

She strained her ears. 'No, Hugh. Excellent timing, actually. I just caught him saying something about "Annie". And look there! That's Giggs squaring up to him.'

Seldon reached for his door handle, but she tugged his arm back. 'Hugh. Let me speak to them. I've learned from my ladies these two are the worst gossips in the village, so it's best you keep out of sight. And don't worry. Neither is the sort to throw a punch in front of a woman.'

He nodded reluctantly.

She ducked around the back of Seldon's car and walked quietly up to the milk cart on the opposite side of the two men. All she could hear as she approached was name-calling. She stepped in front of them.

'Good afternoon, Mr Wilkes, may I purchase an extra— Oh! And Mr Giggs too.' She feigned surprise. 'I didn't see your delightful fish wagon. Mind you' – she looked around – 'I still can't.'

Both men had whipped off their caps, looking abashed. Not for long, however. Giggs glanced slyly at Wilkes and grinned.

'That's on account of my horse bein' fit enough for me to ride, as well as to pull my cart of an evenin', m'lady.' He pointed to where Eleanor could now see his chestnut mount tossing its mane at the milkman's stocky grey. 'Unlike Wilkes' old nag.'

The milkman's jaw clenched.

'Well, gentlemen, at least you're both in robust form after all that food poisoning. Rather too robust, perhaps? Trumping each other in the name-calling stakes? And in public?'

'Trumping?' Wilkes raked his hand through his mop of red-brown curls. 'Not me! I've not one ounce of envy about Giggs that would make me want to trounce him in anything.'

'Liar!' the fishmonger hissed.

'Shut your trap if you can't control your tongue in front of her ladyship,' Wilkes shot back.

She nodded. 'Although, Mr Wilkes, that's rather a case of the pot calling the kettle black, isn't it? Seeing as you were also shouting up and down the lane about poor Annie Tibbets.'

Giggs grinned slyly again. 'Wilkes started it, m'lady!'

'He just won't let it rest!' Wilkes protested.

'Unlike Annie's spirit needs to!' she chided. 'It doesn't need to look down in dismay on you two still fighting over her.'

Wilkes jutted out his chin. 'I never was, m'lady. Had no need, seeing as me and she were a couple. She never fancied this fish-faced dog.'

Giggs scoffed. 'It's sad. Wilkes 'ere just can't accept Annie only had eyes for me. But what's really eatin' him up is it was all on her side, none on mine. I turned her down, you see.'

'You filthy liar!' Wilkes spat. 'That's why I reckon as it was you that poisoned the villagers at the Spring Supper. Just to try and put me out of action so you could get to Annie while I was laid up.'

Eleanor had neither the time nor patience to listen to the two men insult each other any longer. She'd learned what she needed to know. Now she needed to find out if the fishmonger had an alibi for Annie's death.

'It was such a fun evening, before it ended so unhappily, wasn't it, Mr Giggs?'

He stared at her, frowning. 'I don't live in the village, m'lady, so I don't know. It was for locals only.'

'Well, I'd class you as an honorary member, given that you

deliver your tasty fish to us all. So I'm glad you felt you could attend, anyway.'

'But I never did,' Giggs said ardently.

'Someone told me they saw you for sure,' she fibbed, mentally crossing her fingers.

'Then 'twas someone as was mistaken. I only deliver of an evenin' in Little Buckford, but never on Spring Supper. There's no point. Folks are all too busy. And half of 'em aren't even in their own houses, but gassin' away in someone else's.'

She'd check his story later, but it was easy to verify, so she doubted he was lying.

Before she could ask him another question, Wilkes interrupted.

'No one would have wanted your stinking fish anyway, Giggs. Just like Annie never wanted you!'

Eleanor sighed. Clearly, she wasn't going to learn anything more until the two of them calmed down. More though, she had meant what she said about Annie's spirit deserving to be at peace.

'Gentlemen!' she interrupted. 'I hope there's still enough compassion and selflessness underneath your bluster to realise you should be thinking not of yourselves, but of Annie. And Mr Stokes. He was still her husband.' Before either could reply, she spun on her heel, calling over her shoulder. 'I shall leave you to think that over.'

34

Back at Henley Hall, Mrs Butters took Eleanor and Seldon's hats and coats with a sheepish look. 'Welcome back, m'lady. Sir. Only beg pardon for the shocking mess.'

Seldon looked around. 'The terrible two been busy, have they?'

Before she could reply, Tomkins skittered across the marble flooring, Gladstone lumbering behind, gripping the other end of a garland of cream silk roses. Eleanor laughed as she knelt and retrieved their stolen prize.

'It's no good pulling innocent faces, chaps. Not when you're caught red-handed!'

Mrs Butters held up her hands. 'For once, m'lady, 'tis not these two as is the cause of the disorder. Us aprons have all been so busy with the wedding preparations, it's rather spilled out everywhere. I'm so sorry.'

'No, I'm the one to be sorry,' Eleanor said genuinely. 'I should have been here doing a great deal more of it.'

Mrs Butters gave her a motherly smile. 'You're doing your best to help the village, m'lady. We're all just hoping it isn't spoiling your dream of what's supposed to be the most special day ever.'

'Which it won't! And which the day absolutely will be.' Seldon put so much passion into his words, Eleanor's heart skipped. 'So, what can I do to help this afternoon?'

She shook her head. 'Nothing, Hugh. We need to discuss—'

'After some progress on the wedding preparations,' he said determinedly. 'It's only four days away!'

Mrs Butters held out the diary Clifford had given to Eleanor as a wedding planner.

She rolled her eyes affectionately at the note poking out from between the pages. In her butler's meticulous copperplate writing, it read: *Lest distractions should otherwise prevail, my lady, in priority order...*

'Right, Hugh, you and I will hole up in the dining room. That's the centre of wedding operations.'

Mrs Butters gasped.

Eleanor waved her hand. 'Hugh won't even notice whatever mess there is, don't worry. You should see his office desk!'

Mrs Butters winced. 'M'lady, 'tisn't that. There's a few things in there as... you know!'

'Say no more.' Seldon took the list from Eleanor and quickly scanned it. 'Ladies, if you need me, I shall be busy elsewhere. Starting with, ah, finalising the layout of the marquee, seeing as it's underlined twice.'

'Perfect.' She glanced at the tall grandfather clock in the alcove as Mrs Butters hastened off. 'We've three quarters of an hour before Hester Hopcroft is due here to meet us.'

'Meet *you*,' he said resignedly. 'As you're probably thinking, it's best you meet her without me so you can shoehorn in more questions about the poisonings. Specifically, why she really turned down the opportunity to do our catering the first time around.'

He sighed at her nod, brushed his lips over her cheek, and strode away.

Stepping into the dining room, Eleanor gulped. Her housekeeper hadn't been exaggerating. Among the piles of unopened deliveries, swathes of lace, brocade and silk rose garlands covered every chair and most of the table. Capable of seating twenty-four comfortably, there was hardly a glimpse left of its highly polished walnut marquetry.

But it was the canopy of magnolia silk draped over a tall circular frame that beckoned her. She peeped inside.

'My wedding dress!' she breathed.

'Is it coming on as you hoped, m'lady?' Mrs Butters said hesitatingly.

'Oh gracious, more than I dreamed of!' she cried, spinning around. 'When it's finished, I'm going to feel like a true fairy-tale princess. Especially once this basket of exquisitely embroidered ribbons you've worked so hard on are all added. Thank you. I love it more than I can say. The best I can offer in return is to tick off as many wedding prep tasks as possible without adding too much to the chaos in here.'

Mrs Trotman hurried in with a dish of her irresistible salted herb crackers and a glass of sherry. 'Not to worry, m'lady. Us girls will get it all shipshape afore Mr Clifford returns from London this evening. Unless, as you want the fun of watching the steam pouring from his ears, then we won't?' She steered a giggling Mrs Butters out with her.

Eleanor was still chuckling as she finished reading down her butler's admittedly helpful list. Sorting through the stacks on the table, she picked up a beautiful box of ivory ash wood, embossed with two entwined swans, from Dickinson's, a prestigious London stationer. It was held closed by silver ribbons, ending in a pair of tiny wedding bells. She lifted the lid carefully, wanting to preserve the box to use on her dressing table forever. Even more so on seeing the inside was velvet lined.

'Right, number one,' she muttered. 'Make inroads on the stacks of handwritten cards to go with the wedding cake slices everyone will take home.' She checked the boxes themselves had arrived, noting someone had already started fastidiously folding them into shape. Clifford, she guessed. Sipping her sherry and savouring the crackers, she tried to picture the new life that awaited once she and Seldon were married.

Turning, she started. A small bundle on the table had caught her eye. It was wrapped so simply, it stood out among the rich fabrics and luxurious packaging. She recognised it as the parcel on the doorstep she had dashed past that morning.

How had it got inside the house and on the table, Ellie?

She shivered. With the terrible events in the village, even the smallest thing seemed to unnerve her. She fervently wished Silas was back on duty to keep an eye on who came and went up at the Hall.

Giving herself a mental shake, she tutted. Obviously one of the ladies had seen it and put it there. Feeling foolish, she was opening it as Lizzie popped in with more deliveries.

'Ach, that's a darling wee posy, m'lady.'

She smiled weakly. 'Isn't it, Lizzie? Such... such a pretty variation on the first one I received.'

The white peonies and ferns were set among different yellow flowers this time. Even more striking with their orange-dipped petals in clusters radiating like stars. The same cream ribbon encircled them.

'They're from Lucetta Moore, the florist, I'm sure now,' Eleanor said firmly. 'She said she would send me some samples for the arrangements to adorn the pews down the aisle of St Winifred's. But there isn't a hair decoration as well, is there, Lizzie?'

Her maid checked through the tissue paper. ''Fraid not, m'lady. It must be to follow. Would you like Mrs Butters to telephone Miss Moore and check?'

'Gosh, no, thank you. You're all far too busy already. We've plenty of time left,' she said airily.

Clearing a space on the mantelpiece next to the ornate gold and red tortoiseshell clock, she set the posy down. Then fetched the first one from her bedroom. Together, they looked...

Lovely, Ellie.

As she stepped back to admire them side by side, she felt another wash of panic. In only four days, she would be walking down the aisle, holding the larger bouquet her wonderful gardener was making for her.

But what sort of wedding is it going to be, Ellie, if all the preparations aren't finished and half the guests are at each other's throats?

She caught the sound of the telephone ringing. A moment later, Mrs Butters flustered in. ''Tis Constable Fry, m'lady.'

Eleanor grimaced. 'Hopefully not with more bad news?' She glanced at the clock. 'I'd better take it in Uncle Byron's study in case Miss Hopcroft arrives when I'm in the middle of speaking to him.'

She hurried down the long glass-canopied passageway, the left wall of which was filled with a fresco of Henley Hall set among the verdant Chiltern Hills. The right-hand wall was a continuous run of tall arched windows overlooking the rear terrace and the lawns beyond. She couldn't help pausing to enjoy the sight of Seldon mucking in with the marquee work-men. Especially as the company had finally located a new panel to replace the torn one. Having removed his jacket, Seldon looked too divine for words in his fitted charcoal-grey waistcoat with his shirtsleeves rolled up as he carried a stack of chairs inside.

Stepping into the study, she closed her eyes and blew her beloved late uncle a heaven-sent kiss as always. Then she hurried past the acres of oak panelling inset with bookcases to the telephone on the desk.

'Hello, Constable, it's Lady Swift. Any news from Doctor Browning?'

Fry's voice came down the line. 'Yes, my lady. He said to tell you that fellow Villin seems to have died from the same poison as poor Annie. Only as he didn't have a weak heart, Doc said his symptoms seems like... like *respiratory paralysis*, that's it.'

'Monkshood seeds again, though?' she said gravely.

'Doc seemed to think more than likely, my lady. And I've the information you asked for. About Hester Hopcroft.'

'So quickly too, Constable. Well done.'

'To be fair, Sergeant Brice found out about her credit in Chipstone. I checked quietly with the shopkeepers in the village.'

'And?' she said hesitantly, her fingers crossed Seldon had been wrong.

'Perfectly good on both counts, m'lady. She might not have enough to splash out on unnecessaries, but there's not a whiff of debt to her name.'

'That is a tremendous relief, Constable. Thank you, again. Keep up the excellent work.'

'I found a bit more on a different score, mind,' he said quickly. 'Hester and Annie used to help each other out with their catering contracts. As little or as much as was needed. I got that from my good lady wife.'

Having thanked him profusely, Eleanor headed back to the dining room but paused to see if Seldon was free so she could update him. This time he was deep in discussion with three workmen as they struggled with an unwieldy section of staging. She'd booked two surprise bands for the villagers to dance to after they'd eaten.

She walked on. For now, she would have to work out what Hester's game was for herself. And whether it had anything to do with a double murder!

35

Eleanor had almost completed the first stack of thirty cake box cards at the dining-room table when Mrs Butters appeared.

'Miss Hopcroft is here, m'lady. And she's brought that Miss Dunne, the schoolmistress from across the bridge. She said as you suggested so?'

'Yes, I did. Please, can you show them in here while I finish the last of this pile? Then I'll take them off to see the ballroom so Hester can get an idea of how she'll arrange the evening menu. We'll chat through ideas for all the other refreshments in there too.'

The sound of awed voices speaking in hushed tones reached her a minute later.

'Good afternoon, Hester. And you, Joyce. Welcome, both of you.'

The two women stepped in, wide-eyed. She came around to greet them with a welcoming smile. The schoolmistress was dressed conservatively in head to toe navy as before, her pinned-back brown hair the definition of neat and professional. Her rather old-fashioned drawstring bag made her look even more like an elderly spinster before her time, Eleanor thought sympathetically. The more wiry-haired Hester had arrived in what was likely her best cotton day dress of green and white gingham. A pristine apron was folded just so over her arm, a thick notepad clutched to her chest.

Eleanor waved her arms across the overflowing table with a wince.

'Rest assured, on the day this room and the adjoining one will be completely cleared so you can lay out all your finished culinary masterpieces in here. The outside waiting staff Clifford has hired will collect the platters and dishes and ferry them to the appropriate serving rooms. One for the marquee, another for the ballroom. But you can see just how much I need your expert help. We're all up to our necks in wedding preparations, including my wonderful ladies who will all deserve a year off when it's over!'

'I thought as it might have been your cheeky pussycat and doggie having run riot in here,' Hester said with a smile. 'Thank you kindly for the replacement slippers, by the way, m'lady. They're so much warmer and softer than my old pair. Or any I've ever had.'

'My pleasure. And I'm so grateful to you for helping too, Joyce.'

Eleanor made a mental note to buy her a thank you gift.

The schoolmistress smiled. 'Honestly, the treat is all mine, my lady. I mean, if I can help Hester while doing a little of what's needed on this side of the bridge, I'll sleep happy.'

Eleanor beamed back in gratitude. 'Then let's go to the ball-room to talk.'

'I'll bring some tea in a trice, m'lady,' Mrs Butters said before leaving them.

Eleanor led the two women along the first of the long passageways, pointing out the shortcut to the stairs down to the kitchen. And the quickest routes between the doors out to reach the marquee.

'And most importantly, this is the central cloakroom and facilities for you to avail yourselves of.'

Joyce hesitated. 'On that note, would it be rude of me to ask if I might, umm... avail myself of it now?'

'Of course not. The ballroom is past the portrait gallery, through the orangery, then left. We'll meet you there.'

Eleanor smiled, hoping she hadn't sounded too keen. After Fry's telephone call, the chance to have a quiet minute alone with Hester was too good to miss. She hastened her step to reach the ballroom.

Thankfully, the workmen who had been ferrying in the innumerable potted rose trees, tables and stacks of chairs had evidently paused for a well-earned cup of tea. She closed the doors and led Hester around the other side of the tall scaffold tower set beneath the vast central chandelier to prepare for its imminent cleaning.

'Hester, forgive me raising this rather directly,' she started in apologetically. 'But can I ask why you really turned down the opportunity to do my wedding catering the first time?'

Hester's cheeks coloured. 'Why, 'twas as I said, m'lady. It seemed too big just for me to do. Even with the few women in the village I get to help on occasion.'

'Even with Annie Tibbets' help? Because she was often one of them, I was told. And she was, of course, used to catering for parties. So between you, it would have been manageable, wouldn't it? So why didn't you ask for Annie's help when asked the first time to cater for my wedding?'

Hester hung her head. 'M'lady, 'tis true. Annie used to help me when I needed. And me, her. But then we... we had a falling-out. That's why I didn't go around the Spring Supper with her, but with Joyce instead.'

'But it wasn't over my wedding contract that you fell out, was it?' Eleanor bluffed in a tone that suggested she already knew the truth.

'No. It... it was because Annie confided in me she was thinking of getting back with Percy.'

'Percy? Oh, you mean Mr Stokes.'

'That's right. Well, I told her it was a bad idea. She left him for a reason, didn't she? But without a word to me, she suddenly went to see him and told him straight out.'

'I wonder how he took that?'

'Not good, m'lady. 'Specially as it came out of the blue, like. Not surprising they had such a terrible row. He said as it caught him so on the hop, he blurted out that he was already seeing someone else.'

Ah! So that was the real cause of the argument Reverend Gaskell overheard, Ellie.

She winced sympathetically. 'No wonder you and Annie fell out too, then. Because the lady Stokes was seeing was you, wasn't it?' she said evenly.

Hester cast her eyes down. 'Yes. But it's not like he left Annie for me. She was the one who left him. And anyway, Percy knew she was seeing someone else. Only trouble was, I'd been trying to find the courage to tell Annie about him and me, but hadn't. So when he told her, it hit her like a brick.' She looked up, her gaze intense. 'I hope as you won't cancel me doing your catering now, m'lady?'

Eleanor couldn't work out if Hester was upset at having been caught out. Or angry?

'Good heavens, no,' she said reassuringly, quietly feeling a tinge of uncertainty.

Before she could question Hester any further, the door opened and Joyce stepped in, Mrs Butters following with a large tray of tea things.

'M'lady, before we start in on the menu ideas, might it be alright if Mrs Trotman shows me the ovens, so I have an idea what I'm working with?' Hester said.

'Yes, of course.' Eleanor wondered if it was partly an excuse to regain her composure.

Mrs Butters beckoned to her. 'I'd best show you the way.'

As the door closed, Eleanor heard Hester insisting she remembered how to get to the shortcut to the kitchen and would find it just fine.

Left alone with Joyce, Eleanor couldn't afford to waste time. Hester wouldn't be that long.

'You've become a good friend to Hester in a short space of time, Joyce. It's not easy to make a friend so quickly. Especially when still sore from losing one, perhaps?'

She frowned. 'Hester told you about her falling-out with Annie Tibbets, then, m'lady?' She paused. 'Please don't tell Hester I told you, but I feel so guilty, it would be good to confess to someone.'

'I'm listening.' Eleanor held her breath, wondering what was coming next.

'The night of the Spring Supper, I was only in the old part of the village for a short time. But not to attend the supper. No. You see... I went there to see Annie.'

Eleanor tried to keep her features neutral. 'I hadn't realised you were friends with her too?'

Joyce shrugged. 'I wasn't. But I saw how upset Hester was at losing her as a friend and I wanted to try and help them make up. But it was in vain, anyway. Annie told me she wouldn't be the one to say sorry. She was afraid Hester would reject her apology, you see?'

Eleanor was moved by the schoolmistress' compassion. 'That was beyond kind of you.'

Joyce shrugged again. 'When you've been without friends for what feels like forever, not really. I told you I'm a lone island among everyone at the mill.' She looked up. 'It must be wonderful having your fiancé here all the time.'

Eleanor nodded. 'It would be, if he were. Unfortunately, he has to go back to his Oxford office tomorrow to work all day.'

'I see.' Joyce shook her head sadly. 'In the end, you know, Lady Swift, I just made it worse for Hester! Then I heard Annie had passed away while I was still in hospital. I felt terrible. I... I still do.'

Eleanor patted her hand. 'You can't blame yourself. Other people's responses are theirs to choose. You—'

She broke off as Hester stepped back in, letting in the sound of the doorbell ringing.

Who can that be, Ellie?

'We were just talking about Annie, Hester,' she said, not wanting to pretend otherwise. 'I can't help wondering who will inherit her little cottage and possessions now. Have either of you heard?'

Hester shook her head. 'Annie did mention once as she had no blood family still living. And she added that she was thinking of leaving her house to her neighbour, that Miss Ingelby, on account of her being good to her.' She looked scornful. 'Or so she thought. Not that I'm one to listen to gossip, but word in the village has long been that Miss Ingelby is a right conniving mare. Wouldn't surprise me if she made Annie reliant on her to seem like the most deserving of her house and things!'

Eleanor winced. This was the second time Hester had been uncomplimentary about Annie's neighbour. Thank goodness she wasn't there to hear!

Mrs Butters popped her head around the open door.

'Miss Phyllis Ingelby,' she mouthed, obviously having heard the tail end of the conversation.

Eleanor blanched. 'I'll see her in the left tower drawing room in a few minutes.'

She nodded in thanks for her housekeeper's discretion.

Once she had detailed the array of timings the food would

be required, she left Hester to continue discussing menu ideas with Joyce, and hurried to the drawing room, wondering why on earth her visitor had called.

'Miss Ingelby. Hello,' Eleanor said brightly as she entered. 'Please, have a seat. And tell me what I can help with?'

Phyllis sank down onto one of the Wedgwood-blue settees. She looked at Eleanor anxiously.

'I don't know as you can, m'lady. Short of trussin' up folks' tongues tighter 'n a chicken ready for roastin'.'

'Why? What are they saying?'

Phyllis pulled a tissue out of her handbag. ''Tis all the rumours. They're so upsettin'. And to think none have given a thought that I might be upset at losing my friend.' She dabbed her eyes.

'Do you mean Annie?'

Phyllis nodded glumly. 'That's what's makin' it harder to bear than I know if I can, m'lady. Folks is sayin'...' She broke off, fumbling in her handbag.

'Take your time.' Eleanor stepped over to the drinks table and poured a small sherry. 'Here. Maybe this will calm your nerves enough to tell me.'

'Oh, lummy, m'lady. Fancy the likes of me sittin' on your beautiful furniture. Drinkin' your sherry. Folks would have a field day makin' up all manner of stories about that.'

'Well, perhaps they need never know. Now, you were saying about the rumours?'

'Yes. Mean and cruel, they are, too. Sayin' as I only befriended Annie so as she would leave me her cottage. But it's not true! How could she, anyway?'

'Well, why couldn't she?' Eleanor said cautiously.

''Cos she was still Stokes' wife! They weren't divorced. He'd have got her cottage, even if she signed in blood as she wanted me to have it.' Phyllis shifted her formidable form like a ruffled hen.

Eleanor silently admitted she had overlooked that. Something about what Phyllis was saying didn't ring quite true, though.

'Surely, therefore, you can point that out? And mention that you had something considerably less than her house to gain?'

It was a long shot. But one she could make without fear of offence if she was wrong.

Phyllis' flushed cheeks, however, told her she wasn't.

'It's true, m'lady. She did leave me something. Her catering business. I used to be a cook in a fine house back in my day, you see. Not as fancy as yours, m'lady. I gave up cooking many years back, but Annie knew I could make it work.'

'Does her bequest to you include her business bank account, if she had one?' Eleanor said lightly.

Phyllis nodded. 'That's what she told me she'd do anyhow.' She looked Eleanor in the eye for the first time. 'But you believe I'd never have courted Annie's friendship for any gain, don't you, m'lady?'

'Of course,' she said as sincerely as she could.

Having seen one of her visitors out, she slowly walked back to her other two, brooding. It now seemed Wilkes, Giggs, Stokes or even Hester could have poisoned Annie out of jealousy. Or Miss Ingelby, out of greed.

So was their poisoner on this side of the bridge? After all, Annie was murdered first. Or did the answer still lie over the other side? With Villin's death? Maybe the mill meeting Oxdale was so keen she shouldn't find out about would finally provide a clue?

Or simply deepen the mystery...

36

Eleanor was heartened that one small part of her day would have nothing to do with the ongoing poison and murder investigation. Nor the still fearfully long list of unfinished wedding preparations. Instead, it would be occupied by something equally important and the perfect tonic to both stressful matters. Quality time with her best friend! And where better than Winsome's tea rooms in Chipstone.

As she and Seldon approached the door, Constance appeared.

'Hello, love! And Hugh! What a wonderful surprise you've come as well.'

Constance bobbed up on her toes and planted a kiss on Eleanor's cheek, laughing as she tugged Seldon down to her height to do the same.

'It's lovely to see you too, Constance.' He straightened up with an embarrassed smile. 'Aside from Gladstone there, you're the only one who gives me such a, er, keen welcome.'

Eleanor laughed. '"Thankfully", he means. Honestly, I can't take you anywhere, Constance!'

'But you can Mr Sausage Monster, Eleanor?' She knelt

down and made a fuss of Gladstone, whose tail was wagging furiously. 'Hello, Mr Cheeky, as you should be known.' She placed her hand under the bump of her baby as she stood up. 'Anyway, I had to kiss Hugh to make sure I'm not hallucinating, and he's actually here for once. Eleanor, I'm impressed. Not even married yet and you've managed to drag him away from his doubtless mountains of work to join us for tea. Good girl!'

Seldon ran his hand around the back of his neck, 'Actually, ladies, I need to catch up with Sergeant Brice over at the police station. So would it be awfully rude if I didn't accompany you?'

Eleanor clapped her hands teasingly. 'No. It would be rude if you did! Because you'd witness just how much of Winsome's irresistible fruitcake Constance and I intend to devour.'

He hesitated. 'Oh! I'd forgotten about their fruitcake, though.'

She laughed again. 'Be off with you! I'll join you at the station after I've seen Lucetta.'

'Goodbye, Hugh. See you at the wedding!' Constance called, waving him off.

Eleanor smiled as she noted Constance's less matronly attire than the last time. Her friend's pretty, dark-peach silk jacket and skirt suited her still-bobbed blonde hair, although that too was now more flattering, being fluffed around her English rose features.

The ding of the tea room's doorbell prompted all five of the smartly aproned waitresses to look over with a welcoming smile. The only one not serving hurried over.

Eleanor smiled at her. 'Hello, Grace. How are you?'

The young woman blushed. The contrasting cream lace of her frilled cap and apron tied over her fitted black dress made her neat bun of dark hair and large eyes even more striking. 'Just fine, m'lady. 'Tis too kind of you to ask.'

'How's your young man, too?' Eleanor said in a sisterly tone.

Grace beamed. 'Willie's great. He's got a new job. Proud as

punch he is. Mind, it would never have happened without you believing in him. We're so grateful.'

'My friend is the kindest, most selfless person I know,' Constance said emphatically. 'Everyone loves her.'

Eleanor bit her lip thinking back to the frosty reception she'd recently had on both sides of the bridge!

'I'd best show you to a table. For two, is it?' Grace said.

Constance nodded. 'Yes, please. Up in the gallery. And two of your special cream teas with lashings of everything.'

She slid her arm into Eleanor's as they followed Grace, Gladstone straining on his lead, trying to say hello to everyone they passed.

In keeping with the tea room's vanilla damask wallpaper and cream wall sconces, the atmosphere was its usual haven of calm and cosy charm. The hum of companionable conversation mingled with the delicate chink of fine china as they climbed the short flight of steps to the gallery. Eleanor and Constance settled into the comfy button-backed chairs in the corner booth, which was perfect for laughing, sharing, consoling and hugging.

Constance reached across and took Eleanor's hands in hers. 'You know, I've never seen any chap actually radiate such impassioned love as Hugh does when he looks at you. And he's far too deliciously handsome for words with it, too.'

Eleanor's heart swelled. 'Isn't he, though? I keep wondering how I'm going to manage not to pounce on him every day once we're finally married and able to share a room together.'

'Eleanor!' Constance giggled. 'How am I going to sit in the pew now and watch you walk down the aisle without me thinking about that and blushing? Then I'll probably cheer far too loudly when you say "I do". And follow it up with "Watch out, Hugh!"'

'Oh, please do. If only to see the look of horror on Clifford's face.'

They put their heads together and laughed like schoolgirls.

'That's better,' Constance said, as they finally broke apart.

Spotting Grace's lace-capped head bobbing up the stairs, Constance leaned forward and lowered her voice.

'But I want to hear what's troubling you the minute we're alone again. Because I know it can't be Hugh that's taken that little bit of shine off your irrepressible self!'

The table was soon set with a pot of Darjeeling and two-tiered stands bursting with finger sandwiches, oven-fresh fruit scones, pots of cream and jam, and the all-important fruitcake. As a regular visitor, Gladstone had been treated to a bowl of water and his own dish of ham and beef trimmings, which he started in on with gusto.

While Constance poured them each a cup of the delicately floral tea, Eleanor told her about the poisonings in the village.

'And Hugh's investigating it with me. But on the quiet, as we can't risk inflaming the tension between the two sides,' she ended in a whisper.

Constance shook her head in horror. 'How awful for the villagers! And how equally awful for you, love. You're supposed to be thinking of nothing but your most magical day ever!'

'I know. It's only four days off now!' Eleanor's face split into a smile. 'You should have seen Hugh mucking in with the marquee workmen earlier, though. And then fussing around my ladies in the kitchen, trying to do as much as he could in the all too limited hours we've managed to scrape together. He's so excited. Honestly, it's letting him show the side he's buried for so long as a policeman mired in gritty crimes all day. Which is why I know we'll get there. And in time. With the investigation. And the wedding,' Eleanor said determinedly.

Constance still looked mortified, however. 'I so wish I hadn't agreed to leave with Peregrine tonight. Then I would have been free to come to yours for the next couple of days and muck in too.'

Eleanor shook her head emphatically. 'Your husband needs

you by his side.' She winked. 'Besides, he's equally as handsome as Hugh. And you'll be in some gorgeous hotel room together...'

'You are terrible.' Constance laughed, eyes bright. 'And right. So we will! Now, tell me all about your wedding dress...'

The two of them could have chatted all afternoon. And carried on all night too. Among other topics, Constance filled Eleanor in about her new charity and action committee. And how she was feeling better and had stopped avoiding mirrors after Eleanor's heartfelt pep talk last time. But after an hour and a devoured cream tea, they both needed to be elsewhere. With yet another hug, and Eleanor blowing kisses to Constance's baby bump, they finally parted, Eleanor heading for Lucetta Moore's florist shop.

As she walked down the road, she wondered why she'd waited so long to find a best friend. It really was the most wonderful thing in the world! She wondered if Annie had ever had a best friend? According to Miss Ingelby, it had been her. Despite not wanting to be uncharitable, somehow she doubted it. Her mind turned towards Hester and her unlikely friendship with Joyce. Would it survive the trouble between the two sides of the village? Equally pressing in its own way, would Hester's new resolve to cater for her wedding survive any revelations her next meeting with Stokes might uncover? Or would she, once again, be without a caterer only days before the big event?

37

As Eleanor reached the florist's, she felt a weight lift from her. A second meeting on the same day that had nothing to do with confronting suspects over murder was bliss! With a smile in her heart, she strode into the florist, delighting that the next half hour wouldn't mar any of the buoyant mood her time with Constance had restored.

'Good afternoon, Lady Swift. And Master Gladstone too,' Lucetta said as Eleanor paused on the threshold to delight in the fragrant air.

Lucetta tugged on her long, fair curls, which today were loosely embraced by a delicate ring of soft silvery leaves. 'I'm so terribly sorry Alvan disturbed us last time.'

Eleanor joined her at the counter, shaking her head. 'Goodness, please don't be. I'd honestly forgotten all about it. I hope whatever it was has stopped troubling him, though?'

Lucetta sighed as she knelt to accept Gladstone's snuffling kisses. 'Not so as you'd notice, m'lady. If anything, it's got... Oh, but I don't want to bother you with that. You're here to make sure you have exactly the floral displays you're dreaming of for your wedding.' Her face lit up. 'Which I am so thrilled at the chance to have a small hand in.'

'A vast amount more than that, I hope!' Eleanor said hurriedly. 'I have no artistry at all when it comes to flowers. Partly, perhaps, because I think they're all so beautiful. Left to do this alone, I'd probably end up with a hundred vases of just... cornflowers, tulips and honeysuckle!'

Lucetta smiled. 'And you would do more than well enough with those particular flowers having called to you. Although cornflowers are unexpected. But that's why flowers mean so much. So much more than their exquisite beauty. They even have their own language, you know?'

'How wonderful,' Eleanor said, thinking Lucetta could never be lonely, given her shop was crowded with blooms with whom she evidently felt she could converse.

Gladstone had pulled his lead to full stretch to poke his head through the curtain at the back of the shop.

'Let him potter free, m'lady. There's nothing important in there.'

As Eleanor unclipped him, Gladstone bounded through the curtain, wearing it like a cape as he disappeared to the other side.

Lucetta took a notebook from the pocket of her calico apron and moved a part-finished posy aside to make space for it.

That reminded Eleanor of the two posies she had received. 'I almost forgot again. Thank you for—'

She threw her hands over her head at the crash of splintering glass as the shop window exploded, showering her and Lucetta in sharp shards. A red brick tumbled to a stop in the middle of the floor.

For a nerve-wracking moment, Eleanor was transported back to Yorkshire the Christmas before, where she'd been involved in a similar attack, but with much deadlier missiles.

'Gracious!' she gasped. 'Someone threw that on purpose!

Gladstone, stay!' she called to the wrinkled nose which had poked tentatively out from under the curtain. Shielding her face in case another brick came hurtling through the window, she crunched her way hurriedly over the broken glass and peered cautiously out of the door. The street was empty except for an old woman, leaning on two walking canes several shops down and two young boys just coming out of the alleyway opposite, eyes wide.

'Lucetta, are you alright?' she called back from the doorway.

'I am. But goodness, I'm shaking.'

'I'm not surprised. We need to get the police here right away.'

She hurried across the street, calling, 'Boys! Please, run to the police station immediately and tell them what's happened. You saw, didn't you?' They nodded. 'Good. Say Lady Swift sent you. There's a penny each in it for you.'

'Cor, no trouble, miss!'

'Now, hurry! You'll get another when you come back here and see me.'

Back in the shop, she put an arm around Lucetta's shoulders to try to stem the woman's tears.

'Do you have any means of making a cup of tea through your curtain there?'

Lucetta nodded.

'Then let's put the kettle on while we wait for the police. I'll keep watch on your flowers and till, don't worry.'

In the little back room, she sat Lucetta on the upturned crate with a cushion which obviously served as her chair when resting, and then lit the one-ring gas burner. Gladstone launched his top half into the florist's lap, offering soft whiffles of comfort. Quickly checking the shop again, Eleanor scooped up a teapot and cup.

Once Lucetta's sobs had lessened, she asked gently, 'Do you have any idea who might have thrown that brick?'

Lucetta wiped her eyes and sniffed. 'No, m'lady. But 'tis not the first problem I've had since the Spring Supper.'

Eleanor was baffled. 'What possible connection can the smashing of your shop window here in Chipstone have with the poisonings in Little Buckford?'

Lucetta smiled weakly. 'Simple. I live in the village and went to the Spring Supper, but didn't get sick. But you know it's because I didn't eat anything, as I confessed to you last time you were here. Only then the police found the poison in Mr Shackley's flour was dried seeds. So folk started pointing their fingers at me.' Her tears spilled over again and down onto Gladstone's forehead. 'You've only got to look through the curtain to see I've got lots of dried plants, some with berries or seeds, among my displays. Folk have put two and two together and made—'

'Twenty!' Eleanor said angrily, remembering that was exactly Doctor Browning's prediction the evening he came with Brice to persuade her to investigate. 'Lucetta, is that what's been causing Alvan trouble recently?'

She nodded. 'Poor lad. He's already the butt of any trouble others can foist the blame on to him for. Now, he's getting hassle for being the son of a... a poisoner!' Lucetta broke off into uncontrollable sobs.

'Eleanor? Eleanor!' Seldon's anxious voice called from the front of the shop.

'In the back, Hugh,' she called.

He strode through the curtain and pulled her to his side, scrutinising her face. Seemingly satisfied she was alright, he released his grip and turned to Lucetta.

'Any injuries, Miss Moore?'

She blew her nose. 'Only to my shop. And my nerves.'

The sound of heavy boots and even heavier panting was followed by Brice's shocked voice. 'Lummy, whatever next?'

'Almost certainly nothing,' Seldon said pointedly, discreetly gesturing at the crying florist as the sergeant entered the back room. Brice's cheeks coloured.

'Ah! Course, these things is usually a one-off, sir.'

'Did you see who did it?' Seldon said to Eleanor.

'No. Whoever it was must have turned and run the minute they'd thrown the brick.'

'I know who's caused it to happen, though!' Lucetta cried.

Seldon spun around. 'Who?'

'The owner of the *County Herald*. It published today. The report on the poisonings mentions me! Look.'

She held out a copy of the newspaper in a tremulous hand.

'Elijah Edwards! The worm!' Eleanor muttered. She'd run up against the owner of the *County Herald* before and knew how clever he was at taking advantage of a situation and sensationalising it. While, unfortunately, staying just the right side of the law.

Quickly scanning the story, she frowned. Edwards had indeed pointed the finger at the florist. But indirectly by mentioning, as if purely in passing, that her shop was precisely the sort of place where dried seeds could be found easily.

'Disgusting!' Seldon slammed the newspaper down. His brow furrowed. 'How did we miss seeing this, though?'

'By being caught up trying to juggle a surreptitious investigation and our wedding preparations. That's why my ladies haven't spotted it either,' Eleanor said ruefully. 'And Clifford left for London with Kofi hours before our copy would have arrived.'

Seldon tapped the newspaper. 'Eleanor, do you know this *County Herald* man?'

'Unfortunately, yes. He wrote and published my obituary once! To sell more of his wretched newspapers.'

'I'll run him through his own printing press for that!' he growled.

'And I'll enjoy watching you, trust me. But at least wait

until we've given him the appropriate dressing-down for the
damage his report has caused.'

Brice shook his head. ''Tis bad. Very bad, m'lady. I said at
the start, I was worried the trouble in Little Buckford might
spread. But I meant only to the other side of the bridge there.
Not to here in Chipstone.'

'Well, it has, Brice,' Seldon said forcefully. 'And it's still
your case as the officer in charge. I have no wish to wade in,
but—'

'Wade, sir, wade! Lummy, if as you will, I'd be ever so
grateful.'

Eleanor stepped over and gave Lucetta another reassuring
squeeze. 'Sergeant Brice, please find whoever you can to board
up Miss Moore's shop so it's one hundred per cent secure
tonight. And as soon as the glaziers open, instruct them to come
and make everything as good as new. With all bills sent to me.'

'Oh, but m'lady! 'Tain't your responsibility,' Lucetta
flustered.

'To help out when needed? I think it is. And on that note,
Sergeant Brice, please take Miss Moore back to your police
station. Ply her with lots of sweet tea while she waits for Charlie-the-Carriage to collect her in his taxi and take her home.'

'With pleasure, m'lady.' Brice's brow furrowed. 'But how
will Charlie know as he's needed?'

'Because you will have telephoned him to let him know he
is, Brice,' Seldon said firmly.

As Seldon left the florists carrying Gladstone across the
broken glass littering the floor, Eleanor followed, the offending
newspaper tucked tightly under her arm.

Her two messengers were waiting with hopeful expressions.

'Well done, boys.' She reached into her bag for four pennies.
She put one in each of their eager hands, holding the others
back. 'Now, tell me. Did you see who broke this window?'

The two boys looked at each other, downcast. 'Can't say as

we did, miss,' one said. 'I knew it was a window breaking 'cos it sounded just like when I kicked a football through old Mrs Pembleton's front window.' He coloured. 'An accident it were. Anyways, we ran to see but when we got here the flower shop window were already broken, then you comes out. Didn't see nowt else.'

The other boy shook his head vigorously. 'I did. I saw an old lady.'

Eleanor smiled. 'I hardly think it was her. Now, I only asked that you be honest. So, the pennies are yours.' She placed them in their eagerly outstretched palms.

They shot off, calling back, 'Ta, miss!'

She cupped Gladstone's chin where he was still nestled happily in Seldon's arms. 'To the *County Herald* office, next, old chum. Where we'll likely all need to help each other keep our tempers in check!'

As she stood up, she stared down the empty street and blinked.

Where had the old woman gone? And why hadn't the old woman heard the florist's window breaking?

Perhaps she's deaf, Ellie? Or... she groaned. *Perhaps she wasn't an old lady!*

38

Having futilely searched up and down the street for the mysterious old woman, Eleanor and Seldon abandoned the search and headed for the print works.

Inside, the newspaper's reception area was functional in the extreme; white walls, no seats, and a brick floor. The air was thick with the cloying smell of forests of paper overlain with the acrid tang of ink. A rake of a man in angular spectacles blinked at them from behind the glass partition spanning the austere space, giving him the air of a disgruntled ticket inspector. Behind him, the bank of whitewashed windows shook with the raucous clatter, whoosh and clanks of the printing presses.

'Announcements page is full for the next two weeks. Good day,' he said brusquely.

Eleanor passed him her calling card. 'Mr Edwards. Please.'

He shook his head. 'Not a chance. Too busy, Miss...' The clerk held her card up to his glasses, then lifted them to peer at it harder. 'Oh! *Lady* Swift.'

'Well, naturally, Jenkins!' a gravelly voice barked.

She turned to see Elijah Edwards leaning in the doorway in a bold green suit. He ran his thumb and forefinger over his thick moustache, which he'd trimmed to follow the downward curve of his lips. The first time she had met him, she had fleetingly thought he looked like the world's best-groomed frog. But that was before she'd realised he was actually a toad. And an unprincipled one at that!

Gladstone let out a low growl as Edwards stepped up to her.

'Lady Swift,' he purred. 'It's no good pleading with me for more than four pages.'

She was baffled. 'What?'

'Really, even your wedding can't dominate the entire week's news.'

'Mr Edwards,' she said crisply. 'My fiancé, Mr Seldon here, and I have no intention of having you, or any of your so-called reporters, cover our wedding!'

'Oh, come, come. Every bride wants to see herself in glorious print for prosperity.'

His oily tone made her shudder. 'Glorious print, yes. But among pages of irresponsible scandalmongering, no thank you.'

'How harsh the lady scolds,' he mocked. His expression hardened. 'Slanderously so, one might say?'

'Then we'd be even. Although you are guilty of poorly disguised libel!' She whipped open the newspaper she'd brought from Lucetta's and the report of Little Buckford's Spring Supper poisonings. 'This article was intended to inflame a most unfortunate situation. And it has succeeded. With dangerous consequences!'

He looked at her condescendingly. 'But that is my duty, Lady Swift. To keep the local populace abreast of facts in their area.'

Seldon stepped forward. 'The only *fact* in this report is that a number of people in Little Buckford were ill at the same time. The rest, Mr Edwards, is speculation, muckraking, and frankly defamatory insinuations! And it has led to serious consequences.'

After Seldon had told Edwards about the attack on Lucetta's shop, Edwards stared between them for a moment, a thoughtful look on his face. Finally, he nodded slowly.

'Alright. If you play ball with me, I'll play ball with you. I'll publish an article about Mrs Moore's florists being vandalised, as it were, and mention that it seems misguided in light of lack of... direct evidence the lady has anything to do with the recent poisonings. But in exchange, you need to promise to let me be the first to know when the culprit is caught. Is it a deal?'

Seldon glanced at Eleanor, who nodded reluctantly. 'It's a deal, Mr Edwards.'

'Good.' He turned to Seldon. 'And by the way, my reporting of the poisonings wasn't just speculation and whatever else you inferred. It was based on more than that.'

Eleanor's breath caught. 'You have an informer?'

Edwards grunted. 'Had! For a few pounds he was feeding me little titbits of what was going on. And it's no use asking me if I checked what he told me. I can't check every source.'

She glanced sideways at Seldon who looked as if he was about to scornfully rebuke the newspaper man on that point. She hastily interrupted. They were there for more important matters.

'You say "*had*". If he's not divulging any more "titbits" to you, Mr Edwards, would it hurt to pass us his, or her, name? We won't reveal it came from you, I promise.'

Edwards shrugged. 'Doesn't matter to me if you do. His name was Villin. Lucas Villin.'

An hour later, Seldon drew his car to a stealthy stop just short of the bridge over to the mill complex. It was already dark, but he was taking no chance of them being spotted. He glanced at his watch in the ribbon of moonlight.

'Twenty minutes before the meeting is supposed to start.

We'd better get across and then find out exactly where it is.' He pulled her to his side gently. 'Eleanor, I shan't waste breath asking you to be careful. Even though it now seems certain Villin was murdered because the poisoner found out he was feeding Edwards information, whether it was correct or not. Instead' – he kissed her tenderly – 'I shall simply remind you that I have waited a painfully long time to make you my wife!'

She batted his nose. 'Resorting to emotional exhortations now, Chief Inspector? Tsk! That's hardly fair.'

'But effective, I hope.' He came around to open her door and then closed it as quietly as he had his.

In another snatch of weak moonlight that found a fleeting gap in the shroud of cloud, he tucked a few of her stray curls back up under her ebony tam-o'shanter hat. Stroking his chin thoughtfully, he murmured. 'Lady Swift, I prefer you in your customary green, but you're no less bewitchingly beautiful in head to toe black.'

'And you look just as delicious in Clifford's onyx wool cape and broad peaked cap we pilfered from the downstairs cloakroom. So, let's go,' she whispered, wishing they could risk turning on a torch.

As they stepped onto the bridge, the clouds parted again. Now she could better make out the sprawling mill complex. Dominating the night sky like a formidable citadel, its soaring central chimney resembled a medieval fortress tower.

When they'd almost reached the other side, she turned to Seldon. 'We'll head for the main courtyard and then search from there.'

'Won't do you no good though, woman!' a rough voice said menacingly.

Four men emerged out of the dark in front of them. As the hairs on the back of her neck stood up, she was aware of Seldon stepping protectively to her side.

Whoever the men now bearing down on them were, they

had malice in their posture and malevolence in their slow, threatening walk.

Let's hope they haven't got murder in their hearts, Ellie!

They stopped about six feet in front of them. One of the men stepped forward and pointed a vicious-looking bat at them.

'Sling yer hooks back to yer own side. And stay there!'

She held up a hand. 'A slight point of local geography. The land and buildings on both sides of this bridge are part of Little Buckford's parish. And I'm a parishioner.'

The man laughed mockingly. 'Yeah. And we're the patrol to keep all yer poisonous lot the hell out!'

'On whose authority, exactly?' Seldon said coolly.

'Mill management. Not that it's any of yer business. But since yer've asked, no one, and that means *no one*, crosses this bridge without permission from Mr Oxdale.'

She shrugged, convinced nothing she could say would sway them. 'Alright, gentlemen. Seeing as you are so determined to make things difficult, we'll leave.'

She led the retreat with Seldon watching the men over his shoulder.

'I don't think they have any intention of following us, Hugh,' she whispered once they had retraced their footsteps back over the bridge and were out of earshot. 'So, we're not licked yet. However, I'm pretty sure one of them will already be sprinting to the mill to inform Oxdale. Which is why we need to hurry!'

She slid down the steep bank with her coat tucked tightly under her. At the river's edge, she managed to stop her descent before she took a late evening dip in the inky water.

The sound of Seldon sliding down to join her made her spin around to grab him from falling in too. His feet were twice the size of hers, and the narrow riverbank was nowhere near wide enough.

'Thank you. I think,' he said wryly. 'Although I'm not

convinced landing head first in the river would be less uncomfortable than whatever you're about to lead us into. Which is?'

'Finding another way to get into the mill, naturally. Whatever Oxdale is planning, I have to find out.'

'We, Eleanor. *We* have to. But how do we intend to creep past that patrol?'

'We're going to swim past.' At his groan, she nudged him. 'Joke, Hugh. Now, quietly does it.' She started along the muddy bank, silently cursing she hadn't worn her wellington boots because it was treacherously slippery.

A volley of shouts broke out. They quickly hunched down. Grabbing hold of a sturdy sapling, she risked leaning out over the water to peer up river. She spotted a flurry of lanterns spread out on the mill's side of the river. Clearly, she had underestimated Oxdale's determination to keep old Little Buckford out. Including her.

'It's no good!' she whispered, urging Seldon back the way they had come. 'There's no other way into the complex in time. The next bridge is miles away. That's round one to Oxdale, Hugh.'

As they trudged dejectedly to the car, she shook her head. Just what was going on in that meeting that Oxdale would go to such lengths to keep anyone from old Little Buckford from finding out?

Whatever it is, Ellie, one thing is for sure. Unless you can solve these poisonings and catch Annie and Villin's killer in the next forty-eight hours, matters are going to get uglier than they already have. Much uglier!

39

As Eleanor sat down at the kitchen table, her heart swelled.

'Thank you for breaking your precious rule once more about the mistress of the house eating with the staff, Clifford. It feels like a wonderful restorative.'

He had announced outside her bedroom door that breakfast was prepared and waiting. On reaching the morning room, however, she had found nothing but a note directing her to the kitchen. There, the familiar faces beaming back at her were all the more welcome as Seldon had already left to tackle the overflowing case files on his desk.

Clifford arched a mischievous brow as he fussed with a plump cushion behind her. 'Though customarily, titled ladies manage with a soupçon of barley gruel or sliver of calf's foot jelly if indisposed.'

She shuddered. 'I'm not ill, you terror.'

'Yet,' he said gently. 'However, strained nerves cannot be endured for too long without succumbing. Even by an apparently indomitable rhinoceros, hmm?'

She laughed. 'I hear you, Doctor Clifford. So, I shall dutifully adhere to your prescription by laying waste to whatever delectable spread Mrs Trotman has created.'

And beyond delectable, it turned out to be. Her cook's breakfast masterpiece, the Trotters' Tugboat, was served in hearty portions. Its artfully formed puff pastry shell was filled with baked savoury egg custard infused with piquant cheese and hints of chive, all encasing succulent pieces of bacon, mushroom, tomato and black pudding. Accompanying it were baskets of oven-fresh bread rolls and bowls of the creamiest porridge topped with damson jam, that being Kofi's absolute favourite. Tomkins and Gladstone had their own special dishes too.

'Before anything else, we want to hear all about your day out in London yesterday, you two?' Eleanor said as everyone tucked in.

Kofi beamed at her. 'It was such fun! Where to start?'

Clifford stroked an imaginary beard. 'Young friend, given our audience, perhaps omit our shopping and food odyssey in favour of the exhibits at the afternoon's science and engineering exhibition?'

The young boy nodded. 'Good idea, Mr Clifford.'

She laughed. 'Clifford's ribbing you, Kofi. That's exactly what we *don't* want to hear about! Tell us about all the fabulous shopping you did, and food you ate. Not the baffling fingle-fangled whatnots and doodahs you saw!'

Kofi nodded solemnly. 'As you wish. Then it all started in Harrods, where Mr Clifford and I rode on their amazing moving staircase! Did you know it is a continuous belt of woven leather and the motor is a most ingenious—'

He broke off into giggles as Eleanor clapped her hands over her ears. She didn't miss her butler's eyes shining with delight at Kofi's irrepressible sense of fun.

'Close to a mirror image of your mischievous self, hmm?' she murmured to Clifford.

'Two against one, now there's an idea!' he parried in a whisper.

'And then we went to Fortnum and Mason,' Kofi continued. 'And checked on the wedding order of caviar, champagne and...'

As the young boy recounted the day up in London, they all tucked in to breakfast with gusto again. Except, of course, Clifford, who barely sipped his tea while attending to everyone else. Eleanor shook her head fondly. Her butler really was incorrigible.

'... and we went to the speciality chocolatiers, where we had to try a great many samples to choose for your wedding guests,' Kofi said enthusiastically. He paused and looked over at Clifford, receiving a nod in reply. Skipping like a lamb, he disappeared. Returning a moment later, he presented Eleanor and each of the ladies with beautiful miniature boxes of luxury chocolates.

'For us aprons, too?' Mrs Trotman cried.

Polly gasped as she reverently lifted the lid of hers. 'But they're too special to eat,' she breathed.

'I suggest you decide otherwise, Polly,' Clifford whispered loudly. 'Or her ladyship will likely swoop in and prove you wrong.'

Eleanor waited for the laughter to subside. 'Thank you, both, for everything you did towards the wedding. But the day was supposed to be just for you two to enjoy.'

Kofi glanced at Clifford again. Receiving another nod, he left the table with a polite, 'Excuse me, please.'

When he returned, Eleanor's eyes welled up. He was wearing a tailored morning suit of striped grey trousers and matching waistcoat, with a black, long-tailed jacket, tie and top hat. Once he had stopped twirling and posing for the ladies to 'ooh' and 'ahh' over, she beckoned him to sneak out to the settee in the adjoining staff sitting room.

'Kofi, I've been wanting to ask you something. But please

don't say yes, unless you really want to.' She slid her arm around him to whisper in his ear.

His face lit up with a glow of pride and happiness. 'Me? To be your ring bearer? I could not be happier!'

After breakfast, Clifford helped her complete more wedding preparations in his usual methodical manner. He was just ticking off one more task completed in his notebook when Mrs Butters flustered into the drawing room, her face etched with worry.

Eleanor sprung to her feet. 'What's the matter?'

Her housekeeper held a handkerchief to her lips. 'It's... it's. Well, you'd better come and see, m'lady.'

She followed her along the corridor into the dining room and up to the tall circular frame that hid her wedding dress. Only the canopy of magnolia silk had been pulled back, revealing...

Her hand flew to her chest. 'Oh, my!'

Mrs Butters nodded. 'I've asked Polly and Lizzie and they both swear they have no idea how it happened, m'lady. I only discovered it just now.'

She stared in horrified fascination at the red stain in the middle of the bodice just below the bustline. It looked as if it had been stabbed in the heart and a single drop of blood spilled out. She shook her head. It was no time to be morbid. Or fanciful.

'Well, Mrs Butters. However it happened, accidents do. The most important thing is; do you think you can have it cleaned in time?'

Her housekeeper nodded. 'I'll move heaven and earth if needs be, m'lady.'

'Thank you so much. Because right now, I must get down to the village.'

As she left, she tried to shake a feeling of growing unease.

How could something like that have happened in her own home?

Once in the Rolls, however, she was able to focus again on the investigation, grateful to have her favourite sounding board and voice of reason beside her as they went.

'So, that's where Hugh and I are up to, Clifford. Which I wish felt more conclusive,' she ended with a groan as he parked up at the start of Little Buckford's high street.

'Yet progress has been made, my lady. And strong motives discovered, too.' He ran his finger around his starched white collar. 'Along with an eye-opening number of secret, ahem, dalliances unearthed. If I might therefore be excused accompanying you when further probing of those particular persons, and matters, is required?'

She smiled innocently. "But, Clifford! I'll have to drink alone with Mr Stokes in his public house.'

'Again!' he tutted.

Outside the door into the pub's parlour, she nudged him on ahead. 'Go work your infallible soothing magic. Stokes has had a face full of me lately,' she hissed.

'Poor fellow,' he whispered back with an understanding nod.

'Get in there, you toad!'

'Ah, Mr Clifford! Managed to tear yourself away from the wine, women and song of London town, then?' Stokes' genial welcome reached her ears.

Whatever her butler replied, the landlord roared with laughter.

She waited as long as her limited patience could stand, then stuck her head around the door as if looking for someone. Luckily, the place was deserted save for the two men.

'Oh, Clifford, there you are! No, no, please finish your

drink. It's so rare of you to indulge in even half a pint of your favourite porter.'

Smiling at Stokes, she received a hesitant one back.

'Will you... er, be staying too, m'lady?'

'What a lovely offer. Thank you, Mr Stokes, I will.' She slid onto the high stool Clifford was holding out for her. 'A small gin and tonic, please. Luckily, I managed to tick off a fair number of wedding tasks yesterday because Clifford wasn't there to get under my feet. So I have some free time.'

Clifford's lips quirked at her teasing. He turned to Stokes. 'Her ladyship deciding the most important task is a great comfort, Mr Stokes,'

The landlord leaned on the bar. 'What was that, then?'

'The caterer. Such a relief!' Eleanor said, grateful for her butler's lead in. 'Hester Hopcroft was kind enough to spend ages up at Henley Hall with me yesterday. Oh, but she probably told you that already, Mr Stokes?'

He jerked upright. 'Hester? Miss Hopcroft, I mean. Can't imagine why as you'd think that, m'lady?'

Clifford glided away with his drink and busied himself studying the framed rogues' gallery of photographs. She leaned in to Stokes. 'Because she told me about you and her... you know.'

The colour drained from his face. 'Lummy, did she, by crikey?' he muttered.

She smiled. 'Don't worry. It won't go any further. But it was a shame you felt the need to tell me a tall tale before. About the reason for your row with Annie.' She took a sip of her drink, holding his gaze.

He eyed her apprehensively. Then, with a long-suffering sigh, slid the hatch through to the main bar closed. 'Didn't sit right with me when I did, m'lady. I'm sorry. But I was trying to do right by Hester. And Annie...' He tailed off with a shrug.

'By not mentioning that Annie was seeing someone else, you mean?'

'Yes. Well, no. Because she wasn't. She said as she'd broken things off with Wilkes.'

'But that wasn't all, perhaps? Although she didn't come to ask you for money, did she?'

'No. She... she came saying as she wanted to get back with me.' For a fleeting moment, he smiled. But it quickly faded into a sorrowful frown. 'Truth is, I missed her. And a mighty lot, too. But I never thought she'd dream of comin' back. That's why I got involved with Hester in the end.' He rubbed his work-sore hands over his face, which looked like he hadn't slept for a year. 'Quietly, 'tween you and me, m'lady, I wish I never had. Because I still loved Annie. But it's too late now,' he ended glumly.

Eleanor's heart went out to him. 'I hope at least you can draw some comfort that she wanted to start again with you?'

He nodded. 'It's sinking in better now, m'lady. After Wilkes and Giggs came round yesterday.'

That was so unexpected, she floundered for words.

'Wilkes and Giggs. The milkman and fishmonger,' he said, evidently misunderstanding her confusion.

'Yes, but what did they come for?'

'To bury the hatchet about Annie. Wilkes was good enough to say as Annie split up with him because she still had feelings for me. And Giggs put his hands up and confessed he'd tried everything to lure her and failed.'

'Stout men! That was probably hard to admit all round.'

She sipped the last of her drink, fairly sure she believed Stokes had finally told her the truth.

Thank the heavens there's been one bit of goodwill in the village, Ellie. Maybe it's an omen of better things to come?

. . .

Back in the Rolls, Clifford nodded as they drove out of the village.

'Indeed, my lady. I, too, felt Mr Stokes was being truthful with you. Not that I was eavesdropping on your conversation, of course.'

She smiled. 'I hope you were. What's the point of your wizard's trick of blending into the wallpaper otherwise?'

He tutted. 'It is a basic prerequisite for any butler worthy of his uniform.'

'But still jolly useful for earwigging unnoticed if you're also a scallywag.' She watched the hedgerows passing. 'You know, it's a funny thing. Normally, finally feeling that people are telling you the truth feels like progress.'

He raised an eyebrow in silent enquiry. She sighed.

'I mean, I think Hester was honest with me yesterday. And we both believed Stokes just now. And I assume Wilkes and Giggs were also genuine, as it must have been hard for them to admit to him what they did. But if so, then none of them had a reason to kill Annie, let alone poison their fellow villagers. Which seems to just leave Phyllis Ingelby.'

He nodded. 'Which should be a positive, my lady. But?'

She grimaced. 'You're quite right. I feel there is a "but". A great, big, ugly one. Frustratingly, I just don't know what it is!'

40

Eleanor stepped into Henley Hall's marble hallway to see waves of workmen criss-crossing every passageway. Some carried stacks of chairs and tables, others lattice screens adorned in silk roses. A dozen more shouldered a long ivory sausage of material.

'The ruched silk canopy for the ballroom, my lady,' Clifford said. 'Everyone has been very busy in our absence, it seems.'

'Me too, Mr Clifford.'

Kofi's excited voice floated down to them. Looking up, she saw him waving a pad of paper from the galleried landing. With the exuberance of youth, he bolted down the stairs with a wild-eyed Tomkins, and a panting Gladstone following.

As the young boy sprang off the last step, Eleanor whispered, 'I find it quicker to slide down the banisters. But only when a certain someone isn't watching.'

'Would that were a joke,' Clifford said drily.

Kofi's delighted giggle rang around the hallway. 'I will try it next time!'

She laughed. 'Tell us what you've been busy with, then?'

'Mr Clifford gave me permission to answer the telephone. I have taken three messages already!'

'Well done, young friend.' Clifford's praise clearly delighting his ward. 'The first message?'

Kofi consulted his pad. 'From a most helpful gentleman at Fortnum and Mason's. He said the orders you placed yesterday, Mr Clifford, will arrive in two days. In their special hamper baskets.'

'Oh, the ladies would be over the moon to make use of those afterwards,' she pleaded.

Clifford nodded. 'One each for their quarters, my lady. Message two, Master Kofi?'

The boy turned the page of his notebook reverently. 'From Sergeant Brice. Of Chipstone Police Station.'

'Yes?' she said tentatively.

'The sergeant said the tests Chief Inspector Seldon wanted to be completed quickly were as expected.' He looked crest-fallen. 'I did ask which tests, but he would not say.'

'That's alright, Kofi. He wasn't allowed to.' She shared a look with Clifford, whose flinching brow told her how quietly horrified he was, too. The tests had obviously found traces of dried monkshood seeds in the empty medicine vial taken from Annie's house, as they'd expected.

Kofi was still speaking. 'Sergeant Brice did tell me that a Mr...' He read from his pad. 'Mr Shackley did ask a supplier in Chipstone about expanding his product line but didn't seem serious as he never got back to him again after that. Also, Mr Shackley's bank confirmed his credit is not extensive by any means, but still good.'

So Jared was only half right, Ellie.

'Did Sergeant Brice say anything else, Kofi?'

He nodded. 'Yes, my lady.' He read from the pad again. 'That Chief Inspector Seldon told him he had checked out...' He stared at the page. 'Villin and Kemp.'

She bit her lip. Any information on Lucas Villin was probably a little late given he was now dead!

Kofi was still speaking. 'He found out both men have been in trouble before coming to Little Buckford. For petty crimes. Brawling and suchlike, but nothing serious. So they are two tough customers not afraid to get their hands dirty!' He held up a finger. 'Whereas the sergeant could find nothing on Mr... Mr Oxdale.'

The young boy beamed. 'That is all the message. It took me a long time to write it down. Sergeant Brice was most patient!'

She squeezed his arm. 'Thank you, Kofi. You did excellently.'

Totally absorbed in thought, she walked away.

'I have not told you message number three, my lady,' he called. 'It was for you personally.'

She turned back. 'Gracious, sorry, Kofi. I was miles away. Do tell me, please?'

The young boy nodded. 'Chief Inspector Seldon asked me to tell you the cake looks delicious. But he has not had time to try it yet. But he will the first chance he has for a break.'

She was mystified. 'What cake?'

He waved his pad. 'The trial wedding cake Mrs Trotman must have been making.'

She frowned. 'But she hasn't made one. Perhaps you misheard the message?'

He looked affronted and pointed to his page. 'I wrote exactly what Chief Inspector Seldon said.'

'Are you sure, Master Kofi?' Clifford said.

'Yes, Mr Clifford!'

Eleanor offered the boy her hand. 'Of course you did, Kofi. Let's go and see what Mrs Trotman has to say about Hugh's confusion, shall we?'

They arrived hand in hand, with Clifford gliding ahead.

Her cook looked as mystified as Eleanor. 'I haven't made

any *trial* wedding cake, m'lady! Your actual wedding cake's been soaking for ages now. And even if I had made a trial cake, I wouldn't have had the cheek to send a piece to the chief inspector at his police station without asking you first!'

Kofi shook his head politely. 'Please excuse me for saying, Lady Swift, but you have misunderstood. Chief Inspector Seldon *knows* it was not Mrs Trotman who sent the cake. Because of your very lovely message in the box with it.'

She felt a creeping chill. 'I never wrote any note!'

Clifford raised a brow. 'Surely the chief inspector would have recognised your writing, my lady. Unless...'

They stared at each other for a moment, then ran together to the telephone in the study.

'Oxford Police Station? Chief Inspector Seldon urgently!' she said into the mouthpiece. 'It's his fiancée, Lady Swift. I have to speak to him. Immediately!'

The voice at the other end stopped explaining senior officers did not accept calls from the public and asked her to wait while he put her through.

'Oh, come on! Hurry, hurry!' she pleaded, listening to a series of infuriating clicks and silences.

'Hello?' the same voice came back. 'Lady Swift, are you there?'

'Yes! Where's Hugh... the chief inspector?'

'I'm sorry. You've just missed him. Apparently, he left five minutes ago for Wimbourne Underwood.'

'Wimbourne Underwood?' She stared at Clifford. He nodded, striding over to check the framed map on the wall behind her uncle's desk.

'Whereabouts in Wimbourne, Constable?' she urged.

'There's been a nasty matter over at the new building site next to the windmill, Lady Swift.'

About to drop the handset, she gripped it again. 'Ask

whoever you spoke to in his office if he's eaten a piece of cake he received. Quickly, please!'

Another nerve-jangling wait followed.

'Strange question, m'lady. But I got the answer,' the same voice said a moment later. 'He's taken it with him, apparently.'

She let out a long breath. 'I'll telephone the public house.'

Clifford took the handset from her and hurried her to the door. 'The windmill is not the name of a public house, my lady. It is an actual windmill. And miles from any telephone!'

How she got into the Rolls and was roaring down the driveway with Clifford at the wheel, her tear-filled eyes didn't see.

'How far is it?' she asked apprehensively.

'From Henley Hall, ten and a half miles. From the chief inspector's office, almost fifteen.' He held up a finger at her relieved gasp. 'His route being on much faster roads than we have access to, however. As we have no choice but to cross over the Chiltern Hills. Or take the twenty-three-mile route around them.'

'Then put your foot down, please, Clifford. Please! It might be nothing. Or...'

He nodded grimly.

The hedgerows had never flown past at such speed. Nor the long sweeping rises and dips of the Chilterns. And they had been in some tight spots before. Hamlets flashed past. A series of narrow bridges had her breathing in as the car streaked over only inches from the stone walls on either side. In contrast, a ford made for painfully slow progress. All the more, as Clifford insisted on testing the brakes afterwards.

The feeling of icy dread deepened. 'Clifford, suppose...'

'Let's not, my lady.'

'But he might, though? I'd eat it going along if I was him.'

She struggled to hold in a sob. 'And we know he... he never actually takes a break.'

Clifford's silence said it all.

After a blur of steep, narrow roads later, he pointed ahead.

'There! Wimbourne Underwood windmill. And the adjacent building site.'

'But where's Hugh's car?' She hung out of her window, scanning the scene of shouting workmen, rumbling lorries, and roaring cement mixers.

'Perhaps we have beaten the chief inspector here?' Clifford urged the Rolls up the last few yards of the precipitous rise.

'No! He's here. Somewhere. I can... feel him somehow.' As the ground levelled out, she pointed. 'There!' She grabbed Clifford's arm. 'He's sitting on that bench just down the other side of the grass slope.'

'And he's unwrapping something...'

Before the car had slewed to a stop, she was out and running.

'HUGH! STOP!'

But the building site noise drowned her out.

She watched in horror as, oblivious she was even there, he lifted the cake to his mouth and bit down...

41

It was still a good hour before the sun's rays would creep from the evening sky. Until then darkness held its breath. And up on the top of the hill, Henley Hall stood as silent as a mausoleum. Inside, nothing stirred.

Eleanor jerked bolt upright, a scream frozen on her lips. Her chest constricted. She tried to shout, but no sound came out. She was paralysed.

Soft lips pressed against hers.

'Hugh!' She buried her face in his neck.

'Darling, you were having a flashback!' He hugged her. 'You're in the snug sitting room at Henley Hall. With me. All safe. See?'

She looked around her, slowly registering where she was. His brown eyes were filled with loving concern as he pressed a glass of brandy into her hand, wrapping his fingers over hers.

'It's just the shock coming out.'

'The memory was so... so awful! I... I couldn't get to you, Hugh.' Her teeth chattered against the glass as she sipped the brandy.

'But you did! You ran towards me on the bench. You were screaming.'

She nodded shakily. 'The construction noise drowned me out. And Clifford too.'

'Yes. And I was about to take a bite of that cake. But then my heart fluttered as I thought of your beautiful red curls walking down the aisle to join me. And I looked up and there you were, haring towards me. Your panic told me—'

'To spit it out!' she gasped with relief, snuggling further into his neck, relishing his familiar scent.

He cradled her tighter, enveloping her in his arms.

'Hugh,' she said shakily. 'These awful events are getting away from us. And getting terrifyingly worse!'

'I know,' he said gravely. 'That cake being sent to me was a completely unexpected turn.'

'A nightmarish one!' she added with a shudder.

She didn't miss the reluctance in the knock at the door.

'Come in, Clifford,' she called. 'But know I can't let go of Hugh yet.'

He stepped in. 'I should hope not, my lady. I fear it might be necessary for just a moment, however. There is a telephone call for you, Chief Inspector. It is Sergeant Brice.'

'Lead the way, Clifford.' Seldon wound his long, strong fingers in hers. 'Eleanor, come with me. I can't let go of you either yet.'

In the study, he scooped up the handset. 'Brice? Chief Inspector Seldon here.'

'Ah!' The sergeant's voice boomed out loud enough for Eleanor to hear. ''Tis good to hear your voice, sir. I'm in Little Buckford. At Constable Fry's house. He called me after Mr Clifford dropped off that box of cake and reported what almost happened to you. Lawks, but for her ladyship...!'

Seldon squeezed Eleanor's hand. 'Yes, Brice. I'm a very

lucky man. In every way. And I want that blasted cake tested as quickly as possible. Understood?'

'Already under way, sir.'

'Good man. Is that what you telephoned for?'

'No, sir. I telephoned to check if you're happy with me, Constables Fry and Lowe patrollin' the village? Both sides, mind. I can't be sure if as it will inflame the situation or not, but I'd feel a lot happier about innocent folk havin' some kind of police presence now.'

Seldon covered the mouthpiece and looked at Eleanor, who nodded.

'I don't think we can take any more chances, Hugh,' she said earnestly.

'I agree. Who knows what the wretch behind all this awfulness will do next? And we can't risk the situation escalating to all-out war between the two sides of the village.' He uncovered the mouthpiece. 'Good initiative, Brice. Well done.'

As Seldon replaced the handset, she let out a long breath. 'Hopefully, their presence might at least interfere with whatever the poisoner is planning next. Which gives us the chance to better focus on catching whoever it is.' Her cheeks flushed with anger. 'You were wrong about one thing just then though, Hugh. There *is* going to be all-out war. Between us and that wretch!'

'That's the spirit. Now I know you're going to be alright,' he said, sounding relieved.

'Better than alright, Hugh. Our fighting back starts by holding our own council of war. *Now*. And we have the best people on hand!'

He slid his arm around her waist with a smile. 'The motley collection who make up your extended family, by any chance?'

. . .

The atmosphere around the table couldn't have been more different from the one she had enjoyed at breakfast. But they were all just as unified. Her four ladies sat in a line opposite her and Seldon, all with fixed determination etched on their faces. Clifford, his features impassive, was beside Eleanor with Kofi next to him. Even Gladstone and Tomkins were sitting upright together in their quilted bed, ears pricked.

Seldon held up a hand. 'Just before we start, I need to say one thing.'

Eleanor bit her tongue, hoping that after this session he would realise her staff, and Kofi too, were made of stern stuff. And whatever cautions and caveats he was about to issue might be the last. To her surprise, however, he rose and stepped around to Kofi, holding out his hand. 'Young fellow, I owe you a huge debt of gratitude.'

Kofi's dark eyes shone equally with delight and confusion as he shook it. 'But, Mr Seldon, I only took your telephone message.'

He grinned. 'And then managed to convince a certain lady in this room she was wrong! For which you deserve a medal. Because I've never achieved such a feat!'

'Nor I!' Clifford muttered.

'Thank goodness you did, Kofi,' she said fervently, reaching around to squeeze his shoulder. 'Because this attempted poisoning of Hugh changes everything!'

Seldon nodded as he retook his seat. 'We need to rethink everything from scratch. Concentrating on the few facts we have. So, all and any input welcome.'

Eleanor thought for a moment. 'At the Spring Supper, the original villagers of Little Buckford were poisoned. We think to cover up the intended murder of the real target, poor Annie Tibbets. Next, the new villagers were poisoned in a second attack and Lucas Villin was murdered. We are assuming because he was becoming a threat to the killer by feeding

Edwards of the *Herald* information. But that's only supposition. All we can be certain of is that the poisonings on both sides of the village were smokescreens. To confuse and cover up the wretch's real intention. Murder. But why, we need to work out fast!'

Polly was frowning, eyes fixed on the ceiling, her lips moving. She put her hand up tentatively.

'Just speak up, Polly. It's fine on this occasion,' Clifford said reassuringly.

'Yes, sir. Only beg pardon for suggestin' but them poisonings may have been a smoke...'

'Smokescreen, Polly?'

'Yes, Mr Clifford. But maybe those two poor people that died was a smokescreen, too?'

Eleanor gasped. 'Well done, Polly! You may have something. Could it be that the wretch's target all along was not someone either side of the bridge in Little Buckford? But someone here at Henley Hall? You, Hugh?'

Clifford nodded. 'Perhaps we've been caught entirely off guard, Chief Inspector?'

'And with Silas away, it could be all or any of us next!' Mrs Trotman muttered.

'You ladies, and Kofi too, will be absolutely safe,' Seldon said firmly.

'Unquestionably,' Eleanor added.

'If as you both think so, then us aprons do, too,' Mrs Butters said. The other three women and Kofi nodded. 'Only it makes Annie and that other gentleman's passing more tragic than ever. Now it seems like the terrible person doing all of this might have needed them to die just to keep us looking the wrong way.'

Eleanor sighed sadly. 'Possibly, Mrs Butters. But why on earth is Hugh, it seems now, particularly significant in all this?'

She jumped as the back door opened.

It's only Joseph, Ellie. Calm down.

Her gardener raked off his cap. 'Beggin' your pardon for interruptin', m'lady. Only with that cake business and Silas bein' away, I couldn't leave it.'

Eleanor waved him in. 'Don't bother with your boots, Joseph. What is it?'

'Couldn't say, m'lady. But it had been left in a rummy spot. The step below the side door into the boot room. As if whoever was deliverin' got interrupted. And with Silas bein' away, like I said, and the nastiness goin' on, I admit I was too nervy to leave it until Mr Clifford was free to happen upon it.'

'Well done, Joseph. And thank you. Let's have a look at it,' she said.

He passed the parcel to Lizzie, who leaned across the table to give it to Eleanor.

She took it and smiled. 'Ah! Actually, I think after the last two being innocent parcels, we're worrying unnecessarily this time.' She started unwrapping the tissue paper. 'I'm relieved to say it looks like I've still got one well-wisher among the villagers! Lucetta Moore. She's sent me another sample posy... Oh my!'

Everyone around the table craned forward, their frowns deepening as they took in the posy. Unlike the previous two, the ring of white peonies was horribly withered and set among dead, yellowing leaves. And in the middle was a single, jet-black rose.

'Its nae very cheery for a weddin' posy this time, m'lady,' Lizzie muttered.

'No, Lizzie.' Eleanor swallowed hard. 'In fact, it looks more suitable for a... funeral!'

42

Eleanor barely noticed the rain running down the inside of her coat collar. Beside her on Lucetta Moore's doorstep, Seldon lifted the iron knocker and gave it another sharp couple of raps.

'Who is it?' Lucetta's muffled voice carried out to them nervously.

'It's Lady Swift and Mr Seldon. We need your help urgently,' she called.

'Lady Swift? Oh goodness!' A bolt was shot back. The door swung open. 'I'm so sorry. I had no idea it was you. Please come in out of the rain.'

For the first time, Lucetta's long fair curls were unrestrained by any form of floral decoration and cascaded around her face like a veil.

Eleanor stepped inside, clutching the three wrapped posies. Seldon followed. Lucetta closed the door hurriedly as Eleanor turned to her.

'We're the ones who need to apologise, Lucetta. For calling at your cottage unannounced so late. Especially after that incident with the brick being thrown through your shop window.'

'Yes. How are you, Miss Moore?' Seldon said.

The florist smiled weakly. 'Just a little nervous. That's why I wasn't going to answer at first. After all the nastiness that's happened in the village, and then at my shop, I don't know what will happen next.'

Eleanor shook her head. 'Neither do we.'

Especially since someone tried to poison Hugh, Ellie!

'But,' she continued, 'with your help, hopefully we will.'

Lucetta looked startled, but nodded. 'I can't imagine how, m'lady. But, of course, I'll try. Please come sit by the fire while you explain.'

Eleanor crossed the fern-green rug and perched on the edge of the small floral print settee. Seldon remained standing.

'I need you to tell me about these posies. I thought they were samples you'd sent me.'

Lucetta stared at the three bundles, shaking her head. 'Those? I never sent them, m'lady.'

Her breath caught as Eleanor peeled back the wet tissue paper of the first one. As the second and third were revealed, her confused frown turned to a look of horror.

Eleanor exchanged a glance with Seldon.

'It seems they mean something to you, Miss Moore?' he said.

The florist was still staring at the three posies, seemingly mesmerised. 'Not... not exactly. I can read them, though.'

Seldon's brow furrowed further. 'Read them?'

'Yes, sir. Each one is a... a message. Written in the language of flowers.'

Eleanor's thoughts flew back to her conversation with the florist just before the brick had showered them both in broken glass. 'Now I hear you mention it again, the language of flowers sort of rings a bell.'

Lucetta spread her hands. 'It's been around for a long time, although no one knows exactly where it first came from. And, of course, there can be a few different meanings to some flowers.

But people used it to send each other a sort of secret love letter. Some still do.' Her cheeks coloured as she looked at Seldon. 'Especially a gentleman wanting to court a lady without her mother, or guardian, knowing, if you see what I mean?'

Seldon nodded. 'I understand. But does that mean you know this language well enough to interpret the messages in these flower arrangements?' He pointed at the posies in Eleanor's lap.

Lucetta paled. 'Yes, sir. Only, I almost wish I couldn't. Because the language of flowers was used to send other messages in secret as well. And' – she pressed her hand to her chest – 'there's no mistaking what these are saying.'

'We're listening,' Eleanor said earnestly.

Seldon leaned closer.

Lucetta hesitated. 'Well, the white peonies that are in all three posies have long been popular wedding flowers, as I'm sure you know, Lady Swift. In the language of flowers, they represent love, honour, wealth, romance and beauty.'

Eleanor and Seldon both nodded for her to continue.

'Before I tell you more about the main flower in each posy, can I ask what order they arrived in, m'lady?' Lucetta said.

'Just as they are in my lap, from left to right. One, two, three.' Eleanor gestured to them in turn.

'I see. Then I'll tell you in that order. Among the maiden-hair ferns, these yellow flowers in the first one, with the clusters of emerald leaves, are coltsfoot.' Lucetta winced. 'And they mean... *justice will be done unto you.*'

Seldon's expression was filled with concern. 'But you said some flowers have more than one meaning?'

'Yes, sir. But not that one. Or the other main ones in each posy. I'm terribly sorry to say it so harshly, though.'

Eleanor shook her head. 'No, don't worry. We just need to hear whatever it is. Please go on.'

'If you're sure.' Lucetta was looking more uncomfortable by

the second. 'In this next posy, the second one you received, the peonies are combined with these yellow flowers with orange tints. See how each cluster looks like a star? That's birds-foot trefoil.'

'And what does that mean?' Seldon said guardedly.

'*Revenge*, sir. It doesn't have any other meaning. Just... *revenge*.'

Lucetta rose and stepped over to a set of shelves. They were filled with floral jacketed books. She picked one out, looking reluctant, but came back with it to the settee. 'This is a copy of *The Language of Flowers* that was published a long time ago. But it sold widely. All over Europe, as I learned when I worked at Kew Gardens.'

'Let's tackle the last posy,' Eleanor said, despite the increasing apprehension she was feeling.

'Yes, m'lady. The peonies, all being withered, suggests the things they stand for will... wither away for the person who receives them.'

You, Ellie.

'Love being the main one, if I've remembered correctly?' Seldon said soberly.

Lucetta nodded. 'You have, sir. But it's what they are combined with which is most troubling. The black rose...' She tailed off, turning the pages of the book. 'I'm sorry. I can't bear to say it.' She pointed to a line. Eleanor leaned forward and read aloud.

'"Whereas a rose normally symbolises love, a black rose symbolises... death!"' Feeling her throat constrict, she followed Lucetta's finger, '"*Or death to your love*"!'

The florist stared at Seldon in dismay, but he shook his head firmly.

'Miss Moore, it's imperative you don't tell anyone of our visit. Or what we've spoken about.'

Lucetta nodded vigorously. 'Goodness, I won't breathe a

word, sir.' She handed the book to Eleanor. 'It might be best if you take this with you, Lady Swift. Just in case you get any more of those awful posies.' She squeezed her arm apologetically. 'Although after the message in that last one, I shouldn't think you will. Because, well...'

Because in the language of flowers, there can be nothing left to say after 'death', Ellie!

43

As they arrived back at Henley Hall, Eleanor and Seldon agreed to keep the worrying information Lucetta had given them to themselves until they could make sense of it. And in truth, until she felt she could talk about it without being overcome by another disturbing flashback.

Her staff, however, obviously had other ideas as she shrugged out of her coat to find them in a line in the entrance hall. Without waiting for Clifford's nod of permission, Mrs Butters flustered forward.

'M'lady, your face always gives you away to us who care. We can see as you've learned something troubling from Miss Moore.'

Kofi slid his hand into Eleanor's. 'It is true, Lady Swift. If you will excuse me for saying, but sometimes I think your words are not necessary.'

'Perceptive fellow,' Clifford murmured, relieving her of the posies and Lucetta's book.

Eleanor was immensely grateful for everyone's concern and felt she owed them some sort of explanation. 'Miss Moore explained the posies each bear a message. I can't pretend any of the three messages are good news. Nor that the whole thing makes any more sense than before we went, unfortunately.'

Mrs Trotman stepped forward. 'Perhaps it might do so, m'lady, if we *all* tried to unravel it?'

'Together!' Polly and Lizzie chorused.

Kofi nodded determinedly and slid in between the two maids. 'We are eight. The bad person is but one!'

At least you hope so, Ellie.

She smiled. 'Well, when faced with that level of irrefutable logic, how could I say no?'

Seldon nodded. 'Let's hurry to the kitchen then, investigation team. And see how we can defeat this monster.'

Once they were all seated, Eleanor started straight in, there being no time to lose. 'The most significant thing is there's little doubt that the last posy I received. It was intended to mark... a death.'

'Mine. As it almost was,' Seldon said, managing a far more matter-of-fact tone than either of them felt about the hideous truth of his words.

In the shocked silence that followed, Kofi spoke up first.

'Joseph said the parcel had been left on the side step the same day Mr Seldon was supposed to become the next victim. Is that a clue?'

Seldon put his hand on the boy's shoulder. 'Very possibly, young fellow. Eleanor, when exactly did the other two arrive?'

'The first one arrived on the afternoon of the Spring Supper. The same day, the old Little Buckfordites were poisoned and Annie then died,' she said with a sense of dread.

Clifford's brow flinched. 'And the second one was delivered the same day as the workers at the mill were poisoned and Mr Villin died.'

Mrs Butters gasped. 'Lawks, m'lady! Doesn't that sound as if the monster behind all this was letting you know more than just whatever the message is in each posy?'

'Now that you say it, yes.' Eleanor nodded sombrely, her breath catching. 'It seems the murderer was letting me know they were the one who poisoned both sides of the village. In advance of them doing it. But only just. Oh, if only I'd worked out the significance with the first posy, I might have stopped them! And poor Annie and Lucas Villin would still be alive!' She felt her heart squeeze with guilt.

Seldon's expression was tender but firm. 'Eleanor, you couldn't possibly have worked out any such thing. And the wretch knew that. Whoever it is has a truly evil streak. It's feeling more and more like they are enjoying all this. As if... as if it were a game?'

'A very calculated and deadly one at that, Chief Inspector,' Clifford said gravely.

'Then if we can work out why—' Eleanor blurted out.

'We can work out who,' Seldon finished for her.

She jumped at the telephone ringing, her hand flying to her chest.

Your nerves are as jangling as that bell, Ellie.

'Oh lummy, what now?' Mrs Trotman said.

'Perhaps your presence, Chief Inspector?' Clifford called as he strode out towards the butler's pantry.

Seldon nodded and whispered to Eleanor. 'Please double-check your ladies and Kofi aren't too unnerved by all this. Worrying about them is making it hard for me to think clearly.'

When Seldon stepped back into the kitchen the ladies and Kofi were reassuring her it was more of a comfort to be part of the conversations than be left fearing the worst. She noted with dread her fiancé was looking even graver than before the call. She could also tell Clifford was struggling to maintain his usually imperturbable composure as he followed behind.

'Let's hear it, chaps,' she said resolutely.

Seldon ran a troubled hand through his chestnut curls.

'It was Sergeant Brice. He did an excellent job of getting the test on that cake rushed through.'

'And was it poisoned?'

'Yes. Though not with monkshood seeds this time. But a variety of deadly mushroom similar to death cap mushrooms.'

'Lummy!' Mrs Trotman said. 'Sounds like the clue was in the name of it.'

He winced. 'You're quite right. If ingested, it can be fatal in even tiny amounts. And that slice of cake contained anything but tiny amounts it seems! Without your collective efforts, and Eleanor and Clifford racing to find me' – he swallowed hard – 'I definitely would not be here.'

Hurling all regard for decorum to the floor, Eleanor fell against his chest. 'Oh, Hugh!' The reality of just how close she had come to losing him renewed her resolve as if it had been shot through with electricity. She jerked back upright and slapped the table. 'We need to put our brains to working out why the murderer used a different poison. It has to be a clue.'

Seldon nodded. 'I agree. Because apparently the variety of deadly mushroom used is not commonly known either.'

Clifford's already furrowed brow deepened. 'Odd. Did the report say anything else, Chief Inspector?'

'Nothing that can help. Only that it's got one of those old folklore type names.' He consulted his notebook. 'Destroying Angel or Angels, I believe.'

'Angel?' Eleanor murmured. 'Destroying... *Angels!*' Her hands flew to her mouth.

It can't be, Ellie!

But she knew in her heart, it was.

44

It was a chapter of her life she had tried her best to forget. As had countless others.

'The war, my lady?'

Eleanor nodded. 'I didn't realise that you knew the story I'm about to tell, though, Clifford?'

'I do not, my lady. However, his lordship, your late uncle, craved even the merest snippet of news about his beloved niece. And during that dark time, he was able to learn a few fragments from his numerous army contacts.' His brow flinched. 'Hence my being more than disconcerted on hearing the folklore name of the poisonous mushroom added to the cake sent to the chief inspector.'

'Destroying Angels,' she muttered again, feeling the same wash of dread.

Seldon was staring anxiously between them. 'Eleanor, please tell us what this is all about?'

Everyone around the table leaned forward.

She took a deep breath. 'The short version is that I had been living and working in South Africa for several years when war was declared. As you know, I was brought up by my parents on a sailing boat, so I'd spent very little time in England, except at boarding school once Uncle Byron took me in. So I felt it more fitting I offered my services to the country I was resident in at the time. There was no actual fighting in South Africa itself, but nurses were in short supply everywhere. So I volunteered for the Military Nursing Service and stayed with them for the remainder of the war. One of my first and longest postings was to a hospital in Abbeville, France, that dealt with soldiers injured at the front.'

'And blessed were those poor wounded men you would have treated so kindly, m'lady,' Mrs Butters said ardently.

Eleanor sighed. 'They all deserved so much more than any of us nurses, or doctors, could do. Most of them were in a terrible way and needed constant dosing with the strongest painkillers we had. Which... which made it too awful to bear when the supplies on my ward started to run out. And the same on other wards too.' She rubbed her forehead to try to erase the images of the suffering the soldiers had endured.

'You mean as the hospital hadn't ordered enough, your lady-ship?' Polly breathed.

She shook her head. 'No, Polly. I mean, the drugs were being stolen wholesale. And, I found out later, being sold on the black market.'

Seldon's look of disgust was mirrored in the other faces around the table.

'What did you do, m'lady?' Mrs Butters said.

'I went straight to the senior medical officer in charge. But he told me that they had been trying to find the culprits for months without success. And the few military police in the area were too stretched to be able to do any more. Everyone was working way beyond their capacity, night and day, you see. The hospital had been set up on a rundown sprawling site that had been taken over without time to even equip it properly. It had been planned as a temporary emergency unit. Conditions were harsh, makeshift in the extreme in parts. Just keeping it running was a Herculean task in itself. Especially with the number of casualties flooding in every day.'

Seldon squeezed her hand under the table. 'So, let me guess, Eleanor, you decided to take matters into your own hands?'

She nodded vehemently. 'What else could I do? I couldn't let my patients, and those in other wards, suffer like that.'

Kofi frowned. 'And did you discover who was stealing the medicines, Lady Swift?'

'I did. But I won't waste time now telling you how. We've more important matters to sort out.'

'What happened then, m'lady?' Lizzie said.

'I went to the military police with the culprit's name, along with the evidence I'd gathered.' She shook her head again. 'The guilty party was the very man I'd gone to originally; the senior medical officer! Anyway, they set a trap to catch him red-hand-ed.' She felt a wash of cold envelop her. 'One of them told me later the man tried to flee. So, naturally, they shot him. It was wartime.'

'And it was no less than he deserved!' Seldon discreetly threaded his arm around her waist.

She shrugged glumly. 'Maybe. But I never intended for that to happen.' She ran her hands down her arms. 'The good part of all that hideousness is that the military police found a large stash of the stolen drugs he hadn't sold yet. Which was enough to treat my patients, and several other wards' worth until fresh supplies arrived.'

Clifford nodded. 'Which now explains the moniker the soldiers gave you. His lordship was overcome with pride when he heard of it. And eaten up with not knowing why. Likewise, myself.'

'What was it the soldiers called you, m'lady?' Mrs Butters said.

Eleanor's cheeks flushed. 'It was undeserved, but the

soldiers in my ward, and most of the others in the hospital if I'm honest, nicknamed me the "Angel of Abbeville".

'And righter 'n right they were as well, m'lady!'

'That's beautiful,' Polly breathed.

The frown that had been on Seldon's brow while she told the tale deepened. 'That explains why the poisoner used Destroying Angels, yes. But not why they targeted *me*, in order, it now seems, to get at you, Eleanor?'

'It will in a minute, Hugh. You see, the culprit had an accomplice, who the military police rooted out. I had no hand in that. I never even met her. She was a nurse, I found out later, in another wing on the opposite side of the hospital to my ward. The military policeman who told me the culprit had been shot also told me the culprit was—'

'The nurse's fiancé,' Seldon murmured, realisation dawning.

She bit her lip. 'Exactly, Hugh. They shot him three days before she was due to walk down the aisle with him.'

Seldon blanched. 'Just as today is three days before you will walk down the aisle with me!'

'Did you hear what happened to her, m'lady?' Lizzie said.

Eleanor thought for a moment. 'I heard she was tried and jailed. But after that, I've no idea. Honestly, I was just glad it was all over, and could get straight back to tending to the sick and injured soldiers on my ward.' She failed to hide the shiver that took hold of her. 'Well, now we know why the posies spelled out the messages, "Justice will be done to you", "Revenge," and "Death to your love".'

Seldon squeezed her hand again. 'At least we've narrowed the suspects down to a woman. And despite what I said before about it being a myth that poison is largely a woman's weapon!'

She grimaced. 'Have we narrowed it down that much, though? The murderer could be any of the women in the village who moved here within the last, what? Almost eight or nine years. Depending on how long a sentence she got.'

Clifford cleared his throat quietly. 'Or perhaps half that timeframe if she followed you here, rather than having ended up in the same village by coincidence, my lady?'

'Oh gracious, you're right!'

Seldon ran his hands over his cheeks. 'She maybe doesn't even need to live in the village to have poisoned everyone, actually.'

The room lapsed into deep and uncomfortable thought. Clifford broke the silence. 'I wonder...?'

She glanced at him in hope. 'What have you realised?'

'That we can, in fact, narrow the potential suspects down substantially more. Because they must have had access to Henley Hall to have copied your handwriting.'

'Of course!' She paused, then winced. 'But I've written dozens of things down in the village and in Chipstone. And misplaced innumerable shopping lists, too. They could easily have used one or more of them to copy my handwriting.'

'I think not! If you would follow me?'

Eleanor hurried after him, followed by the rest of the table. In the dining room that had been set up as the centre of wedding preparations, Clifford carefully counted out the stack of cards she'd written and then the cake boxes next to them.

'You see, my lady, the perpetrator copied your handwriting from one of the cards you wrote out. And placed the cake in one of the boxes I made up. There are only twenty-nine cards and boxes. I had made up thirty so far—'

'And I wrote out thirty cards!' she said indignantly. 'One for each box. So they must have stolen one of each!'

Seldon stroked his chin. 'Did you write them all out in one go?'

She nodded. 'Yes. Only yesterday.'

'Ah! The culprit wouldn't have known that. The cards could have been written days, or even weeks ago.' Seldon's eyes glinted. 'But they slipped up, we now know. This narrows it down to someone who was in Henley Hall *after* you wrote those cards. And a woman at that!'

Mrs Butters slapped the table, making them all jump. 'I knew as there was something about that last posy that was troubling me. Can I see it again, m'lady?'

'Of course.' Lizzie quickly fetched the withered posy with the single black rose and placed it in front of her housekeeper. She pulled out her sewing spectacles and looked it over, nodding to herself.

'I thought so! The blummin' cheek! That's a length of the special wedding ribbon I only finished embroidering yesterday morning for her ladyship's dr—' Mrs Trotman clapped her hand over the housekeeper's mouth. Eleanor's ladies stared at Seldon in horror.

'Dressing gown,' Clifford said smoothly. 'Which means the poisoner made a second error in taking that particular ribbon, not realising you had so recently personalised it, Mrs Butters.'

'Brilliant, everyone!' Eleanor cried. 'That means we've narrowed the culprit down to a woman who was here only...' She tailed off, her frown deepening.

'Yesterday, your ladyship.' Polly slid her arm into Lizzie's. 'And only three ladies called, I think,' she said breathlessly.

Mrs Trotman's eyes narrowed. 'Yes! Hester Hopcroft. Joyce Dunne. And Phyllis Ingelby.'

Seldon reached for his notebook. 'Were any of them left alone for any length of time?'

Eleanor's thoughts flew back to the confusion of the busy afternoon. 'All of them, Hugh. Joyce used the facilities, then made her way to the ballroom alone. Hester made her own way to the kitchen to check the ovens she could use on the day. And Miss Ingelby, Annie Tibbets' neighbour, was waiting for me for several minutes before I got to her.'

'So any one of them could have stolen the card, cake box and ribbon,' Seldon mused.

'Although Trotters and me know as Miss Ingelby never left the village during the war,' Mrs Butters said.

Eleanor's cook nodded vehemently.

Kofi cocked his head. 'One suspect less then, yes?'

'Yes, I believe so, young fellow,' Seldon said. 'Agreed, Eleanor?'

'Agreed. Which leaves us Hester and Joyce.'

'So which one is it?' Mrs Butters said.

Seldon pursed his lips. 'Unfortunately, at this point, we simply don't know.'

A grim smile spread slowly across Eleanor's face. 'Actually. We do.'

45

As the kitchen clock struck three in the morning, Eleanor was finally feeling confident that, between them, they were close to having a promising plan.

Clifford set down another pot of strong coffee, a hot chocolate for Kofi, and a mountain of buttered toast and jam. She waved around the table.

'Don't stand on ceremony. Dive in, everyone. And that includes you, Joseph.' Even her gardener had joined them. 'So, please think of anything we might have forgotten,' she said passionately. 'Anything at all that might trip us up?'

Seldon's troubled frown deepened. 'The fact we'll be acting alone, Eleanor. Without any police backup whatsoever.'

'We have to, Hugh. We can't risk taking Brice, Lowe, or Fry from patrolling the village.' Her jaw clenched determinedly. 'And even if we could, I wouldn't.' She turned to him, her eyes alight. 'This wretch has attacked everyone I love and care about. She's abused my hospitality and home. We have to end this together. We're going to make certain that creature wishes she never had!'

'Spoken like a true Henley, my lady. His lordship, your late uncle, would be beyond proud,' Clifford said ardently.

Joseph and her ladies all nodded.

She smiled at them, feeling eternally thankful she had inherited such robust and resolute staff.

'And I agree,' Seldon said. 'For once, procedure and protocol can go hang!'

'Thank you, Hugh,' she said sincerely. 'That means the world.' She thought for a moment. 'Now, is there any way our intended prey can have worked out what's awaiting her?'

Clifford shook his head. 'None of us have breathed a word outside these walls about the attempted poisoning of the chief inspector, my lady. Except to Constable Fry, who only told Sergeant Brice. Both of whom we can categorically trust to keep quiet.'

'And I haven't left Henley Hall since we returned here in the Rolls from Wimbourne,' Seldon said. 'So my car is still over there.'

'Good!' She struck the table emphatically. 'So, she'll be stewing over not hearing any news, Hugh. She'll have to keep this evening's appointment for fear of looking suspicious. And I'll warrant she'll feel compelled to turn up to find out what went wrong, or not, with her plan.' Her heart faltered again at almost having been too late.

'And to have another attempt, if she can, I'd say,' Seldon said soberly.

She shook her head emphatically. 'She'll get no second chance. With us. Or, later, with a jury!'

He spread his hand on the table. 'Which is a point worth reiterating. Without any firm evidence, even if I make an arrest, the culprit will likely walk free. We need a confession.'

'Don't worry, Hugh,' she said quietly. 'You'll have it. So, let's check we're all sure of the plan one more time. Clifford, you're going to drive the back way through the lanes to Oxford and

pick the item up. Hugh, you'll make the telephone call ahead of
him arriving so they'll let him have it. And Mrs Trotman, you'll
be ready for when Clifford returns. Yes?'

The three of them nodded.

'Chaps, ladies and Kofi. We're all happy with who will be
where this evening?'

Around the table, everyone nodded again.

She took a deep breath. 'Then all we can do now is wait...'

The doorbell rang at eight minutes to seven that evening. In the
dining room, Eleanor crossed her fingers that their prey hadn't
baulked at coming at the last minute. And Clifford was about to
usher one woman, rather than two, in from the drizzle outside
into the entrance hall.

On cue, Polly and Mrs Butters arrived in the doorway
carrying chair sashes and boxes.

'Beg pardon, m'lady. But both dining tables are overflowing.'

Eleanor waved at the half-written cards spread across her
lap. 'Well, we'll just have to put them on the floor then. I'm sure
whoever was at the door will excuse the mess.'

'Miss Hopcroft and Miss Dunne, my lady,' Clifford
announced from the threshold as Polly and Mrs Butters began
laying out the chair sashes, starting with the settees nearest the
French doors.

Eleanor sighed inwardly with relief both had come and
stood up, seemingly oblivious to the flurry of cards falling from
her lap. 'Good evening, ladies. Do come in.'

Hester stepped in first, followed by Joyce.

'Good evening, Lady Swift,' they chorused.

'Will you require tea, my lady?'

She nodded. 'Yes, thank you, Clifford.' Glimpsing a figure
passing the French windows, she shrugged to herself. Clifford
had conjured up such a perfect labourer's disguise for Seldon,

he blended in with the marquee workmen so well she simply couldn't spot him among them. Joseph, however, looked commonplace in his gardening sou'wester and broad-brimmed hat at the corner of the flower beds. Beside him, Gladstone and Tomkins sat eager-eyed under a tarpaulin in his wheelbarrow.

'Ladies, please excuse the untidiness and take a seat,' she said, retaking hers, her heart pounding just a little faster. 'It was good of you both to brave the weather. Now, I had my notebook somewhere... oh dear, whatever have I done with it?'

Clifford glided level with the doorway and gave his customary quiet sniff. 'I believe it may have become embroiled among the confusion of cards you have managed to complete, my lady. Several of which, ahem, have joined the pattern on the Wilton rug.'

Eleanor noted two pairs of eyes flit to the dropped cards, but one linger a little longer.

'I'll get 'em, Mr Clifford. And find her ladyship's notebook while I'm about it,' Lizzie said, placing a tray of tea things on the table.

Mrs Butters stopped unpacking one of the boxes and came over with a cluck of disapproval at the maid, who was now kneeling on the floor picking up the cards.

'Hurry, Lizzie, my girl!'

'Sorry, Mrs Butters.' She handed the cards to Eleanor, who counted them carefully, then frowned.

'One moment. There's one missing.'

From the corner of her eye, she carefully watched her two visitors as Lizzie checked under the chairs.

'I'm sorry, m'lady. But that's all I can find.'

Eleanor's frown deepened. 'But I distinctly remember writing out thirty cards to go with the same number of cake boxes.'

'I'll go and check, m'lady.' Mrs Butters returned a moment

later. 'There's only twenty-nine boxes. I counted them carefully.'

Eleanor shrugged, catching a stiffening on the settee out of the corner of her eye. 'I must have been mistaken. Now.' She turned to Hester and Joyce. 'Shall we start while Clifford serves, if you don't mind? We haven't got very far with discussing the menus. Hester, your finished list of suggestions for the marquee refreshments, please?'

'Of course, Lady Swift,' Hester said. 'I suggest—'

'Polly, my girl,' Mrs Butter's voice came from the hallway. 'Have you found that special ribbon for her ladyship's... you know what?'

'No, Mrs Butters. But I'm sure I put it back in the basket on the dining-room table with the others, like you told me,' the young maid's voice replied.

Eleanor allowed herself the luxury of a small smile. There was a distinct unease in the room.

'Beggin' your pardon for interruptin',' Mrs Trotman called, bustling up to the doorway as Mrs Butters walked away. 'But you did say as it would be alright to get a second opinion from your guests, m'lady.'

'Did I?' Eleanor tapped her forehead, spotting Kofi helping Polly unpack the boxes by the door to the adjoining reception room. 'I fear my brain is completely full of wedding preparations. I seem to be forgetting everything. I think I just need a moment's air.'

She went to the French windows and poked her head out. As she returned to her seat, she left the doors slightly ajar.

'Now, Mrs Trotman, please do tell what it is you want Miss Dunne and Miss Hopcroft's opinion on while Clifford tops up everyone's tea?'

Her cook turned to her visitors. 'Ladies, honest words only, if you would. Polite ones won't help as it's a taster of what I'm planning for her ladyship's wedding cake.' She lifted the lid of the dish to reveal two half slices of cake. The very same as had been sent to Seldon.

Joyce stared at it. 'Cake? Cake isn't really my thing, I'm afraid. I'm the last person to ask.'

Eleanor noted two bright spots had appeared on Hester's cheeks. 'Lummy. I... I couldn't pass judgement on your expertise, Mrs Trotman! The very idea.'

Eleanor shook her head. 'I'm sorry, but I absolutely insist. You will both be working directly with Mrs Trotman, so all three of you need to trust each other's judgements. And, just as importantly, be able to take each other's constructive criticism. After all, this is one of the most important days of my life.' Her tone hardened. 'You're not going to *destroy it* by refusing such a reasonable request, are you?'

Reluctantly, Hester took hers. But Joyce held her hands up. 'I... I can't, Mrs Trotman. Sorry. Special diet, still, you see, after that awful food poisoning.'

'Yet you managed plenty of biscuits when you were here yesterday, Miss Dunne,' Eleanor said grimly, her pleasant demeanour gone. 'Go on. Just... one... bite. Be an... *angel*.'

Joyce's eyes widened. Then she bolted for the French doors.

46

By the time Eleanor had caught up with Joyce on the terrace, their fugitive was surrounded by Clifford, Joseph, and Gladstone, teeth bared, hackles raised. She whirled around, but Eleanor blocked the French windows back into the house. In perfect unison, her ladies and Kofi stepped out from the other doors onto the terrace and formed a second ring around her.

'It's over, Miss Dunne,' Eleanor said coolly.

Seldon loomed out of the gloom.

'You!' Joyce gasped, staggering backwards. 'You're supposed to be dea—!' She broke off, looking daggers at Eleanor.

'Really?' she said mildly. 'Why would you think that, Miss Dunne?' She frowned. 'Let's continue this discussion inside like the civilised people we are. Well, some of us are.'

Joyce stayed where she was, a defiant look on her face.

Seldon waved a set of handcuffs.

Eleanor nodded. 'We can do this the hard way or the easy way, Miss Dunne?'

The fight seemed to leave her. Her face crumpled as she allowed herself to be led back inside to the sitting room where she was sat on a wooden chair in the middle of the room. Seldon locked the French windows. Then Joseph took up guard in front of them with Gladstone, while Clifford guarded the door into the rest of Henley Hall. The ladies and Kofi stood around the walls like silent witnesses, Hester joining them, shock etched on her face.

'Miss Dunne, you are officially under arrest on seven counts,' Seldon said in an uncompromising tone, holding his notebook. 'The murders of Miss Annie Tibbets and Mr Lucas Villin. The attempted murder of a senior police officer, myself. Two mass poisonings of the population of Little Buckford. Pilfering from Lady Swift's estate, Henley Hall. And malicious damage to Lady Swift's wedding dress and marquee and Miss Lucetta Moore's florist shop window. You were the "old woman" seen by two young lads, I'm sure. A confession now to all of the above may go in your favour with the court.'

'I've... I've nothing to confess,' she mumbled, the stress in her voice giving away her frayed nerves.

'Just the reply I hoped for,' Eleanor said smoothly. 'Because you don't deserve the possible leniency a confession may give. Whereas the noose has no leniency!'

Seldon nodded. 'Lady Swift is right. And just so you're clear, your arrest is the one I will relish most, no matter how long my police career.'

Joyce raised her head, a flicker of fire still in her eyes. 'I've nothing to say!'

Eleanor fought down her disgust. 'Can't you understand it's over, Miss Dunne? My staff saw you steal that cake box, letter and ribbon,' she lied smoothly.

Joyce's eyes shot to the other side of the room where Mrs Butters and Lizzie nodded solemnly.

'And you made the mistake of attempting to murder a senior police officer of Scotland Yard! One who has access to the very latest scientific methods to catch criminals just like you. He's already had those three items fingerprinted.'

Joyce's eyes shot to Seldon, real fear in them now.

'And, Miss Dunne,' he said levelly, 'they are being checked at this moment against the prints my men recovered from your last cup of tea here. And those found on the missing vial we recovered—'

'There can't have been any!' Joyce cried. 'I wore gloves! You're lying!'

'Wore gloves for what?' Eleanor said quietly.

'Annie's medicine vial! There can't have been any...'

'How did you know we were talking about Annie's medicine vial?' Eleanor said quietly.

Joyce's eyes flashed between her and Seldon, a haunted look in them. 'I—'

'And,' Seldon interrupted smoothly. 'The monkshood seeds found in that vial matched the ones in the cake you—'

'Lies! More lies!' Joyce spat. 'There weren't any seeds in that cake you were supposed to eat! They were mushrooms...' The light in her eyes faded. She held her head in her hands, sobbing. Finally, she lifted her head slightly. 'Alright. I confess. I killed Annie. And Villin. And tried to poison your fiancé. And whatever else he said.'

Seldon wrote in his notebook, then nodded to Eleanor.

'The truth is, Miss Dunne,' she said coldly. 'In reality you weren't any cleverer than we painted you, fictitiously I must confess, a moment ago. Your arrogance and overdramatic sense of revenge led you to leave cryptic messages in flowers and the names of the poison you used against my fiancé. Once we'd deciphered these, it didn't take a genius to figure out who the culprit was from my past. And on that note, how long were you in prison for?'

Joyce's eyes flashed briefly again. 'Two years! If it hadn't been for the bomb that fell on the hellhole I'd still be there! But it allowed me to escape and after the war, make my way back to Britain with a new identity. I got work as a private tutor, then in a school. I dreamed of getting my revenge on you! It was the only thing that kept me going. Then the job of schoolteacher came up at the mill down south. It was better money than I was earning so I took it, little realising the Lady of the Manor was... you!' She glared malevolently at Eleanor, then continued. 'I found out as much as I could about you and those nearest and dearest to you. And then your marriage was announced in the local paper and my prayers were answered. I knew just how to get my revenge!'

'It would have been better for you, and all of Little Buckford, if you had stayed in that jail,' Eleanor said coldly. 'Anyway, where was I? Oh, yes. Then we only had to match the culprit from my past to one of our present suspects. And again, you helpfully gave us the clues we needed to narrow it down to three by arrogantly taking that note, cake box and ribbon from here. In fact, two, as one suspect, for irrelevant reasons here, couldn't possibly have been responsible. So that left only you and Hester.' She shook her head mockingly. 'It was dim of you to confess you'd only been at the Spring Supper a short while, you know, visiting only a few houses. Because that meant you ate less than most and yet you were more ill. To the point of hospitalisation. Strange? But, of course, that's because you never got ill at the Spring Supper, I realised last night. You simply waited until you got home and then took a carefully calculated dose of the remaining dried monkshood seeds you had used to contaminate Shackley's flour. A dose rather like the one you gave Annie, wasn't it? Only the one you gave Annie was much larger. Fatally so!'

Miss Dunne hesitated, then her shoulders sagged again. 'Like a fool, Hester refused the catering contract for your wedding. I *had* to get it back. It was my only ticket into Henley Hall. So I added monkshood seeds to Annie's medication the night of the Spring Supper.'

Eleanor nodded as Seldon wrote down everything Joyce said. 'And Villin? You found out he was snooping around and passing information onto Edwards of the *Herald*?'

'He was too cocky!' she said without remorse. 'The fool should have minded his own business.'

'Miss Dunne, how did you know enough about poisoning to kill Miss Tibbets and Mr Villin?' Seldon said.

She laughed bitterly. 'I learned in prison. It's hell, but a wonderful place for meeting people who know the deadliest of things. The woman in the cell next to me was in for selling potions. Deadly potions. Mostly to other women, wanting to rid themselves of their husbands. Maybe even their fiancés! She taught me the language of flowers too.'

Seldon made another note and nodded for Eleanor to continue.

'And lastly, Miss Dunne, when we first met, I was talking about my upcoming wedding. You mentioned cryptically that you'd never walk down the aisle yourself. Which clinched it for me, when we learned of the Abbeville connection. *You* were the culprit.' Her expression darkened. 'You thought you could destroy the most precious things in the world to me and then turn up at my house and gloat. But you were wrong.' She swallowed to contain the rush of fury threatening to overcome her. 'Your undoing is that you thought you could have your cake and eat it!'

She reached for the two halves Lizzie had fetched from the adjoining drawing room. Slowly, she lifted one piece to her mouth and bit down. As she swallowed, she savoured the cake and the expression of disbelief on Miss Dunne's face.

'You see, my cook, Mrs Trotman, makes an exceedingly

good *replica* wedding cake when I ask her to. Minus the poison mushrooms, of course!'

Miss Dunne's mouth gaped open. You—!'

'Beg pardon for interruptin', m'lady,' Polly panted, running in. 'But 'tis Jack at the back door. He needs to speak to you, your ladyship. Urgently!'

47

'Jack?' Seldon looked enquiringly at Eleanor.

'He's a young man from the village, Hugh.' Her gaze flicked to Joyce. Whatever the news was, Polly thought it important enough to interrupt her at such a critical time. 'I'll see him straight away. You and Clifford had better come, too.'

'Us three aprons and Joseph will guard this evil mare, m'lady,' Mrs Trotman said, throwing the now handcuffed Joyce a fierce glare.

'Me too!' Kofi added determinedly.

'She won't get away,' Mrs Butters added, as she, Lizzie, Kofi and Joseph joined Eleanor's cook in forming a formidable ring around their captive's chair.

'Polly, please bring Jack to the main drawing room next door.'

'Yes, m'lady.'

As her maid rushed off, Eleanor, with Seldon and Clifford in tow, swept into the drawing room. A moment later, she spotted Jack hovering anxiously outside the French doors, turning his cap in his hands.

She hurried over to the door, beckoning him in. 'Gracious, Jack, come in out of the rain. You look soaked through.'

The young man's Adam's apple bobbed as he did so tentatively. 'Beggin' your pardon for bein' so brazen, m'lady. Only, I didn't know where else to go.'

'Whatever it is, you've done the right thing, I'm sure.' Seldon stepped over from where he'd been keeping an eye on the situation next door.

'Hugh, this is Jack Browne,' Eleanor said. 'A "friend" of Polly's and a fine chap. Jack, you probably know this is my fiancé, Chief Inspector Seldon?'

Jack stared at his boots. 'Yes, m'lady. Only as I didn't realise he was here... I mean, I see now as I shouldn't haven't come. Beg pardon.' He bobbed his head apologetically and turned to leave.

Clifford stepped in his way and gently held him by the shoulders. 'Jack. You came to her ladyship for a reason. To say what?'

He hesitated. 'What... what I'm not supposed to tell anyone, Mr Clifford! Especially the... the police.' His gaze flicked to Seldon and away. 'That's why I didn't go to Constable Fry. Or the other two from Chipstone, that have been patrollin' the village.'

Eleanor gestured to Seldon it might be best if he left. He strode back into the adjoining room, leaving the door ajar.

Eleanor gave Jack an encouraging look. 'It sounds as if you've taken a big risk coming here. So there's no point not speaking up now, is there?'

He nodded, but his troubled frown deepened. 'I heard summat, m'lady. From... some of the men as live in the old part of the village.'

'You don't need to name anyone to her ladyship, Jack,' Clifford said.

The young man looked relieved. 'Thank you, Mr Clifford. 'Tis on account of word of what the millworkers are plannin', m'lady. They're makin' ready to attack this side of the bridge at eight o'clock tonight 'cos of their lot gettin' sick and one of 'em dying!'

She gasped. 'Gracious! So that's what the secret meeting at the mill was all about! But how did their plan leak out?' She glanced towards the dining room. 'Of course! Miss Dunne!' She returned her attention to Jack. 'Tell me quickly. When you overheard the men on this side talking, what was their reaction to the news?'

His lean face paled. 'That's why I came, m'lady. They plan on attackin' the mill complex first. They were callin' all the men in the village to a meetin' as I raced up here quick as I could.'

'Where's the meeting being held?'

'In old Cobber's barn.'

Clifford clapped him on the back. 'Well done, my boy. Her ladyship will know what to do.' He nodded to Polly. 'Take Jack to the kitchen and get a hot drink in him before he returns to the village. And be quick in case he is missed.'

As Polly left with a relieved-looking Jack, Seldon strode in and over to Eleanor's side. The mantelpiece clock chimed the quarter to.

'I heard it all,' he said gravely. 'And this time—'

'We need to call in police reinforcements, I agree. Come with me.' She hurried to the telephone in the entrance hall and dialled.

'Fry, answer, please,' she muttered.

But the only reply was the intermittent ringing the other end. She exchanged a look with Seldon then rang off and dialled another number. Her intuition was telling her something was off. Badly off. And she was hoping this time the person she was calling *wouldn't* be there.

'Chipstone Police, Sergeant Brice speakin',' the voice on the other end boomed.

'Blast it!' Seldon muttered, holding his hand out for the

handset. 'Brice, what in blazes are you doing there? You're supposed to be patrolling the village here, man!'

'Chief Inspector? Ah! I got called back by the desk here, sir. On account of receivin' an alarm raised 'bout a nasty muggin' in Brackley Road. Only, well, it turns out—'

Eleanor groaned. 'It was a false alarm!'

'Ah, her ladyship's there too. Right you be on that, m'lady. How did you know, mind?'

She raised her voice. 'Because we've more trouble in Little Buckford than ever. And the person responsible made sure you would be out of the way!'

'Miss Dunne, again?' Seldon gritted.

She nodded. 'Just before she left to come here, I imagine, given the timing.'

'The last act of a defeated woman!'

Maybe, Ellie.

'Er, Chief Inspector?' Brice's voice came back. 'I... I brought Constable Lowe with me as the caller suggested it might take several officers to contain the mugger who was holed up... though, of course, when we got there...'

Seldon grunted in exasperation. 'Just get back here immediately, Brice! And bring Lowe with you and anyone else you can spare. All hell's about to break loose in Little Buckford, and we can't contact Constable Fry.'

He slammed the handset down.

Eleanor pointed at the grandfather clock. 'They'll never get here in time, Hugh. We'll have to go ourselves.'

They sped back to the reception room to find the chair Joyce had been in empty.

'No!' Seldon cried. 'I should never—'

'Underestimate my staff,' Eleanor said calmly.

As they hurried into the kitchen, Clifford was striding out of the passage to the larder, holding their hats and coats, already dressed in his.

'Miss Dunne is being held securely, locked in the cellar. With Joseph and the ladies standing guard, Chief Inspector. Shall we go?'

'Empty!'

Eleanor looked around the barn in panic. 'Are you sure this is the meeting place Jack said, Clifford?'

'Cobber's barn, my lady. There's only one. Here at the far end of Pippin's Swoop.'

Seldon bent down and picked up a formidable-looking cudgel. 'Whoever was here, was armed!'

Eleanor's stomach clenched. 'We must intercept them before they get to the mill!'

The tyres of Seldon's Crossley shrieked on the wet cobbles as he spun the car around and bounced agonisingly slowly back up the road towards the bridge. The unmetalled surface was peppered with axle-breaking potholes, now filled with water, making it impossible in the gloom to gauge their depth.

As they neared the last of the sweeping curves which followed the river, Eleanor half-turned to Seldon and Clifford. 'Well, we're almost at the bridge and haven't met an angry mob. So, it looks like we're in ti—'

She lurched forward as Seldon braked abruptly. As she sat up, he pointed through the windscreen.

'I doubt they could have got through that lot!' he said grimly.

Eleanor flinched at the throng of men marching onto the bridge from the mill side. Forty or more in number, most yielding wooden bats or thick sticks. The lanterns held by the others were enough to light the men's faces with an eerie glow.

'Get out. Quickly!' As Seldon shook his head at her words, she grabbed her door handle resolutely. 'They surrounded this very car over at the mill and stopped us getting out, remember?

And trying to reason with them through an inch of open window didn't work, so I doubt it will now.'

Without waiting for a reply, she leaped out into the rain.

Before she had taken two steps, Seldon and Clifford were either side of her.

'Just be careful, Eleanor,' Seldon murmured as they reached the middle of the bridge. They stopped about ten feet from the irate horde, who had also halted. One man stepped forward.

'Ah! Mr Oxdale,' she said with no surprise and more calmly than she felt. 'First question is, what have you done with Constable Fry?'

Oxdale laughed. 'No idea. Haven't seen hide nor hair of him. Besides, he's one of yer lot, so why should I care?'

Dash it, Ellie! I bet Fry received a bogus call like Brice.

She waved at the armed mob. 'You must know this isn't the way to settle differences.'

'Scores, you mean!' he growled back. 'And yer not one of ours! Neither are those two suited goons. So none of yer is crossin' over to this side. But we're comin' over to yers! And right now!'

'Over our dead bodies, you are!'

Eleanor spun around to see a crowd of familiar faces gathering onto the other side of the bridge. Like the millworkers, the men of old Little Buckford all carried weapons or lanterns. Stokes stepped forward. 'You're not stoppin' one of ours comin' over there if she wants to! So we're comin' over right now with her ladyship!'

'Stop!' she called. The shouts dwindled. She addressed the mob led by Oxdale. 'You are right. I'm not one of yours!'

The old villagers cheered raucously. As it died down, she turned to them and shook her head firmly. 'And I'm not one of yours, either!'

Stunned silence fell. She looked from one side to the other.

'Let me tell you all, the person responsible for the poisonings, and the murder of Annie Tibbets and Lucas Villin has been caught. Chief Inspector Seldon here has the culprit secured in handcuffs.'

'Which of yer lot is it?' one of the millworkers yelled.

'You mean which of you interlopers is it?' someone from the other side shouted back.

'Listen! All of you!' Eleanor called. 'It doesn't matter who it was. Or which side of the bridge they came from. The truth is, they were only able to commit their crimes for two reasons.' She held her hands up in admission. 'First of which is because I neglected my responsibilities as lady of the manor. For which, I'm heartily ashamed.'

As Clifford's brow furrowed, Seldon shook his head at her in disagreement.

'And secondly,' she continued, once the muttering had died down, 'because there was no cooperation between the two sides of the village. To be blunt, gentlemen, you were too busy looking after your own interests. And spreading lies and fear about each other to see you were destroying the very thing you proclaimed to be protecting!'

Angry mutterings broke out in both mobs, rising to a crescendo of shouts, accusations and threats.

She held her hands up higher this time. Once silence had fallen, she took a deep breath. 'Even though it breaks my heart to say it aloud, unless you bury your differences and unite as one village, I... I don't want to be your lady of the manor any more. And I'll want nothing to do with any of you. Little Buckford deserves better. Far better. Let me know when you've decided.'

Turning her collar up against the rain, she gestured for the old villagers to part, barely making it back to the car through the tears streaming down her face. As the three of them drove off, her last view was of the two warring factions still facing each other on the bridge.

48

Eleanor stepped into the breakfast room and sipped her coffee as mechanically as she had dressed. Shaking her head apologetically at Clifford's subdued introduction to each of the morning's offerings, she headed for the dining room to bury herself in wedding preparations.

Seldon had left the minute they'd returned from the village the previous evening, taking Miss Dunne with him. So the cellar no longer housed a malicious poisoner. Henley Hall was empty of workmen. And her ladies were keeping out of the way. Doubtlessly on her butler's orders.

Even he only appeared twice after breakfast, both times with more coffee and an update on the weather. Apparently, the rain was easing. Or had it already stopped? She couldn't recall. She glanced out of the window. Stopped. Gladstone lumbered in shortly afterwards and nudged her hand with a soggy leather slipper. Then left with his tail at half mast.

As the mantel clock struck midday, she switched from wedding tasks to making a list of things to pack for her honeymoon.

'Dresses. Shoes. Hats. Underthings. And toiletries too, I

suppose,' she mumbled as she wrote the five items in a line. She closed the notebook. 'It's too special a trip to go at like that. Perhaps it's a job for later, Ellie?' she murmured.

Tomkins jumped up onto the table with his toy mouse in his teeth. Dropping it on her page, he batted it half-heartedly. Then left without it. She nudged it aside.

'Wedding vows, Ellie. You haven't practised those,' she said to her reflection in the coffee pot. It shook its head back at her. 'You're right. They'd be better later, too,' she muttered.

She roused herself and wandered to the two-storeyed library that was usually one of her favourite rooms in the house. Selecting a book on the strength it had a green cover, she drifted back. The printed words probably told a wonderful story. She didn't register much of it.

A walk around the garden? No, the grass was still wet.

'Two o'clock,' the mantel clock announced.

Clifford glided in with a small parcel. For a moment, she froze, staring at it in horror. Then she remembered and relaxed.

Opening it, she found it was her long-awaited hair accessory from Lucetta; a garland of beautiful wildflowers only just opening so they would still be fresh for the wedding. She hurried to the hallway to find Clifford waiting with her hat and coat. He held up the key to the Rolls.

Apparently, he can still read your mind, Ellie.

'Chipstone, please,' she said unnecessarily.

They took the long way, avoiding the village altogether. He offered her his trusty blue and white striped paper bag of mint humbugs. She took one, and they sucked in silence. The puddles in the road splashed muddy water up the side of the Rolls. Her butler's leather gloves creaked as he reached inside his jacket pocket. His hip flask appeared in her eyeline.

She shook her head. 'I'm fine, thank you.'

His raised brow said otherwise.

The start of Chipstone High Street arrived.

'Lucetta Moore's florist shop, please, Clifford.'

'I was unaware you had made an appointment, my lady?'

'I haven't.'

As he pulled up outside, she was pleased to see the window had been repaired.

He opened her door, she stepped out and up to the shopfront. On the door was a note stuck on the inside.

'"Closed for today. Sorry",' she read aloud. She sighed. 'That's that then.'

Clifford joined her. 'Was it for something special you wanted Miss Moore?'

'Just to say thank you for the hair garland.' At his sideways glance, she tutted. 'I know I could have rung, but...' She shrugged.

'As the lady is not here, and you have come all this way, perhaps some... shopping?' He gave her a hopeful look.

She tried hard. 'I just can't think of anything. Can you?'

'Aside from seating my mistress in her favourite seat at Winsome's tea rooms and ordering disgraceful amounts of fruitcake...?'

'That sounds wonderful. Only would you mind if we took it home to eat?'

'Very much,' he said, to her surprise. 'I suggest we add it to the small picnic your ladies pressed upon me before we left instead. If that would suit?'

She smiled. 'It would.'

On a bench in the greenest folds of Buckinghamshire's countryside, she nibbled. Clifford fiddled. They packed up. And took the long way back to Henley Hall.

Early house pyjamas, as Clifford referred to her grey silk ensemble, were usually her favourite comfort clothing. In her bedroom, she reached for her soft cashmere trouser suit instead. Then shook her head and laid it on the bed. Her Ryeland wool skirt and matching cardigan? No. Her sage, wide-legged trousers and matching long, buttoned-tunic top? Too faffy. The pile grew as her wardrobe emptied. She scooped it all up and hung it back up. Her house pyjamas won.

Later that evening, as she picked at her supper in the snug, soft lips brushed her neck.

'Hugh!'

He bent down and ruffled Gladstone and Tomkins' heads, both of whom had come bounding over at his arrival.

'Where have you hidden the woman of my dreams, you monsters?' he whispered in their ears.

She frowned. 'What do you mean?'

He waved his hand in front of her eyes. 'You're here in person. But nothing like in your usual spirits, my love.'

'Yes, I am. I'm just... tired, I imagine.'

'Hmm!'

Clifford glided in with Seldon's generously loaded supper tray, which also sported two glasses of brandy. She sipped hers, watching Seldon savouring the warmed slice of beef pie with rich gravy while gently batting away Tomkins' greedy paw. Clifford retrieved the tomcat with an apologetic wince.

Having finished eating, Seldon led her to the settee.

'By the way,' he said casually, 'Fry confirmed that his wife received a call like the one Brice got. Miss Dunne admitted it was her again, just making doubly sure there was no one to interfere with the, er, intended mayhem.'

'Oh. That explains that, then.'

'It does. I also checked just before leaving the office with Brice and Fry for any reports of any further incidents in the village.'

She jerked upright, catching Clifford turning his head too. Tentatively, she asked, 'And?'

'Nothing. It seems at least each side of the bridge are holding off for the moment.'

'Or they're planning something even more awful,' she muttered.

Clifford topped up her brandy more than normal and glided away without a word.

'Perhaps you need an early night, Eleanor?' Seldon said gently.

'Perhaps we all do.'

He nodded, rose, and kissed her goodnight.

She lay down under her bed covers, which were soothingly warm, Polly evidently having been sent up earlier to switch on her new electric blanket. Her staff were all so thoughtful. Clifford had also left a small, tissue-wrapped parcel on the bedside table.

Inside was a sleeping draught and a book. A new penny dreadful novel, featuring a swashbuckling pirate. Usually her absolute favourite. She turned the pages. The first chapter came and went. The sleeping draught won.

She awoke to a bird singing. And a patch of early morning sun painting slowly swirling patterns on the inside of her still closed eyelids. With a sigh, she reached out and stroked Gladstone and Tomkins, snuggled together on her bed. She swung her legs out from under the covers and stumbled to the window. She stood there for a moment. Then rubbed her eyes.

Her foggy brain couldn't make sense of it.

That sleeping draught must have been stronger than you thought, Ellie.

She threw open the window and... gasped.

Not pausing to put on her slippers, she ran down the stairs two at a time and out the door. The gravel pinching at the soles of her feet went unnoticed as she bent down on the front lawn and picked up ...

A bouquet, Ellie. Such sweet yellow catkin fronds, tied with a green ribbon.

She looked up and her breath caught again, felt the hot prick of tears at the magnitude of it. For all around on the lawn and stretching as far down the drive as she could see were hundreds of identical bouquets, of all sizes.

'They are boughs of blossoming hazel, my lady.' Clifford materialised at her side.

'But... why? And why so many?' She shook her head in disbelief. 'What do they mean, do you suppose, Clifford?'

'There is no supposing about it.' He held up *The Language of Flowers* Lucetta had lent her in case she ever received another bouquet. Opening it, he ran his gloved finger under a line.

'Hazel symbolises...' she read aloud. Then sobs of happiness overcame her voice, tears of relief coursed down her cheeks. '*Peace and... reconciliation,*' she whispered.

She blinked up at Clifford, laughing through her snatched sobs. 'But how?'

'Suffice to say, Silas returned just after midnight to see almost the entire population of old and new Little Buckford herding towards Henley Hall's gates. He alerted me to check if I wished to let them in. I did. It was a spectacle I shall never forget.'

She felt Seldon's arms encircle her shoulders from behind, making her heart skip.

'Little Buckford adores their lady of the manor, Eleanor,' he whispered. 'They can't bear the idea of life without you. Just like me.'

THE WEDDING DAY

The beauty of the morning promised that everything was now right and beautiful in the world. It was warm, windless, and bathed in glorious sunshine from an azure sky. To Eleanor's delight, Clifford had arranged a surprise champagne breakfast for her to enjoy with her staff and Kofi.

But even before that, he had whisked her away to give her an unexpected gift. An arched, arbour love seat in the rose garden, carved by his own hand. And inscribed with her and Seldon's names and the date of their wedding, to sit together in for all eternity. It meant more than the world and started her first stream of happy tears of the day.

After breakfast, the seven of them toured the settings for the afternoon and evening festivities amid excited chatter and laughter.

Inside the marquee, the tables were beautifully dressed in cream linen with shimmering silver-lace edging. Every chair back was adorned with a peach-coloured rose and eucalyptus wreath, all tied with a vanilla satin bow. At every place setting, the napkins and cutlery were set in a blue-striped or pink-flow-ered calico pouch with a button closure. A handwritten note awaited under the flap: *Please take me home if you wish.* A useful thank you gift the villagers would love.

Garlands of silk roses looped down from the marquee's Arabian style roof. More adorned the stage where the two dance bands booked would play alternately all afternoon and evening, one jazz and one traditional. Even the flooring was beautiful, being an acre of striped emerald and moss-green matting.

At the wedding party table, the speeches sat ready to be shared with everyone; heartfelt sentiments and jokes in equal measure. Most likely all manner of mischievous ones in Clifford's case, Eleanor was sure!

At one end of the giant marquee was a games and craft table for the children. At the other, a free bar for the adults, which was to be manned by Stokes, by his own request.

Eleanor was over the moon. It was a captivating setting. One just right for the villagers to feel like honoured guests and friends, yet modest enough that they wouldn't be too overawed to truly let their hair down. Their welcoming glass of fizz would be sure to start them off, while the hearty wedding fayre Hester had prepared would fortify them well into the small hours.

And inside Henley Hall itself, lavishly decorated in ivory and gold, the grand two-storeyed ballroom looked ready to receive titled guests in the evening like royalty. With its ruched magnolia canopy, trimmed with ostrich feathers, velvet seating adorned with silk sashes and potted roses arranged by her meticulous butler, it was the definition of sumptuous elegance. Lucetta Moore's exquisite tall floral displays adding so much on top. The crystal glassware shone as invitingly as the silver napkin rings and specially ordered cutlery. The vast nine-tiered champagne fountain centrepiece sat ready to start proceedings, which would be followed with the speeches being repeated from that afternoon. And then, Eleanor and Seldon would have the first dance while the twelve-piece orchestra played.

At just the right magical moment, Mrs Trotman's stunning five-tiered wedding cake would be wheeled to the awaiting linen-dressed table in the centre of Henley Hall's rear terrace. There, all the guests would gather around and cheer while she and Seldon made the first cut. And silently, their wishes.

But all that was for later. Before leaving for the church, Eleanor twirled in her lovingly tailored wedding dress around the entrance hall with Kofi in his darling suit and top hat, setting all of her ladies off in tears again. And left even Clifford struggling with his composure.

Mrs Butters' expertise had captured Eleanor's dream to perfection; all signs of the stain removed, the ivory beaded bodice and delicate full-length lace sleeves made her feel feminine and beautiful. The intricately embroidered pairs of doves swirling up from the base of the gown's cascading skirt folds and down the length of her silk train were too special for words. Particularly as the last pair were making a nest, she spotted.

On her wrist, she wore something she would treasure forever. Kofi had also surprised her with a gift, in the tradition of weddings in his native Gold Coast; a three-banded bracelet of exquisite glass beads threaded with mesmerising swirls, graduating through every shade of green, her favourite colour, and held with a delicate silver clasp. Something, Clifford whispered to her, the young boy had politely insisted he wasn't leaving London without finding the parts for. The two of them had then secretly worked together to make it for her, which made it even more special.

Her skin glowed as if to tell the world that she was bursting with happiness. Her red curls shone as they bounced around her lace veil. While the beautiful hair garland of delicate white buds and soft emerald leaves Lucetta had made for her brought out her own natural beauty. There was no getting away from it; today she truly was, and felt, every inch a princess.

. . .

Clifford eased the Rolls to a stop outside the picturesque stone
and flint church of St Winifred's that had served Little Buckford since the twelfth century. She hadn't expected it, but he
had decorated the car with ivory satin ribbons running either
side of the stately bonnet to the silver lady emblem, from which
a horseshoe hung. Looped along the car's sides were more silk
rose garlands and extravagant bows.

She stepped out to the regal hum of the organ and the
choir's rejoicing voices filling the air.

'Ready, my lady? Or are we all to be kept waiting another
half decade before we can toast your marriage to the finest, most
upstanding gentleman I have ever met?' he said mischievously.

She laughed. 'I'll race you inside, Clifford. Does that answer
your question?'

As the two of them reached the middle of the quaint
vaulted porch, he gestured into the anteroom where she would
go first.

'Ah, perfect timing. Lord Langham is waiting, my lady.'

She stopped. 'Yes. But not for me. For you, Clifford.'

'My lady?'

She nudged his arm. 'Please don't feel pressured. But from
the moment Hugh and I set the date, I've wanted to ask you
to... to give me away. Lord Langham already knows I'm going to
and is happy I do.' She held her breath. 'Will you, Clifford?'

For the first time, her ever-inscrutable butler looked
completely overcome. Then her heart clenched as he shook his
head, his expression filled with regret.

'Forgive me, my lady. I cannot. Since you came to live at
Henley Hall, I have tried to respectfully step in where his lordship, your late uncle, regrettably no longer can. But this...' His
gaze fell to the floor. 'I cannot actually take his lordship's place.
Most especially in regard to the most significant event in your
life. My abject apologies.'

'Aren't needed. I understand,' she said gently. 'But I don't think you understand. Clifford. I'm not asking you to give me away in Uncle Byron's stead.' As he looked up in confusion, she nodded. 'If he could be with us today, as we both wish he could be, I would ask him to take one arm. And you, equally, the other. Maybe one day you'll realise that... you're just as precious to me as he is, you know.'

His eyes swam as he slid his arm over hers, then placed her other hand over his wrist.

Lord Langham poked his head out of the anteroom. 'Hurrah! Good man!' He slipped away to take his place beside his beloved wife.

She wiped her eyes. 'I only wish Silas would have agreed to come. Even though I've still never met him, he's the only part of Henley Hall not here.'

'On the contrary, my lady. He would not have stayed away for anything,' Clifford said.

She gasped. 'You mean?'

'Yes. He is among the congregation. Watching over you. But alas, you will not see him. Such is his way.'

Her shoulders rose with happiness. 'Of course. Please thank him for me.'

Inside the anteroom, her ladies looked so beautiful in their matching rosy-peach silk dresses, and Joseph, her treasured gardener in his smart new suit, she had to hug them all. Which necessitated Clifford hurriedly whipping out more pristine handkerchiefs.

Bending to cuddle her excited bulldog and tomcat, she felt another wave of affection for the people she adored, as much as they clearly did her. In amongst all the chaotic wedding preparations, Mrs Butters and her maids had found time for a further surprise; Gladstone and Tomkins were sporting bow ties and striped waistcoats to match Clifford and Kofi's. Even having the detail of the same silver buttons, handkerchief in the tiny breast pocket, and carnation in the buttonhole.

Joseph stepped to the side table and returned with her bouquet, which made her breath catch; lily of the valley sprays nestled among double-bloomed cream and yellow roses, framed by a fan of flowering myrtle stems.

'Joseph, it's even more beautiful than I imagined,' she choked.

Her ladies arranged the train of her dress, while Kofi proudly held the velvet cushion on which the two gold rings rested. Tomkins and Gladstone whirled excitedly either side of him.

'Shall we, my lady? To the most unorthodox wedding of the century?' Clifford said.

She nodded. 'Yes!'

'On that note, are we going for elegant gliding or cart-wheels?' he teased to ease her nerves.

She pretended to mull it over amid the ladies' giggles. 'Elegant gliding, I think. I'll save cartwheels for the way back with Hugh once we're married.'

Reverend Gaskell bounded up, clapping his hands with elation. 'Blessed be the bride on this wondrous day. And blessed are we all, for she truly has the heart of her village. Who have handkerchiefs aplenty, I've spotted.' He chuckled before disappearing again.

Joseph bobbed his head to Eleanor and shuffled off to take his place in the front pew.

As the organ began the traditional wedding march, the ladies cooed with excitement.

'On three, bridal entourage?' Clifford said.

As she started up the aisle, every head was turned, every face lit with a smile. But the only one she really noticed was that of her betrothed. Standing at the altar, Seldon looked more irresistibly divine than ever in his morning suit. His striped grey trousers highlighted those long, athletic legs that had given her butterflies the first time she had met him. Likewise his kind brown eyes. And his chestnut curls. She was overjoyed to see he had left them just as she loved them, not raked into submission by his comb but free to frame his far too handsome face.

As she progressed up the aisle, she recognised all the familiar faces of a now clearly united Little Buckford. The villagers from either side of the bridge were mingled together across the bursting pews, standing areas, and above in the gallery. Constance blew her a teary-eyed kiss as she drew level with her and Peregrine. Her uncle's oldest friends, Lord and Lady Langham, sat arm in arm, both dabbing their eyes and beaming at her as if she was the daughter they never had.

As she reached the altar, she felt Clifford gently squeeze her arm before passing her hand to the man she loved more than she had ever thought possible. Seldon's lips moved, but no sound came out.

'Too... too beautiful, Eleanor,' he finally managed in a whisper. 'I really don't deserve you.'

Reverend Gaskell held up his Bible. 'Dearly beloved, we are gathered here today in the sight of God to join together this man and this woman in Holy Matrimony.'

The readings and hymns were perfect, poignant and personal.

'I do,' Seldon said, through a smile that lit his face and the entire church.

'I do,' she cried, feeling her heart leap up to heaven.

Kofi stepped forward with the rings. Seldon slid hers onto her finger with a whispered, 'I love you, Eleanor. With all my heart. And I always will. Grow old with me, my love. In my arms, forever.'

She slid his onto his finger, failing to stem the trickle of ecstatic tears running down her cheeks. 'You make me whole, Hugh. And you've healed the hole in my heart I thought no one ever could.'

'I now pronounce you man and wife!' Reverend Gaskell

said. He smiled at Seldon. 'You may now kiss the bride, young man.'

The little breath she had left, her new husband took away with the perfect soft kiss.

Reverend Gaskell led the cheer that rang up to the vaulted rafters. Then the organ started up with a tune that she vaguely recognised, but thought unusual for the end of the ceremony.

Seldon took both of her hands and led her down from the altar. 'I asked Reverend Gaskell for permission, and he was tickled pink to say yes.'

'To what?'

'This.' He looped the train of her dress carefully over his arm before waltzing her slowly and elegantly back up the aisle. 'This is the music we had our first ever dance to. In Brighton. Five years ago. I've hummed it every morning since, thinking of you,' he whispered. She thought she might actually pass out with happiness as he added, 'I'm going to waltz you around wherever we are at least once, every single day of our married life, my love.'

They reached the end of the aisle and turned to see the entire congregation standing, waving, and wiping their eyes.

She beamed up at her husband through the ecstatic tears swimming in her own eyes. 'You said you had a surprise, Hugh. And that was the most wonderful and special one you could have thought of. I'll still be swooning over it when I'm ninety years old.'

'Then I couldn't be happier. Although that wasn't it.' He linked his fingers in hers and led her out towards the Rolls and her waiting butler. 'I fibbed about the honeymoon I had planned for us. After all the celebrations tonight, we're off to... Paris. For two weeks.'

'Paris?' she gasped. 'Two weeks? But, Hugh, the cost...'

His handsome face was filled with tenderness. 'Paris is my second surprise. The first is that I've sold my house, Eleanor.'

Her jaw fell. 'But you've so many special memories there!'

'Not any more. I'm starting my new life right now. With you as my darling wife.' He picked her up and twirled her, wrapping them both in the embroidered nesting doves of her gown's silk train.

A LETTER FROM VERITY

Dear reader,

I want to say a huge thank you for choosing to read *A Recipe for Murder*. If you did enjoy it, and want to keep up to date with all my latest releases, just sign up at the following link.

Your email address will never be shared and you can unsubscribe at any time.

www.bookouture.com/verity-bright

I hope you loved *A Recipe for Murder* and if you did I would be very grateful if you could write a review. I'd love to hear what you think, and it makes such a difference helping new readers to discover one of my books for the first time.

I love hearing from my readers – you can get in touch through social media or my website.

Verity

www.veritybright.com

facebook.com/veritybrightauthor
x.com/BrightVerity

RECIPE FOR ELEANOR'S WEDDING CAKE

(AS MADE BY MRS TROTMAN)

When Eleanor relays Kofi's message about Mrs Trotman making a trial wedding cake and sending Seldon a slice, she refutes the suggestion. Quite rightly, too. An experienced cook like her would have no need to make a trial cake. Any good Edwardian cook would make the cake months before so it could soak properly. Often in oodles of brandy! In fact, having learned her trade in the Victorian era, Mrs Trotters makes Eleanor the same wedding cake Queen Victoria favoured for most royal occasions, not just weddings. Up to seven-foot high, it was so liberally doused in brandy that it would keep for up to two years!

Here's as close as I could get to the wedding cake recipe Queen Victoria favoured and Mrs Trotman used for Eleanor's wedding:

Ingredients: Twelve eggs, 1 1/2 pounds of white sugar, 1 pound of butter, 1 cup of brown sugar, 1 pound of flour, 1 pound of almonds, 2 pounds of citron, 4 pounds of raisins, 2 pounds of currants, 1 nutmeg, 2

spoonfuls of cloves, 2 spoonfuls of cinnamon, 1 quart of
brandy, 1/2 cup of boiled milk.

Method: The almonds must be blanched and cut in
strips; the raisins seeded; the citron sliced; the currants
washed and dried the day previous to the mixing.

The flour, sugar and almonds are dried and slightly
browned in a slow oven; the eggs must be separated and
beaten stiff; the butter and sugar must be beaten till
creamy, then add flour and eggs alternately, then milk
and spices — then with a wooden spatula beat in the
fruit, add 1 pint of brandy, and cook four hours in an
evenly heated oven.

The pan should be raised from the bottom of the
oven. After the cake is baked and cold, turn over it the
remaining pint of brandy. Wrap in paraffin (waxed)
paper and box.

Once a year the cake should be removed from the
box and another pint of brandy poured over it. It will
keep and grow better for several years.

The Queen's Wedding Cake by Mrs Guy Magee from
*The North End Club Cook Book. A Collection of Choice
and Tested Recipes*, compiled and arranged by ladies of
the club. Published 1905.

HISTORICAL NOTES

SPRING SUPPER

Little Buckford's Spring Supper is based on real traditions in various villages around England, including where I used to live. One evening a year the villagers would have 'open house'. They'd bake some food, leave it on the table, leave the front door open and visit all the other houses in the village who did the same. Everyone would meet passing in the street, or eating at each other's houses. It is a lovely tradition and up to this point as far as I know, fingers crossed, there has never been a mass outbreak of food poisoning!

EDWARDIAN WEDDINGS

Weddings of the super rich and famous in Britain have always been extravagant affairs, as everywhere, but it wasn't really until Victorian and Edwardian times that everyone down to the middle classes started to imitate them and they became the weddings we know today. Everything from white wedding dresses and playing the 'Bridal March' as the bride walks down the aisle came from royal weddings of the time. Eleanor, as always, doesn't quite conform to custom at her wedding, but at least for Mrs Trotman's sake, she only had one wedding cake. It wasn't unusual to have up to three, one of which wasn't eaten at all at the actual wedding. And Seldon keeps their honeymoon destination a secret from Eleanor until the wedding. Often, no one at the wedding knew where the bride and groom were honeymooning except the best man who was sworn to secrecy.

ELIJAH EDWARDS AND THE *COUNTY HERALD*

When Elijah tells Eleanor he's not willing to extend his newspaper reporting of her wedding to more than four pages, he is bluffing. But in Edwardian times, the papers covered every detail of weddings. And not just high-society weddings. Local papers like the *County Herald* would publish details of weddings between any reasonably well-known people in the area. As well as a detailed report of the wedding itself, it would often include a list of all the guests and a list of every wedding present and who gave it.

THE EDWARDIAN PUBLIC HOUSE

The Dog and Badger public house run by Stokes is the focal point of Little Buckford. Despite the small size of the village, not that many years earlier, most similar ones had several such establishments. In fact, many villages and towns had a public house per hundred residents or fewer! However, a campaign from around 1903 to persuade magistrates not to renew licences led to many local pubs like Stokes' Dog and Badger being forced to close.

ACKNOWLEDGEMENTS

Thanks to the fabulous team at Bookouture whose enthusiasm to make sure each and every publication is as good as it can be still shines through, even though *A Recipe for Murder* is book twenty-one in the Lady Swift series!

PUBLISHING TEAM

Turning a manuscript into a book requires the efforts of many people. The publishing team at Bookouture would like to acknowledge everyone who contributed to this publication.

Audio
Alba Proko
Melissa Tran
Sinead O'Connor

Commercial
Lauren Morrissette
Hannah Richmond
Imogen Allport

Cover design
Tash Webber

Data and analysis
Mark Alder
Mohamed Bussuri

Editorial
Kelsie Marsden
Nadia Michael

Copyeditor
Jane Eastgate

Proofreader
Liz Hatherell

Marketing
Alex Crow
Melanie Price
Occy Carr
Cíara Rosney
Martyna Młynarska

Operations and distribution
Marina Valles
Stephanie Straub
Joe Morris

Production
Hannah Snetsinger
Mandy Kullar
Ria Clare
Nadia Michael

Publicity
Kim Nash
Noelle Holten
Jess Readett
Sarah Hardy

Rights and contracts
Peta Nightingale
Richard King
Saidah Graham

Printed in Great Britain
by Amazon